"A promising new writer!"
"Elrod is a writer who gets b...

Thrill to the bloodcurdling n... P. N. Elrod as she introduces you to the chronicles of the vampire Jonathan Barrett . . .

"Wonderful! I found myself enthralled!" —*Onyx*

His amazing history of bloodshed is born in
RED DEATH

He learns what price he must pay to live as the undead in
DEATH AND THE MAIDEN

In searching for his immortal love, he finds great mortal evil in
DEATH MASQUE

And don't miss P. N. Elrod's acclaimed vampire mystery series
THE VAMPIRE FILES

"An entertaining blend of detective story and the supernatural."
—*Science Fiction Chronicle*

"Four stars!" —*Rave Reviews*

The Vampire Files include:
BLOODLIST
Meet Jack Fleming, investigative reporter—
and vampire.

LIFEBLOOD
The living vs. the undead—
but who's hunting whom?

BLOODCIRCLE
Vampire meets vampire—
and the stakes are life *and* death.

ART IN THE BLOOD
Blood is thicker than paint—
and easier to spill.

FIRE IN THE BLOOD
Diamonds—and vampires—
are a girl's best friend.

BLOOD ON THE WATER
Never put out a contract on a vampire.

DANCE OF DEATH

P. N. ELROD

ACE BOOKS, NEW YORK

If you purchased this book without a cover, you should be aware that this book is stolen property. It was reported as "unsold and destroyed" to the publisher, and neither the author nor the publisher has received any payment for this "stripped book."

DANCE OF DEATH

An Ace Book / published by arrangement with
the author

PRINTING HISTORY
Ace edition / March 1996

All rights reserved.
Copyright © 1996 by Pat Elrod.
Cover art by Mark Garro.
This book may not be reproduced in whole or in part,
by mimeograph or any other means, without permission.
For information address: The Berkley Publishing Group,
200 Madison Avenue, New York, NY 10016.

The Putnam Berkley World Wide Web site address is
http://www.berkley.com

ISBN: 0-441-00309-5

ACE®
Ace Books are published by The Berkley Publishing Group,
200 Madison Avenue, New York, NY 10016.
ACE and the "A" design are trademarks
belonging to Charter Communications, Inc.

PRINTED IN THE UNITED STATES OF AMERICA

10 9 8 7 6 5 4 3 2 1

*For Mark
and exhausting times.*

*A very special thanks to
Teresa Patterson,
for all your support on and off the field;
The Fort Worth Writer's Group,
for the help at the start;
Nigel Bennett, Deborah Duchêne,
and the great gang at Dead of Winter II
for the dose of totally wonderful fun;
and to Hershey's Chocolate U.S.A.,
for without certain of their products
portions of this book would not have been possible.*

As this story was written to give entertainment, not instruction, I have made no attempt to re-create the language spoken over two hundred years ago. There have been so many shifts in usage, meaning, and nuance that I expect a typical conversation of the time would be largely unintelligible to a present-day reader. Having had to "shift" myself as well to avoid becoming too anachronistic in a swiftly changing world, modern usage, words, and terms have doubtless found their way into this story. Annoying, perhaps, to the historian, but my goal is to clarify, not confound, things for the twentieth-century reader.

Though some fragments of the following narrative have been elsewhere recorded, Mr. Fleming, an otherwise worthy raconteur, misquoted me on several points, which have now been corrected. I hereby state that the following events are entirely true. Only certain names and locations have been changed to protect the guilty and their hapless—and usually innocent—relations and descendants.

—JONATHAN BARRETT

CHAPTER
~1~

London, December 1777

"You're certain that he's all right?" asked my cousin Oliver, shifting closer in an anxious effort to see better. "He looks like a dead fish."

Which was a perfectly accurate observation; however, I had no need to be reminded about the effect of my special influence on another person. I really had no need for Oliver's interruption, either, but he'd asked to watch and at the time there seemed no reason to deny his request. Now I was having second thoughts.

"Please," I said in a rather tight voice. "I must concentrate."

"Oh." His hushed tone was contrite, and he instantly subsided into silence and went very still, enabling me to put forth my full attention on the man sitting before us. Focusing my gaze hard upon his slack face, I softly spoke into his all too vulnerable mind.

You must listen very carefully to what I say. . . .

In this moment I truly felt myself balanced on the edge of a knife. With Oliver along to witness things, I was steadier than if I'd been alone, and yet I was very much aware of the

1

lamentable consequences should I make a mistake with this fellow. A single word on my part or a brief surge of uncontrolled rage let loose, and the man would most likely be plunged into a madness from which he might never recover. I'd done that once before—unintentionally—and would be a liar not to admit this present circumstance offered me a great temptation to repeat the action. God knows, I'd more than sufficient cause to justify such a malfeasance.

His name was Thomas Ridley, and last night he and his cousin Arthur Tyne had done their damnedest to try to murder me. For this and other crimes they'd committed or participated in, I had been informed it would be too much to expect a just retribution by means of the law; therefore I'd taken upon myself the responsibility to guarantee that they would commit no further mischiefs. Arthur had already been dealt with and would soon be sent away home when he was fit enough to travel. I'd drained quite a lot of blood from him last night—purely for the purpose of survival, not revenge— and he'd been but half awake and easy to influence.

Ridley was another matter.

We'd confined him to one of the more remote cellar storage rooms far beneath Fonteyn House, well away from any ears with no business hearing his bellowed curses. When I'd awakened that evening, had finished with the befuddled Arthur, and was ready to deal with Ridley, he'd worked himself into a truly foul temper, if one might judge anything by the coarsely direct quality of his language. Much of his invective involved both general and specific profanities against myself and my many relatives for his treatment at our collective hands.

Coming down to the cellar together, Oliver and I had dismissed the five footmen detailed to stand watch, and announced our presence to Ridley through the stout oak timbers of the door to his makeshift prison. He responded with a statement to the effect that it would be his greatest pleasure to kill us both with his bare hands. He saw no humor in Oliver's comment that he'd just given us an excellent reason for keeping him incarcerated until he was starved into a better disposition. Ridley's reaction was another tirade against us, accompanied by a solid crashing and thumping to indicate that he'd found something in his cell with which to make an assault on the door.

"I think we should have the footmen back," Oliver advised, casting a nervous eye at me. "We won't be able to handle him alone, he's far too angry for reason."

"He'll not be difficult for me once I'm inside."

"That's a proper lion's den in there and I must remind you that your name's Jonathan, not Daniel."

"And I must remind you that I have a bit more than just my faith to protect me in this instance."

"From the sound of things, you'll need it."

Ridley roared and smashed whatever weapon he'd found upon the door, causing it to rattle alarmingly. I hoped that his improvised club was not made of wood. For reasons unknown to me, wood presents a rare difficulty to my person when brought to bear with violence, and to it was I as susceptible to bodily harm as any ordinary man; I'd have to take care not to allow Ridley the least opening against me.

Easier said than done, Johnny Boy, I thought, steeling myself to enter. More out of trepidation of what was to come and to put it off just a bit longer than out of concern for Oliver, I paused to make an inquiry of him.

"You know what to expect, don't you?"

Ridley's commotion must have distracted him. "I expect he'll pulverize you, then come after me."

"He won't be able to. I was asking if you remembered what I was going to do to get inside."

"Oh, that," he said with wan enthusiasm. "Yes, you've mentioned it, but I'm not so sure that I've quite taken it in."

"I've never had cause before to demonstrate it for you. You're not going to swoon or do anything silly, are you?"

"For God's sake, how bad can it be?"

"It's not bad, just something of a surprise if one is unprepared for it."

"I should be able to manage well enough. Once one's witnessed a few amputations there's little enough the world can do to shake one's calm. Nothing like seeing a man getting his leg sawed off for putting you in a proper mood to count your blessings and to ignore most troubles life has to fling at you." As if to give lie to his statement, Oliver jumped somewhat at Ridley's next fit of hammering.

"Steady on, Coz." I found myself near to smiling at his discomfiture and wondered if he was playing the ass on purpose just to lighten things.

He scowled, jerking his head in the direction of the clamor. "Well, get on with it before he has the whole house down. Do what you must—just promise you'll try to come out in one piece."

"I promise." And with those words, I picked up one of the lighted candles left behind by the footmen and vanished.

Oliver emitted a sort of suppressed yelp, but held his ground as far as I could determine without benefit of sight. My hearing was somewhat impaired while in this bodiless state, but I could clearly sense his presence just in front of me—or what had been my front but a moment before. Now I floated, held in place by thought alone, and by that means did I propel myself to one side, find the crack between the cellar bricks and the wooden door, and sweep down and through to become solid once more in the little room beyond.

I say little, for Ridley seemed to fill the whole of its space. I was a tall man, but Ridley was just that much taller, possessing a large and fit body heavy with muscles and all of them full charged with his anger. The remains of some bandaging circled his head; he'd suffered injury last night and taken a shallow but colorful wound. It had probably opened again because of his exertions; the blood had soaked through, and I instantly picked up the scent of it. His right arm had been in a sling the last time I'd seen him. The sling was gone now and his arm hung slack at his side. He still had much energy in him, for he slammed at the door again using his good arm and called us cowards and damned us thrice over. His back was to me when I caused myself to reappear.

The candle I held yet burned, and its sudden radiance drew his instant attention upon me. He whirled, one hand raised holding what had once been a table leg and the other shading his eyes from the brightness of the flame. We'd left him in the dark for the whole of the day lest he work some damage by having fire, and so my tiny light must have been utterly blinding to him. Despite this, he was very game for a fight, and without warning threw his improvised club right at me with a guttural snarl. I wasted no time vanishing again, an action that plunged his room into full darkness once more since I still clutched the candle.

He must have been so lost to his emotions that it had made little or no impression on him that I'd appeared from nowhere and departed in the same manner. I'd held some hope that the surprise alone might slow him enough for me to soothe him to quiescence, but was forced to abandon it as he charged over to the spot where I'd been standing and tried to grab hold of me. I felt his arms passing this way and that through my invisible and incorporeal body. He, I knew, would feel nothing but an unnatural coldness.

Now he blundered about trying to find me, cursing like a dozen sailors.

"Jonathan?" Oliver called out in a worried voice.

I could not answer him in this form, nor could I count on him to be especially patient. We were as close as brothers, and his concern for me would soon cause him to fetch the footmen and come to my rescue. Even with the odds at seven to one Ridley would probably break some heads before being subdued.

I didn't care for that prospect one whit. When Ridley had crossed again to the door in his blind search, I allowed myself to assume a degree of visibility, but not solidity. He saw the candlelight immediately as before, but this time it was pale and watery, the brass holder in the hand of a ghost, not a man. This was so startling that he finally paused long enough to take in a good view of me. I was fairly transparent yet; doubtless he could see right through me to the damp brick wall at my back, an alarming effect that more than served. In the space of a moment Ridley went from a man who looked just short of bursting a blood vessel from his fury, to a man frozen with a profound astonishment beginning to edge into fear.

It was as close as I'd likely be able to come to a favorable condition for what needed to be accomplished. Quick as thought, I assumed full solidity, fastened my gaze unbreakably on to his, and told him to be *still*. Perhaps fed by my own heightened emotions, my order to him must have had more force to it than was necessary for he seemed to turn to cold marble right then and there. An abrupt twinge of dismay shot through me, and for an instant I thought I might have killed him, but this eased almost as quickly as it had come when my sharp ears detected the steady thunder of his heartbeat. I sagged from the relief.

"*Jonathan?*"

"I'm fine," I said loudly so Oliver could hear through the slab of oak between us. "It's safe now. You may unlock the door."

I heard the clink and rattle of brass, and the barrier between us swung hesitantly open. Oliver, his lanky frame blocking the lighted candles behind him, stood braced for trouble with a charged dueler in his hand.

"Where on earth did you get that?" I asked, staring.

"F-from my coat pocket, where d'ye think?"

"You won't need it; Ridley's asleep on his feet, as you can see."

Oliver narrowly examined my charge, then reluctantly put the pistol away. "He's under your influence, then?"

"For the moment."

His gaze alternated between my face and Ridley's. "First you're there and then you're not, and now this. You should have a conjuring show. It's just too uncanny."

"I quite agree," I said dryly.

"Something wrong?"

"I'm tired and I want to have done with this."

And more than that I wanted to feed again. Though outwardly I'd fully recovered from the attack Ridley and Arthur had made upon me the previous evening, I was still mending within. My vanishings just now had depleted my strength more than I cared to think about; my very bones felt hollow.

Perhaps Oliver realized something of this. He stood well aside allowing me to lead Ridley to sit at the table the footmen had recently used for their supper. I sat opposite him, checked on the number of lighted candles, and decided there was enough illumination for me to work by. The single one I'd used in the cell would have been insufficient for the sort of detailed project I was about to attempt.

Finally settled—as well as unable to put it off any longer—I began the dangerous process of rearranging another man's thoughts.

Oliver, after his initial question, was content to leave me undisturbed as I cautiously worked. Whenever I had to pause and think on what to say next, I'd steal a glance at my cousin and find him watching with rapt attention. Since first learning of them he'd been highly curious about my unnatural abilities; I hoped this demonstration would content him, since I wanted it to be the last one for the time being. I had no liking for forcing my influence upon another and took such a liberty with people only when dictated by dire necessity. At the worst it was a terrible and sometimes hazardous intrusion upon another and at the least any lengthy encounter like this one always gave me a god-awful headache.

But for all our sakes and his, Ridley very much needed to forget certain past events, as well as remember to abide by a new pattern of behavior in the future. Though presently un-

der my control, he was as hearty in mind as in body, and I
found it a difficult and exhausting task. I not only had to constantly maintain my hold against his strength of will, but labored hard to keep my own perilous emotions in check lest I
cause him a permanent injury of mind.

*You're not to pick any more duels, Ridley, do you under-
stand that? It's past time that you assume more peaceful pursuits than harassing honest citizens. No more violence for
you, my lad.*

Light enough words, but it was the force I put behind them
that counted. He blinked and winced a few times, a warning
to me to ease off. I did, but damnation, I'd come so *close* to
dying again . . .

*You know well enough how to cause trouble, so you must
certainly know how to avoid it, and that's exactly what you'll
be doing from now on. If I hear about you being in any more
rows . . . well, you just behave yourself or I'll know the reason why.*

When I'd run out of things to tell Ridley, which were
mostly instructions I'd already given to Arthur but requiring
much less of an exertion, I leaned back in my own chair to
pinch the bridge of my nose and release a small groan of sincere relief that it was finally finished.

"Now you're the one who looks like a dead fish," said my
good cousin.

"Then serve me up with some sauce, I'm ready to be carried out on a platter after all this."

Oliver pressed the back of his hand to my forehead. "No
fever, but it's clammy down here, so I can't be sure."

"I'm not feverish, only a bit worn down. A little rest and
some additional refreshment and I'll be my own self again."

"Which is something more than amazing from what
you've told me about your adventure."

"Less adventure than ordeal," I grumbled, rubbing my
arm. Arthur had nearly severed it with his sword last night,
and though muscle and sinew were knitted up again with

hardly a scar to show for the injury, it still wanted to ache. Another visit to the Fonteyn stables might help ease things.

"And I want to hear the full story of it, if you would be so kind. Elizabeth's only been able to repeat the high points you'd given her."

But I'd told my sister all that there was to tell and said as much now to Oliver.

"That's not the same as hearing from the source. Besides, I'm full of questions that she was unable to answer."

"Such as?"

"I'll ask 'em as they occur to me, so expect to be interrupted. For the moment, all I want to know is what do we do with Mr. Ridley here?"

Our guest was still blank-eyed and slack-jawed. Perhaps the experience was tiring to him as well. One could but hope. "Take him upstairs and put him with his cousin, then pack the two of 'em off as soon as Arthur's ready to travel."

"Tomorrow, whether he's ready or not."

That suited me very well. Wearily I stood and instructed Ridley to do the same and follow us out of the cellar and upstairs. He did so, as docile as a sheep. Oliver, leading the way with the one candle we'd not extinguished and left behind, cast a worried look back at our charge.

"We'll not have any more trouble with him? You're sure?"

"Quite sure." At least for the present. Ridley and Arthur would behave themselves for a time, but past experience told me that even the most firm suggestions would eventually erode away and be forgotten. I'd have to make a point of visiting them from time to time to strengthen what had been constructed in their minds tonight. My hope was they would eventually embrace my compelled guidance as their own desire, and no longer have need of my influence to keep out of trouble.

"Seems unnatural, that," Oliver muttered.

"I can readily agree."

"It also doesn't seem . . . well, enough, somehow."

"In what way?"

"After all that he's done and tried to do, just to tell him to run along and sin no more hardly seems fitting. He should be hanged."

"Did Edmond not explain to you how unlikely an occurrence that would be?"

"In rare detail if nothing else about this business. He also said the scandal would be bad for the family, though I'm getting to the point where I think a scandal would do the lot of 'em a world of good."

"I could almost agree with you, except for how it would involve and affect us. I am content to put it all behind me and get on to more rewarding pursuits."

"Damn, but you almost sound like him."

"I suppose I must. After all, think how much we have in common." I meant it as a light jest, but it didn't come out right. Oliver looked back again, eyebrows high with shock. "I'm sorry, Coz. That was very rude of me."

"Think nothing of it. You've had a hard time of things."

Wasn't that the grand understatement? And not just for last night but for the last year or so of my life. Oliver's sympathy coupled with his kind dismissal of my poor manners crushed me down as much as the weight of recent events seemed to be doing. My death, my return to life, my search for the woman who had made such a miracle possible, all pressed close, crowding out any other thoughts in my brain for the next few moments. So thoroughly did they occupy me that I was genuinely surprised to come to myself in the central hall of Fonteyn House with no recollection of how I'd gotten there.

"Now what?" asked Oliver, setting his candle on a table.

As an answer, I looked hard at Ridley until I was certain I had his full attention. "You are a guest of Fonteyn House and will conduct yourself in a gentle and honorable manner. The servants will see to your needs, and don't forget to give them a decent vale when you leave tomorrow morning.''

Ridley responded with a slight nod of acknowledgment, and I cocked an eyebrow at Oliver. He regarded each of us with no small amount of wonder.

''He can stay the night in Arthur's room,'' I said.

Taking the suggestion, Oliver called for a servant. One of the household's larger footmen appeared, stopping short in his tracks to give Ridley first a surprised, then highly wary look. He'd apparently heard tales from the men who had been on duty in the cellar. Of course, Ridley's appearance might have had something to do with it, what with all the bandaging, blood, and damage his clothes had taken from last night's fight and this day's incarceration. Add to that his abnormal *calmness* of manner and you had the makings of what promised to be some very speculative and animated belowstairs gossip.

''Show Mr. Ridley here to his cousin's room,'' Oliver instructed the man as though nothing at all was or had ever been amiss. ''He'll take his supper there, and see that he's cleaned up and has all he needs to stay the night. And be sure to have someone fetch along a very large brandy for me to the blue drawing room.''

The fellow looked ready to offer a few dozen questions, but was too well trained to make the attempt. Oliver's mother, the previous mistress of Fonteyn House, had not been one to encourage any kind of familiarity between servants and their betters, and her influence still lingered. The footman bowed and cautiously invited Ridley to follow him upstairs. Our prisoner, now our guest, went along as nice as you please without a backward glance at us. Oliver breathed out a pent-up sigh and let his shoulders sag a trifle. He exchanged a quick look with me; I gave him a short nod meant to reassure him that all was well and would remain so.

We watched until they reached the upper hall and turned into one of the rooms off the stairs where Arthur Tyne had been placed. More heavily concussed than Ridley and missing a goodly quantity of blood, he was slower to recover from his injuries. Bedrest and broth flavored with laudanum had been prescribed and administered, and he'd slept the day away under the watchful eye of one of the maids. The girl, her duties no longer required, soon emerged in the company of the footman and both quickly crossed our line of view to take the back way down to the kitchens. They were doubtless in a great hurry to carry the latest startling developments to the rest of the servants.

"Wonder what they'll make of all this?" I mused.

"Who knows, but we may be certain it will in no wise even remotely approach the truth."

"Mmm, then shall I thank God for such a mighty favor."

We moved along toward the blue drawing room, Oliver's favorite lair, to await the arrival of his brandy. By now I was in very sore need of a restorative as well. That hollow feeling in my bones had progressed to my muscles, and the pain in my head from all the influence I'd exercised against Ridley seemed worse than before. I wanted a deep draught of blood in me and fairly soon; the dull pounding that had taken up residence behind my eyes was threatening to become a permanent lodger.

"Please excuse me for a few minutes," I said as we approached the room. "I'd like to get some air to clear my brain."

"Go out to the stables for a drink, you mean," he corrected. "Of course, you've more than earned it. Would you object if I watched?"

"Good God, why on earth would you want to?"

"I am impelled by scientific curiosity," he stated, full of dignity.

"The same curiosity that allows you to sit through amputations?"

"Something the same as that, yes."

I shrugged, not up to trying to talk him out of it, and, as before when he wanted to see how I was to influence Ridley, there was no reason to deny his request. "Come along, then, let's get it over with."

"Such eagerness," he remarked. "You weren't like this that time with Miss Jemma at the Red Swan."

"That was for pleasure, this is for nourishment. There's a difference."

"So you've said, but don't you look forward to a nice bit of supper as much as any other man?"

"I do, but how would you feel having someone closely watching while you eat?"

"If you really mind that much—"

"I don't, I'm just reluctant lest the process disgust you. But then if you can witness an amputation without so much as batting an eye . . ."

Oliver went somewhat pink along his cheeks and ears. I'd caught him out, but decided against pressing him for embarrassing details. We found a maid to fetch our cloaks and wrapped ourselves against the outside chill, then ventured forth into the night.

The air was cold and clean as only a newly born winter can make it. My lungs normally worked just when I had need of breath to speak; now I made a real bellows of them, flushing out the stale humors lingering from the cellars. Oliver must have felt the same rejuvenating effect, for like schoolboys we contested to see who could make the greatest dragon plume as we crunched our way over the frozen earth to the stables.

Last night's sleet had transformed the world into a silvertrimmed garden that turned the most mundane things magical. My sensitive eyes found delight wherever I looked, a happiness that was somewhat dampened when I realized Oliver was unable to share in it. After my second attempt to point out an arresting view was accompanied by his complaint that he couldn't see a damned thing except that which was in the circle of his lantern light, I gave up and kept my appreciation for nature's joys to myself.

My cousin's presence was not unwelcome to me, though, particularly concerning this errand. In the London house that my sister Elizabeth and I shared with him, the servants had all been carefully influenced by me into ignoring some of my more singular customs, especially any after-dark excursions to visit the stable. The retainers at Fonteyn House were not so well prepared, making me glad of Oliver's company as an insurance against discovery. He was master here now, following the sudden death of his mother, and should anyone interrupt my feeding, he'd be the best man to deal with the problem.

He then demonstrated his own keen understanding about my need for privacy, for when we encountered some of the stable lads, he invented a minor household duty to take them elsewhere.

"Will you be long at this?" he murmured, watching them go.

I shook my head. "Having second thoughts?"

"No. Not trying to discourage me are you?"

"Hardly, since you're doing a fine enough job of it on your own."

"Am not," he stoutly protested, eyes all wide with mock outrage.

Laughing a little, I led the way in, picking out an occupied stall. Within stood one of the estate's huge plow horses. Placid to the point of being half asleep, the beast would hardly notice what would be done to him, and his vast body would provide far more sustenance than I could possibly take in.

Oliver fussed a bit to make sure he was in a position to have a clear line of observation and that his lantern was well placed for the best light. I spoke to the horse in my own way until I was utterly certain of its tranquillity. The inner anticipation I felt building within had swiftly prepared me to sup. My corner teeth, sharp enough to pierce the toughest of hides, had budded to a proper length for the work they were to do. I knelt, closing my eyes, the better to hear the heavy beat of the animal's great heart, the better to shut away my awareness of Oliver's presence. His own heart was thumping madly away, but the sound quickly became a distant triviality as my immediate bodily need was at last free to assert its supremacy over all outside distractions.

Now did I cut hard and fast with my teeth into the thick skin of the animal's leg to tap the vein that lay beneath. I was dimly aware of Oliver's strangled gasp somewhere to one side, and then I heard nothing else for a brief and blessed time as I sucked in all I needed and more of the fiery red vitality that had become my sole nourishment for life.

The night before I'd drunk deeply from another of the animals here, but then I'd been weary beyond thought, hurting, and in need of haste. There'd been no time to savor, no enjoyment to be had beyond the basic sating of appetite. Now could I hold the rich taste in my mouth and revel in it and give wordless thanks for its roaring heat as it rapidly suffused throughout my chilled flesh. The injuries, the worries, the cold failings of a harsh world thawed from my soul and melted into nothing.

Would that all the problems of life could be dealt with so easily.

I drank for as long as necessity dictated and beyond. No imbibing only enough to sustain myself for an evening or two, tonight I felt like playing the glutton. Perhaps I could take in enough blood to hold me for a whole week—an interesting, but questionable accomplishment. To achieve it might mean that my present enjoyment would be less frequent in occurrence. There had ever been a touch of the Hedonist in my nature, and, knowing that quality would not suffer, but quantity would, it seemed most reasonable to bring things to a stop.

But not until many, many delicious minutes passed by.

Reluctantly drawing away, despite the fact that I was full near to bursting, I pressed the vein above the point where I'd gone in and waited until the seeping blood slowed and finally clotted. My handkerchief took care of the few stains on my face and fingers. Practice had made me very tidy in habit.

The pain in my head was quite abated, and the strength had returned to all my limbs. Satisfaction, in every sense of the word, was mine.

Then I looked over at Oliver.

The golden glow of the lantern light lent no illusion of well-being to his face, which had gone very pasty, nor did his cloak seem to be of any use keeping him warm. He shivered from head to toe, exhibiting a misery so palpable that I felt its onrush like a buffet of wind.

Contrite that I'd caused him such distress, I raised one hand, but did not quite touch him for fear he might flinch away. I'd expected him to be affected in some adverse manner, for it is one thing to hear how a thing is done and quite another to watch, but I'd not expected his reaction to be *this* adverse.

"It's all right," he said quickly, his staring eyes not leaving mine. "Give me a moment."

"I'm sorry," I whispered.

"Sorry for what?" he demanded after taking in a few deep draughts of air. "You do what you must to live. If that involves drinking a bit of blood now and then, what of it?"

What, indeed? I thought. *What am I?* I had no name for my condition except for one fastened on me by a terrified Hessian soldier. *Blutsäuger.* Never liked the word. It made me think of spiders and how they sucked the life from their living prey. Ugh. No wonder poor Oliver was having a hard time of it.

He went on. "Pay no mind to me, I'm just cursed with a vivid imagination."

"What's *that* to do with anything?"

He gave a ghastly imitation of a smile. "Most of the time it's well in check, but tonight what with one thing and another . . ."

"What are you on about?"

"The bane of my life as a doctor, but only if I let it get away from me. Have to keep a tight hold on it when I'm dealing with a patient, else I'd be no good at all."

"Oliver—"

He waved a hand to quell my mild exasperation. "While you did your work just now, the physician in me was doing his. I was fine at first, observing, noting everything there was to note. Then I began to wonder what it might be like to be in your boots, downing all that blood like it was so much ale night after night, like it or not. Once my mind fixed on *that*, on all that blood drinking, and on the smell and taste of it . . . well, I couldn't seem to shake it off, so this foolish reaction is my own damned fault."

"I should not have allowed this."

"God's death, man, you think this is bad? Then you should have been there to see me at that first amputation. Five of the students fainted, and I was one of the dozen others who lost his last meal. Sometimes I can still hear the poor wretch's screams and the rasp of the bone saw. By comparison, this was nothing. Well-a-day, but I'd say I'm doing rather splendidly this time around."

"Oliver, you're—"

"A complete ass? And babbling his head off? Oh, yes, I'm sure of it, but even an ass needs to learn things now and then to get on in the world. Sometimes the lesson is easy and pleasant, and sometimes not, but it doesn't matter, knowledge is the goal."

"And you've gained knowledge from this?"

"Indeed I have, and from now on I'll not take it so lightly when you try to present a warning about any given aspect of your condition. That disappearance you did in the cellar fair gave me a turn, y'know. Thought my poor heart would stop then and there."

"Why didn't you say anything?"

"I thought if I did you'd get the wind up and not let me watch. I'm quite ashamed of myself. To be like this after all the bleedings I've done . . .'' He trailed off, shaking his head. ''But enough on me, tell me what happened to your teeth. One minute they're normal and the next . . . and I want to know how your eyes feel right now.''

''My eyes?''

''They're redder than a sunset—does it hurt? Does it affect your sight?''

''No, not at all, and I can see perfectly well.''

''Why do they get like that?''

''Damned if I know. I once asked Nora about it, for hers did the same when she fed, but she said she didn't know, either.'' Or she chose not to tell me about it as she'd done with a thousand other details.

His mouth twitched at the mention of Nora's name. ''And damned funny that she never told you what to expect after . . . well, we've talked that one over often enough. Let me see your teeth.''

I obliged and opened my mouth. He muttered that the light wasn't good for a proper examination, and I suggested that we remove ourselves back to the warmth of the house where there were plenty of candles. I also reminded him that a large brandy still awaited him there. Either enticement was enough to inspire him to action; together both inspired him to haste.

Once back in the house, and ensconced before the blazing hearth in the blue drawing room, I found myself to be better disposed to undergo a doctor's examination. Though Oliver had known about my changed condition and the story behind it for some little time, this had been the first opportunity he'd had to really look into things. I harbored a small hope that his training in medicine might yield up some explanation for my unusual physical state.

Since Nora Jones, the woman I had loved—still loved—the woman who had gifted me with this strange condition, had seen fit not to provide me with anything in the way of preparation on how to deal with it, I'd had to learn about my

advantages and limitations by many trials and much error.
Certainly I'd used what knowledge I recalled about her own
habits as a guide, but after more than a year of it, I was still
full of many important questions and singularly lacking in
answers. The urgency to see her again and to obtain those answers had drawn me from my lifelong home on Long Island
and back to England again in an effort to find her.

Unhappily, she was not to be found. Oliver had done his
best, moving through his wide circle of friends and acquaintances in London, writing to others on the Continent trying to
locate her, or at least a hint of her presence. The only clue I'd
had of her passing had come from a madman named Tony
Warburton, and it had been less informative than frustrating
and the cause of a profound unease on my soul. He'd said
she'd been ill. So impervious was I to sickness and injury I
could not imagine what she might be suffering from. I also
tried very hard not to imagine that she might have suc-
cumbed to it. My success at this endeavor was indifferent at
best. If not for the support of Oliver and my sister, Elizabeth,
I might have turned madman myself. They distracted me
from my melancholy fits and helped me to maintain hope,
but it was hard going for all of us.

When he'd initially learned about my change, the shock
had put Oliver's innate curiosity off for a time, and after that
family events and troubles had supplanted all other matters.
Only last night we'd interred his mother in the Fonteyn mausoleum, a miserable occupation for everyone concerned, but
particularly so for my poor cousin since he'd hated the old
harridan.

Because of this hate, he'd had a difficult time dealing with
her death. The world expected one kind of response from
him and his heart poured forth quite another. He'd retreated
into a shell filled with nebulous self-censure for several days,
until I'd had enough and took a firm hand, giving him a good
talking to about it.

I'd managed to coax him away from his guilt in this

very room. The servants had done a remarkable job of cleaning up the mess. Only a bit of scraped wood on the floor, a
few dents in the frame of a painting knocked from the wall,
and a missing vase broken during our "conversation" gave
the least evidence that anything had happened. My injuries
from the encounter were all healed, and so, I hoped, were his,
particularly the old ones his mother had inflicted, the ones
that had threatened to swell and fester upon Oliver's soul.

His reawakened curiosity seemed to be a good sign of his
spiritual health, and had been one of the points I'd considered before giving my consent to let him watch me feeding.
Whatever adverse reaction he might draw from it could hardly be worse than anything he'd had to deal with while growing up in the dark halls of Fonteyn House.

"Now just you open wide," he told me, looming in close
with a candle.

I opened wide, baring my teeth, then squawked when he
brought the flame uncomfortably near. "You'll singe my
eyebrows off!"

"No, I won't," he insisted. "Oh, very well, hold still and
I'll try something else." He pulled a small mirror from a
pocket and employed it in such a way as to reflect the candlelight where he wanted. Unfortunately for the purposes of his
science, both his hands were occupied and he could not conduct a proper examination. "Damn, but if I could only get a
good look in proper daylight," he complained.

"Impossible," I said, hoping he wouldn't insist on trying.
The sun and I were no longer friends, but if Oliver's zealous-
ness overtook his sense, he might forget that vital detail and
take action.

"Don't talk." He put the candleholder on a small table
and asked me to lean in its direction. I did so. Holding the
mirror steady in one hand, he used the fingers of the other to
grasp one of my corner teeth and tug. I felt it slide down. Surprised, he released it and gaped as it slowly retracted into
place.

''Like a deuced cat's claw, only straighter,'' he said, full of wonder and repeating the action. ''Does that hurt?''

''No.''

''What does it feel like?''

''Damned strange,'' I lisped.

''You should see how it looks,'' remarked a new voice that gave us a start. ''The servants will think the both of you have gone mad.''

My good sister Elizabeth stood in the open doorway regarding us with a calm eye and a curl of high amusement twisting one side of her mouth.

''Hallo, sweet Cousin,'' Oliver said, a grin breaking forth upon his mobile features. Elizabeth's presence always had a hugely cheering effect on him. ''You couldn't come at a better time. I need you to hold this mirror so I can give your brother's teeth a good looking over.''

''Whatever are you doing?'' she asked, not moving from her place by the door, God bless her.

''Scientific inquiry, my dear girl. I want to thoroughly examine the workings of Jonathan's condition, and since the good God did not provide me with three hands, I should like to borrow one of yours for a moment.''

''Scientific inquiry? How fascinating.'' With a wicked smile, she determinedly moved in on poor helpless me.

''Now just one moment . . .''

But I had no chance to further object. In a twinkling she was next to Oliver, holding the mirror and watching with avid interest as he poked and tapped and tugged my teeth with happy abandon. I endured it for as long as I could, then made a garbled protest loud enough to inform them that the examination was, for the time being, over.

''Before heaven, I think you've dislocated my jaw,'' I complained, rubbing the offended area.

''I just wanted to see if the lower teeth were also capable of extension,'' he explained.

''Next time ask. I could have told you that they don't.''

"Sorry, I'm sure, but there's so much that you don't know about yourself that I've gotten used to your negative answers every time I do ask about anything. It seemed simpler just to go ahead and experiment."

"There's no harm done," Elizabeth told him. "But I think we've tried Jonathan's patience sufficiently for this night. Besides, he's needed elsewhere now. That is, if you have concluded your business with those two Mohocks."

"Messieurs Ridley and Tyne have been dealt with, dear sister. I doubt they shall ever resume their destructive activities with their old crowd again."

"Thank God for that. Now straighten your neckcloth, dust off your knees, and let's get along. Nanny Howard's been waiting for more than an hour on you."

"Nanny Howard?" said Oliver, then his expression abruptly altered. "Oh, I'd quite forgotten about that. Really, Jonathan, you should have reminded me. Or did you forget as well?"

"No, that is to say . . ."

"Don't tell me you've been putting it off."

"Not precisely, but there's just been so much to think about that I—"

"You *have* been putting it off."

"I have not, I've just . . . well . . ."

Elizabeth stepped in. "Don't badger him, Oliver. Can't you see he's terrified?"

"Terrified? *Him?* After all he's gone through?"

"Do please make allowances, Cousin. He's never been through this before."

Oliver frowned and shrugged. "I see what you mean. Come to think of it and given the choice, I'd probably be hiding in the cellar about now, or be halfway to France. It's a hard road you've picked for yourself and no mistake."

"Surely not that hard," I said.

"Consider how much of the way of it you'll be walking with Cousin Edmond, then tell me that again."

He'd made a good point there, but I'd deal with Edmond later.

"Edmond can keep," said Elizabeth. "Our concern is with young Richard. Come along, little brother, put your best foot forward. It's not every day a man gets to meet his son for the first time."

CHAPTER
-2-

This was not strictly true. I had met the child last night, though he'd not been awake for the occasion. It was probably for the best, since the knowledge of his existence had been a frightful surprise for me. Coming as it did some four years after his birth, I was hardly prepared to deal with it in an intelligent manner. For the most part, I'd simply stared in wonder at the little boy asleep on his cot—the little boy bearing my features—that his mother had been so careful to keep insulated from the rest of the family lest they discover his true paternity.

Even now, with Elizabeth and Oliver there to take me in hand, I hardly felt ready to deal with the mere prospect of meeting my natural son, much less a face-to-face encounter. It was enough to make the bravest man's resolve tremble and collapse upon itself. Who was I if not a child myself, surely unable to assume the responsibility involved.

But Elizabeth adjusted my neckcloth, I saw to the dusting of my knees, then out we marched with Oliver to the upstairs rooms that served as the house nursery. My feet threatened to transmute into leaden weights along the way;

if left to myself, this few minutes' walk might have turned
into an hour's journey. Their company forced me to keep
to a normal pace. Before them I had to pretend to an enthusiasm I did not possess as I had no desire to draw additional attention to myself.

*Why so reluctant, Johnny Boy? It's not as though you
haven't met him already.*

True, but until then I'd no knowledge of the child's existence and therefore no time to think about things. Besides,
he'd been safely asleep. Now that the initial surprise and
shock had worn off somewhat I was just beginning to com-
prehend the enormity of what I was about to face.

I *could* give the child a looking over, then leave him to
Edmond and have done with it, but my heart, quailing as
it was at an unknown future, firmly told me that that was
not the honorable course to follow. I'd already given Edmond to understand that I was interested in the boy's welfare, something that had surprised him at the time. After
thinking about it, my reaction was something of a surprise
to me as well, but the words had been said, and I'd have
to stand by them. For it was my duty . . . obligation . . . burden . . .

Good God, but Elizabeth and Oliver were positively
alight with anticipation for what was to come. I was hard
pressed to keep my own shameful cowardice well-hidden—
an achievement made particularly difficult because of a craven voice within urging me to bolt and run from the house
while I could.

Then I seemed to hear my father's voice as sometimes
happened when I most needed his counsel.

*Always move forward, laddie. We're all in God's hands
and that's as safe enough place as any in this world.*

It helped steady me, helped to drown out my disgraceful
whining.

Would that he could be here, though. Of course, *then* I'd
have to break the news to him. . . .

Later, I promised myself.

Most of the family members who had stayed overnight after Aunt Fonteyn's funeral had gone home today, taking their own offspring back to more familiar surroundings. It might have been easier to leave the children at home to begin with, but those parents with long-reaching plans found weddings and funerals to be ideal times to allow the coming generation a chance to meet. Thus were advantageous matches often made a dozen years prior to the actual nuptials.

My son's mother—and Edmond's wife—Clarinda Fonteyn, had gone with custom and brought the boy with her. I could assume that it was done for the sake of form so as not to draw attention to him by his absence. Certainly she would not have shown him off to the other adults. His resemblance to me was unmistakable and the reason why she had incited her lover Ridley into murdering me. She'd not wanted me around as a living reminder of her past indiscretion; it would have spoiled her plans for her future.

Clarinda had had ambitions—dangerous for me and for her husband, and entirely fatal for Aunt Fonteyn. Edmond and I had survived them, but what effect the aftermath would have on young Richard was yet to be determined.

"Here," said Elizabeth, pausing and touching my arm. "I thought you should have a present to give him." She drew a parcel from a hidden pocket in her wide skirts and thrust it at me.

Nonplussed, I accepted it, staring as if I might see through the wrappings and string to what lay within.

"It's a toy horse," she explained before I could ask. "Oliver's idea."

"If that's all right with you, Coz," he added. "I mean, I had one myself. You don't mind, do you?"

I spread my hands, deeply touched by their consideration. "Before God, I think I've got the best family that ever was."

"This small part of 'em, anyhow. I'd not be too certain about the rest of the lot if I were you. They're all mad in one way or another y'know. Hope the boy takes after you and not Clar—well . . . that is to say . . .'' He suddenly went very red.

"Oh, let's not be silly about this," Elizabeth said, regarding us both with a severe eye. "All right, so young Richard's mother is what she is. That need not affect him in an adverse manner unless we do it ourselves by behaving strangely every time her name comes up in conversation. Jonathan, do you not recall how Father dealt with the subject whenever we inquired after Mother as children?''

"Vividly."

"How?" asked Oliver.

"He'd tell us that she had to be away from home because she was ill and did not want us to become sick as well," she answered.

Was that not the stark truth of it? I thought. Later, when we were much older, Father explained that Mother's illness had to do more with her mind than her body. Now did we understand the extent of damage that might have been done had she remained with her family and not gone off to live far away from us as we matured.

"Since Jonathan wants to make himself a part of Richard's life, then I think it best that we decide here and now how to behave ourselves concerning Clarinda. I had a long talk with Edmond about it today—''

"Edmond?" I yelped, leaving my jaw hanging wide.

"Certainly, little brother. You weren't in a condition to do so, and as the boy's aunt, I think I have a justified interest in his future."

Clarinda's husband. With all my physical advantages over normal men and despite the fact that we were on reasonably amicable terms considering the outrageousness of the situation, even I was subject to a tremor or two when it came to facing Edmond Fonteyn. That Elizabeth had done so and apparently emerged unscathed raised my already high respect for her capabilities to a yet loftier elevation.

"We had a very constructive conversation about the whole business," she said, "and he promises to be quite reasonable about how to deal with Richard concerning Clarinda. In fact, he thought that Father's example would work perfectly for him in every way as well."

"You told him about Mother?"

"Certainly, since he knew all about Aunt Fonteyn and her ways. He expressed great curiosity to me over how we managed to turn out to be so sensible, so I thought it the polite thing to inform him."

Unspoken was my thought that Edmond might have been comparing us to Oliver and found my cousin somewhat lacking. Not that Oliver was a fool; it just suited him to assume the role when the need arose. The need, unfortunately, seemed to occur most often whenever Edmond was around.

"Is it agreeable to you both that we should follow this direction?" she asked, knowing full well we'd have to say yes. We did not dare disappoint her. "That's resolved, then. Are there any other points that we need to discuss?"

"I have one," said Oliver. "What does Edmond plan to do when the rest of the family twigs on who the boy's real father is?"

"We did not precisely address that issue, but I got the impression he'd stare them down and dare 'em to say a word to his face."

"That's fine for him, he can take care of himself, but when people start whispering and the other children start bullying the lad—"

"I think that will be best worked out as it happens," I cautiously put in.

Elizabeth favored me with an approving look and turned again to Oliver. "Anything else?"

"One more thing, I fear. What are we to tell the boy? He'll have to learn about his true parentage, y'know."

For this, Elizabeth made no response. Both of them looked expectantly at me. I raised and dropped my hands, giving in to pure helplessness. "I'll have to talk to Edmond about it, I suppose. But for now, the boy's only four, the knowledge will hardly mean anything to him, nor would it do him much benefit. Such a topic can wait until the time is right for it to be addressed."

"Well said," Oliver commented. "I suppose I worry too much and too far ahead of myself for anyone's good."

"I believe that it has become your lot to have to do so. You're head of the family now, aren't you?"

He snorted, rolling his eyes. "Yes, God help me. They're already coming forward, wanting me to settle disputes—or should I say take sides. You'd think I was a judge and not a doctor the way they go on about their squabbles."

"You'll do all right."

"Humph. Easy for you to say, Coz, you're well out of it for the day. Wish I could hide in the cellars when they come calling with a new problem."

"No, you *don't*," I told him with such absolute sincerity that he laughed.

"What? You've no liking for sleeping the day through and avoiding its troubles?"

"I told you that it's not really sleep—"

"Bother it, you know what I mean."

"Indeed I do, but I'd gladly take on a bit of trouble if a bit of real daylight went with it, too."

My wistful tone turned him instantly contrite. "I'm sorry, I should have thought first before—"

"No, you shouldn't. You're fine just as you are." Best to curtail *that* kind of thinking, or my poor cousin would end up apologizing every time he opened his mouth for a jest. "I'm the one who's too serious around here. My point was that it is a wise thing to have a care on what you wish for. Now if you *really* want to spend the day skulking in a damp cellar and never ever taste brandy again—''

He raised both hands in a horrified shudder. "Enough, enough already! You make my skin crawl. Ugh!''

Good humor was with us once more. "Right then. You've reminded me of something. I've a question for you, Elizabeth.''

She tilted her head expectantly.

"Tell me, dear sister, was it you who went home and fetched some of my earth today?''

Because of all the many distractions the night before I'd had no time to return to my usual sanctuary under Oliver's house in town and had to seek shelter from the dawn in the cellars of Fonteyn House. Safe enough from the hazards of daylight it was, but when denied the comfort of my native soil I was always subject to an endless series of bad dreams and powerless to escape them until the setting of the sun. This time, though, the infernal dreams had mysteriously curtailed themselves, and against all expectations I'd achieved a decent day's rest. Upon awakening this evening I discovered that someone had placed a sackful of earth next to me where I'd made a bed on the floor of an unused wine cupboard.

"I could not go myself—with so much work to do it was just impossible to get away," she said, "but I did dispatch a note along to Jericho to send over a quantity. What a blessing it was that you taught him to read and write. To have given such strange instructions to the footman verbally—well—there's enough gossip belowstairs as it is. No need to add to it.''

"Indeed not, and for your trouble you have my thanks. You spared me no end of torment today.''

"I'd like to study that aspect of your condition, too,'' Oliver put in. "There must be some reason behind it.''

"Perhaps later," I said, hoping he'd notice my singular lack of eagerness.

Fortunately, he did. "I see. There's better things afoot than having your doctor plague you with questions for hours on end. Come along, then, let's go meet this brat of yours."

"He's not a brat," I objected.

"How do you know? Weren't you a brat at that age? I was, when I could get away with it, and what fun I had, too." Eyes aglow, he tucked Elizabeth's hand over his arm and continued down the hall, leaving me to catch up as best I could.

The nursery looked quite deserted now. The cots and bedding were folded and put away, and all their occupants long gone home except for one. Nanny Howard, the tiny woman in charge of this most important post, sat by a sturdy table with some sewing in her lap, working by the light of several candles. She glanced up as we entered and without saying a word managed to communicate to us that we were very tardy and no excuses would be accepted for the transgression.

Hers was a kind face, though. She'd been Oliver's nanny once upon a time, and his regard and respect for her ran very broad and deep. Certainly she alone had provided him with his only real source of love and protection when he was growing up under the cold eye and critical tongue of his mother. His expression softened and warmed as he looked at her. He silently excused himself from Elizabeth and went over to take the other woman's hand, bending to kiss her cheek.

"Hallo, Nanny. I was a bad lad last evening, or so they tell me."

"Indeed you were. No chocolate for you tonight."

He ducked his head in mock shame, then she tapped his wrist twice with her free hand in an equally mock slap. "There now, all's forgiven. Stand up straight and tell me what you've been about today."

"Oh, just seeing to business. What with all that's hap-

pened there's quite a lot of it going around—like an out-
break of the pox.''

She nodded. ''I've not been able to tell you how sorry I
am about your mother's death.''

His mouth worked. Her expression of sympathy for him
was genuine, probably making it that much harder to accept. He did, though, murmuring his thanks to her.

''Are you also here to see Richard?'' she asked him, her
eyes glancing over toward me and Elizabeth.

''I should say so. Past time it was done, don't you
think?''

''Well past time. I was about to put him to bed. He gets
cross when he's kept up too late.''

''Oh, but I meant—oh, never mind. Bring him out and
let's have a good look at him.''

She stood and rustled into an adjoining room.

If my heart was still capable of beating, now would be
the time for it to recommence that duty; perhaps then my
chest would not feel so appallingly tight. A great lump was
trying to rise and lodge in my throat, and I found myself
swallowing hard and repeatedly in a vain effort to push it
down.

Elizabeth slipped her hand into mine. ''It's all right. He's
only a little boy.''

''I know, but—''

''It's all *right*,'' she said, squeezing my fingers.

Another unsuccessful swallow. What would he think of
me? *Would* he even think anything? Would he like me?
What would he call me?

Nanny Howard provided an answer at least for the last
of the many panic-inspired questions bombarding my over-
active brain. Herding her charge into the room, she said,
''Come along now and meet your cousins, there's a good
lad.''

He tottered hesitantly in ahead of her, and such a little
creature he seemed to me with his diminutive limbs and

overly solemn expression. Thick black hair, fine pale skin, huge blue eyes, and rosy lips, he hung back by Nanny Howard, frowning a bit at this formidable gathering of adults. He came in nonetheless.

"He's your living image," Oliver said under his breath.

"In miniature," said Elizabeth in the same hushed tone. "Oh, he's beautiful, Jonathan."

As if I could take much credit for the boy. All I'd done was provide seed for his mother to conceive him. Despite the hasty and imprudent circumstances of that illicit joining, I had to admit that the results were astonishing.

Mrs. Howard urged him forward. "Richard, this is your Cousin Oliver. Remember how you were taught to greet people?"

Mouth pursed in concentration, Richard nodded and made a deep bow, hand to the waist of his petticoats. "At your service, sir," he said, the seriousness of his manner making an appealing contrast to his light, piping voice.

"And yours, young master," Oliver gravely responded.

"Oliver's the head of the family now, did you know that?" Mrs. Howard asked of the boy.

Whatever it might mean to Richard, he decided that another bow was in order and so executed one in good form. This time Oliver returned it with a dignified nod of his head, but he was struggling hard not to smile.

Mrs. Howard turned the boy slightly to face his second visitor. "And this is your pretty Cousin Elizabeth."

"How do you do, Cousin Richard?" Elizabeth asked. She was positively quivering from inner excitement. Above all the others I could hear her heart pattering away as she extended her hand toward him. He bowed deeply over it.

"Very well, thank you." There seemed to be a hint of guarded interest in his eyes for her.

"How old are you?"

"I am four, and next year I shall be five. How old are you?"

This brought forth an admonishment from Mrs. Howard that that was not a proper question for a gentleman to ask a lady. He then inquired why it was so.

"We'll discuss it later. Now you must greet Miss Elizabeth's brother. This is your Cousin Jonathan, and he's come all the way from America to meet you."

Reminded of his social duty, Richard bowed and I returned it. Doubtless our respective dancing masters would have been well pleased.

"What's 'Merica?" he demanded, looking me right in the eye.

"It's a land very far from here," I told him.

"Is it farther than Lon'on?"

"Oh, yes. Very much farther. Right across the ocean."

"What ocean? I can tell them all to you, the 'Lantic, the Pacific, the Ind'n . . .''

"Stop showing off, Richard." said Mrs. Howard.

He subsided, pouting at the interruption of his recitation.

"You're very well up on your geography, aren't you?" I asked.

He nodded.

"Do you know your letters and numbers, too?"

Another nod.

"Mr. Fonteyn is most particular that the boys have their lessons early and regular." Mrs. Howard had not referred to Edmond Fonteyn as Richard's father. I wondered if that was a conscious effort on her part.

"Boys? Oh, yes. Richard's older brother." I recalled Clarinda mentioning him, but not his name.

"Away at school, bless his heart. And then this one will be off himself in a few short years. They grow up much too fast for me."

I vaguely agreed with her and found myself first staring at Richard, then trying hard not to stare. Shifting from one foot to the other, I experienced the uncomfortable realization that I'd run out of things to say to him.

Elizabeth came to my rescue with a gentle tap on the package I held in one arm and had quite forgotten. I shot her a look of gratitude and knelt to be at a better level with Richard.

"Do you like presents?" I asked him. "If you do, then this one is yours."

From his reaction as he took the package, I gathered that he very much liked presents. The string baffled him a moment, but Mrs. Howard's sewing scissors removed it as an obstacle. A few seconds of frenzied action accomplished the release of his prize from the wrappings, and he crowed and held up a truly magnificent horse for all to see. Shiny black with a brightly painted saddle and bridle, it was very lifelike, carved in a noble pose with an arched neck and tail.

"By George," said Oliver, "if it doesn't look like that great beast you brought over with you."

Elizabeth beamed. "The very reason why I picked that one over the others in the shop. It reminded me so much of Rolly."

"You're brilliant," I told her.

"Aren't I just?"

"Who's Rolly?" asked Richard, his bright gaze momentarily shifting toward us.

"Rolly's my own horse," I said. "He's a big black one with some white on his face just like the one you have there. I'll . . . I'll give you a ride on him some day, if you like."

"Yes, please!"

"Not so loud," Mrs. Howard cautioned. "A gentleman never raises his voice to another, you know."

"Yes, please," he repeated in a much lower pitch.

"And what do we say when we get a gift?"

"Thank you very much."

"You're very welcome, I'm sure," I said, feeling all shaky inside. *'Fore God, what was I getting myself into?*

Oblivious to my inner turmoil, Richard darted away and began playing with his new toy, strutting back and forth through the room as if practicing the art of dressage. He provided a variety of horse noises to go with his imagined exhibition, from whinnies to the clip-clop of hooves.

"A success," Elizabeth observed, leaning toward my ear.

"To you goes the credit, if not the thanks."

"I got my thanks when I saw the look on your face."

"Don't you mean his?"

"I mean yours while he opened it up. You looked ready to burst."

"I'm sure I don't know what you mean."

"Do you not?"

Oliver, not to be excluded, got Richard to pause long enough in his parade to ask if he liked chocolate.

"Yes, please!" he bellowed, drawing Mrs. Howard's mild reproof again.

"Well, let's see what I have in my pocket," Oliver said, digging deep. "Here we are—I think. Yes, there it is." He produced a fat twist of paper, collecting a thanks from Richard, who carried off this second prize to enjoy on his own in a far corner of the room.

"You're not to be spoiling him, Mr. Oliver," Mrs. Howard said, hands on her hips.

"Just this once won't hurt."

"Only this once. More than that and I don't care how big you are, I'll put you over my knee just like I used to years ago."

"No doubt. Then I shall consider myself warned off. Does that rule against spoiling infants apply to Jonathan and Elizabeth, too?"

He had her there, and knew it, though she continued to favor him with an arch gaze.

"Of course, we won't presume to infringe on what you deem to be best for the boy, Mrs. Howard," Elizabeth promised. But I knew my sister and had seen that particular look on her face many times before. Richard was going to reap a bountiful crop of gifts from his aunt in the future.

"Thank you, Miss Elizabeth." By her tone, I gathered that Nanny Howard was not for one moment fooled, either. "Well, custom says that first meetings should be brief and polite, and it's past his bedtime . . ."

"I don't want to go to bed," Richard announced. Chocolate smeared the lower part of his face and coated his fingers. Mrs. Howard moved in on him, pulling a handkerchief from her apron pocket. There followed a short struggle as she tried to clean away the worst of it before the stains wandered to his pinafore. She must have dressed him in his best for the occasion, and so her anxiety to spare his garment from damage was most understandable. It reminded me of my own tribulations in the nursery and how glad I'd been to forsake my child's petticoats for my first suit of boy's clothing. He was at least two years away from that glorious rite of passage. I wondered if he'd lie awake nearly all night as I'd done, too excited with anticipation to sleep.

"You seem pensive, little brother."

"Oh, not a bit of it. I was just watching."

Duty done, Mrs. Howard invited Richard to bid us good night. He did so with notable hesitation, but I thought it had less to do with parting from our company than with a natural reluctance to give up the day and go to sleep. Mrs. Howard took him in hand and led him off to the next room. They'd just reached the door when with a cry he broke away from her and darted over to where he'd left his toy horse. He seized it strongly in both hands, hugging it to his body, and marched back.

Then he paused, turned, and looked me right in the eye as before, and flashed me the devil's own grin.

Then he was gone.

My mouth had popped open. What breath I had within

simply left, as if it had other business to attend. I stood as
dumbfounded as one can be and still have consciousness,
though there was little enough evidence of that in my frozen brain. I was dimly aware of Elizabeth exclaiming some
words of approval to Oliver and his own reply, but blast
me if I was able to discern anything more of their speech.

I felt all light and heavy at the same time, and if my
heart no longer beat, then surely it had given a mighty lurch
when that exquisite child had smiled at me so. My sight
misted over for a second or two. I blinked to clear it, wondering, wondering what on earth was the matter with me.

And then I knew, as clearly and as brightly as if lighted
up by a thousand candles. I knew in that moment that I
loved the boy. The boy. My child. My *son*.

Just like that.

"Jonathan?" Elizabeth pressed a hand on my arm.
"What's wrong?"

I shook my head at her foolishness. And at my own
foolishness. "Nothing. Absolutely nothing at all."

"Come on, Elizabeth, you must have something to cel-
ebrate meeting your nephew," said Oliver. "Since Jonathan can't join in, you'll have to make up for his place in
a toast."

"I should be delighted to try, but if you give me anything
stronger than barley water or better yet, some tea, I shall
fall asleep here and now."

"Asleep! After all that?"

"Especially after all that."

We'd returned to Oliver's drawing room to find the fire
was in need of revival. Eschewing the employment of a
servant, Oliver set himself to the task, being full of considerable energy and needing to work it off. He did ring for
someone to bring in some form of refreshment, though. He
chose port for himself and dutifully ordered a pot of tea for
Elizabeth.

"You'll be awash with this later when dinner's done," he warned her after a maid had come and gone leaving behind a loaded tray.

"I'm tempted to avoid dinner altogether and have something sent to my room," she said, pouncing on the teapot like a she-cat on a mouse.

"What? Leaving me to face the remaining crowd on my own?"

"Hardly a crowd, Oliver. There's just a few elderly aunts and uncles left, after all."

"And the lot of 'em starin' at me the whole time like a flock of gouty crows. Don't you think they aren't interested in the goings-on last night, because they are. I managed to keep out of their way so far, but there'll be no escaping them at dinner." He shuddered, pouring himself a generous glass of the port, then downing the greater part of it.

Elizabeth was not without pity. "Very well, for your sake I'll play hostess and talk about the weather should anyone ask you an embarrassing question."

"Thank you, dear Coz. The weather! Excellent topic! There's nothing they like better than to discuss how bad it's been and how much better it was when they were younger. We'll give 'em a real debate on it. Well, that's all solved. Now, about young Richard . . ."

"What about him?"

"I was only going to say what a fine lad he seems to be. What about you, Jonathan? We've not heard a peep from you since we came down."

Both looked at me, but I really had nothing to say. I was so full of feeling that words seemed pointless.

"I think my brother is still in the thrall of shock," Elizabeth observed.

Smiling, I shrugged in a way to indicate that she was more than a little correct.

Oliver's face blossomed with sudden anxiety. "You don't dislike him, do you?"

My sister answered for me. "Of course he doesn't, that's why he's in such shock. Give him some time to get used to the idea, then you'll hear him talking about nothing else."

I shrugged again, adding a sheepish smile.

Oliver raised his glass, saw that it was nearly empty, and took the opportunity to fill it again. "Then here's to the very good health of my cousin Jonathan and his son Richard."

Elizabeth raised her teacup and joined him in the toast. I spread my hands and bobbed my head once, modestly accepting the honor. I was yet unable to offer coherent conversation and quietly eased into a comfortable chair near the fire. They occupied themselves with their own talk about Richard, not excluding me so much as allowing me time for my own reflections and speculations. I folded my hands and watched the flames, content with all the world and my lot of it in particular.

"Heavens!" Elizabeth hastily set down her cup and gestured sharply at the mantel clock. "See the time—I'll be late for dinner if I don't go up now and dress for it. You, too, Oliver, unless you want to pique family curiosity even more about what you've been doing today."

"No," he said, sighing deeply. "Can't have that, though it's bound to be a rotten tribulation. Jonathan's the lucky one, he can do whatever he likes while we sit chained to the table for the next few hours."

"Or at least until the ladies take their leave," she reminded him. "Then you and the other men can get as drunk as you please while I drown in tea." Custom held that all ladies had to eventually retire from the table for their tea or coffee until it was time for the gentlemen to rejoin them for the serving of dessert.

"Well, I did warn you. Tell you what, I'll see if Radcliff will sneak some brandy into the teapots for you. That should help you pass the time more merrily."

"Dearest Oliver, it's a wonderful idea, but we ladies have already long made a practice of it."

"Have you, by God! First time I've heard of it. Perhaps I should forsake keeping company with the gentlemen and fall in with your troop."

"Cleave to your duty," she advised him. "Except for me there's not a woman left in the house that's under sixty. You'd be bored to death in five minutes for that's ever been my fate. Now I really *must* go." So saying, she swept out, skirts swinging wide and bumping against the doorframe, and we heard her quick progress down the hall.

"A damn fine girl, your sister," said Oliver. "A pity she didn't find a man worthy of her."

"She probably will, given time and inclination," I murmured. "But whoever she may settle on will have to behave himself with the two of us as her guardians."

He laughed. "Now, isn't that heaven's honest truth, especially with your talents. Tell me, though, if it's not too impertinent, why did you not question that Norwood fellow first before she married him—just to be sure about him?"

What a sore wound it was he'd struck. I actually winced. Oliver started to withdraw the question, but I waved him down. "No, it's all right. All I can say is that it seemed an ungodly intrusion at the time. She was so in love with him that I hesitated to tamper with her happiness. As it turned out, my hesitation damned near got her killed. Be assured, I will not make the same mistake again. Should she seriously take up with another suitor I'll be able to tell soon enough if he's a right one or a rogue."

"Now there's a good idea for an occupation."

"Hmm?"

"It just occurred to me that since you can't practice law because of your condition, you could busy yourself as some sort of inspector of marriage proposals. The ladies could come to you to have you ferret out the truth about their gentlemen prior to committing marriage. That way they can find out the worst about them before it's too late.''

"The gentlemen might also be interested in such a service,'' I pointed out.

"True . . . then it's an idea best forgotten. If engaged couples knew all there was to know awaiting them, then none would marry, and humanity would die out for want of progeny. Unless they do what you've done and father a child by—er—ah—that is to say—well, no offense.''

"None taken. Get on with you, Cousin, and ready yourself for dinner. You wouldn't want to leave Elizabeth all alone with the crows, would you?''

"No. But given a choice I'd prefer to leave the crows all alone with themselves, then they could feed on each other and soon disappear altogether.''

"Dreamer,'' I called to his back as he left to prepare himself for the endeavor to come.

Alone and comfortably settled before the revived fire, I let forth a satisfied sigh. Now could I finally give in to my own dreams for a little time. Not the bad ones I'd endured for a brief interval early that morning, but the light and fanciful ones that possess a man so filled with good feeling that it overflows his heart and makes the very air about him seem to hum from it.

I'd met my son, and all was well.

The trepidation and apprehensions had fled. I was so encompassed with warmth for the boy that it seemed impossible I'd ever been worried at all. Whatever problems the future might hold would solve themselves, of that I had no doubt.

There was much work ahead, of course, but it would be easy enough labor. Facing down the disapproval of the family, dealing with the scandal of the boy's conception, dealing with Edmond, even dealing with Clarinda, tribulations all, to be sure, but not terribly important so long as I could spend time with Richard. I could hardly wait to see his face again, to see it glow with another smile like—

If Edmond would even allow it. Before God, he could tell me to go to hell and be well within his rights and then I'd never see . . .

My moment of panic came and instantly passed. He *would* allow it. I'd make certain of that no matter what. If I could turn the likes of Ridley into a lamb, then I could just as easily convince Edmond to cheerfully welcome me into his home. Elizabeth would probably disapprove—she usually did when it came to forcing my influence upon another person, but this was a special circumstance. Surely she'd not object to my making life a bit smoother for all concerned by the use of this strange talent.

Then the only limitation I'd have against being with Richard would be my inability to see him during the day. Damnation, but there was one obstacle I could not influence my way around. Half a loaf was better than none, but it irked me all the same. Ah, well, I'd just have to live with it until he got older and could stay up later. By then he'd be away at school, though . . . but he'd be home for visits between terms . . .

So much to think about, so much to dream and plan. I stared at the fire until my eyes watered, blinked to clear them, but they only watered all the more. To my astonishment, first one tear then another spilled forth.

"You're being ridiculous, Johnny Boy," I said aloud, wiping at them with my sleeve before remembering my handkerchief. It was the one I'd used in the stable, the one bearing evidence of my last feeding in the form of some small bloodstains. *No matter*, I thought, scrubbing away at my wet cheeks.

Though in a way it did matter, for now did I realize why I wept. Mixed with my happiness was the certain knowledge that Richard was the only child I would ever father, thus making him immeasurably precious to me.

Because of my changed condition the male member of my body, though still capable of providing enjoyment to any lady so desiring to make use of it, was now incapable of producing seed. Though it could come to glad attention, allowing me to roger away as happily as any other man, it was no longer at all necessary for the achievement of a climax to my pleasures. That sweet accomplishment was only to be found when partaking of the lady's blood, a process we could both enjoy to its fullest for as long as we could stand the ecstasy. Wonderful as it was and superior as it was to the more common way of making love, it had a wretched price. The joys of having a wife and a hearth might yet be mine in the future, but my present state tragically precluded any possibility of ever having a family of my own to cherish.

Why was it so? I wondered. The question had long occured to me prior this night, but never before had the lack of an answer seemed so hard to endure.

If I could only find *Nora*.

Seeing her again had ever been the focus of all things for me since that summer night when I'd awakened in a coffin deep beneath the church graveyard. For all its limitations, though, the condition she'd bequeathed upon me had its favorable side. I was grateful for the advantages, but needed to know more about the drawbacks. Ignorance had caused me grief in the past, so I harbored a very reasonable desire to learn all there was to learn before committing additional blunders. If I could just speak with her, even once, and put to rest all my questions, then might I find a bit of peace for my troubled heart.

I'd have to tell her about Richard, of course. There was no way around it. I hoped she would not be too awfully upset.

If I found her.

Oliver and I would just have to take on the task with renewed vigor. I could have another look through her London house on the slender chance that I'd missed something earlier, and Oliver could track down the agents who had sold it to her. Perhaps they had records on where she'd lived before. . . .

I quelled the speculations. Firmly. They'd had their race around inside my head far too often before to offer any new approach to this particular hunt. Time to let them rest and cast my mind back to better, more productive thoughts. Like Richard.

Alas, it was not to be. Just as I was summoning the energy to forsake my comfortable chair to build up the dwindling fire, one of the footmen came in with a message for me. Damnation, if it wasn't one thing it was another.

He handed over a small fold of paper, then stepped back a pace to await my reply. I more than half expected it to be from my valet Jericho, who was probably wondering if I planned to return home tonight. An excellent question, that. I opened the thing, but did not recognize the bold, flowing writing within.

For God's sake, will you come speak with me? I beg only a moment.

The signature was a large, florid *C* placed in the exact center at the bottom of the sheet.

Clarinda, I thought, my spirits sinking. What the devil did she want? And did I really wish to find out?

Edmond Fonteyn had taken full charge of his wife to make sure she was securely confined for the remainder of their stay at Fonteyn House. Had he not been forced by his injuries to rest, he would have swept her away to their own home by now.

A temporary prison for her had been improvised from one of the more distant upstairs rooms. I understood it to be cold, bare of all furnishings except dust, and horrifically dark and stuffy since it had no window. Oliver's description of it, given earlier when he filled me in on the day's events, was vivid, as the chamber had served well enough as a place of punishment for him when he was a child. His mother had a great fondness for shutting him away there for hours at a time whenever she deemed any given transgression of correct behavior to be serious enough to merit it. That meant most of them, he'd added with heartfelt disgust. Nanny Howard hadn't approved, but was forced to comply with orders or risk a dismissal with no reference. To mitigate the worst of it for poor Oliver, she'd sit just outside the door and keep him company, talking and cheering him while pretending for his parent to play the stern and watchful guard.

Clarinda had no such companionable warden. Edmond had instructed two of the footmen to keep a close eye on her locked door, and see to it she didn't make too much noise. He had been up twice today to see she got her meals, but no one else had come since he'd put the story about that she'd fallen ill from the strain of the funeral and needed complete quiet to recover. That and the long climb up the stairs had been sufficient to discourage the remaining elderly relatives from paying any calls, though Oliver reported that speculation on the real nature of her illness was rife. Some took Edmond at his word, but others maintained that he'd gotten tired of her infidelities and had finally decided to lock her away. Though close enough to the truth, the chief mystery for them was why Edmond had chosen this particular time and place to take action.

They would most certainly connect it with the row last night: Edmond and Arthur Tyne's injuries, Ridley being held prisoner in the cellar, Oliver getting roaring drunk, and all the other odd goings-on that had taken place in the wee hours after Aunt Fonteyn's funeral. I grimly wondered how Oliver and Elizabeth would ever manage to hold fast to a topic like the weather throughout the ordeal of supper. The gouty crows would likely be disinclined to ask a direct question, but there was always a chance one of them might pluck up the nerve to try. Just as well for me that I was missing it all, for I'd find myself hard-pressed to keep a neutral and sober face.

I dismissed the footman, thanking him with a penny vale. He had most surely gotten the note directly from Clarinda, and even if he could not read might have some clear idea of what it was about. The fellow would likely go just far enough along the hall to acertain the direction of my own movements. Though the servants of Fonteyn House were fairly trustworthy, they were not above taking an avid interest in the antics of their betters. Would I go to see her or stay? I had intended to have a talk with her, but not really planned out when. It was rather like having a tooth drawn, sooner or later it would have to be done, but neither haste nor delay would make the process the least bit pleasant to endure.

Well, I thought, heaving out of my chair with a groan, *mustn't disappoint the belowstairs gossips.*

CHAPTER
-3-

Edmond had told the footmen on guard to ignore anything Clarinda said or promised on penalty of a prompt discharge from service and the pain of a sound thrashing that he would administer personally. Either threat was enough to ensure a close observance of his orders; together they had the effect of inspiring a formidable dedication to duty. When I first approached and made known my intention to visit the lady, the fellows were thrown into a painful dilemma. Passing on Clarinda's correspondence—that is to say, the note to me slipped under the door along with a penny bribe—was one thing, but they had no idea on what to do about visitors. Another bribe to grant me admission was out of the question because Edmond possessed the only key to the room. It would seem my one choice would be to confront him and ask if he might grant his consent to this call.

Well, that was one course of action I wasn't too keen to follow. Clarinda was asking much if she expected me to go that far for her. She probably wasn't aware of the business of the solitary key—that or she anticipated conducting a conversation through the locked door. Hardly wise, considering the footmen would hear all and be only too glad to share a detailed recountal with the other servants. Perhaps she would think I'd simply order them out of earshot. Indeed, I could do so, but possessed no enthusiasm for crossing Edmond's instructions.

With a grimace for my own weakness, I chose the lesser of several evil options and quietly persuaded the men on guard to avail themselves of a short nap they would not remember taking. I borrowed one of their candles and stalked up to the storage room door, pausing before it to reflect that this was also a not very wise action. However, it would be easy enough to cause Clarinda to forget anything inconvenient. I vanished, candle and all, and resumed solidity on the other side.

Oliver's description was accurate; it was a depressing little closet right enough: cold, dark, and with a chamber pot smell to it, but not totally bare. A narrow bed with several blankets had been crammed in, along with a small chair and table. The latter held the leavings of her latest meal, paper, pen, and ink, and several candles, though only one was currently lighted. Unlike Ridley, Clarinda could be relied upon not to try burning the house down, though I wasn't sure I would have given her the benefit of the doubt. Perhaps Edmond based his trust on her acute sense of self-regard, and he knew she'd not attempt anything that might miscarry and endanger her own skin.

She faced the door, apparently having heard me outside with the footmen and had composed herself to receive, standing in the small space between the bed and the desk, hands folded demurely at her waist. Still wearing yesterday's black mourning clothes, her dress was the worse for wear with some tears and dried smears of mud, so the suffering dignity she strove to affect was somewhat spoiled.

Of course, she could not have possibly expected me to make the entrance that I did, but before she could do more than widen her eyes in reaction, I bored into their depths with my full concentration.

Forget what you've just seen, Clarinda.

Her mouth popped open and she swayed backward one unsteady step as though she'd been physically struck. Had I been too forceful? Bad business for us all if that proved true. Fear of the dire consequences made me turn away from her until my composure was quite restored.

When I had nerve enough to look again, I saw her shake her head and blink as she regained her balance and her senses. Until this moment I'd taken care not to examine my feelings about her; now came the realization of just how strong they were and how dangerous they could prove. If I held mere anger in my heart for Ridley's actions, then Clarinda's had inspired white hot fury. With all this night's preoccupations I'd managed to thoroughly bury it, like heaping earth upon a fire. But instead of smothering the flames, the burial had only served to preserve, if not increase, their heat. I couldn't trust myself to keep my temper under strict control with her. No more influencing for me; that state brought the true wishes of my deeper mind too close to implementation for comfort.

"Jonathan?" Her voice was none too firm, but I found it distinctly reassuring. It would seem that no permanent damage had been done to her mind if not her body. The fight last night had left its mark on her. Her jaw was bruised and swollen where I'd struck her unconscious.

"I got your note," I said in as flat and as discouraging a tone as I could summon. It wasn't at all difficult.

"Thank you for coming."

"What do you want?"

"I—I want nothing. That is to say—"

"Clarinda, you didn't ask me up here without a reason," I said wearily, putting my candle on the table.

She snapped her mouth shut.

"Just speak and have done with it."

She lifted her chin, her eyes steady. "Edmond said that you were well, that when I shot at you I'd missed."

She had not missed, not at two paces, but I'd been able to vanish for a crucial instant, and the darkness and flash of the powder had served well to cover things.

"I thought he might have lied to me. I am glad to see he did not."

"Are you?"

"You can believe what you like, Jonathan, but I never wished you any harm."

"Oh, indeed?"

"What was done was done only to protect my child."

"And what rare pleasure you took from it, madam, trying to murder his father."

"That was only a sham for Thomas Ridley's benefit. All of it. If I hadn't pretended such for him he would have killed me on the spot."

"You were most convincing."

"I *had* to be!"

"Of course."

Her hands formed into fists and dropped to her sides. "I can't expect you to understand, but I did want you to at least know why I was forced—"

"Clarinda," I said in a clear cold voice. "If you want to waste the effort telling me this rot, that's your business, but I have better diversions to occupy my time. I am not a fool and neither are you. I recall exactly everything you tried to do last night and how close you came to success, and nothing, no distortion of truth, half-truth, or outright lie from you will change that memory."

That stung her good and square. Were we in another place, she'd have probably slapped me soundly and marched out. Here all she could do was stand and stare and fume. Not that it lasted long. She recovered beautifully, smooth as a cat. Her fists relaxed and she assumed a rueful expression.

"Very well, no more pretense. Is it possible that with you I may be able to speak the whole truth?"

A cutting reply concerning my sincere doubt that she would know how hovered on the tip of my tongue, but I held it back and gave a brusque nod, instead.

She may have seen or sensed my skepticism, but chose to ignore it. "Edmond doesn't know you're here, does he?"

There. She'd just correctly read one of the other reasons behind my abrupt manner. I should have to take extreme care dealing with her. "It seemed the tactful thing to do for the moment."

"No doubt. He's a formidable man."

I offered no comment, though I could easily agree with her on that point.

"He said that you'd seen Richard."

"Took me by last night."

"Did you like him?"

"What does it matter to you?"

Another sting for her, which was something of a surprise. By now I'd thought her beyond all tender feeling.

"It does matter. I'm afraid for my child. Our child."

"In what way?"

"I'm afraid that because of what's happened Edmond might do him harm. He could punish Richard for the things I've done."

Clarinda was shut away in a most disagreeable spot with only her own dark soul for company, so hers was a reasonable fear, but not one I seriously harbored. Edmond could be unpleasant, but I sensed he would not purposely harm the boy. Even so, I had an excellent means of dealing with him to guarantee Richard's well-being.

"I'll see that the child is safeguarded from any harm." Instinct told me to preserve a cool and indifferent front before her, but she was perceptive enough to see through it.

"You really do care for him, don't you?" she asked with more than a hint of rising hope.

It seemed better not to answer, though my silence was answer enough.

"I'm glad of that. What I say now, what I ask now, is not for my sake, but for the sake of that innocent child. You're a part of this family, but you haven't lived long with them, you don't

know them as I do. Richard will need a friend. Will you look
out for him?''

A fair request, and certainly for something I'd be doing regardless of her intercession in the matter. ''I shall do what I
can. What about your other son?''

She looked away briefly. ''He's already lost to me. He's
away at school, his life has been ordered and set out for him.
Edmond saw to that. Edmond and Aunt Fonteyn.''

''Whom you murdered.'' Edmond and I had worked as
much out between us, that Clarinda had killed Oliver's
mother, but I wanted to know for certain.

Clarinda's lips twitched in a near smile. ''If you think I regret helping that evil old harridan along to her place in hell,
then please do reconsider. You—any of you—could get away
from her. I could not. It was an ill day for me when I married
her favorite brother and worse still when I gave him a son. She
was always there, interfering, sharp as a thorn, and never once
letting me forget who controlled the money.''

The Fonteyn money. The inspiration and goal behind all of
Clarinda's trespasses. ''How did your first husband die?''

''What?'' The apparent change of subject first puzzled her,
then she divined the reason behind it. ''For God's sake, do you
think—''

''I don't know what to think, so it seemed best to make a direct inquiry.''

''He dropped dead from a bad heart,'' she answered with
no small disgust. ''I had nothing to do with it. A pity his sister
did not follow his example, else life would have been easier
for all of us.''

''Then you married Edmond?''

''I needed his protection and he needed my son's money,
but what a farce that turned out to be with the lot of us still subject to Aunt Fonteyn's whims. When Richard was born sooner
or later she'd know Edmond was not his father, all of them
would *know*, and then what would happen to us? She'd have
put me out on the street quick enough or packed me off to Bed-

lam and done God knows what to my baby.''

I didn't see Edmond or even Aunt Fonteyn for that matter
allowing things to go so far. The offensive prospect of a scandal would have likely mitigated any judgment she made once
her initial outrage had passed. Clarinda had the intelligence to
know and play upon that weakness. No, she'd ever been after
the family money; it was just that simple.

''So you got the likes of Ridley to be your protector, to be
subject to *your* whims.''

Various thoughts were clearly flickering back and forth behind her eyes, too fast to interpret. She paused a goodly time to
search my face and finally shook her head. ''You don't understand,'' she said with genuine incredulity, then softly
laughed.

There was a sound to make my skin crawl. The room
seemed to shrink around us. ''I think it's best that I don't.''

''Or you might have some sympathy for me? For what my
life has been like? Don't bother yourself.''

''As you wish.''

A baleful silence grew between us, filling this dank and
chill closet right to the ceiling like smoke. There was no room
in it for me. My questions were all satisfied; therefore I had no
need to remain. I made to pick up my candle.

''No, wait!'' Her hand shot out to seize mine. Because of
the restricted space we'd been close enough to easily touch,
but had managed to avoid it.

Five years past I'd been more than eager to touch her. Just
last night I'd fought off the temptation to do so again only with
the greatest difficulty. I saw her still as a very beautiful, desir-
able woman, but any craving I'd ever fostered for her was now
stone dead.

I shook her off. ''I'll leave the candle if you like.''

''It's not that. I have one more thing to ask of you.''

Tempting as it was to point out that I owed her no favors, I
waited for her to go on.

''Jonathan, do you know what Edmond has planned for

me? What he will do once we're home?''

"He has not communicated that information to me, nor is it really my business.''

"He'll have me shut away in a room that will make this seem like a palace.''

"There are worse spots, madam. Would you prefer Bedlam or Bridewell?''

"You speak that way because you're angry, but please, try to see things through my eyes, just for a moment, I beg you.''

Again, I waited.

Outwardly, she calmed herself, but her heartbeat was very loud to my acute hearing.

I sensed that the earlier talk and questions about Richard had never been a real concern for her. It had been but a useful means to sound me out; was she finally coming to the real reason why she'd asked me here?

"There may be worse places, but I can't think of a single one,'' she whispered. "I am to be shut away forever and ever. I will be completely alone. After tomorrow, I will never see the sun or even the warmth of a candle flame again. It will be always dark and always cold. He's promised as much. Those are his very words.''

I thought that she was lying again, for it would be easy to verify the truth with Edmond, but her fear was genuine enough. I could smell it. I could almost *taste* it.

"He full well knows that it will drive me mad, giving substance to the story he'll tell others. No person with an ounce of compassion in them would treat a mongrel dog with such cruelty, but that's what he's sworn is in store for me.''

No sunlight, not even a candle. God, but could I not thoroughly appreciate what kind of darkness *that* was? "Very well, I'll speak to him,'' I said heavily.

"No! I want you to help me get away from him!''

My turn for a bout of incredulity. "By heaven, I think you're mad already.''

"Not yet. Not *yet*! I don't ask you to help me escape, but

just to get me away from him. Devise whatever prison you like for me, let me be totally alone, but if I can have but an hour of daylight I'll ask nothing more of you.''

An hour of daylight. What would I not give to have as little for myself? Most of the time the lack did not grieve me. Not much. But then I had diversions aplenty to fill the hours. I had some choices left. Clarinda had none.

''If . . . if that's impossible,'' she continued, faltering as her gaze dropped away, ''then I would ask you to give me the means of making another kind of escape.''

''What means?''

She raised her eyes to search mine and licked her lips. ''I've heard it said that if one takes enough opium—''

''Good God, Clarinda!''

''Otherwise I can tear up the bedclothes and find a way to hang myself. It would please Edmond very well, I'm sure.''

''There's no need—''

''Is there not? I mean this, Jonathan. You still seem to have a heart left, that's why I thought to talk to you. I can trust no one else. I'm not asking a great deal. You'd put a mad dog out of its misery, would you not?''

''I would, but—''

''But what? It's that or take care of me yourself—or help me escape altogether.''

She waited and waited, and for all her skill at deception could not completely keep a sharp little spark of hope from showing in her eyes, but I did not deign to remark on that last absurd suggestion. Any or all of her talk of another prison with me as keeper or of taking her own life might have been meant to soften my resolve so perhaps I would agree to help her escape. Well, I'd already told her I was not a fool. I shook my head. ''There's another way of handling this. I'll see to it tonight.''

The spark flashed once, then dimmed. ''What is that?''

''I'll talk to Edmond—''

''But that won't—''

"He'll listen to me, I assure you."

She made a choking sound.

"You may think otherwise, but I will make him. That's really the best I can do for you, and I believe you're well aware of it."

Obviously this was not what she'd hoped to achieve for herself; on the other hand, it was better than an outright refusal. But however much disappointment she showed, I still had a strong impression that she had accomplished *something* with me and was calculating its eventual effect on her. Mildly worrisome, that, but nothing more.

She abruptly lowered her gaze, shoulders slumped as if in defeat or acceptance. "Yes, I am aware of it. For what it's worth, I'm grateful to you."

For what it's worth, I thought. Very damned little, but as she'd said, I'd do as much for a mad dog.

Being more unsettled than angry, it was less perilous now to influence her into taking a restful sleep; thus would she have no memory of my egress from the room. I suggested nothing more than that, though, preferring caution over calamity in the event that I'd misjudged my present state of mind and gave in to error. Leaving her reclining peacefully on the narrow bed, I seived past the door and back out into the hall, turning solid again before thinking to remove myself from the immediate view of her guards.

Thankfully, I found the footmen were still lost in their doze, sparing me additional exertion. It struck me that I should wake them and tell them to forget they'd even seen me, but that was too much of an effort for so small a detail. They could tell Edmond what they liked, if they dared. I didn't care one way or another. Whatever they said would be little enough. I quietly made my way down the stairs, for I had much to think about and wanted to be as far away as possible from Clarinda. All the relatives and servants would be busy with supper, so privacy was no problem; I had the pick of Fonteyn House's many rooms.

Only one appealed to me, though.

The nursery.

Not only would I have another look in on Richard, which in itself was sufficient enticement to go there, but the superb idea of plying a few questions to Nanny Howard had popped into my mind.

Clarinda was as full of lies as hive has honey. Some I'd picked out without trouble, others were more elusive, and by God, but didn't the woman have more than her share of brass? Wanting me to take Edmond's place as her warden or to go so far as to help her escape . . . ugh. That was right out. It was also something of an insult since she'd so badly underestimated me. She was not without considerable wit; why had she even proposed such a ludicrous action? Likely it had to do with the theory of venture nothing, gain nothing. I hoped as much, for then it would seem less offensive to endure.

She was unquestionably afraid, but was her fear for the threat of a dark imprisonment or for imprisonment alone? Either one would be more than alarming, and certainly Edmond would make a stern and alert keeper, but I found it difficult to believe he would be as extreme as she'd claimed. Perhaps he'd been giving vent to his own anger with her, making threats he'd probably not fulfill. More likely she'd simply lied to me. Again.

Still and all, I'd have to sort fact from fancy just to be sure, and could think of no better person to consult than Nanny Howard. If she was as intelligent as she looked, then she'd know all the happenings of this particular branch of the Fonteyn family tree and be able to provide any number of necessary details.

She might be reluctant to talk with an outsider, though, for I was just that despite my relationship to Richard. I made a face, not liking the idea of having to influence her. I didn't like it, but would do so if nothing else would move her.

"What a sneaking rogue you're turning into, Johnny Boy," I said aloud, but not too very aloud. Echoes tended to carry far along these dark corridors, and I had no wish to announce my self-reproach to any stray upstairs maid who might be lurking about. Best to remove my mind from the subject until the time was right to approach it.

So I cheerfully speculated on the prospect of slipping in for another peep at Richard. If nothing else, Nanny Howard would gladly tell me all about *him*. What did he like to do? What were his favorite games? Did he have other children to play with at Edmond's estate? Did he have a pony yet? Probably not, considering his reaction to the painted one now in his possession. My heart seemed to quicken with a kind of life again at the splendid thought of eventually giving him a real one. I recalled clearly the delicious excitement that had possessed me on one of my early birthdays with Father's gift of a fine white pony. No more sharing rides with others on the front of the saddle, I'd had a brave charger of my own to play out my daydreams. More than that, I'd learned much on the care and coddling of equines, and had taken to my lessons in dressage like butter to hot bread. Richard looked to have some of that enthusiasm in him, and what a pleasure it would be to nurture it and . . .

Father.

Dear me, but I'd *have* to sit down to write and *somehow* tell him what had happened.

But later, I thought, bounding lightly down the last of the stairs and taking the final turn needed to reach the nursery.

Unfortunately, just outside the nursery door, I encountered my son's *other* father, Edmond Fonteyn.

He was a big man, nearly Ridley's size, and usually as robust, but last night's activities had left him with a gaunt white face, one arm in a sling, bandaging 'round both hands, and an unnatural slowness to his movements. Fire still lurked in his dark eyes, though, and he favored me with some of its heat.

I hauled up short, rocking back on my heels in a most undignified way, at the same time cursing myself for such absurd behavior. After all, what had I to fear from him?

''Where have you been keeping yourself all day?'' he growled, not bothering with the courtesy of a greeting beyond a slight raising of his chin. Had he always had that mannerism or taken it from Clarinda? Or had she gotten it from him?

''My doctor recommended rest.''

''That fool Oliver.''

''He's not a fool,'' I said mildly.

Edmond chose not to argue the point. ''What are you here for? Mrs. Howard said you'd already come and gone.''

''And I've come again. What else did Mrs. Howard have to say about my visit?''

His lips parted as though to answer, then snapped shut. I'd caught him out and he was well aware of it. ''Come along then. We need to talk.'' When I hesitated to jump at this command, he added, ''The boy's sound asleep and will look just the same later on.''

When first we'd met, his brusque manner had intimidated me, for I'd attributed it to the fact that he was aware of my past intimacy with his wife. True enough, but now I was able to understand that such was his manner with everyone and counseled myself to tolerance. I followed as he led off up the hall to again take the stairs to the ground floor.

As he slowly paced along, an uncomfortable foreboding began to assert itself on my spirit, and I soon found my somber expectations fulfilled when he turned into the one room in this whole dismal house I least wanted to visit.

Its fireplace held a hearty blaze; that was the chief difference between my present intrusion and the very first time I'd come here with Clarinda. Then it had been rather cold and cheerless—until she made it her business to warm things up for me. We'd consummated our fit of mutual passion on that settee under the eye of that same bust of Aristotle—or perhaps it was one of the Caesar's—sitting on the mantel. Good God, what did Edmond think he was about in bringing me here?

But as he eased his heavy body down on the settee with an audible sigh, I comprehended (and not without considerable relief) that he did *not* know what had happened here those few short years ago. His present occupancy must be because of its privacy and because this had been Clarinda's room during the funeral. Some of her things still lay scattered about—small things: a handkerchief discarded on the floor, a comb forgotten on a table, a pair of slippers peering shyly out from under a chair. Of her other belongings there was no sign; perhaps they'd been packed and taken away to their home already.

"Sit," he ordered, gesturing to one of the chairs.

I did so.

He had a brandy bottle close at hand and some glasses. Without asking my pleasure, he poured out two portions and nodded for me to take one. I did this without hesitation, for if need be I could alter his memory about my lack of thirst.

He did not trouble to make a toast, but partook himself of a draught that would have done credit to Oliver's reputation for swilling down spirits. That gone, he filled his glass again and emptied it just as swiftly, then availed himself of a third libation. I thought he might deal with it as with the first two, but he contented himself with only half before putting the glass to one side.

"Something disturbs you?" I ventured, indicating the brandy.

He grunted. "Life disturbs me, Barrett. I've been harshly served."

"If you want an apology from me, I should be happy to give—"

He waved me down, shaking his head. "There's no need, what's done is done. I had quite a talk with Clarinda today and got the truth out of her concerning her liaison with you. I think it's the truth, anyway. At long last she has no more reason to lie to me."

"Sir, if you wish the truth, then by my honor, it's yours for the asking."

"That won't be necessary. You need not tell the husband how enjoyable you found his wife's favors."

I winced, recovered myself, and spoke through my teeth. "But I did not *know* she was anyone's wife."

He looked long and hard at me, not moving a muscle. By very slow and small degrees the lines of his face relaxed. "That makes a difference to you?"

"It does."

"Then by God, you're probably the only man in England who can say so."

"Like Clarinda, I have no reason to lie to you, nor would I if I did." I let him think on it a moment, then said, "You wanted to talk. Was this the subject you had in mind?"

"Not quite, but it is directly related to my wife. And you."

"Richard."

"Our mutual son," he rumbled.

"What about him?"

"You surprised me last night. Most fathers want nothing to do with their bastards."

Like a runaway fire, hot anger rushed through my body. One bare instant later and I was on my feet and looming over him. It was only by the greatest effort of forbearance that I didn't haul him up and toss him across the room as he deserved. He flinched, eyes widening, taking in my red face and trembling fists. Apparently my reaction surprised him once more, almost as much as it startled me. "You will *not* refer to him in that way ever again," I whispered, voice shaking with rage.

"Or what?" His eyes had narrowed; his tone was dangerous.

"Or . . ." A number of obvious, violence-oriented threats occurred to me, but I was starting to think once more and knew that none of them would be taken seriously by this man, not without an immediate demonstration, anyway. "Or I'll make it my duty to instruct you on the subject of good manners."

We locked gazes for a goodly period, but there was no need to rely on my unnatural influence this time. Edmond could see just how earnest was the intent behind the temperate words.

Then he smiled.

It was a mere tightening of the straight line of his mouth and very brief, but a smile nonetheless, and enough to give me pause. Had this thrice-cursed villain been *testing* me?

He leaned back upon the settee. "Thank you, but I've had sufficient instruction to last me a fortnight. Thought you had as well, but you seem to have recovered. Sit down, Cousin, there's been enough blood spilled in this family already."

I backed away, not to sit, but to pace about the room and work off the sudden energy that had set my limbs to quivering. Had he always been like this to Clarinda? If so, then though I could not excuse her crimes, I could easily understand one of the reasons why she'd committed them. Certainly continual contact with his abrasive manner could not have done her much good. Or had it been Clarinda's endless infidelities that made him like this? Had they driven him to live in what was apparently a constant state of bitter exasperation? Perhaps by now he knew of no other way to express himself to the world.

"Why am I here, Edmond?" I asked, when I'd gotten my temper under control.

"Because I wanted to have a good look at you. Your sister and I had quite a talk earlier today . . ."

"Yes, she said something of it to me."

"She was most informative about your high sense of honor and good character, but I needed to see for myself what you're made of. A man usually shows one face to women and another to other men, just as they do for us. It would seem that for you there's little difference between the two."

"You have an annoying way of fashioning and bestowing a compliment, sir, if that was your intent."

"The shortcoming has been mentioned to me by others, but for the sake of accuracy think of it as less of a compliment and more of an observation."

I paused by the fireplace. "So you've observed that I seem to be a man of honor and good character. What of it? I thought you wanted to talk about Richard. I am more than willing, provided that you refrain from insulting him.''

He snorted. ''The truth is not an insult, and you'd best get used to hearing such once news of this gets out. There are others ever willing to make a cruel cut when the fancy strikes 'em. Then what means will you take to improve their manners? More duels?''

''Only when it's impossible to avoid. That business with Ridley—''

''Was all part of Clarinda's scheming, I know. You're damned lucky he didn't kill you. Now that you've raised the subject, how the devil are you to be rid of him without another fight? However right and pleasing it may be, we can't keep him locked in the cellar forever.''

''Put your mind at rest on that. I've already dealt with him. He's presently upstairs in Arthur Tyne's room, and they'll both be leaving in the morning.''

Before he could master himself I had the great satisfaction of seeing a look of boundless astonishment seize control of Edmond's features. ''*What* are you saying?''

''It's all cleared up and put away, so to speak. He and his cousin will trouble us no more. I have his word on it.''

''His word!''

''It was all quite easy, once I got him to settle down and listen to reason.''

In light of the quarrelsome nature of his character, and not forgetting the implausibility of what I was telling him, I was convinced that my very best assurance would not be enough for Edmond. Even as the words tumbled easily from my mouth, the corners of his own turned markedly down, and he looked ready to offer a considerable debate and a number of bothersome questions I was not prepared to answer. Consequently, I made sure to come close and lock eyes with him again, guaranteeing a successful imposition of my will over his own.

''*You don't have to worry about him at all. . . .* '' I whispered into his mind.

He was not easy to influence; for that difficulty I could blame the brandy. It was very like talking to a wall—a rather stoutly made one composed of brick. Several moments passed without my noticing any visible effect beyond a slight deadening of his countenance, but I'd seen that face on him before, usually prior to the delivery of some trenchant remark. Just as I thought my efforts would come to nothing, I observed that he had ceased to blink his eyes quite so much. For that good blessing I allowed myself a small sigh of relief, but continued to concentrate the greater part of my thought and will upon him. There was a kind of instinctual feeling within me that if I let my focus wander for even a second, I'd lose him.

"It's all been sorted out...."

When finally finished, I'd acquired a nasty, droning ache behind my eyes, but at least there would be no more discussion of Ridley for now and probably for good. It was well with me; I was altogether sick of the subject. Returning to my post by the fireplace, I pinched the bridge of my nose trying to diminish the pain. Though fading, it was an annoyance. I hoped I could get through the rest of the night without having to resort to that handy talent again.

"Now what about young Richard?" I asked upon seeing Edmond very much needed the prompting.

"Yes. Well . . ." He rubbed his face and neck like a waking sleeper. I was happy enough to wait him out for it had been hard going for us both. "You've seen him. According to Mrs. Howard you seem to like him. So what do you want to do?"

A vague enough question, requiring a general sort of answer, though in my heart I'd already made a thousand plans for the boy. "What's best for him, of course. You're his father as well; what do you recommend?"

"Father? Father in name only," he rumbled, coming fully awake. "I knew he wasn't mine the moment I clapped eyes on him. She used to delight in pretending—oh, never mind. It's all over." He made a throwing-away motion with one hand.

I frowned at him. "Did that child ever suffer because of his mother's betrayal of you?"

His snapped-out answer told me he spoke the truth. "I've never laid a hand on him. God's death, I only saw the boy when it was necessary. He never took to me."

That I could understand.

His gaze canted sharply over to meet mine, and he correctly interpreted my expression. "What would you have? For me to play the saint and clasp him to my bosom as my own? Then wish on, for such sham is beyond my ability."

"My wish . . ." I began with a return of hot anger, but trailed off and made myself cool down. There was no point to it now. There was no point in wishing the child had had even a vestige of kindness from the man he perceived as his father. Whether or not ignoring the boy was better than pretended affection I could not judge. It was just so unutterably *sad*.

"What is your wish?" he finally asked.

"Nothing. As you say, it's all over."

For several more minutes neither of us spoke. I was now abrim with dark perturbation, and Edmond seemed in no better shape. I could almost feel the restless shift of our combined emotions churning through the room like some sort of fog composed of feeling instead of mist. Very much did I want to remove myself from its ill effect, but there was no help for it; I'd have to see this through.

"Edmond."

He didn't move; only his eyes shifted.

"You've asked me what I want. Tell me what it is that *you* want."

He laughed once, softly. "Another life might serve me well, or fewer mistakes in this one."

"I meant concerning Richard."

"I know what you meant. You said you want what's best for him. On that we are in full accord; we should certainly try to do what's best for him. It's not his fault that his mother's a murdering sow."

The brandy must be having its way with him, else he might not be so free with his speech, but after looking up the muzzle of a pistol aimed at him by his own dear wife, he was more than entitled to call her names. Indeed, I could respect him for his extreme restraint in the matter.

He glowered at the fire. "For as long as she lives I'll have to be her keeper. It's my just punishment for marrying the wrong woman and hers for marrying the wrong man. We're stuck with each other, she the prisoner, me the turnkey, not unlike most marriages, I suppose."

Just the subject I'd have to question him about, but it would have to hold for a bit longer, for this one was far more important to me. "What has this to do with Richard?"

"I'm attempting to give you an idea of what sort of growing up awaits him once we're all home again."

He allowed me time to think on it. I didn't much like the images my mind was busily bringing forth for consideration.

"What's best for the boy," Edmond said, reaching for his unfinished glass, "is to not be in a house where his mother must be locked away like the lost soul that she is. What's best is for him to be with his real father."

"Wh-what?"

He caught hold of the glass and downed the last half of his drink. "Would you consider taking him away?"

"To where?" I asked stupidly.

"To any place you damned well please."

I shook my head, not as an answer to his question but from sheer disbelief. The longer I stared, though, the more certain I became that he was utterly serious. "You'd be willing to make such a sacrifice?"

Now it was his turn to favor me with his disbelief. "Sacrifice? Haven't you yet gotten it through your head that I care nothing for the boy? Did someone stuff cloth in your ears when I wasn't looking? God help me, but knowing the things I know I can hardly endure the sight of him anymore. D'ye think I'm making a sacrifice? Don't flatter me."

"But—"

"If it's true that we both want what's best for him, then that's for him to be well away from my house."

"But for you to give him up just like that?"

"Damnation, I'm giving him to a man who might be able to provide better for him than I ever could. I know my limit, Barrett, and I've long since reached the end of mine."

"This is the brandy talking—"

"Brandy be damned, I'm trying to do something right for once. If you don't want him, then I'll find someone else who does and bless him for the favor. I'm trying to give the misbegotten brat a chance to know some kindness and love. I've none of it left in my heart; that bitch I married burned it out of me." He hurled the empty glass across the room. Though aimed nowhere near me, I still instinctively ducked as it flew past, so savage was the force behind his action. Next he picked up the brandy bottle and seemed for a moment ready to send it crashing after the glass, but the moment passed. He collected himself and fell back on the settee.

"D'ye want 'im or not?" he asked, his voice drained of everything except weariness.

There was no need to think on my answer. "Yes, of course I do. I should be more than delighted to take care of him."

"Good." He took a long drink right from the bottle. "You can sort out the details with Mrs. Howard. Take her along as well if you like. I can give her an excellent reference if you need it."

"That won't be necessary. I'm sure she will do admirably with us." God, the man must truly be distracted if he thought I'd separate Richard from the one person who had been his chief source of affection and guidance from the cradle. "What about Clarinda? What if Richard should want to see her?"

"No." There was a finality in his tone reminiscent of the gallows. "Your sister and I discussed that already. Until he's old enough to understand better, his mother is ill and that's the end of it.''

"It's a hard business never to see his mother again."

"I cannot perceive that it would be of much advantage to him in the future, since he saw little enough of her in the past."

"Hard for Clarinda, too."

"Indeed it would be if she cared a fig for him. For either of them,'' he added, reminding me of the other child who was away at school. I wondered if that boy was a true son of Aunt Fonteyn's brother or the first of Clarinda's changelings. Now was not the time to make an inquiry, though. Besides, this was in direct opposition to the impression Clarinda had given me on her feelings for either of them and wanted sorting.

"How can a mother not care for her children?" I mused in a way meant to draw him out. Even my own mother, twisted in mind and heart as she was, cared after a fashion for her two children. She'd removed her damaging presence from us all those years ago, after all. Not unlike what Edmond was trying to do now for Richard.

His answer was curt and lacking in interest. "Ask her sometime, you'll find out soon enough that she hasn't a jot of regard for anyone but herself. But if it were otherwise with her, it still wouldn't matter. She forfeited all rights to them when she did her murder.''

I looked at the stone bust on the mantel. On impulse I picked it up and turned it over to see if anything might be marked on the base to indicate who it represented. Neither Aristotle nor a Caesar, the neatly carved inscription identified it to be Homer. That little mystery explained, I put it back in place.

Since Edmond had ascertained for himself the fact of my honor, now would be the time for me to return the favor, to make sure that all would be reasonably well for Clarinda, if not for her sake, then for Richard's. "With you as the turnkey how will she be treated?" I asked very quietly.

"A damned sight better than she deserves. Don't worry yourself. It won't be a Bridewell, she'll not want for creature comforts, but I'm going to make damned sure she has no opportunity to kill ever again."

I believed him. He was as he presented himself. Perhaps Clarinda's constant lies had created in him a need to cleave to the absolute truth. So said all my instinct as I studied his hard face. It was no small reassurance to me that my growing respect for him was not misplaced.

He took another long drink, then glared at me.

"What is it? You want to toast her health or something?" He nodded toward my untouched brandy.

Damnation, but I was tired. "No. Nothing like that." Just the prospect of trying to pierce through his brick wall again was enough to renew the ache behind my eyes. He could think what he liked about my not drinking his brandy, to hell with it.

"What, then?"

For all his roughness, his willingness to do well for Richard spoke of an innate decency in his heart. This told me that Clarinda would be all right for the time being. Complete confirmation of it could wait for another night.

"I just wanted to say that should you ever feel differently about the boy, then you're welcome to come visit him any time."

He seemed on the verge of tossing the invitation back in my face, if I could judge anything by the sneer that briefly crossed his own. Then he visibly reigned himself in. "I'll consider it," he muttered. "Now get along with you. I need my rest."

I took this servant's dismissal in good grace. The man was in pain and only wanted the privacy to get thoroughly drunk. God knows, I'd do the same were I to find myself in his shoes. I wished him a good night, getting no reply beyond an indifferent grunt, and shut the door on him.

Halfway along the hall I had to stop for a moment, staring at nothing in particular while my thoughts finally caught up with events.

Good God in heaven . . . *Richard was going to come home with me.*

Then I clamped my hand over my mouth to keep from shouting the house down.

CHAPTER
~4~

"Faster! Faster! Faster!" Richard screamed into my right ear. "Yah-yah-yah!"

I did what I could to oblige him, though things nearly came apart when I made a sharpish turn into the parlour. Our progress was nearly defeated by the high polish on the floor causing my shoes to lose a bit of their grip on the turf so to speak. I just managed to gain the safety of the parlour rug in time to keep us from taking a slide into an inconveniently placed chair. We flashed by Elizabeth and Oliver, who were sensibly sitting and having their tea before the fire, whooped a hallo at them, then shot out the other door and into one of the narrow back halls where the servants usually lurked. It was a straight path on this part of the course, so I stepped up the speed and galloped hard and with lots of needless bounce, much to the delight of my rider. Richard giggled and gasped, tightened his stranglehold around my neck, and dug his heels more firmly into my flanks.

"Have a care," I told him, making sure of my own hold on his legs. "We're coming to a hill."

He shrieked encouragement to his steed and I carried us

up the back stairs three at a time, wound my way through the upper back hall to the upper front hall, then jounced roughly down to the front stairs landing, startling the one maid in the house who hadn't heard our noisy progress. She let forth a satisfying screech, throwing up her hands, an action that amused Richard mightily. He yelled out a view-halloo, told her she was the fox, and we gave roaring chase as far as the entry leading to the kitchen. Showing an unexpectedly fleet turn of foot, she ducked through to safety, smartly shutting the door in our faces just in time.

"Outfoxed!" I cried in mock despair to my laughing rider. "She's gone to ground and the dogs can't find her. What shall we do now? Another steeplechase?"

"Yes, please!" he bellowed, freshening his hold 'round my neck. I took us through the house twice more as we pretended each corner was a church steeple we had to make in time to stay ahead of a pack of pretend horsemen who were hot on our heels. We naturally won each race, for I was a steed of superior stock, a point I'd confided to him when I initially proposed our horseback riding game.

This was his first night in London, and it was proving to be a memorable one—for us both. I could not have been happier, and never before in my life had I felt this particular kind of happiness. No plans, no speculations, nothing I'd ever imagined had remotely prepared me for the actuality of his constant and immediate presence. He filled the house, he filled the whole world for me. At times I could scarce take in that he was real, and at others, it seemed that he had been with me always from the very moment of my own birth.

Once he'd learned that Edmond had given Richard over to my care, Oliver generously opened his house to the lad and welcomed him in. Elizabeth was just as keen about having the boy in as well and managed within the space of a few days to turn a couple of the upstairs rooms into a very fine bedroom and nursery for Mrs. Howard and her charge.

That lady was not herself adverse to moving out of Edmond Fonteyn's no doubt gloomy household and into ours, but with all the row going on, I was certain she'd be having second thoughts soon enough. Past personal experience with nannies had taught me that they prefer routines of the quiet, restful sort, something that would likely be lacking during those hours when I was up and around.

My time with Richard was short owing to the limits of my condition, but happily for the present, the winter nights started early and lasted long. Even so, on this first evening the instant I was awake I anxiously bolted from my cellar sanctuary to rush upstairs and see him, taxing the patience of Jericho, my valet. His inviolable custom was to lie in wait in my room, then seize upon and subject my person to an interval of grooming and dressing so I wouldn't shame him before polite company. As Richard and I galloped past, we surprised him emerging from my doorway, razor in one hand and cloth in the other, indication that I was in for a shaving tonight. Jericho's mouth popped open in startled disappointment before he hurriedly retreated out of the way.

The rest of the servants had simply been told that Richard was our cousin and committed to our care. If anyone chose to make anything of his uncanny resemblance to me, Jericho was to report such murmurings, and I'd have a little "talk" with the person to discourage idle gossip. Like Nanny Howard, Jericho knew all about the boy's true paternity, and both could be trusted to keep it to themselves. We'd all planned that Richard would also be informed but only when he was old enough and when the time was right. It seemed best to curtail any possibility of him overhearing something he wasn't ready for by making sure all the other servants were just as discreet.

Richard and I made another circuit of the upper rear hall

and emerged into the front again but were forced to abruptly rein in. Nanny Howard stood square in our path, hands on her hips, and a stern cast to the look on her face.

"Mr. Barrett!" she said in a tone to match the look.

"Oy-oy-oy!" Richard yodeled, thumping the top of my head with one fist while the other twisted the remnants of my neckcloth around. "See me, Nanny! We're having a race!"

"You'll race yourself into an upset stomach with all that shouting," she told him, fulfilling my expectations about nannies and their preference for a quiet routine. Her eye fell upon me like the hand of doom. "Mr. Barrett, it will be his bedtime soon and now he'll be hours settling for it."

Not at all contrite, I nonetheless came up with a pretty speech of apology and volunteered to help in that task. "What's your best settling remedy, then? We'll get him fixed right up. How about a tot of hot milk with a little honey for taste? That always worked for me."

This mollified her somewhat, but she still showed some reluctance to let go her chagrin. "You needn't trouble yourself over such trifles, sir. I can see to things."

"Hardly a trifle. Besides, I got him stirred up; it's only fair I stir him down again."

"But, sir—"

"This isn't what you're used to, I'm sure, but we run things differently in this house. I'm very interested in the lad's well-being, so you might as well get used to the fact that I'm going to be underfoot quite a lot. You've got him to yourself all through the day, but for an hour or so at night it's my turn."

She pursed her lips in swift thought and being every bit as intelligent as I'd estimated, decided cooperation was preferable to argument. "Very well, Mr. Barrett. But I must remind you that Richard is not yet used to such excitements. Perhaps it's best to ease him into things a little at a time."

It sounded reasonable to me, and I wasn't one to cross her on anything as important as a growing lad's bedtime. Not yet, anyway. Richard groaned a protest as we ducked into the nursery and pulled on my neckcloth again in an effort to turn his steed back to the beckoning fields of the rest of the house. The fabric came all undone and slipped free, and not wasting the opportunity, he waved it like a banner, then whipped it around my eyes.

"What's happened?" I gruffly asked, blundering about with one arm extended to feel my way. "Who blew out the candles?"

This game went over enormously well with him. I played it to the limit, pretending to smash face first against a wall resulting in a crash to the floor—a slow and gentle one— with much loud moaning, despair, and calls for caution. We ended up rolling and tussling like puppies until he was breathless. One advantage I had over any other adults he'd ever play with was that I didn't get tired.

"I think you need a carpet in here, Nanny," I said, still lying on the floor because Richard had decided to hold my legs down by sprawling over them. "A nice thick one. Don't want the boy to get any more bruises than necessary."

"It's sure to get very dirty, sir."

"Then let it get dirty, we can always get another. I'll put my sister onto it tomorrow. London's full of shops; the three of you can go pick one out. Does he need anything else—clothes, furniture, that sort of thing?"

"Toys!" Richard shouted, taking off one of my shoes and measuring it against the other, sole to sole.

"He is well supplied with all that he needs, sir, with more than enough, I think."

The furnishings from the nursery at Edmond's home had been carted over and put into place in these rooms. Moving from my childhood home to London had proved to be a bad wrench for me, and I was full grown and well prepared for it. I'd hoped that the sudden change for Richard would be lessened with the presence of having his own familiar things around him. It must have worked, for he seemed carefree enough.

"Well, you be sure to tell us of your least little need, y'hear? The big needs, too. You have any problems, you come straightway to any of us so we can fix 'em."

"Yes, sir."

"One's bigger than the other," Richard observed of the shoes. He looked at me for some sort of reaction. "One's *bigger* than the other."

"So it is," I agreed, propping up on my elbows to see. "By a fraction of an inch. I'll have a word with my shoemaker."

"What's a fraction?"

"A portion of something, usually very small."

"A portion of what?"

"Anything you like."

He now measured my shoe against one of his own. "It's bigger by a fraction of an inch," he pronounced.

"So it is, by lots of fractions of inches. I'll teach you properly about them if you like."

"Yes, please."

"Nanny, have we got a measuring stick about the place?"

"I'm not sure, sir."

"Then perhaps you'd be so kind as to ask Jericho to find one. He usually knows where everything is."

"But, sir, about Richard's bedtime—"

"Oh, bother, I suppose if we must. Tell you what, have Jericho bring a measuring stick, and you go turn up that hot milk and honey. I'll give Richard a lesson in fractions. With any luck, the combination will put him to sleep. It always worked for me."

She tucked in her lower lip in an effort not to smile and whisked out. A moment later Jericho appeared in the doorway bearing the required stick and a pained expression when he saw the state of my clothes.

"Good evening, Jericho. Have to hold off on the nightly wash and brush up for the moment."

"I think it is just as well, Mr. Jonathan. Had you taken the time earlier, it would have all been for nothing."

Richard giggled. "Jericho."

"And what about it?" I asked. "That's his name."

I got another giggle for a reply.

"I believe Master Richard is referring to the unfortunate habit Londoners have of calling the back garden privy a 'jericho,' sir," my excellent friend said with unsuppressed distaste.

Another giggle from below.

Well, I had to put a stop to that. "Richard," I said, fully sitting up and addressing the boy in a serious tone. It took a repetition or two before he calmed down sufficiently to give me the solemn sort of attention the occasion required. "Making fun of a person's name, no matter what it is, is very rude and not at all becoming of a gentleman. You understand that?"

He pouted and nodded.

"Very good. Now I want you to promise not to make fun of anyone's name ever again, particularly Jericho's."

I'd had to deal with this subject before with the servants. Jericho was the true head of this household when it came to all practical matters, and it wouldn't do to have anyone finding amusement in his name and thus undermining his authority. His was an excellent name, after all, and certainly not his fault that it had been corrupted by the locals into something that might be thought basely amusing.

"I promise."

"What an excellent lad you are! Now can you tell us where Nanny keeps your little nightgown? If you're all dressed and ready for bed when she comes back, then she might not be cross with me for keeping you up so late."

Put this way, he had no objection to helping me avoid Nanny's wrath and readily pointed out a chest with drawers. We searched through its contents and discovered a suitable garment.

"I can take over from here, sir," said Jericho. "Perhaps if you would use this time to put yourself into order as well . . ."

I obediently set to work on myself as he turned to take care of Richard.

"Won't that come off?" Richard said, pointing to Jericho's dark skin.

"I assure you it will not, Master Richard. See for yourself." He held his hand out for the child's close inspection. Said hand was peered at, rubbed, and pinched. "See, just like yours but with more color—and a good deal cleaner. A trip to the washbasin is in order, I think. Come along."

He gently guided Richard away, and from that so subtle action smoothly assumed the same position of command he held over me when it came to proper grooming. Jericho could be quite formidable when he chose, but in this instance he was careful not to bowl the lad over by overdoing his grand manner. A soft word here, a delicate recommendation there and he had Richard painlessly scrubbed and dressed for bed before the boy knew what had happened.

"I'll take my turn as soon as I'm done here," I told Jericho.

"One would hope so, sir," he replied, raising an eyebrow at my lackluster turnout. Since all I'd done was replace the shoe on my foot and straighten my waistcoat, he was entitled to all the eyebrow raising he wanted. He plucked my discarded neckcloth from the floor and stalked out just as Nanny Howard returned with a small cup of hot milk in hand.

"All ready," Richard announced to her, showing off his clean hands, face, and change of clothing. "Don't be cross with Cousin Jon'th'n."

The woman was becoming adept at adjusting to changing circumstances, and her look went from questioning to acceptance. "Very well, I won't. Have you had your lesson in fractions yet?"

"We were just about to get down to it," I answered for him.

"Very well," she said, and put the cup of milk on a low table next to a miniature stool. Richard plopped himself onto the latter and gave the cup and its contents a suspicious eye.

"It's too hot," he said decisively.

"No doubt, but it will cool off in a moment. Now where's that measuring stick?" I quickly found it and sat cross-legged on the floor next to him to more easily explain the basic principals of fractions.

For all the fatherly pride that was fast burgeoning in my swelled bosom over his many talents, I couldn't say that he took well to this first lesson. To be fair, he was still very lively from all his hard riding and full of questions for everything except the subject at hand. It didn't take me long to twig to this, so I obligingly did not force him around. Instead, I did my best to answer why I preferred not to wear a wig, where I'd come from, the general location of America in relation to England, and conjectured just how wide and deep the " 'Lantic Ocean" might be. By then his milk was of a suitable drinking temperature, and I managed to coax most of it into him.

"Doesn't taste like real milk," he said.

"That must be the honey in it."

"He's used to fresh cow's milk, sir," Nanny Howard put in. "All the kitchen had was ass's milk."

"Yes, Oliver is particularly fond of it, says it's more wholesome than what comes from a cow."

"Indeed it is, sir, for I shouldn't care to trust any cow's milk bought in the city. Too many things can make it go bad."

"Perhaps if we got our own cow—"

"Oh, no, sir, for it would still be in the city. Better to have ass's milk or none at all."

"You don't care much for the city, then?"

"It's not my place to say, sir."

"Certainly it is if I ask you."

"Well, then, it's fine enough for me, but in all truth, I don't think raising a child in the city is at all wise."

"What have you against it, then?"

"The bad air for one thing, the bad water for another."

I could offer no argument on those points and motioned for her to continue.

"That's more than enough to stunt growth and turn them sickly. There's also soot everywhere you step, rotten food sold by people you don't know, disease, low women, wicked men, and too much noise. How can a child get any sleep with all the constant row?"

"There's low women and wicked men in the country— or so I've heard," I said, dodging the question.

"Perhaps that is so, Mr. Barrett, but I've yet to see any and I've lived in the country considerably longer than you've been alive. But all that aside, I've seen more country children reach their majority than city ones. Raising children is not unlike farming, sir. You need a bit of room to grow, sunshine, and sweet water. Take any one of those away and you'll end up with a failed crop."

Damnation, but she was making perfect sense. "Then you see nothing favorable about the city at all?"

"I'll allow that it has some passable distractions and entertainments, but the nature of such things holds little interest to a boy of four years." Her observations were entirely sensible, but I didn't know what to do about them. The first idea that came to me—and the first one to be discarded—was for Richard to return to Edmond's country home. As for the second idea . . .

"I could possibly look around for a place of my own,"

I said, without much enthusiasm.

She picked up on that and offered an alternative. "What about Fonteyn House? It's not too far away and has more than enough room."

That was my third idea, and I wasn't too keen on it. "I don't think it would prove very practical. You see, my father and mother may be on their way to England at any time, and I rather expect Mother will want to live in Fonteyn House."

"That's only natural, it being her late sister's home."

"Natural, yes, but to have her sharing it with a young and rowdy child would not be the best for either of 'em."

"But there's more than room enough—"

"Room is not the point, Mrs. Howard. It's best that you know about my mother."

"Indeed?" She assumed a carefully neutral face, having also picked up on a darkening in my tone of voice.

"She's just as horrible in her way as Aunt Fonteyn was." I paused to allow her to take in that bit of blatant honesty, giving her a suitably somber look. "I think we all know what might have happened had Aunt Fonteyn lived to learn about, let us say, certain irregular circumstances in the family progeny. Now multiply that by a factor of ten and you'll have an idea of how my mother might react should she learn of it."

"Oh, dear."

"In truth, her hold on reason is altogether infirm, and when her grasp slips she is capable of the most violent fits imaginable. I would be loath to expose an unprepared innocent to such an irregular temper."

Mrs. Howard nodded. "Yes, old Judge Fonteyn suffered the same sort of malady. Many's the time I had to keep Oliver out of his way when the spell was on him."

Oliver and I had had a lengthy talk about what the old judge suffered from, an entirely horrifying topic. Though she gave me the impression she knew something about it,

I wasn't going to pursue it with Mrs. Howard at the present and certainly not while the boy was listening.

"Having my own home might be the best for all concerned, then," I said instead. "But I shouldn't like to be too far from London."

"I'm sure there are any number of suitable places, sir."

I had my doubts, but only because I was reluctant to move from Oliver's comfortable house and assume the responsibility of looking after my own. On the other hand, there was a decided appeal to being one's own master. "You know, if Oliver hadn't invited me and Elizabeth to live with him, I'd have had to find one for us, anyway. It probably would have been in the city, though, and I'd still have the same problem to face now."

Then perhaps it was past time I gave serious thought to finding a separate accommodation for myself, or rather for the Barrett branch of the Fonteyn kindred. And I hadn't exactly come to England empty-handed, being still in the possession of a half dozen cattle that had survived the ocean crossing. They'd originally been put aboard ship to provide me with a fresh source of blood for the long journey, but my condition had changed that plan by causing me to fall into an unnatural sleep for the whole trip. My unnerving hibernation had provided no end of worry for Elizabeth and Jericho at the time. The only favorable thing that might be said of the phenomenon was that it spared me from two months of constant and exhausting *mal de mer*.

Soon after our arrival in England, the Barrett cows had been turned out to mix with Fonteyn stock. My property would soon be in need of a permanent home if they bred as planned. It was my fond hope that when Father arrived he'd have the start of a fine herd to keep him busy if he wanted to retire from his law practice.

Now there was something *else* to think about. "Another thing you need to know about this coming household," I continued, "is that my father and mother are estranged, and

I rather think both would be more comfortable if there's some goodly distance between 'em. If I find something suitable, then my father will likely be sharing it with me.''

"How will he feel about the—ah—irregularities? That is, if I may be so bold as to ask.'' She nodded her head very, very slightly in Richard's direction, not looking at him.

"Ask away, dear lady. As for your answer, once he gets over the shock, I think he will be utterly delighted.'' I hoped for as much. Elizabeth and I had come to that happy and comfortable conclusion after much lengthy discussion. During moments of weakness, I was subject to the occasional doubt or two, but that was from my own inner discomfiture, not because Father would fall short of our expectations. We knew him to be a very wise and compassionate man. Certainly he would welcome a grandson, even one from the wrong side of the blanket.

"There's a comfort,'' said Mrs. Howard. "I remember him as being a most sensible young fellow.''

"You do? You knew him before he left England?''

"Not to speak to, I should say. It wasn't my place, of course. But there was many in the servant's hall who were glad he stood up to the old judge and won Miss Marie away from Fonteyn House. Best thing that ever happened to her. I'm so sorry to know that—that things worked out as they did.''

"What was she like then?'' I asked, feeling a sudden tightness around my throat at this chance to look into another's past. Part of me wanted nothing to do with Mother, but a different part wanted to know everything. It was like picking a scab to see if it would fall away clean from a healed wound or peel painfully off only to start it bleeding again.

"Oh, she was a very beautiful girl. Sometimes quiet and sometimes very headstrong. Not what I would call too knowledgeable about the world, but then the judge didn't

have much use for women learning any more than they
needed to run a household. She used to do very clever
needlework."

"Mother? Quiet?"

"Silent, then. There's a difference," she said with a sad
face.

"I'm done with my milk," Richard announced. His eyes
had grown wide and his expression pensive with concern.
Even if he didn't understand much of our talk, he was keen
enough to perceive the dark emotions running beneath it
and be worried.

"What a good lad you are!" she exclaimed approvingly,
with a swift brightening in her manner. "Are you ready to
go to bed, now?"

"No, please. I want to play with Cousin Jon'th'n."

Nanny Howard shot me a dangerous look, one that I took
to heart. "We'll play again tomorrow night, my lad, or
we'll both be in trouble. We have to do what Nanny says,
y'see. She knows best."

Reluctantly he allowed himself to be led to his bed, and
she tucked him in.

"A story, please?" he asked, as appealing as only a four-
year-old can manage. I found my throat tightening again,
but for a far different reason than before. Mrs. Howard
correctly read my face and upon selecting a chapbook from
a pile on a shelf, thrust it into my waiting hands.

The book's subject had to do with the alphabet, being
full of instructive rhymes of the "A is for Apple" sort.
Richard and I went through it together, with him pointing
out the letters and naming them and muttering along as I
read the rest of the text. He seemed to know the book by
heart, but that didn't matter. I'd been told I'd had my favorite stories, too, never tiring of their repetition. He was
asleep by the time I'd gotten to the "M is for Mouse"
rhyme.

"Thank you, Mrs. Howard," I whispered to her as I prepared to tiptoe out.

"Bless you, sir, but you're the one to be thanked. I think you're the best thing that could ever have happened to the child."

"I can hope as much. I'm new to this and don't mind saying that I should highly value your guidance if you would be so kind."

"Certainly, sir."

"And about the food, I'll have Oliver arrange it so the pick of Fonteyn House's country larder is at your disposal. Will that be satisfactory until such time as I can find my own home outside the city?"

"More than satisfactory, sir."

I fairly bounded down the hall to my room where Jericho waited to repair the damages of my recent romp. Our conversation was a bit one-sided at first, with me rattling on about Richard with hardly a stop except when it was time for my shaving. Jericho had a light touch with a razor, but years back we'd both agreed that any unnecessary talk from me might prove to be a dangerous distraction to his concentration on the task. I was close-mouthed as a clam for the duration.

He took the respite as an opportunity to catch me up on the day's events within his own sphere, reporting about who had paid calls and what their business had been. An invitation had arrived for Elizabeth and me to dine with the Bolyn family. It was worded in a flexible enough manner so as to include Oliver if he chose to come. He was still officially in mourning for his mother and not expected to participate in social gatherings, though an exception could be made for a private informal supper. Considering the restrictions of my diet, it was just as well for me. At least then Elizabeth would not be without an escort if she accepted.

Once Jericho had my chin scraped clean and clothed me

in something presentable, I was released from the nightly ritual and free to go about other civilized pursuits. I had to promise not to indulge in additional boisterous play before he let slip the leash, though. Since Richard was safely asleep, it was an easy enough pledge to make.

I found Elizabeth to be alone in the parlour, very much at her ease on the settee staring at some book. All the tea things were cleared away. It was that space of time where most people enjoyed the quiet comfort of their home and family while awaiting the arrival of the supper hour.

"Hallo, where's Oliver got to?" I asked, idly glancing about.

"Off to his consulting room for a bit of work he missed during the day." She put the book to one side on top of a pile of well-thumbed copies of *The Gentleman's Magazine.*

"Is he going to be busy for the whole evening?" Our cousin could disappear for hours on end into his medical studies when the inspiration was upon him.

"I don't think so. He wanted only to read up on a treatment for a complaint he thought too delicate for mixed company."

That sounded interesting. "Delicate?"

"Apparently even reading about it with a female in the room was of considerable discomfort to him, so he excused himself. I can't see what his problem might be, since it was only something in a past issue of a magazine about a new method of cutting into the bladder to remedy the suppression of urine."

"Ugh! Really, Elizabeth!"

"Oh, now don't you object to what is or is not proper for a lady. The article was right there plain and open on the page for anyone to examine." She tapped the stack of publications next to her with her fingertips.

"And bladder operations are the sort of thing you enjoy reading up on?"

"Hardly, but it caught my eye. I was really looking for

news about the war and was distracted away by the account.''

"So how is the war going?" I asked, eager for a change of subject, any change at all. I vaguely recalled reading the bladder article myself and had no desire to have my memory refreshed.

"It was a September issue, so their news was very dated. All they had was what we already knew when we left, that, and some account of the rebels indulging in a paroxysm of prayer and fasting last July fourth to aid their ill-considered cause. But the December issue is no better. There's not one word in it about General Burgoyne's defeat.''

I threw myself into a chair, hooking one leg over its arm. "They're probably afraid it will prove to be too disheartening to the public. Too late for that, though. I'll wager the King and his cronies know all there is to know, and they hope by keeping quiet the whole nasty business will be forgotten.''

"Then they are bound to be disappointed, especially if all the rumors in the papers are true.''

"Oh, I'm sure they are. I overheard quite a lot during the funeral.'' A few of the men in the Fonteyn and Marling clans possessed an inside ear to the private workings of the government and when closely questioned, became rather free with their information, most notably after the Madeira started flowing.

"So did I,'' she said, one corner of her mouth curling down. "If it's true, then we may be here for good.''

"I thought we were, anyway. That's what Father—or did he tell you differently?''

She made a sour face at me. "Father's moving here for good, but it doesn't necessarily mean that I have.''

This was more than startling news to me. My belly gave a twist as I sat up straight to face her. "What? You want to go back? Into the middle of a war?''

"Certainly not, but the war can't last forever.''

"And then you'd go back?"

"I don't know. London's just wonderful from what I've seen of it, but I do get so homesick sometimes."

"But you might return to Long Island after the war finishes?" This came out as less of a question and more like a woebegone whine.

"I've thought of it. But please don't excite yourself yet, little brother. All I've done is *think* about it."

"Then thank God for that." But I was still very much unnerved.

"Your concern is most flattering."

"I had no idea you felt this way."

"Normally I don't, but it caught up with me today after reading this rubbish. I came suddenly all over homesick. Mostly I miss Father and worry for him. Perhaps once he's here in England, things will brighten up for me."

"I'm sure they will." I sincerely hoped as much, being very attached to my sister. Though ever considerate for her happiness and comfort, the thought of her moving back, perhaps forever, to Long Island made a cold and heavy knot in my heart. I should not like that to happen at all. "I miss Father, too," I added lamely. "Once he's here everything will be all right for you."

"Have you written to him yet?"

"Well . . ." I hedged. "I've started a letter, but there's been so much to do with Richard—"

"Bother that." Some of her dark mood appeared to drop away, and she favored me with a severe eye. "I've heard you complain time and again how heavy the early morning hours are before your bedtime when you've gotten tired of reading and there's no one to talk to except the night watch."

I favored her with a sour face in return. "Be fair, Elizabeth, how do you think I can put all that's happened into a letter? 'Dear Father, Cousin Clarinda murdered Mother's sister, and damned-near got her husband and myself as well. By the way, I've taken in Clarinda's boy, who's turned out to be my son, so congratulations, you're now a grandfather. How are things faring with you?' He'd burst a blood vessel.''

Elizabeth found a cushion on the settee and threw it with a great deal of force, catching me square on the nose. ''If you send him such a letter *I'll* burst a blood vessel—one of yours.''

The cushion dropped to my lap, and I punched it a few times, feeling quite cheered by her show of temper. ''All right, all right, I know better, but it's still anything but an easy task. If you're so keen to let him know what's happened, why don't *you* write him?''

''Because it's all concerned with your business; therefore it's your responsibility.''

''But you're the eldest, as you so frequently remind me. Besides, yours is the more legible handwriting.''

''Jonathan, if I were a man I'd call you a coward and issue a challenge here and now.''

''And you'd never get satisfaction, because I'd here and now freely admit that I'm as craven as a rabbit.''

''And properly ashamed of it, I hope.''

''Dreadfully ashamed. In fact, I'm quite paralyzed from it, so much so that I don't think I could *possibly* lift pen to—''

Elizabeth reached for another cushion.

''That is to say . . . never mind.''

She put her potential missile back, smiling a cat's smile. Now *that* was a very good sign.

Teasing done and peace preserved, I continued. ''It would be easier for me if we heard from him first. Surely he's written us by now.''

''I'm sure he must have, but with the war going on, his letters might be delayed or stopped altogether. Those damned rebels have ships and guns, too.''

''Oh, I'm sure he'd find a way to get something through.

He's got enough well-placed friends to help him. What I'm thinking is that he might have sold the house by now and already be on his way here.''

"I hope not—a winter crossing . . .'' She shivered, expressing a very real concern for the dangers. "But all that aside, you still have to do something about this yourself. Oliver and I will help all we can, but in the end, it is your task.''

"I know. But making a proper job of it requires a lot of thought and I'm not sure I'm up to it.''

She made no effort in the least to stifle her laughter. I threw the cushion back, but missed. It landed harmlessly on the magazines next to her.

"Very well,'' I grumbled when she had control of herself again. "I'll make a real start on it tonight, though what I'll say to him will be anyone's guess.''

"I'm sure the simple truth in the order it happened will be fine.''

"But there's such a deuced lot of it and—oh, heavens— what if Mother should see it?'' We both knew Mother was not beyond opening and reading her husband's letters when the chance presented itself.

Elizabeth's mouth crimped into an unflattering frown. "If she's determined to commit such a trespass, then she should be prepared to accept the consequences.''

"I'm all for it, but my worry is what the consequences will be for Father.''

"I expect that should the worst happen, he'll just call Dr. Beldon to give her a draught of laudanum, then Mrs. Hardinbrook will pat her hand and offer shrill sympathy as usual.''

"If he manages to keep the letter from Mother, I hope Father won't tell her about Richard.'' My description to Mrs. Howard of Mother's likely reaction was no exaggeration. Far better for all concerned that she never learned of the child's existence.

"He probably won't, but all you need do is ask for his discretion."

"Be assured of my utter determination to do so. But I'm tired of all this, let's talk about Richard instead."

"I wondered how long it would take for you to get 'round to him. Sooner than this, I would have thought."

"Don't fret, I'll make up for the delay. We had a wonderful time tonight."

"So Oliver and I observed whenever you came hurtling through. Did you win your race?"

"Oh, dozens of 'em." Taking this as an invitation, I told her every detail of what we'd done. "He's very smart, y'know." I concluded, sometime later, after letting her know all about the attempted lesson in fractions and the chapbook.

"I know."

"I think he really was reading along with me. He knows all his letters, at least up to M, anyway. I'll take him through the rest of the alphabet tomorrow night."

"That should be nice."

"Something wrong?"

"I hope not." But her face was all serious again. I feared a return of her earlier melancholy.

"Then what is it that you hope is not wrong?"

"Perhaps I'm too much the worrier, but I need some assurance from you."

"On what?"

Her ears went pink. "This is entirely foolish of me. I *know* you, but I can't seem to quell the worry."

"What worry? Come now and tell me."

"It's just that Richard is tremendous fun for you right now. Everything's all new and exciting. But I have to know that you'll be there for him when he needs more than a playmate. That you'll look after him when things are serious as well, the way Father's always done for us." Her words came out all in a rush, clear evidence of her embarrassment.

In my own heart I'd already thought along those very same paths. I'd worried over the fear that once the novelty of Richard's presence wore off, I'd find other pursuits to occupy me. After a lengthy heart search, I'd concluded the fear to not be worth further examination. "Of course I will," I answered quietly. "Elizabeth . . . know this: That boy is part of my very soul and always will be. That's as certain as the sunrise."

Her face cleared somewhat. Then she smiled, a small one, and gave an equally small sigh. "Thank you for not being angry with me."

I shrugged. "If you care for Richard half as much as I do, then hearing your concerns for him is my duty and pleasure. You've nothing to fault yourself with. I won't pretend to assume I'll make as good a job of it with him as Father did for us, but certainly I'll try my best."

"I don't understand why I thought you might do anything less. I just needed to hear you say it, I suppose."

"It's because you're my sister. You've seen *me* as a child howling away over scraped knees and a bloody nose, and it's hard to accept that the boy you hold in your memory can handle a man's business when he's grown. Good heavens, there's many that can't no matter how old they get."

"Too true." We regarded each other, peace restored—I hoped—to her heart and mine. For all the fun and frolic I had with Richard, I held a keen and clear awareness of the attendant responsibility. In odd moments I sometimes gave in to fear and quailed at the enormous weight of it, of raising a child, but then I'd had a more than decent raising and could draw upon memories of my father's example when necessary. With this and guidance from others I had a more than reasonable expectation of not making a mess of things.

Still and all, I would be very, *very* glad when Father arrived in England.

Perhaps I should wait a bit before seeking out a house, on the chance that he would want to help in the choosing. Much of his law practice had been occupied with the details on the buying and selling of property and boundary disputes. I'd very much welcome his vast experience. Damnation, but there would be a thousand decisions to make. The place might even require extensive furnishing. Elizabeth would be of excellent help there. Furnishings . . .

"I was just thinking, dear sister . . . "

Her glance up at me was sharpish. I only used that particular form of address when I wanted something from her and well did she know it.

"Do you think you could teach Richard to play the spinet?"

"I could try, if I had a spinet upon which to teach."

"I was planning to get you one."

"I'm pleased to hear it. But isn't he a bit young, yet?"

"Oh, it's never too early to learn. They say that fellow Mozart started just as young, and he ended up playing before all the royal courts."

"Mozart was born with musical talent—what if Richard takes after you?"

"Then I'll teach him to ride horses instead, and you'll have a fine instrument left over as a souvenir of the attempt. Tomorrow I want you to run out and find the best spinet in London and have them cart it over right away. But all that aside, I miss hearing you play."

Her expression softened. "Why, thank you!"

"And get a carpet, too."

Now did her expression abruptly pinch into blank perplexity. "A carpet?"

"Yes, a nice big thick one, the thickest you can find. I promised Mrs. Howard one for the nursery and said the three of you could go shopping for it tomorrow. Richard should have a say in the choosing, too, I thought.''

"How kind of you to find so many enjoyable things for me to do," she said dryly.

"Not at all. I suppose you'll need to take measurements or something so it will fit. You'll find a measuring stick up there, unless Mrs. Howard has given it back to Jericho. I was teaching him about fractions—Richard, that is, not Jericho—with it, if you'll recall. Perhaps you can find a carpet for Mrs. Howard's room, too. An excellent woman, we're so lucky to have her, and I want her made as comfortable as may be."

"Heavens, Jonathan, I don't even have a carpet for *my* room!"

I waved a careless hand. "Then indulge yourself at my expense."

"Don't worry, I will," she muttered darkly.

Dear me, but I knew *that* look. Time for a bit of placation or I'd have another pillow in my face. "Well, I've gone on quite long enough, why don't you tell me everything *you* did today?"

Elizabeth sighed, apparently exasperated by this latest sudden change in subject, then composed herself to give a summation of the day's events. As with Jericho, it had become a regular custom between us for her to tell me all the news I'd missed while lying oblivious in the cellar.

"Well, to start with, Charlotte Bolyn has invited us to—"

"No, no, no, I don't mean that rot! Tell me all that happened with you and *Richard*."

She picked up the cushion and once more—and with considerable force—managed to strike my nose dead on.

In an effort to preserve my battered countenance from additional damage, I decided to intrude upon Oliver's ruminations, hoping he wouldn't be too far gone in study for a bit of company. Upon hearing my knock he grunted something that might loosely be interpreted as an invitation to enter. I took it as such and pushed the door open.

His own sanctuary was part study, part consulting room, to be used on those occasions to interview patients when he was not out making calls on them. His practice wasn't a busy one, but he kept himself very active with it. Most of his patients were from within his broad circle of friends, and being a gregarious sort, he often as not paid visits as much to socialize as to render aid. Unless his services as a physician were actually required, he never charged for those visits, claiming he was content enough with the distraction of agreeable company. This made him popular, but it was just as well for him that he had income inherited from Grandfather Fonteyn or he'd not be living in his present comfortable circumstances.

At the moment he was very comfortable, indeed, having pulled his favorite chair close to the fire and treated himself to some port while reading. Like Elizabeth, he had a respectable stack of *The Gentleman's Magazine* nearby and held one in his hand.

"Hallo," he said, looking up. "Is the house still standing?"

"Was it too much row for you?"

"Not at all. You should have heard us earlier when Richard and I were playing hide-and-seek. I was just wondering whether the walls were still intact after the races."

"Intact and likely to stay solid," I said, easing into another chair. "But we'll be more stately tomorrow night if you like."

"Please say you won't. I grew up being forced into stateliness and can't recommend it. Let the boy laugh and shout his head off; I like that kind of noise. The reason I came here was to keep from getting trampled."

"Sorry."

He dismissed my contrition with a wave. "And because I feared you'd invite me to join in and I might not have

the will to refuse. The little brat already tired me to the
point of fainting once today. Once is more than sufficient."

"He did?"

"Well, perhaps not quite so far, but I was pretty blown.
Don't know how Nanny can keep up with him. Paces herself, I suppose."

"She and I had a nice little talk about this and that," I
said. "She managed, during that talk, to throw a sizable
rock into my tranquil pond."

He squinted. "Sorry, but I don't quite follow."

"Because I've not yet explained."

"Then please do so, Coz."

I did so, recounting to him Mrs. Howard's objections to
raising a child in the city.

"Then you also think young Richard would be better off
in a rustic setting?" he asked.

"It didn't seem to hurt either of us or Elizabeth."

"True enough. It may have been hard going for me with
Mother, but Nanny saw to it I got my share of fresh air
and exercise. You'd also be limiting his chances of getting
the pox, too."

My dormant heart gave a sudden and sickening lurch.
"Pox? Good God, I hadn't thought of that."

His normally jocund expression was now as gloomy as
that of a judge. "And well you should. I've seen far too
many young souls carried off before their sixth year from
that curse, and pox aside, there's any number of a hundred
other things that . . ."

Another lurch in my chest. It felt like a great ball of ice
was rolling around inside.

I wanted Oliver to stop talking, to stop filling me with
fears I didn't want, but as hard as the facts were to hear,
they were inescapable.

"He'll have to be inoculated," I whispered.

"Oh, yes, certainly that. I know a good man for it, grinds
'em through a dozen at once."

"What?"

"He's got a big house he's turned into a sort of inoculation mill. Has in a dozen children at a time. They stay for about a week for a bit of purging and bleeding to purify their systems, then he makes the inoculation. They're down sick from it, of course, but he keeps them all bedded up and cared for until they're ready to go home, say after about two weeks. He's very good, very successful."

I recalled my own ordeal had not been quite so involved and said as much.

Oliver frowned mightily, then his face cleared. "Oh, well, that's because it was a few years back and on the other side of the world. There's been a lot of advances made since, y'know. You won't find 'em practicing any wild colonial experimentation here in England! But there's no hurry. The lad needs a little time to grow. Elizabeth made a point of hiring servants who'd already had it, so things should be safe for now. Just make sure it's done before you send him off to school."

If I send him off, I thought. At the moment, the idea of hiring a private tutor looked much more appealing to me. Many other boys, myself included, had not suffered from such schooling in the safety of one's home.

So many plans. So many responsibilities. That ball of ice would turn into a leaden weight and take up permanent residence if I let it.

Always move forward, laddie. We're all in God's hands and that's as safe enough place as any in this world.

"Jonathan?"

I'd been staring at the fire and now gave a start.

"Don't come all over melancholy on me. Everything's going to be fine."

"Yes, I'm sure you're right. It was just a bit of a jolt, don't you know."

"I know, and I'm glad to hear it. Means you'll be doing something when the time comes."

"Upon my honor and before God, you may be sure of it."

"Excellent. There's nothing that breaks my heart more than hearing the parents wailing away because they'd forgotten or had put it it off until it was too late."

"You won't have that with me."

"Excellent." He tapped his fingers along the spine of the magazine in his hand. The silence that now settled between us thickened like a sudden patch of fog. I didn't care much for it and he seemed not to, either. He cleared his throat. "About this idea of moving to a country home?"

I gratefully seized his opening for a change of subject. "Mrs. Howard recommended Fonteyn House, but I'll have to find some other place." I clarified this statement by mentioning the probable situation ahead once Father and Mother arrived in England.

When I'd finished, he was in full agreement with me, adding, "But whether or not your mother takes up residence there, you still wouldn't want Richard shut away in Fonteyn House. It's much too dark and drafty, but there will soon be changes. I'll be making a deal of those when things settle a bit. Changes, that is. Dress up the insides, knock a few holes in the walls and put in more windows and damnation on the window tax. Once I'm done you won't know the old pile. But as for your having a place of your own—"

"There's no hurry yet. I'm thinking I'll wait until Father's here."

He shrugged. "As you wish, but I was going to say I know of a perfectly nice house standing empty that might suit. The land's been fallow for years, but that can be fixed. There's room for your cattle and what not, and it's just a few miles north of the city. The house will need a bit of work; it's been empty a long time."

"Why is that?"

"Oh, one of Mother's grand imperial orders, y'know.

The estate belonged to my late father. Seems when he died, she closed it down hard and fast, wouldn't even rent it out.''

"Strange to do that."

"Consider her nature, old lad. Y'see the whole lot was my father's, free and clear, and in accordance with his will it was to come to me when I came of age. But she shut the house up and let the property go, thereby making sure it would eventually become pretty worthless. I remember her sending Edmond around with an offer to buy it from me a day or two after I turned one and twenty."

"Which you turned down?"

"Not exactly. Edmond didn't say it in so many words, but he gave me to understand that her offer was much too low and that I should hang on to the deed for a bit longer. I didn't at first know what he was up to, but twigged to things after she sent him on a second visit and he managed to discourage me again. Mother had been going on about how she was doing me a favor by trying to take the place off my hands since it was essentially a ruin, so I went out to see things for myself. It seems that Edmond had been less than honest with her."

"In what way?"

"Oh, whenever a storm came through, he'd tell her another shutter had dropped off or there was a new hole in the roof. The truth was he'd made it his business to keep the place in tolerable repair. The doors and windows all hang straight and close snug, and it's dry as a drum inside. The land's all overgrown and that gives it a forlorn, ruinous look, but otherwise everything's sound."

"And Edmond did that for you?"

Oliver nodded. "He took a dreadful risk over the years. I mean, he'd have been out in the street quick enough if Mother had ever taken it into her head to pay a visit to the old Marling hold. He must have hidden the expense of repairs and the taxes from her in some clever way. Edmond's as intimidating as a bear with the gout, but deep down quite a decent chap at heart. We should all have such a fellow handling our business, don't you think?''

"Great heavens, yes. Makes you wonder what other little secrets he's got hidden away.''

"I'll be finding out soon enough, I'm sure. Before he packed himself and Clarinda off home the other day, he said he'd have to soon sit down with me to go over the accounts. Seems there's a lot of legal nonsense that needs my attention now, and I can't put it off much longer. Anyway, if you want to look the place over some night—''

"Certainly, I'd be most happy to do so.'' What a painless way to find a home. By keeping all the business within the family I wouldn't have to wait for Father's arrival to avoid any purchasing pitfalls. "If it takes my fancy, then we can work out some sort of rent—or were you thinking of selling?''

"I was thinking of neither.'' He sat well back in his chair, lifting his chin slightly to peer down his nose. "If you want it—well, then . . . for the price of the yearly taxes you may *have* it!''

For a yawningly long moment I was in complete distrust of my ears. "*What?*''

He repeated it, grinning away like an ass and most certainly because I must have looked exactly like one myself.

CHAPTER
◄5►

He'd utterly stunned me. That was the only word to describe my feelings when the whole import of his proposal finally sank in. For some considerable period I could do nothing but gape, inspiring a good deal of amusement in him.

"But I couldn't," I objected in a faint voice when partial recovery asserted itself sufficiently for me to speak.

"And why ever not?" He was still grinning.

"It's too magnificent a kindness."

"Don't be sure of that until you see the place—it might not suit, y'know. But all that aside, it's my property and I can do whatever I please with it. Besides, I know damned well such an arrangement would have sent Mother into an apoplectic fit, so that's yet another good reason for me to do it."

I argued a little more, but not too terribly hard. A firm and outright rejection of his generosity in the name of good sense would have been very rude and hurtful, of course, but aside from that I found myself partially willing to let him have his way. It was a magnificent gift, but if it proved to be too much so, then perhaps Edmond and I could argue him into something more equitable for all concerned. I had no wish to cheat my excellent cousin out of any of his rightful incomes. For now, deeply moved, I warmly and sincerely thanked him; he clapped his hands, practically crowing, then sat forward and told me all he could remember about the house and lands.

It was a sizable place not all that far to the north and east of Fonteyn House, but not all that close, either. There were fields and woods in the generous acreage, all overgrown and running wild by now, at least one clear running stream, and several buildings. Edmond had seen to the care of the house, but Oliver wasn't as certain about the condition of the barns and stabling. The house itself had been erected not long after the Great Fire of the previous century.

"Was it involved in that in some way?" I asked, fascinated.

"What, you mean burned up and then put something in on top of the ruins? No, nothing like that. The property's not even close to where all the destruction happened. The story is that one of my Marling ancestors liked the look of all the new buildings going up in London at the time and decided to have one of 'em for himself. Found himself a fashionable architect for the job and . . ."

The more he talked the greater waxed my interest and the more eager I became to see the place. Though it promised to involve a lot of work to make the house livable and get the land producing again, the prospect of undertaking such a project was enormously appealing. Now could I understand some of my father's youthful wish to cross a wild and dangerous ocean to a new land in order to create a place of his own.

In my case it would be going to an old land, but still virtually a foreign country from the one where I'd been raised. That had a very compelling appeal as well, for I'd ever been intrigued by the history of my English ancestry.

Who knows but that some famous battle or great event might have taken place on the Marling lands in ages past. Oliver expressed a degree of doubt over this speculation, but that did not dampen my enthusiasm. Even if nothing more exciting than a bit of sheepherding had ever occupied the property over the centuries, what is commonplace to the local is exotic to the visitor.

When Oliver's store of description ran out, we resolved to visit and give the place a thorough inspection within a week if the weather cooperated.

"I'll probably go earlier to have a look 'round in the daylight," he said. "Shan't get much out of it at night I'm afraid, no matter how many lanterns I carry. Are you sure you'll be able to do as well?"

"As well if not better, especially if the sky is clear."

He shook his head. "Amazing business, your condition. That reminds me, I was meaning to ask if I might draw off a bit of your blood."

Again, I found myself gaping at my cousin. "Good God, whatever for?"

"For the purposes of scientific research, of course. A friend of mine has one of those microscope things, and I thought it might be interesting to use it to peep at a sample of your blood and compare it to that of another's, see if there's anything different between the two."

"A microscope?"

"You know, like a telescope, but for much smaller work. I may get one myself now, it's a marvelous toy. You wouldn't believe the things you can find in a humble drop of pond water with one of 'em. Most of my colleagues don't think much of the things, but my friend is always peering through his and making drawings of what he finds. Has an enormous collection of the most fascinating sketches. I don't think he quite knows what to do with any of it, but as a curiosity it'll hold your attention far better than a flea circus."

"And if you find a difference between my blood and another's, what then?"

He gave a great shrug. "It's knowledge and so it must be important. Come to think of it, perhaps I might take a sample from young Richard, then compare it to yours and see what's different and what's the same. I'll wager that might be very interesting, indeed."

"Really, now, Oliver, I don't want you poking at the poor child with one of your fleams unless it's absolutely necessary."

"I doubt that I'll need to; he's bound to get a scrape or two while playing—children are so good at that. I had my share of skinned knees and elbows and know it's only a matter of time for him to turn up with one. All I have to do is wait until he takes a tumble, then sneak a quick sample off him before binding up the wound. He'll never know a thing."

"Oh, you've reassured me to no end," I grumbled, with more than a trace of annoyance. "Now I'll not only be worrying about the pox—which is worry enough—but about skinned knees, broken arms, and who knows what else."

"Yes, the joys of fatherhood. You'll do all right, Jonathan. I've been in many a house where the parents are more concerned about the lapdog than the child, so be glad that you have such a heart in you that cares so. Anyway, God wouldn't have brought the two of you together unless he meant for it to last a bit. Just enjoy Richard one day—I mean, one night at a time, and let the future take care of itself."

"You sound like Elizabeth."

"Well! Thank you! I'll tell her you said that. She's a damn fine girl. Damn fine. I don't mind telling you that if she wasn't my first cousin I'd be sorely tempted to pay her court. With your permission, that is," he quickly added.

This wasn't precisely news to me, for I knew Oliver had

been quite taken with her from their first meeting. Certainly I wouldn't have minded having him for a brother-in-law. "Cousins have married before, y'know," I ventured with an optimistic air.

"I know," he said, rolling his eyes. "For the last century or so the Fonteyns have been famous for it and look where it got 'em. Any rustic huddled in his cottage will tell you about the dangers of inbreeding their stock. No, I don't think the Marlings and Barretts would benefit from such a course. Suppose Elizabeth would even have me, our children might turn out like Mother, and then where would we be? Ugh. No, thank you, I shall content myself with admiring your dear sister from afar only."

"Such an inheritance of temper might not happen. Elizabeth and I aren't in the least way like our mother, after all, and I'm going to do my best to see that Richard doesn't turn out to be like Clarinda."

"If anyone can do it, Coz, then it is you. I say, you mean you wouldn't have objected to me and Elizabeth . . . that is, if she'd . . . that is?"

"Not at all. You're an excellent fellow. Not a bit like your mother, either."

This pleased him to no end, and he told me as much, saying it gave him great hope for Richard's prospects. "It was Nanny Howard that trained me up right," he pronounced. "If it hadn't been for her, Lord knows how I might have ended up. Between the two of you, well, maybe the three or four of us—what with Elizabeth and me hanging about the lad—there won't be so much as a trace of Clarinda left in the boy."

"And that's just as well," I muttered.

"Yes, wretched business. I'd never have suspected it of her, but then I'm likely not to suspect it of anyone. It's just not in me to do so."

"Then you are a very blessed man, Coz."

"Not so blessed that I don't have a dark moment here

and there. Sometimes I don't know if I should condemn Clarinda or thank her for what she did," he mused. "Murder's a horrible, awful thing, but I don't know of anyone in the family who was truly sorry to see Mother gone, myself included, once you woke me up to it. Do you think I'll be damned for even considering such stuff?"

"I think rather that you might need to go dancing on her grave again and purge any lingering remnant of guilt out of your soul."

"Perhaps you're right on that. What really bothers me about the business is that Clarinda's idea to marry me would have probably worked because, damn it all, I *liked* her. Suppose I still do in a way, though it's all mixed up with a sort of revulsion, like Eve and that serpent, y'know. A pretty animal, but so bloody dangerous. I don't envy Edmond's job of keeping her caged for good and all."

"Neither do I."

"What about Ridley? In a way you've become his keeper, too. You're sure that the influencing you did will hold him and Arthur in check?"

His reminder of this unpleasant task waiting in the near future was hardly a welcome one. I found myself rubbing my arm again. The bone ached yet where Arthur Tyne had nearly severed it. That, or it only seemed to ache in my mind whenever I recalled the incident. "They'll be fine for the time being. I'll visit them within a week or so and bolster things up so they'll behave themselves."

"Pity you can't do the same thing for Clarinda."

"Oh, but I probably could. But I don't think it would—"

His eyes widened. "Really? Well, that would take the load off poor Edmond."

"Indeed, but then I'd have to explain myself to him. I'm not quite prepared to do so just now. It's a damned heavy confidence."

"Yes, that's the stark truth right enough. Edmond might think you'd gone mad and toss you out if you ever told

him about your little secret. It's so extraordinary. He'd have
to have proof, y'see.''

''And then I'd have to give it to him, and I'm not too
terribly confident in the benevolence of his reaction.''
Which is a mild way of putting it, I thought, with a nasty
cold twisting in my belly. For Edmond to find out that the
father of his son was some sort of extra-natural blood
drinker didn't bear lengthy consideration. My own immediate family accepted my condition well enough, but then
we were held close together by the ties of our deep, mutual
affection for one another. Not so with Edmond. ''He'd be
within his rights to take Richard away from me,'' I said,
thinking aloud.

''Then you could just influence him into leaving well
enough alone,'' Oliver said, with some little heat. He
seemed ready to enlarge upon the subject, but the look on
my face stopped him. ''Whatever is wrong?''

I'd come all over glum at his idea of influencing Edmond, for the very same one had occurred to me as well
and made my vitals twist in another direction. ''I . . . well
. . . damnation, that wouldn't be right.''

''In what way?''

''Father and I have talked the length and breadth of this
business about enforcing my will upon other people, the
good points and the bad. It all comes down to a question
of honor.''

''Honor? How so?''

''Your suggestion of my influencing Edmond—it's all
very well to talk about it, but to actually carry it out would
be an unconscionable intrusion upon him. To be telling him
what to do just so it's convenient to my needs . . .''

''But you're doing it all the time to keep the servants
from being curious about your eccentric habits,'' he objected.

''Yes, but I'm not telling them how to arrange their very
lives. That's the difference. I don't think you're fully aware

of just how frightening a power this is for me, Oliver. If I wanted to I could make my way right to the bedchamber of the king himself and play him or any of his ministers for a puppet on matters of state.''

"Good God." His color flagged. "I never thought of that."

"Then think hard on it now. I have, and in weak moments it makes me tremble."

"I don't fault you for it," he whispered, then recovered somewhat. "Mind you, it would be a way of settling things out with France. You could take a little trip to Paris, talk here and there with some of old Louis's ministers, and remove the threat of them jumping into the war to help those damned rebels."

"God help us, but I could if I had a mind to try."

"Without the French sticking their noses into that which doesn't concern 'em, the rebellion would die down fast enough." He was fast warming to the idea of my becoming some kind of invisible agent for the crown, quietly managing the direction of foreign powers to suit the policies of the king and country.

"Hold and cease, Oliver," I said, raising both hands palm out in a show of not so very mock terror. "I want no part of any of that."

His eyebrows went up. "But you could be of no end of service to the king. By God, you could even make peace with Ireland if you put your mind to it."

I shook my head and continued to shake it, until Oliver finally saw I was not to be moved by any argument.

"Why not?" he demanded.

"Politics is better left to politicians. I am, or would have been a humble lawyer, fit for arguing the law, but not for recreating it to fit my idea of perfection. Besides, even if I had the guidance of the whole of Parliament for my actions I would still have to listen to the reproach of my conscience should things go wrong."

"You're just being the pessimist."

"I'm being an abject coward," I said truthfully. "Suppose I bungled things and started a war? I'm not prepared to have all those deaths haunting me. Other men are able to stand it, but not me. I'll gladly choose my own path, but will not presume to tell others where to walk themselves."

He scowled. "Well, put that way, I can't really blame you, though one might argue that you would also have an equal chance of preventing a war, thus sparing untold lives."

I shifted, uncomfortable, scowling back at him. "There's that," I admitted. "But I'm not wise enough for such work and know it. Please, Oliver, let's not pursue this subject, it's making me liverish."

He acquiesced, much to my relief. "Very well, can't have you coming down sick on me because there's no tonic you can take but the one, is there?"

"Right enough," I agreed, but I was not feeling especially hungry at the moment. Quite the opposite.

"Then politics aside, what about Edmond? You've no plans for him one way or another if he decided to take Richard away?"

"But he's not going to, I only mentioned that as a remote possibility, born out of my own fears. It's true that I could influence Edmond, or most anyone else to suit to my needs, but where does one stop once one has started? No, sir. That takes it back to the political once more and my liver won't stand for it."

He gestured to indicate his dismissal of that topic. "But then what about Ridley and Arthur? You're doing your best to completely change their lives."

"And don't I wish to high heaven to be free of the responsibility. I've come to take no pleasure in any of it, even if it is to change them for the better. I'm hoping that the need for my influence will eventually cease for—believe me—I've a tremendous dislike of playing the god in men's affairs. I am absolutely stuck having to do this to them for the present, because for the life of me I can't think of any way around it. If there is a way out, I shall take it, and if you've any better ideas I should gladly hear them.''

''None at the moment. But the changes you are making within them are for the better. Surely that mitigates some of your strong feeling against using your talent for influence?''

''Oliver, how many times have you writhed inside when someone told you that they were doing something awful to you simply because it was for your own good?''

He thought that one over, then said, ''Oh.''

''And recall your feelings when you remembered how Nora had dealt with you back at Cambridge. It was for your good as well as hers that you should forget your liaisons with her and what she did with you, but still . . .'' I spread the fingers of one hand, using a gesture to complete the thought.

''Oh.'' He gulped, the corners of his mouth turning earthward in a bleak frown.

''Indeed. And again, where does one stop? Who am I to decide whose soul is in need of improvement and whose is not? Who am I to decide what's best for me is also best for another? Remember how you felt when you found out I was influencing you into not noticing my 'eccentricities,' as you call them? It wasn't so intrusive as to make a major change in your life, but I still hated doing it, especially to you of all people. Before God, as hard as it was to go through at the time, I am most thankful that you walked in on me and Miss Jemma that night in the Red Swan or else I might yet be having to gull you of the truth.''

He went very pink around the ears and nose and made a business of clearing his throat before speaking again. ''No need to be so harsh on yourself, Coz. You did what you thought was necessary and explained things to me quick enough. I don't think badly of you, y'know, for I do understand why you had to do it. All's forgiven and forgot, I hope.''

A little wave of relief washed through me and I nodded.

"Well, then, that's that." He gave a shake and shrug of his shoulders. "But just to end my curiosity on the topic for good and all . . ."

In a comical manner I groaned, raising my eyes to heaven, making us both laugh. We needed it, the relief of it, it seemed. "What is it?" I asked after we'd settled ourselves.

"I was just wondering that since you're already influencing Ridley and Arthur, you might think of it in terms of in for a penny, in for a pound.''

"Think of what?"

"Of influencing Clarinda, of course. You mentioned it as a possibility earlier."

"A possibility I'm not ready to undertake for all those reasons I've just set before you. Besides, before you took the bit and ran with it, I'd been about to add that I'm also very doubtful it would work on her.''

"Why so?"

I hesitated, making a face. "If she's mad—and it is my admittedly unqualified opinion that she is—then it won't work very well—if at all."

"How do you know that? Oh, do stop glowering and tell me."

I stopped glowering and sighed instead. "All right. The first night I was in London I paid a midnight call on Tony Warburton—''

"You *what*?"

"—and tried to find out if he knew anything about Nora's whereabouts." Before being struck down by sudden insanity, Tony had been an especially close friend of Oliver's at Cambridge. He was now one of Oliver's patients.

"The Warburtons never mentioned this to me," he said.

"Because they didn't know about it. I let myself in

through a window and left in the same manner.''

"What, like the way you passed through Ridley's door that time, and how you get from the cellar to your room here?''

"Exactly the same way.''

"And you then influenced him?''

"Tried to. It didn't work. I just couldn't catch hold of his mind—like trying to pick up a drop of mercury with your fingers.''

"But what has this to do with Clarinda? She may be as she is, but she's not mad that I can see.''

"Are there not kinds of madness that are less obvious to the eye?''

"Of course there are.''

"Then my feeling is that Clarinda might be in that number. My mother's like that.''

"But I thought your mother yells a lot, then goes into fits.''

"She does, but most of the time she's merely disagreeable. When she's with people other than her family, she gets on quite well. One might think of her as being somewhat highly strung, but otherwise unremarkable. I've seen her being very cordial, even charming when she puts some effort into it. She's all right as long as she can keep hold of her temper. Only when her grasp slips does she go flying off into one of her fits and shows all that she's kept hidden about herself.''

"I saw no sign of that sort of temper with Clarinda, but then, as you say, her madness must surely be of a different kind. She hides it well enough.''

"It's the madness of being so single-minded that she will overcome all obstacles by any means possible in order to obtain what she wants.''

"But lots of people are like that,'' he protested. "Just look at the House of Commons.''

"True, but for the most part I don't think they normally

run about arranging duels, committing murder, and shutting their spouses into tombs preparatory to shooting them dead to achieve their goals.''

"Granted, but doesn't all that just make her clever rather than mad?''

"Good God, Oliver, listen to yourself!''

Apparently he did, and went flame red in reaction. "Yes, I see what you mean. I believe I've been hanging about with you too much, I'm starting to sound like a lawyer, trying to offer a defense when there is none. Very well then, you're telling me that because Clarinda has a touch of hidden—for the most part—madness, you don't think your influence will work on her?''

"Perhaps for a time, but I'd not want to trust my life or another's on it. I couldn't do anything with poor Tony because his mind just isn't there to be touched; Clarinda's is—but it's much too focused and strong to hold for any length of time.''

I'd been able to make her forget my unorthodox entry to her temporary prison at Fonteyn House; that was one thing, but to change the very pattern of her will was quite something else again. Add to that my own still very caustic feelings toward her and the likelihood of successfully turning her about became a very remote, if not impossible expectation.

"But how can you be sure without trying it?''

"My mother,'' I said, not looking at him.

"You mean you tried to influence her?''

I felt myself color a bit in my turn. "Yes. Once. I tried to get her to stop being so cruel to Father. It didn't last long, not long at all. I'm not proud of what I did, either, so promise me on your word of honor that you'll say nothing to him about it.''

My tone was so forceful he immediately gave me his solemn pledge of silence.

"From what I've heard from you about Nora and the

Warburtons," I continued, "I'm sure that she's been trying to help Tony in the same way, to influence him out of his madness."

"She did spend a goodly time with him when they were all in Italy—or so his mother told me."

"With indifferent results, sad to say." For the present it seemed best I not inform Oliver about Nora causing Tony's madness in the first place.

No, that wasn't precisely true. Not at all true, in fact.

Tony had been mad to start with; Nora's influence merely sent him more deeply into its embrace. Perhaps later I might tell Oliver the whole story of that dreadful night when Tony tried to murder Nora and me, but not just now.

"I wonder why she stopped visiting him?" he asked, leaning well back in his chair to gaze at the ceiling.

A long moment passed as I tried to dredge up the words to answer. It was proving unexpectedly difficult to cast them into speech. They felt sticky, hardly able to release themselves from my throat. "Tony said . . . said that she was ill."

"Ill?" He looked hard at me, brows drawing together. "What from, I wonder?"

I spread my hands. "I just don't . . ."

He perceived the sudden rawness of my feelings well enough and, sitting forward once more, raised a hand to make a hushing gesture. "There now, don't come apart on me just yet, you'll make the most awful mess on the floor if you do."

An abrupt choking seized me. Laughter. Brief, but it seemed to clear things inside. Trust my good cousin to know exactly when and how best to play the fool. "Sorry," I mumbled, feeling somewhat sheepish. "It's just that whenever I think about it, that she might be lying sick and helpless somewhere, I come all over—"

"Yes, I know, it's as plain as day—or as night, in your case. No need to feel badly about feeling bad, y'know. Did

Tony say anything at all about the nature of her illness?''

"Couldn't get anything else out of him. Maybe he didn't know."

"But his mother might. She's very fond of Nora, very touched by her kindness to Tony, y'see. I'll call 'round first thing tomorrow and have a nice talk with her."

"But you've already questioned Mrs. Warburton ages ago."

"And time and again since, lest we forget. She made no mention of Nora being ill, either. On the other hand, that's the one question I managed not to ask her. Can't make promises, though. It's been so long and her main concern is ever for Tony. The lady might not remember anything useful."

I heaved from my chair, needing to pace the room. My belly was twisting around again from an idea I did not care for one whit. "Oh, God."

My manner puzzled Oliver. "'Oh, God' what?"

"Oh, God in heaven, why am I in such a cleft stick?"

"What cleft stick?"

"The one where I spend all this time telling you the worthy reasons why I should abstain from influencing people, and now I see an equally worthy reason to use it again."

"On Mrs. Warburton?" His brows shot upward, his eyes going very wide. "You mean you could influence her into a better memory for a past event?"

"Saying one thing and then wanting to do another," I snarled, but to myself, not to him.

Oliver watched open mouthed as I made a few fast turns about the room. "What are you on about? You *are* thinking of influencing Mrs. Warburton, are you not?"

"I'm a damned hypocrite, that's what I am."

He shook his head at me. "A damned fool, you mean."

"Yes, I'm sure of it. To inflict it upon some innocent woman is—"

"It's positively brilliant! I see where you got the idea, if you and Nora are capable of making people forget certain things, then you're just as capable of helping them to remember others. This is marvelous."

"It's deceitful . . . dishonorable . . ."

"Oh, rubbish! It's not as though you were changing the woman's life—and if not precisely honorable, then it's certainly nothing harmful. Heavens, man, you could even ask her permission to do so."

That stopped me exactly in my tracks. "*What?*"

"Ask her permission," he said clearly and slowly.

"How the devil could I do that? I'd have to tell her all about myself and—"

"No, you wouldn't. You think you have to explain yourself to everyone you meet? Vanity, Coz, beware of vanity. If her memory isn't up to the work, then all you have to do is tell her you have a way of refreshing it and ask if she's willing to try. She doesn't have to know *how* you do it, only that you can and that it is perfectly harmless. I'll be there to back you up. Now what do you say?"

Asking permission. It was so obvious I felt like one of nature's great blockheads. Perhaps I should put myself on display at Vauxhall or Ranleigh for the entertainment of the crowds.

"If she tells you it's all right, then your conscience is clear, ain't it?" he asked in the manner of a person for whom only one answer will suffice.

"I . . . that is . . ."

"Excellent! I knew you'd be sensible. I'll just tell her that it's something you learned how to do in America. People will believe *anything* you tell them about that land, no matter how outré, y'know."

Oliver went off to supper, leaving me alone in his study to find my own amusement. I did not ordinarily join in on any of the evening meals as the odor of all that cooked food in a confined space was overwhelming to my heightened sense of smell. Here, though, I found a degree of relief from its unseen presence, and if things got too much for me I could always open a window. So far, there was no need to let in the winter cold, and when he returned Oliver would find his room as warm and comfortable as he'd left it.

With weary resignation I seated myself at his desk, found paper, a pen with a good clean nib, and opened the ink bottle.

Time to write to Father.

As I began the salutation and paused to gather my wits, the fervent hope stabbed through me that he was already on his way to England, making this missive unnecessary. *Selfish, Johnny Boy*, I thought.

Extremely selfish it was of me to want to place him on a freezing cold ship crossing a dangerous winter sea just to spare me a bit of letter writing. Yes, that was the light explanation for it. The heavy truth was that I very much wanted to see him again, to have his dear face before me, and to hear his voice. Try as I might, I could find no fault in that wish, for I knew it would be his as well.

Like any other chore, the hardest part was in the mere starting, and once this was achieved I was more of a mind to keep at it until it was finished. I began writing steadily, filling page after page with a recountal of events since Elizabeth, Jericho, and I had first made landfall in England. So much had happened, so many details, events, and speculations rushed at me, that I had to make notes to myself on a bit of used paper to be sure they were all included.

I scratched and scribbled away, hoping Father would be able to read my handwriting without too much difficulty, taking pains to go slower over the more involved bits of narrative so it would be clear to the eye as well as to the mind. One memory jogged another as I set it all down, and I was only occasionally aware of my surroundings, now and then noticing a footstep in the hall without, the snap of the coal in the fireplace, or the wind outside trying to pierce its way through the window. Twice I got up to throw coal on the fire, more to give myself a respite to stretch and think what to write next than for any need of warmth on my part.

The candles on the desk burned down to the point where fresh ones were needed. Rather than halt my work by calling for them, or even opening the curtains to the general glow of the night sky, I simply thieved more from the sconces on either side of the mantel, shoving them into the desk holders.

Some portions of the letter were easier to write than others. Surprising to myself, my past liaison with Clarinda proved to be the easiest of all to get through. I'd resolved to tell it plainly and make no apologies for my actions or hers. Father was a man of the world in his own right, having a dearly loved mistress as well as an estranged wife, so I had no doubt he would clearly understand the needs of passion when they so firmly seized hold of me. I did, however, make it clear to him my surprise and regret at finding Clarinda to be married and of my sober intention to avoid a repetition of the circumstance with other ladies. I then told him that there was a very good reason why I had written at all about my encounter with her, and so word by word and page by page, as I told all there was to tell about Clarinda's now broken plans, I led up to the subject of Richard.

Again I surprised myself, for now the ease of writing deserted me. I could not seem to put pen to paper about him for very long. Each time I tried, my mind wandered off in a dreamy speculation of a happy future, rather than framing a solid report of the happy present. How that child could lay hold of my mind and keep hold of it—had my father felt this way about me at my birth? Perhaps, though, he'd have had several months to anticipate the event, thus getting used to the prospect of having another baby in the house. Richard had been—to grossly understate it—a complete surprise.

At least I could and did say with all truth that there was no question in my mind whatsoever about the child's paternity, adding that I considered myself to be one of the most fortunate of all men. I added also that unless upon finding Nora and she told me otherwise, Richard was like to be my only child because of my changed condition. With that in mind I expressed the profound wish that Father would receive the news he was a grandparent as joyfully as I gave it.

After that, I couldn't think of anything else to say. His acceptance of Richard meant much to me. He would or he would not, but I had every confidence in his love for me and felt he would have no trouble welcoming my son into his own heart as well as I had myself.

I blotted the last page and shuffled them into order like a huge pack of flimsy playing cards. They'd make a sizable parcel and would cost a fortune to post. Well, it wasn't as though I didn't have the money for it. I rolled the letter into a cylinder and tied it up with a bit of string filched from a drawer. Then I wrote a short note to Elizabeth, asking her to wrap it up and post it for me.

The thought came to me on the wisdom of making a copy of the thing. That might not be a bad idea, especially should something adverse happen to this pile of paper while en route to Long Island. But to do all that work over again? Ugh. Though I could easily *have* the whole thing copied for a modest fee. . . .

Oh.

Good heavens, no. I snorted at myself for being such a fool.

To hire someone, to allow some stranger a look at the intimate doings of the Fonteyns and their relations? That was impossible—not to mention ridiculous. The schemes, lying, adultery, assaults, and murder? No, no, no, far better and safer to keep all that within the family where it belonged. I'd do the copying myself.

Then all I had to do was hope neither letter fell into the wrong hands.

Well-a-day, maybe I should have used *that* as an argument with Elizabeth against writing the whole lot down to start with and saved myself an evening's toil. Too late now. For that matter, how late was it, anyway?

When I finally glanced up at the mantel clock, the hour shocked me. Listening closely for a minute or so, I determined the whole house was fast asleep and had likely been so for a long time. If I wanted company to help me pass the meager remains of the night it would have to be chatting with the watch again or reading another book.

Or copy work.

I shuddered and pushed away from the desk. It could keep until tomorrow night; I'd devoted quite enough time on the project.

Quite enough and quite a lot, since I'd been left alone for nearly the whole of the night. In this mild form of abandonment, I sensed Elizabeth's hand. Guessing that I might be writing to Father, she'd probably told Oliver all about it and had cautioned him against a return to his study lest he interrupt the task. If I grew tired of the work, I'd be out to visit them in the parlor. Since I hadn't once emerged, she was likely to be quite pleased with me. I thought of confronting her about it tomorrow and teasing her a bit by saying I'd spent the whole time reading old magazines. It would serve her right for knowing me so well as to predict my behavior with such accuracy.

But my inclination for mischief passed; it occurred to me that Jericho might also have had something to do with it. He possessed an uncanny ability for understanding and predicting the actions not only of me but of others if given enough time to come to acquaint himself with them, and he knew me better than I did myself. He would be aware of Elizabeth's wish for me to write—he knew all the goings-on of the house—and would have arranged for me to work on undisturbed. A keen observer of life was my good friend and valet.

I found evidence of this in the central hall. On a narrow settee he'd laid out my heavy cloak, hat, walking shoes, gloves, and stick, anticipating that I'd want to take a turn about the early morning streets before diving into my cellar sanctuary for the day. Not wanting to disappoint him, I donned the things and quietly let myself out without bothering to open the entry door.

It was a fine clear night, if windy. I had to keep a tight hold on my hat lest it go flying. The ends of my cloak whipped about as though alive and trying to make good an escape from my shoulders. Finally giving up on the hat, I held it close to my chest with one hand and bravely walked into the wind with my cloak streaming behind like a great woolen flag. Not an arrangement to protect one from the elements, but I wasn't one to feel the cold as sharply as other people do. My chief annoyance was the way its collar tie tugged like a hangman's rope at my throat. I thought it might be better after all to turn back to the house and fill the time with a book, but I'd been physically idle for hours and my body craved exercise. Though the wind was a nuisance, it freshened the air marvelously, a rare thing in London, inviting me to partake of it while it lasted. Coming hard out of the north, it reminded me of the wholesome landscape of the country and my desire to eventually move there.

The street was empty, though the tumbling of a stray newspaper and the constant dance on either hand of tree branches in the breeze made it seem less so. The creaks and whispers they made unnerved me at first until I grew used to the sound. Not so for a dog I heard occasionally giving vent to his unease by barking.

Most of the houses had lamps burning outside to aid in

the lighting and thus the safety of the street. Oliver's was one of their number because of his profession. Once or twice since moving in, I'd witnessed him being called forth on a late medical errand, and it was best for all concerned that his door be easily found by those in need.

Within the houses all must have been peaceful with sleep, though now and then I'd see candlelight showing through the curtains or shutters. When I did, it was always my hope that it was simply an early riser or another wakeful soul passing the night in study, rather than sickness.

I found the watch, in the person of an elderly man named Dunnett, uneasily dozing on his feet in his narrow box. He wore two cloaks wrapped close about his sturdy frame and a long muffler wound around his hat and head against the bitterness of the night, but the way he huddled in them gave me to understand they were somewhat inadequate to the task. So light was his sleep that he jerked awake at my soft approach, his startled gaze meeting mine in an instant of fearful suspicion until he recognized me.

"Good e'nin', Mr. Barrett," he said, rubbing his red nose with the back of his gloved hand. "Up early or out late ag'in? That is, 'f y' don't mind my askin'."

"Good morning to you, Mr. Dunnett. I'm out late, as always."

"Mus' be rare 'ard for a youngun like you to 'ave such trouble findin' sleep."

"Oh, it comes to me eventually. All quiet tonight?"

"Aye, too cold for the bully boys, I'm thinkin'. Saw 'alf a dozen o' them Mohocks earlier tonight. Gave me a turn. I was afeared they'd be makin' some grief, but they left me alone, thanks be to God."

"I'm glad to hear that." The night watch, mainly composed of unarmed old men, was ever a favorite target for the malice of the city's rowdy element.

"A foolish lot they are, but mebe too cold fer their pranks. 'Tis fine with me."

"Any other visitors aside from them?"

"None as I could see. 'S been rare quiet tonight. 'S I said, 'tis fine with me.''

"What, not even footpads?" I asked, pretending surprise.

" 'Tain't no one out fer 'em to rob," he said with a cackle. " 'Ceptin' me, 'n' I don't 'ave nothin'. There's you, but I 'eard as 'ow you c'n take care o' yerself."

"You have? Where?—if you don't mind my asking."

" 'Eard it 'round o'r by the Red Swan. I done a favor f' the landlord 'n' he sees I get a tot o' rum once a night 'f it's to me fancy." From the look of the many veins decorating his nose, one could deduce it suited Dunnett's fancy very well indeed.

I knew about his favor. The Red Swan's chief business was not the sort to have the approval of the law. According to Oliver—himself a regular customer there—Mr. Dunnett had warned the landlord of an impending raid from the forces of justice and decency in time to save the establishment from serious damage. The story went that the raiding party burst into the place ready to face the worst kind of resistance this side of a battlefield, only to find it occupied by a large group of Quakers having some sort of a meeting.

There was vast disappointment on all sides once they worked out their business—the raiders had no one to arrest, and the Quakers failed to interest any of the newcomers in joining them on the closing prayer. Both sides eventually retired unbloodied from the field to go their separate ways. The next day the Swan was open for normal custom, free now of the harassment from the forces of morality because of a well-placed bribe from the landlord.

Dunnett said, "I was in 'avin' me tot not long back, 'n 'eard some gentlemen drinkin' to yer very good 'ealth."

I smiled, feeling absurdly pleased. "Some friends of mine, I suppose, or my cousin Oliver."

"Friends," he confirmed with a nod. "I know Dr. Marlin' well enough. Many's the time I've seen 'im staggerin'

from 'is coach to 'is front door when 'e's had a bit o' fun.
Always 'as a friendly word for me no matter 'ow much
'e's swilled.''

"That's Oliver and no mistake. But you didn't know
these men to name? If someone's toasting my health it's
only right I should return the courtesy."

"Not to name, nosir, but I've seen one or two of 'em
visitin' the doctor now 'n' then. One was a 'andsome perky
chap with a mole right 'ere,'' Mr. Dunnett pointed to a spot
on his nose. "I noticed 'im special for it, 'n' for 'im bein'
the one t' name you 'n 'is toast. Talked all 'bout that duel
you was in, called you a real fire-eater, sir. Those were 'is
very words. So that's 'ow I 'eard 'bout you takin' care o'
yerself so well."

I felt my face going red, and not from the wind. "I know
the fellow," I admitted. The mole on the nose was the clue;
he could only have been Brinsley Bolyn. Since the night
of my duel with Ridley, young Mr. Bolyn had become my
most devoted admirer and supporter. Good lord, but I'd
have to find a polite way of asking him not to be so free
with his enthusiasm or I'd have no end of challenges from
men wanting to test themselves against me. I could fight,
but had an unfair advantage over them in terms of strength,
speed, and an unnatural ability to heal from even a mortal
wound. Besides, unlike most of them, I had killed before
and found no pleasure in it.

Dunnett noticed the change in my expression. "Not a
friend o' yers, sir?"

I quickly sorted myself and laughed a little. "He's a
friend, but he's doing me no favors with such praise, however well intentioned."

"I see 'ow it is, sir," he said with a quick wink. "Too
much talk like that makes it 'ard to live up to the 'onor."

"Exactly. You're a most perceptive man, Mr. Dunnett."

"I do wot I can, sir."

"And very well indeed."

"Thank you kindly, sir, 'n' bless you," he said in response to the shilling I slipped him. I bade him a good morning and began to walk away, but he hailed for me to stop a moment more. "There's one thing botherin' me 'bout them Mohocks, sir."

He had my full attention. "What would that be?"

"They walked right past me without hardly a look—which as I've said, 's fine with me. But 's been my experience that they always 'ave at least a curse or two to throw at me. Nothin' like that tonight. They just walked past, lookin' at all the houses like a pack o' damned foreigners. It was dark 'n' they was a ways down so I couldn't see too good, but I think they was payin' some extra mind to yer 'ouse—Dr. Marlin's 'ouse, that is."

I certainly didn't like the sound of this. "Staring at it, you mean?"

"That's what I'm not too sure of, sir. 'F it'd been plain I'd 'ave come 'round to let you know about it, but it wasn't, so I didn't. The 'pression I got was they might 'a' looked at it a bit longer than the other 'ouses, 'n' for that I can't rightly swear to on a Bible. Just thought I should mention it now since yer 'ere 'n' all. I don't mean t' be troubling 'r worryin' ye'."

"Not at all, Mr. Dunnett, as I see it, you're only doing your duty. I'm very grateful you told me. Do you recall what time they came by?"

"Not long after midnight, 'f the church bells rang true."

By then I'd have been deeply occupied with my letter writing and the rest of the house asleep. It may have been nothing, but recent events gave me many excellent reasons to be cautious. Also, though I was endeavoring to bring a change for the better to Ridley and Arthur, it did not mean their friends would also be favorably affected by such reformation.

This time I pressed a handful of shillings into Dunnett's hand, and he was sufficiently overwhelmed to start protesting that it was too much. "Not nearly enough," I said. "If ever you see anything of a similar nature in the future, I want you to come straight to the house as soon as you're able and let me know about it. You need have no fear of waking me no matter how late the hour—that is to say, if I'm home. If I'm not, then you be sure to tell Dr. Marling or Miss Barrett or Jericho, understand? I'll see to it they hear what you've just told me."

"You 'specting' trouble?"

"Not expecting, but it suits me to know all I can about anything to do with Mohocks. That duel I fought may not be quite finished yet. Friends of the man who lost might want to reopen the contest, but not on the field of honor, if you take my meaning."

"God bless you, sir, I understand clear as day. Y' can count on me."

I bade him a good morning and continued along the street, wanting to stretch my legs and needing to think. Neither activity took very long. I walked fast and thought faster.

Tomorrow night, before anything else, I'd pay a call upon Ridley and see to it he kept his friends in check. Arthur Tyne would also briefly receive me as his guest, like it or not. I didn't believe either man to be much, if any sort, of a threat to me or my family now, but had learned to value caution over carelessness.

Of course, the Mohocks Mr. Dunnett had observed might have had nothing to do with Ridley. There were dozens, if not hundreds of their ilk roaming the city at all hours of the night. Word of the duel might have reached some kindred group and they'd only come to look at the house out of a sense of curiosity and nothing more.

And, of course, I was not prepared to believe *that*.

Even knowing it was much too late by now to look for any sign of their band, I surrendered to the desire to take in a broader view of the area. Tucking the ends of my cloak

close around my body, I gave the street a quick glance up
and down to make sure it was deserted. Only then did I
vanish. The world faded to a gray nothingness, though I
soon had ample evidence of its continued existence despite
my apparent leaving of it.

Well-a-day, but I'd underestimated the *wind*.

The beastly stuff must have blown me a good hundred
yards before I knew what was happening. It tumbled me
about as easily as that discarded newspaper, and I had to
fight it with more than the usual effort of will required for
this mode of movement. The wind felt every bit as solid to
me without a visible body as with one. After a stint of hard
work I managed to force my way back and upward until I
reckoned myself to be well above the tops of the immediate
houses. Then did I take on the barest amount of solidity to
see exactly where I'd gotten myself.

I was just within sight of Mr. Dunnett's box and silently
crowed with an inward congratulation I certainly didn't de-
serve, for it had all been luck. I hovered over this one place
a moment, decided it was possible for me to continue with
this folly despite the weather, then went higher. The wind
slacked off a bit, easing my work. Doubtless its strength
was worse closer to the ground, being whipped up by its
passage between all the city's many buildings, like that of
a river being forced to flow between the pylons of a bridge.
The more narrow their placement, the greater the speed of
the water.

When I was well over the tops of the tallest chimneys
and holding in one spot like a kite on a string, I gave all
the streets within range of my cloudy vision a thorough
examination. All was as I'd expected, quiet and unremarkable—if one could describe so unorthodox a view as such.
I chided myself for taking this aspect of my miraculous
condition for granted.

Below stretched the walkways and cobbled streets, some
empty, others showing scatterings of people either starting

to wake for the coming day or trudging wearily off to bed from the closing night. None of their number looked to be Mohocks; on that point I was torn between annoyance and relief.

Relief, I finally decided. If I'd spotted any of them from my high prospect I might have been tempted to investigate their business, and that might have led to all sorts of unpleasant and time-consuming complications. The morning would be here soon to send me into another day's oblivion. I'd have my fun tomorrow night. For now, I would have to put away my worry since there was nothing I could do about it and try to enjoy my remaining moments of consciousness.

Not a difficult task, that.

Except for a rare balloonist, no others would ever share this sight; I was one of a tiny number and needed to be more aware of and thankful for the privilege. A cartographer drawing at his map might also have so fascinating a view, though all would have to take place in his imagination. He could measure out the streets and write their names, even add tiny squares to his work to mark individual houses, but could never put in all the details as I saw them. Could he see the shadows of the people coming and going from those houses and wonder how their lives and fortunes fared? Could he fill his flat paper streets with the movement of life that I observed like a god from on high? Perhaps he did to some extent, but he could never actually *see* and know it as I did. It was glorious and at the same time sadly dispiriting. My dismay came from the knowledge I could not share this with anyone. I was doing the impossible and though exhilarating beyond imagining, it was also unutterably lonely.

I thought of Nora. Of all the people of the earth, she was the *only* one who could possibly understand my feeling, could possibly share it, cherish it.

Though she must certainly possess this ability, I'd never

heard her speak of doing it. She was ever careful to keep the differences of her changed nature well hidden, using her own talent for influencing others to maintain the illusion she was no different from any other normal woman.

But she was different. Different because I *loved* her.

The remembrance of her face, her voice swept over me more strongly than the wind. I twisted like a leaf and began to descend. Swiftly.

The need to keep that illusion was important to her. I'd seen how it had been when, with the cruel thrust of a blade, Tony Warburton had torn it away from her.

I spiraled down, down, down, skimming close to the harsh brick of the buildings.

Where are you, Nora? Why did you let me go? Why did you not tell me what would happen?

I took on solidity. Weight.

Perhaps she'd been unwilling to share her knowledge with me because of that need to pretend. God knows she was reticent enough with all else.

I dropped faster.

Perhaps she thought her silence had all been for my own good.

Faster.

Perhaps she'd been unsure of my love for her, or worse, unsure of her own for me.

With a jolt that shot right through my spine I landed hard on the cobbles. The violence of the impact was too great for my legs to bear. A bone snapped. I heard the sickening crack quite clearly. I fell and rolled. The pain followed but a second later, wrenching from me a strangled cry. I sprawled on the freezing cold street trying to writhe away from the torment.

Perhaps . . . she'd never really loved me at all.

CHAPTER
-6-

"Melancholia," Oliver pronounced, glaring at me from his chair by the parlour fire.

I said nothing, only shrugged, though I tended toward full agreement with him.

"It must be from all this black stuff hanging from the windows and mirrors," Elizabeth put in, also favoring me with a dour look as she stirred her tea. "And having the curtains being drawn all the time so as not to offend the neighbors."

"Oh, that will soon change," Oliver said, reaching for a biscuit. "And I'll not care who's offended. God knows Mother never worried about offending people—but back to your good brother's complaint—put those things together with it being winter and all, and without a doubt you have a rampant case of melancholia."

"What will you do about it?" she asked him.

"An outing is in order, I think. Nothing like a change of scenery to change one's outlook. Didn't he say he wanted to go to the bookstalls and hunt for plays?"

"Yes. He promised our cousin Ann . . ."

And so they went on, drinking their tea and talking about me as though I wasn't there. All intentional, of course, sounding almost rehearsed. I stood it patiently.

Melancholia was a fairly close description for my state after all.

Earlier this evening my hour with Richard had helped, but only for that hour. Once he was tucked away and well asleep I tiredly trudged off to my own room for Jericho to repair the damage wrought by playing with a lively four-year-old. He caught me up on the day's events and, as he brushed out my coat, cautiously asked if I'd enjoyed my walk the night before. I told him I had, offering no explanation for the condition of my clothes, made filthy from my fall to the street.

The broken bone in my leg from that abrupt landing had mended with my next vanishing, which had taken place soon after the pain jarred me into a brief period of common sense. Brief, I say, for it fled from me quickly enough. Despondency about Nora seized my spirit once more, slowing my steps toward home even as the vanguard of dawn began to creep over the eastern sky. The watery light was nothing to the early risers I passed, but blinding to me. For all that I held to a perverse need to risk myself—that, or I simply did not care what happened.

Despite my deliberately laggard progress, I managed to reach my bed in the cellar with time to spare. With time to think.

And I did not want to think.

I'd cast off my cloak and shoes and stretched out on the bags of earth that served as my grave for the day and tried very, very hard not to use my mind. And failed. Miserably. Nora's face was the last image I saw before oblivion finally came and the first there at its departure. I could still almost see her, in the corner of my eye, in the flame of a candle, in the shadows of an unlighted corner—almost, for invariably when I looked more closely, she disappeared.

Trying to escape the phantasms, I'd eventually come downstairs to join my sister and cousin, mumbling only the most minimal acknowledgments to their greetings. Oliver immediately remarked that I looked like a dejected grave-digger and inquired why, since last night I'd been fairly cheerful. My vague reply was anything but satisfactory to either of them, and that must have set things in motion.

Their rapport with each other had now grown to the point that with the exchange of a single look they were able to conduct quite a detailed discussion without uttering a word. The conclusion they reached on the best course of action to take soon manifested itself in this rather artificial con-versation about me. I took no offense from it since the overall bent was to eventually put me into a good mood. I wasn't adverse to the idea of a change to a more pleasant state of heart, but my spirits were so low that I couldn't see how they'd ever succeed.

However, their obvious concern touched me enough that I at last roused myself to speak in an effort to at least meet them part of the way.

"I'd prefer not to go Paternoster Row," I said, inter-rupting them. Both looked at me expectantly. "Not yet, anyhow. Perhaps a little later."

"Where, then?" asked Elizabeth.

"The Everitts house."

She raised her brows slightly, knowing the Everitts to be one-time neighbors to Nora Jones.

"I just thought I could look in, find out if they've heard any news about Nora since Oliver's last visit."

She promptly expressed her full approval of my errand. Being familiar with all my moods, she was fully aware of the usual reason behind my past despondencies, and saw the proposal as a means to lift this one.

"Would you like some company?" Oliver asked, trying to hold to a neutral tone, but still managing to express hope-fulness.

"Very much so, Coz. What about you, good sister?"

"I've had more than my share of London for now, thank you very much." She'd spent nearly the whole day out with Mrs. Howard and Richard, shopping for carpets. Their choices were to arrive sometime tomorrow along with Elizabeth's new spinet.

"Probably just as well," I said. "I'll feel easier knowing you're here to look after things." It was then I told them about my conversation with Mr. Dunnett and the men he'd seen looking at the house last night.

"Damned Mohocks," Oliver growled, for once forgetting to apologize to Elizabeth about his language. "Something should be done about 'em."

"Not to worry. If I see them, I most certainly will do something about them," I promised.

"Well, it can't be safe leaving Elizabeth on her own with those louts lurking about."

Elizabeth snorted. "I'll be safe enough if Jonathan loans me his Dublin revolver. Besides, the staff here has nearly doubled in the last week. I'll just warn them to keep their eyes open, the doors bolted, and have a club handy."

"It's a disgrace," he complained. "Decent people having to go about in terror of a lot of worthless bullies with no more manners than a pack of wild dogs—it's just not right."

"No, but I'll be fine, nonetheless."

"One of us should stay here with you."

"Leaving the other to wander the city all unprotected? I think not, Coz. Now you both go along before it gets too late to visit and find out what you may about Miss Jones, and I wish you the best of luck at it."

With this combined blessing and firm dismissal upon our heads, Oliver rang for someone to tell the driver to ready his horses and carriage, then shot off to his room to ready himself. He didn't get past the lower hall; Jericho was coming down the stairs with our cloaks, hats, and canes. He must have heard my proposal for an expedition out and made suitable preparation.

"You're even more uncanny than your master," Oliver remarked, staring at the things.

Jericho's eyelids dipped to half-mast and his lips thinned into a near-smile. I understood that look; he was insufferably pleased with himself. He helped us don the cloaks—he'd long since retrieved mine from the cellar and brushed it thoroughly clean—and handed over our canes. Oliver's was topped by a fine knob of gold, marking him as a medical man; mine was less ostentatious, but still identified me as a gentleman of means. Hidden within its length was a yard of good Spanish steel that would also identify me as a gentleman of sense to any footpad or Mohock. I thought of carrying along one of my duelers as well, but decided it was unnecessary. The two of us, along with the driver and two footmen, would likely be safe enough even on London's dark streets.

Of course, they were not at all dark for me. Another advantage in our favor.

The carriage was brought along to the front, and I took this time to excuse myself, passing quickly through the house as a shortcut to the stables. They would be empty of activity for a short time while the men and lads were busy. I slipped inside, patting Rolly and by way of a greeting slipped him a stolen carrot from the kitchen. Forbidden fruit—or in this case vegetables—must taste best, for he crunched it down with obvious relish. Moving on to Oliver's riding horse, I offered him the same treat. The bribe was greedily accepted. In return, I just as greedily supped on a quantity of his blood and felt the better for it. Last night's efforts and injury had used me up, leaving my body in sore need of refreshment.

This admirable provender, on top of the prospect of our outing, was beginning to have a favorable effect on me already. I didn't really expect the Everitts to have any fresh

news, but it felt good just to be able to make the effort to
find out for certain. Besides, whatever the outcome, the trip
we'd planned afterward to Paternoster Row held more at-
tractions for me than mere shopping for plays. This was
London, a city all but bursting with women and opportu-
nities to share their company. If I could not immediately
find Nora and settle my questions with her, then I might,
for a while at least, find distraction with someone else. Not
the same, of course—of that I was very well aware—but
passing time with a pretty lady had ever been the best way
I'd found for gladdening a sorrowful heart.

Yet another excellent reason to refresh myself. Should
things work out as I hoped, I'd not want my prospective
liaison spoiled by the needs of my body confusing lust with
hunger. I could and had fed on human blood before when
forced to by dire need, but when partaking the pleasures of
a woman, it was best for us both that I kept control over
my appetite. Thus could I prolong our mutual enjoyment
without worrying about causing harm to my partner by taking too much from her. Such was the way of it for most
men, food first, then love, and so I was unchanged from
my fellows in that respect, at least.

Necessity seen to and finished, I hurried 'round the house
and climbed into the carriage with Oliver.

"What kept y—oh!" he said, when he caught a glimpse
of my reddened eyes in the lantern light.

"They'll be all cleared up by the time we get to the
Everitts," I assured him.

"I'm glad to hear it. Most alarming when one doesn't
expect it. You sure it doesn't hurt?"

"Can't feel a thing."

He grunted, then called directions to the driver, who in
turn called them to the two footmen. They ran with their
torches just ahead of the horses, lighting our way. The lot
of them had come from the staff of Fonteyn House. Rather
than dismissal, since for the time being there was little work

for them there, Oliver had moved them to his house in town
and kept them busy. He was still getting used to the idea
of having to deal with his vast inheritance, and taking the
weight of it in this manner, a little at a time.

I didn't talk much during the ride, content to let Oliver
rattle on about his day. He'd paid a call on Tony Warburton
and chatted with Mrs. Warburton about her son. Eventually
he'd led the conversation around to Nora.

"I made out that Tony had muttered something to me
about Nora being ill," he said. "Then I asked his mother
if she knew what he was talking about. She didn't."

"You're certain about that—I mean—she's certain?"

"Very certain. There's no need for you to jog her memory with your influence, so your conscience may rest easy
now. Her recollections of Nora's time with them in Italy
are most vivid. What with the girl's kindness for Tony,
Mrs. Warburton was quite taken with her. Hung on her
every word, if you know what I mean. Anyway, the last
she recalled, Nora was fair blooming with health, though
perhaps a bit troubled over something."

"Over what?"

"That I could not say, for the lady herself could not say.
She asked if all was well with Nora, and was told that
things were fine. Still and all, she was a bit surprised when
Nora didn't turn up in London that summer as she'd practically promised to do so in order to look in on Tony. I
know it's all the same as I'd written before, but at least
you know Nora isn't ill."

"It could have been something sudden," I said, unwilling to relinquish the worry so easily. "Something to keep
her on the Continent."

"It could," he admitted. "But you must try to be optimistic, old lad. Your constitution's as tough as a country
bull's. Who's to say that Miss Jones is any different?"

Who, indeed?

We arrived at the Everitts, where I came up with a suggestion. "What about you going in and paying your respects while I give Nora's house another quiet looking over? It'll save some time."

"Save time for what?"

"As long as we're out, I've a mind to visit Ridley and Arthur tonight. Maybe we can catch them while they're at supper. If those Mohocks that came by have anything to do with them—"

"Say no more, Coz. I'll hurry things through. I'll say I have other calls to make, else old Everitt will have me up to his study to look at his beetle collection again."

We left the carriage and went our separate ways. As it was still somewhat early and the streets busy with evening traffic, I quietly slipped into the shadowed space between the Everitt's house and Nora's. Free from observation and hidden in the darkness, I vanished and sieved my way into her former home through a shuttered window, returning to solidity in what had once been a music room. Nora hadn't been much for playing herself, but delighted in letting her guests indulge themselves. In one corner crouched the rectangular shape of a spinet and close to it stood a tall harp, both protected by musty shrouds. Similar sheets covered the remaining bits of furniture.

I held still and listened, but already knew that I'd hear nothing but the scurry of rats and mice. She was not here.

My last visit had left me very downhearted. Things were only a little improved now, the chief difference being that my hopes were almost nonexistent; therefore any disappointment awaiting me would not be such a crushing blow.

With the shutters all closed fast the house was almost too dark for even my eyes to see. This time I'd thought to bring a candle and, after a bit of work with my tinderbox, soon had it lighted. As before, I moved ghostlike through all the rooms, and as before I found no sign of recent occupation. There were only my own footprints in the dust.

I'd been wrong about the disappointment. Any blow,

even one that's expected, hurts just as much as another.

Dragging from one room to the next and up the stairs, I checked the whole place over. I knew I would find nothing, but went through the motions regardless, just to be thorough. The overall gloom of the house gathered heavily on my soul as I seeped into her own bricked-up sanctuary in the cellar. There she had slept during the day on a large chest that held a store of her home earth. Everything was the same as before. The bags of earth were undisturbed, the air around me still and stuffy and wholly silent. I eased the chest lid down, but my fingers slipped, and the sound boomed off the hard walls of the chamber like a cannon shot.

Damnation.

Noise of any kind was all wrong here. It was like laughing in church. A strict one.

The hair on my neck was all on end. I knew there was nothing and no one else in here with me, but my imagination provided the fancy that this place was occupied by some disapproving guardian who had just been awakened by my clumsiness.

I fled by the fastest means, reappearing again just outside the cellar door, candle still alight, but unsteady because of the tremors in my hand. And I thought I'd conquered my fear of dark, closed-in spaces. It would seem I needed to conduct more work in that area, but not tonight. I scuttled away from the door, firmly denying the frightened child in me from giving in to the strong inclination to glance behind. Nothing had followed me up, because nothing was there in the first place. I wasn't so sure about Oliver, but if Elizabeth had been with me, by now she'd likely be doubled over with laughter at my cowardly flight, I was sure of it.

The last stop was the downstairs parlour to look at the note I'd written and left for Nora on my previous visit. I pushed open the door and my gaze went straight to the mantel . . . but the folded and sealed square of paper I'd placed so carefully there was missing. My heart, suddenly coming to a kind of life again, gave a painful leap against my ribs. It was all I could do to hold on to the candle, and then the flame nearly guttered out in my rush to cross the room for a closer look.

The note was gone, truly, truly gone.

"You're sure a rat didn't eat it?" Oliver asked once he'd come back to the carriage. I'd impatiently given him the news of my discovery twice over, having babbled it out too fast the first time. "I don't mean to throw a blanket on your fire, but one must be certain about these things."

"I understand, and believe me, I did consider it, but if it had been a rat I'd have seen signs in the dust. No, I checked the mantel very carefully, and it was untouched except for a thin line where the paper had rested. I also found footprints in the floor dust. A man's shoes by their size and shape." Possibly one of her servants, I thought, sent to see that all was well with her house.

"Might have been a passing thief, y'know."

"I doubt it could be a thief, the house is still locked up tight—I made sure of that. The only person who could get in would have to have a key. That means it must have been a servant or a house agent."

"Or Miss Jones, slipping in the way you did. But then it was a man's shoe. . . ."

I nodded, my mouth too dry for words.

"Or someone *like* Miss Jones. Have you ever considered there might be more chaps about like you, others to whom she's passed this condition?"

I nodded again, trying to clear my throat. "I have. If there are, then I don't know of them; she never mentioned them to me."

"If you don't mind my saying it, your Miss Jones never mentioned a very great number of things. I should be very severe with her about that when you see her again."

The possibility of seeing her . . . it *was* a possibility once more. My poor heart gave another leap, or seemed to, making me gasp with a half-realized laugh.

Oliver grinned and thumped my back. "Well, then, congratulations, Cousin. This must be the best news you've heard all year."

"Just about," I said, with a flicker of warm thought for Richard. "I'd all but lost hope. But . . . but what if she doesn't want to see me?"

"Why the devil shouldn't she? You know in your heart what a great regard she held for you, and probably still does. Even—and mind you it's not likely—if that regard has faded, at the very least she'll be curious about why you're back in London. Of course she'll see you!"

"But she could have had that note a week or more by now. Why hasn't she come by or even written?"

"She might only have gotten it today, it might be en route even, especially if she's still somewhere on the Continent. Patience, Coz, patience. Give the lady some time to pack. You know yourself how difficult it is to travel—especially with your sort of limitations."

"I have to leave her another note. Just in case the first one did go awry. I have to be *sure*."

"Of course you do, but did you bring along any writing paper?"

I made a face. "You know I didn't." Nor pen, nor ink, nor . . .

"Well, then!"

"Well, then, what?" I demanded, growing annoyed.

"It'll have to wait a bit, don't you think? You still have to look in on Ridley tonight, after all."

I let out a thunderous, exasperated sigh. "Damn Ridley and all his cousins—"

"Especially Arthur," he put in brightly.

"—especially Arthur," I echoed. Then I couldn't bring

myself to finish. The laughter bubbling up inside prevented it. We hooted at one another like lunatics.

"You can leave another note anytime," Oliver said when he'd recovered some of his breath. "You'll like as not come back later while all the world sleeps, or am I wrong?"

"You are perfectly right." But my good spirits sagged, dragged down by my ever present doubt.

"What is it?" he inquired, seeing the change.

"Well, just look at things. The note I left is gone, and so I make all these assumptions that she has it and will reply as soon as she can."

He sat back, sobering. "You're right, it's not much, but if the worst happens and nothing comes of this, we can still continue on as we'd planned. I was going to go 'round to more house agents tomorrow. Everitt gave me the name of one I've not tried yet—oh, in your mad rush to tell me of your discovery, I've not had the chance to say what I've learned. No, no, don't excite yourself, because I didn't learn a damned thing that's new. No one in that household has the least idea of Miss Jones's whereabouts, sad to say."

"But there's obviously been a visitor or the note would still be there."

He waved one hand. "Then they just didn't notice his coming or going."

"How could they not?" I was outraged.

"I'm sure it wasn't intentional, but certainly they've better things to do with themselves than stare at an empty house all the time. Anyway, be of good cheer and keep thinking she's got your note and is on her way to see you. The world's not that big; she'll get here eventually. Or we'll find her first."

I wanted to believe that, and Oliver's manner was such as to half convince me of the truth of it. Some of my doubt sloughed away.

"Now, then," he said cocking his head, "what about

you taking care of the vile Mr. Ridley and his Mohock hordes?''

Not much time passed before our driver, following Oliver's directions, guided the carriage to the right street. While Ridley had still been a ''guest'' at Fonteyn House, my cousin had taken pains to get his exact address.

''There, I think.'' He pointed out one in a line of doors as we slowly passed. ''He told me it was the fourth over on the west side of the square. Not a very fashionable neighborhood, I'm sure.''

His disdain was well founded as he looked down his long nose at the row of narrow, dingy houses. Most buildings in London were dingy regardless of their quality because of the soot-tainted air, but these specimens seemed to be a bit more so than most.

''I thought he had money,'' I said.

''He does, but only if he doesn't live with his family. The gossips at one of my clubs say they give him a quarterly payment to be elsewhere as much as possible.''

''Can't be much of a payment.''

''I'm thinking he spends most of it on his pleasures and this is all he can afford on what's left.''

We drove by and had the driver stop a hundred yards down, then I got out to walk back. I might not have otherwise troubled myself with such caution, but Mr. Dunnett's observations inspired me to take greater care than usual. If any of Ridley's friends were lurking about, I wanted the chance to spot them first.

The building housed several flats, all occupied, if I correctly discerned the varied noises coming through the many walls. Ridley's was on the first floor. I hurried lightly up the stairs and gave a jaunty double knock on his door as though I were expected. No one answered. After a moment I found my own way in, slowly reforming on the other side of the threshold with my eyes wide for any sign of him.

He had two small chambers, this one serving as a sitting room, and I guessed the one beyond the half open door across from me to hold his bed. From the untidy condition of things, he had no servant. I listened hard, but heard nothing, not even the soft breath of a sleeper. The place was dark, cold, and empty. Well, that's what comes of it when one doesn't make an appointment. I would have to return later.

On my way down I reflected that though I was interfering in the very direction of Ridley's life, it might not be such a bad thing after all. If I got him to improve himself, he might even be able to do the Prodigal Son business with his family and at least end up in a better place than this to live. The trick was to catch him at home.

But later.

My spirits had lifted—because of this failure, not in spite of it. I'd been spared getting a headache from the work, if only for the moment; there was still a call to make on Arthur Tyne. Perhaps he wouldn't be at home, either. Pleasant thought, that.

I walked up the street toward Oliver's carriage, not in a hurry, but not especially slow. Pacing me on the opposite side were three other strollers in gentlemen's dress. None of them seemed to pay me much, if any, attention, but my guard went up nevertheless. I had the strong impression they were very well aware of me, though none looked in my direction beyond a glance or two. They seemed very comfortable with themselves. That's when I understood why I felt the need for caution; their ease of manner did not fit. Only a gang of bullies confident in their numbers would have such bravado. That meant they were likely to be Mohocks.

A quick look behind confirmed that three more of them followed me on this side of the street. Well-a-day, but I must have walked into a veritable nest of rowdies. I quick-

ened my stride to a trot. Taking this as a signal to drop all
pretense, they set after me like a pack of hounds on a fox.
I broke into a dead run and started yelling at the driver to
whip up the horses. The man turned in his seat, divined my
intent, and called something to the footmen. Those worthy
lads, well used to the rigors of their work, started smartly
away with their torches. I wasn't too very worried about
coming to harm, but felt a distinct a wash of relief when I
tore open the door and jumped onto the carriage. It rocked
from my sudden weight, but kept moving forward as I bellowed for the driver to go as fast as he dared.

"What is it?" Oliver demanded, and though astonished
at this development, he helped haul me in. I sprawled upon
the opposite seat, righted myself, and pulled the door shut.

For an answer I told him to look out one of the windows.
He saw all six of the men running after us, waving their
sticks and shouting abuse. Fortunately, none was as fit as
they might want to be for such exertions and had to give
up the chase after a very short distance. They were soon
left behind, breathlessly cursing and shaking their fists.

"Good God," he said, drawing his head back inside
again. "What on earth was that about?"

"Friends of Ridley, I suppose. He wasn't home, by the
way."

"Just as well. If they'd charged in like that while you
were trying to influence him—"

"I'd have vanished in a blink, dear Coz. Left 'em with
a proper mystery."

He laughed at that idea, but uneasily. After another look
back to make sure no one still followed, he told the driver
to slow to a safer, more civilized speed. "Was Ridley in
that lot?"

"I didn't see him, and he's too large to miss. Of course
they might not be connected to him and only be up to
general mischief."

He shook his head. "I can hardly believe that. If they're

the ones that came by last night, then they must know you both.''

''True, and if so, then I'll have a lot of work on my hands finding them one by one and warning them off. I can get their names from Ridley.''

''This is positively beastly. There's no reason for such unpleasantness, y'know. Not one that I can see.''

''It's bound to be just pure meanness, or revenge. Maybe they've noticed their leader isn't behaving—or misbehaving that is—as usual and have determined I'm somehow responsible.''

''I hope to God Elizabeth's all right.''

''She's fine.''

''How are you so certain of it?''

''If all of Ridley's friends are here then they won't be anywhere near your house.''

''Oh.''

''Well, shall we pay a call on Mr. Tyne?''

''You are a one for taking chances, aren't you?''

''Hardly, but perhaps Ridley's with him and I can catch them both in one go.''

He acquiesced with a short laugh and called fresh directions to the driver. This time our destination was to a long crescent of identical houses in a very fashionable area of town.

''I'd hate to have to find my way home without a guide,'' Oliver commented. ''Look at 'em—like a row of peas in the pod. Too much to drink and you could end up in your neighbor's bed instead of your own.''

''I expect one gets used to it—oh, stop braying, you great fool, or you'll have the watch down on us. I meant it in terms of finding one's own door and you know it.''

For all their similarity, the overall effect of the houses was very grand. Made of white stone with large windows, the wooden trims still looked freshly painted despite London's soots. The people who lived in these palaces took pains to keep them as perfect as possible. They probably even had vicious rivalries going on amongst themselves over the fine points of how to keep everything clean.

"Is this Mr. Tyne's place or his parents?" I asked.

"His own. Arthur must be rather better than Ridley at keeping his carousing within his means, that or he's confoundedly lucky at the gaming table."

"Where are his parents, then?"

"They live in the country and generally take themselves away to Italy at the first sign of winter. Not a very sociable lot, except for Arthur."

As before, Oliver pointed out the right door and we stopped the carriage a distance down the way so I could walk back. And, as before, the object of my quest was not at home according to the servant who answered my knock. He informed me that the master was staying over with one of his friends, but could not say who it might be. The master had a wide circle of friends. I thanked the fellow with a small vale and retracted my steps. This time the street was clear of bullies.

"There it is, then," said Oliver as I passed the news on in turn. "Nothing for it but to enjoy the ride back home— unless you have a mind to go along to Paternoster Row? It's not that far away."

"If you think the bookstalls will still be open."

"Some of 'em are bound to be. Don't you recall there are parts of this city that never close?"

"It has been a while. . . ." The other sort of stop I had in mind I knew would most definitely be open for custom.

"Then you need to become reacquainted with things."

My thoughts exactly.

Navigation through the sometimes cramped and nearly always crowded streets was quite a demanding art. Happily our coachman was a master at it. The two footmen were also skilled, shouting for people to clear the way, their calls getting more frequent the closer we came to our destination.

As they labored, Oliver and I discussed the chances of hunting down some decent plays to send to Long Island for our cousin Ann to read. She'd come to have a fondness for Shakespeare, but wanted to read others. Oliver understood that despite her exposure to such writing she was still not especially worldly, which meant that numbers of the more easily understood modern works would be most inappropriate for her delicate character.

"A pity, really, for some of 'em are quite amusing," he said.

"You mean quite obscene."

"That's what's so amusing about 'em. Here, this place should do, I know the proprietor." He had the driver stop and led the way to a spot that was half shop, half open stall, lighted now by several lanterns. Every horizontal surface was covered with books and manuscripts of all size and description. It was just the sort of place to appeal to my own sense of the hunt, though in terms of knowledge, not for trophies or food. The time fled and so did a goodly quantity of coin from my purse. In a very short hour I had not only a stack of books containing plays suitable for a young lady to enjoy, but several volumes for my own amusement. The weather for the coming year promised to be vile, so I'd probably not be as inclined to fill the early morning hours with outdoor exercise as was my habit. Better to settle before a warm fire with a book when the time came than to brave the fury of the elements.

"I think you bought the store out," Oliver commented, eyeing my purchases.

"Not yet, but next time for sure. Good thing we have the carriage. All this would be a bit much for a sedan chair."

"It may be a bit much anyway. Where are we to sit?"

"I thought we could send the carriage home without us."

"Did you now? To what purpose, other than leaving us stranded?"

I gestured slightly with my head in the direction of a nearby gaggle of trollops who where presently trying to attract business. Some of them were very fine looking, indeed. "Remember at the Three Brewers you suggested we treat ourselves to a real celebratory outing?"

"No, but it certainly sounds like something I'd suggest."

"I was still recovering from the ocean trip at the time, but I gave you my word that—"

He raised a hand. "Say no more, Coz, I take your meaning exactly. Now that you've brought the subject to my attention, it seems to me that we've been denying ourselves a real sampling of the pleasures of life for far too long."

"Have you also a mind to do something about it?"

"More than a mind, though I think we can do a bit better than those ladies, excellent though they may be."

"The Red Swan?"

"Oh, better than that. Since we've been forced to delay celebrating your arrival, I propose we avail ourselves of a place with more sophisticated forms of diversion. What do you say to a few hours at Mandy Winkle's house?"

That surprised me. "I thought you didn't care for Turkish bathing."

"Indeed not. As a doctor I know that frequent indulgence in full bodily immersion in water can be very dangerous to one's health—however, this is in your honor, so we shall yield to your preferences this time. Besides, Mandy has added some dry rooms for her more sensible customers." He jutted his long chin out to clearly indicate himself to be a part of that select group.

"Say no more and lead on, then," I said, laughing. A night at Mandy Winkle's had ever been a favorite diversion during my student days. Not only did I share company with a delightful lady, but had soaked to my heart's content in hot scented water up to my chin. Though free running water had become a nuisance to me since my change, I had no trouble with the contained sort—especially if contained in a large tin tub with a near-naked woman standing close by to scrub my back before proceeding on to other delights.

My heart did provide me a slight twinge of guilt for thinking of having sport with other women when the possibility of seeing Nora again loomed so near. However, she was not near at the moment, and they were. Having a positive horror of any form of jealousy amongst her gallants, she applied the same rules of conduct to herself, so when apart from her I'd ever been free to nourish my carnal appetites without incurring her disapproval. But I was sensible and sensitive enough not to speak of such little encounters as I had to her. That would have been extremely boorish.

Oliver instructed the driver to go home without us, that we'd find our own way back later. If the man held an opinion on the business he kept it to himself, but the footmen exchanged knowing grins with each other, indicating they were well aware of the nature of our plans.

"Rogues," Oliver commented to their backs as they trotted off with the carriage in their wake. "Heavens, but we should have given some message for Elizabeth so she wouldn't worry."

"She won't. She understands these things."

"Indeed? Doesn't that make her a rare jewel? Well, come along, then." He started off in what I first took to be the wrong direction.

"I thought Mandy's was back that way."

"Not anymore. One of her neighbors was a magistrate and getting too demanding for his bribe money. Mandy found it cheaper to move to new digs. Wait till you see the place."

He threaded his way across the square, down one street and up another, finally stopping before an unpretentious door. He knocked twice and was admitted by a half-grown black child. The boy was such as you might find serving in any genteel home, except for his clothes; he wore sweeping silk robes, had a curved sword thrust through his belt,

and perched on his head was a purple and green striped
turban trimmed with glass jewels.

Oliver greeted him. "Hallo, Kaseem. Very busy tonight?"

"Busy, but not too busy, sir," came the reply in a very
London accent, giving lie to his having any possible eastern
origin despite his exotic name. "We have room for you
and your friend."

"More than a friend, my lad. This is my cousin from the
American colonies, Mr. Barrett. If Mrs. Winkle does her
job right tonight, you'll be seeing a lot more of him in the
future. He's fond of bathing, y'see."

A flash of white teeth appeared in the boy's dark face,
and he bowed, indicating the way with one hand while
holding his turban in place with the other. Oliver led me
down a short hall, and pushing aside a dark red brocaded
curtain, ushered me into a most surprising room.

The war between the Turks and the Greeks had created
a vogue for all things eastern in certain quarters, but I'd
never seen so much of it gathered into one place before.
My eye was so diverted by the mass of colors revealed by
the light of dozens of candles that I honestly did not notice
the girls at first. The floor was awash with layers of pat-
terned rugs, low tables of intricately carved wood, and
mountains of pillows, and it took a bit of concentration to
finally pick out the lovely houris reclining over them like
so many flower petals. Once partially accustomed to the
confusion, I spotted one beauty after another, each a sul-
tan's dream, wrapped in bright wisps of scarves, some of
the fabrics so light you could see right through to the
charms of the lush flesh beneath.

The only prosaic element in the whole fantastic chamber
was Mandy Winkle herself, who was dressed in the normal
fashion, and a rather sober version of it. In the past, I'd
learned that such conservative garb often served her well
when dealing with the forces of morality. On those rare

occasions when the law was compelled to take notice of her business, her habit of looking and behaving like any respectable, well-to-do matron was very advantageous. She swore that such affectation had ever kept her out of the stocks.

"Dr. Marling, isn't it?" she said, coming forward, all warm smiles.

"It is, Mandy dear," Oliver replied with a slight bow. "You remember my cousin, Mr. Barrett?"

"Of course I do. The girls still talk about 'the 'andsome infidel from 'Merica.' " She turned her warmth on me. "Where have you been keeping yourself, sir? It's been much too long since we've enjoyed your company."

"He's here to make up for it, I'm sure, so mind you to put forward someone with a hardy constitution."

"My little pets are very sturdy, else they'd not handle all the traveling they've done," she said with a perfectly straight face. Mandy Winkle maintained the illusion for her customers that all her girls had been liberated from the seraglios of various unnamed sultans. Since they knew no other skills than those required for the arts of lovemaking, they were more than happy to exercise that knowledge in order to earn honest living. Some of her customers believed the story, and for the rest of us it was an innocent enough fancy to carry forth.

Mandy did have a fine eye for the exotic, and though none of her girls could have come from farther east than Dover, they yet looked as foreign as one could ask for. Instead of wigs powdered the usual white by rice powder, theirs were made by Mandy's orders to be black as jet. It was at first a shock to the eye, and then a compelling lure to all the rest of the senses, for the dark color made a striking contrast against their pale skin.

"They certainly look to be in excellent form," Oliver said, casting about him with an admiring gaze.

"I'm sure any one of them will be happy to prove them-

selves to you. Would you gentlemen prefer some refreshment for starters? We have tea or stronger if you like.''

With this gentle prompting, Oliver tore his attention from
the girls and settled the business side of things with Mandy.
It was expensive compared to the Red Swan—guineas instead of shillings and lots of them. I protested, but he insisted.

''Think of it as a present to welcome you back to England, Coz.''

''A Turkish *hareem*? Not terribly English, y'know.''

He shrugged. ''No matter, just so long as you feel welcome.''

''No fear of that.''

Several of the girls were eyeing me speculatively. Playacting, perhaps, but ably done and thus quite tempting. My
previous experiences at Mandy's old location had ever been
satisfactory, and it had not been nearly so well trimmed.
This event promised to be even more memorable.

''You may recall that Mr. Barrett is fond of the full treatment,'' he said to Mandy. ''I hope you have room for
him.''

''Him and all his cousins.''

''Ah, no, not this time. I should prefer something a bit
less aquatic for my own entertainment tonight, if you don't
mind.''

''Lord bless you, sir, if I minded anything you gentlemen
did, I'd lose all my custom before you could turn 'round.''

Mandy got things started with a quick double clap of her
hands, and the girls came to their feet for inspection. Unfortunately for me, they all appeared to be equally tempting.

Perplexed for a choice, I appealed to Mandy. ''I recall
you had someone named Fatima the last time I was here.
Might she still be around?''

Mandy was all sympathy. ''She's busy with another gentleman, sir, but if you'd like to wait . . . ?''

Hardly, I thought to myself, shaking my head.

"If I might make a suggestion?"

"Suggest away, dear lady."

"Yasmin over there is enough like Fatima to be her sister."

To be truthful, I wouldn't know Fatima from Yasmin or vice versa, the former having been but a name dredged up from memory to help make a choice, but I promptly expressed my pleasure to become better acquainted with the celestial Yasmin. Mandy clapped her hands again and one of the girls swayed over to take my arm, smiling—as far as I could tell—through the folds of the nearly transparent veil she wore over the lower half of her face.

"Charming," I said, bowing slightly and patting her hand. "Yes, I think we shall get along just fine."

"If I might be so bold . . ." said Mandy.

I reluctantly paused. "Yes?"

"The specialty of the house has been paid for, sir, so if you would care to—"

Shocked, I rounded on Oliver. "You didn't!"

He grinned and nodded. "Welcome back to England, Coz."

Mandy, reading this as a sign to proceed, called for another girl named Samar to come forward. Like Yasmin, the lower part of her face was concealed by a veil, and neither of them wore very much else, only a few scarves with some beads and bangles. Their eyes were thickly outlined in black paint; their eyelids dusted in a soft gold. The effect on me was not altogether different from the influence I used on others, the difference being that I was yet able to rule my actions somewhat. One of the things I could not rule was putting up any and all resistance to being led away by Yasmin and Samar to the inner areas of the house. The last thing I heard as we departed from the receiving room was Oliver calling after us, wishing me to have an excellent good time.

Given the circumstances I didn't see how I could possibly have anything else.

Giggling, the girls took me step by step down a wide hall. I had an impression of more eastern decor, but didn't pay all that much mind to it, not with these two squirming against me. Well-a-day, but I was already primed to make a conquest of them here and now. My body felt very alert and flushed with desire, and my corner teeth were out. I smiled with my lips sealed shut, not wanting to alarm my companions.

I eventually noticed the air becoming warmer and more moist as we progressed, a reminder of the other unique offerings of this particular house. That helped me shake off some of the combined spell these beauties had cast. I was here to loll about and enjoy myself for as long as it suited; it would be ridiculous to hurry things. From the sounds coming from behind some of the doors we passed I could tell some of the other customers might disagree with me. Their loss, I suppose.

I was ushered into a charming room, and Samar cautioned me against falling into the bath. No fear of that, I had to stop in my tracks and gape a bit. Mandy had gone to considerable effort to enforce her illusion of foreign elegance; I felt as though I'd been whisked halfway 'round the world in a blink.

No tin tub for the sultans in this palace—the bath was a great square pool set right in the floor. I'd read descriptions of those used by the Romans, and this seemed to be an accurate recreation of one. Small tiles, carefully placed in intricate patterns, lined the thing, spilling over the edge to cover the floor. Away to one side was a sort of couch, having a very broad sitting area and armrests, but no back. It was covered with shawls and cushions and looked just as inviting as the bath.

"Does the master wish some help undressing?" asked Yasmin.

Oh, but this girl knew her business. I answered that their help would be very welcome, and she and Samar set to work, leisurely removing my clothes. Each piece was carefully placed on a delicate-looking chair that was far enough from the bath to avoid being splashed. They worked their way down through my coat, waistcoat, neckcloth, and so forth, and, once stripped of everything but my growing feeling of well-being, took my arms to lead me into the bath.

Without removing her own insubstantial garments, Yasmin eased into the water first, drawing me after her. The pool was nearly a yard deep and provided with foot-wide steps along one side so that one might have a choice of depth in which to sit. Samar followed, descending into the pool like a swan. The loose scarves she wore spread out on the water, and once soaked through, flowed around her body like feathery seaweed. I thought of mermaids, and if such creatures bothered with clothing, then this would likely be the kind they'd bother about.

As the hot, scented water crept up my bare chest, I knew without a doubt that this bath was to be the second best thing I was going to feel tonight.

Yasmin continued to hold my arm, and Samar backed away to give her room.

"No need to be shy," I told her, drawing her close again.

"Does the wise master desire both of us at once?" Yasmin asked.

"Yes, but I doubt that would prove me to be very wise. But what do you think of making the attempt for a while and seeing what happens?"

"As the master wishes," they whispered in unison, closing in on me.

It was a difficult thing, but I just managed not to cry out for mercy.

CHAPTER
─7─

After an initial frenzied bout of shared kissing and fondling that overwhelmed my senses to the point where I hardly knew which girl was doing what, we paused more or less at the same time to collect ourselves.

"Does the master desire refreshment?" asked Samar, whispering in my left ear. Yasmin was busy putting her tongue into my right.

Oh, how did I desire just that, but not in the form they might be expecting. Still, I was polite and told them to refresh away. Samar clapped her hands twice, and immediately another young lady appeared from behind a brocaded curtain. Instead of a black wig, she wore a turban with a veil attached to conceal her lower face. She also affected a short satin coat with no sleeves or buttons that ended just above her trim waist, and draped around her hips was a length of thin silk that revealed far more than it hid. She carried a huge silver tray loaded with wine, goblets, fruits, and other edibles.

"Have you got any more like her hidden about the

place?'' I asked as she set the tray near the edge of the pool.

''We are your two most obedient servants tonight, but if the master should desire to have more companions . . .''

I knew my limits—at least for the present. ''Very kind of you, I'm sure, but I think you'll both prove just fine for me to be starting with.''

The serving maid giggled and bounced her way out.

Yasmin glided over to the tray and poured wine for all of us. I excused myself from joining in by saying that I wanted to have all my wits about me the better to appreciate their favors, which seemed to please them. However, I insisted they indulge themselves all they wanted. Very soon, both girls had tucked away a goodly portion of several bottles and were feeling very lively, indeed.

They now set to work on me in earnest, first one resting a bit and looking on, then the other, all of which had me stirred up to an uncommon fever. I'd not felt it this strongly in far too long a time, and knew I would very shortly have to do something about it or suffer mightily.

Taking Yasmin by the hips I turned her back to me and guided her onto my lap. The buoyant effect of the water was both a nuisance and a titillation for it was hard to keep her anchored in one spot. She had to clamp her legs around mine and brace her arms against the pool's edge and one of the steps to hold on. By this time both girls were highly interested in what they were doing, a very important element to my pleasure-taking, for my own satisfaction was ever the greater when the lady was pleased as well. Yasmin, leisurely moving up and down on me, was happily occupied, so I felt free in leaning back along the steps to make room enough between us to draw Samar close across my chest, facing me.

I kissed her through her wet veil, then slowly peeled it to one side to work my way past her jaw and down her throat. Running my tongue over her taut skin, I felt the blood pounding just beneath, tempting me to release it from the vein. Yasmin was just starting to moan as I buried my corner teeth into Samar, who gasped and made a short soft cry. Both women writhed with the rapture of the moment, but because of the nature of our joining, Samar's ecstasy, like mine, continued on and on long after Yasmin's was exhausted. I held Samar close and sipped from her like taking nectar from a flower. Though her breath was heavy and fast, she held herself as still as possible in my arms, then every few seconds a gentle shuddering wave over-swept her body from head to toe. Each time she did this, my own flesh responded, gifting me with a fresh surge of rapture that rushed like flames throughout my whole being.

Time ceased to be. The world ceased. I ceased. I was not a man, but a non-thinking creature of pure flesh and carnal appetite. I was joined to another like to myself, and all that mattered was our shared exultation for as long as we could endure the fiery joy of it.

At some point I became dimly aware of Yasmin gently easing away from me, then drifting around to come close to my side. She ran one of her hands through my hair, down my shoulder and back, and with the other caressed Samar. She would not have done this had she divined what I was really doing to her companion and so must have mistaken it for an especially long kiss. As my awareness of her presence increased I first resented it as an intrusion on what I was doing, but as she began kissing us both, I welcomed it as a new path to try. I blindly reached out for her. . . .

Then Samar arched against me, falling into yet another long shuddering climax; as it rolled through us both, she suddenly went limp in my arms. I felt the change take her, but was so deeply enthralled in sensation that I could do nothing right away. It was a heavy waking, a reluctant wak-ing, for me to go from a state of luxuriant gratification to . . . to almost nothing at all. I was still drawing blood from her, but her response to it had utterly ceased. Finally rousing, I put my back to Yasmin to block her view and pulled away in sudden fear. Had I hurt Samar? The wounds I'd made were very small; for all the needs and drives of my passion, I'd taken care to be gentle.

I shook her a little, saying her name, but her eyes remained shut. She breathed normally through her slightly open mouth, and though her heart was not thundering as it had been a moment before, its beat was yet steady and strong.

Then was I flooded with quick relief. She'd only fainted. I heaved a thankful sigh. This had happened once or twice before when I'd shared company with Molly Audy back in Glenbriar. The cause was not loss of blood, but too much good feeling.

I guided Samar's lax form over to one side, lifting her up enough so her head and upper body were well out of the water. She'd waken when she was ready.

"Is something wrong, sir?" asked Yasmin.

"Your friend's just having a little rest, nothing more."

Eyes nearly closed so their red color would not cause alarm, I turned my full attention upon her, hands and mouth moving lower and lower on her body until she expressed the worry that I might drown myself. At my suggestion we quit the pool to make use of the backless settee, throwing ourselves upon its silk pillows with no mind to the water still streaming from our bodies.

Yasmin had already taken her pleasure of me, but I was determined to offer her yet another, and resumed my work on her with this in mind. She moved more slowly than before, probably because of her recent climax and the wine she'd consumed. Oddly enough, I felt myself slowing, too, as though my bones were gradually turning to lead. Puzzling for a moment, until I recognized the symptoms and realized the wine in Samar's blood was responsible. Of all things—I was becoming tipsy. I hadn't been drunk since . . . lord, I couldn't remember. It had been more than a year, at least since my last visit to England. I laughed aloud as I roamed freely over Yasmin's breasts and belly.

"The wise master is enjoying himself," Yasmin said, in a manner to make it half-question, half-observation.

"The wise master is . . ." but I couldn't think how to finish it, so I fastened my mouth on a place just below Yasmin's navel. It must have tickled her, for she gave a slight jump and squealed. I went on kissing her just there, using my hand on her most intimate area in a way that soon had her squirming.

My corner teeth were well extended and it was a sore temptation to use them to gouge into this soft plain of flesh, but recalling my interest—need—to see to Yasmin's happiness, I progressively worked my way up her body. The quickening of her breath and heartbeat were proof that my efforts were all to the good. Hip to hip, I finally burrowed into her in the normal fashion, then sought out her throat. The sharp gasp that came from her at this double invasion of her person was such as to assure me that her gratification was equal to, if not better than, my own. She pressed her hands first upon my backside to push me in more, then my head to drive me harder against her throat. We thrashed and groaned together like animals in a fever of rut.

She twisted under me, shaking her head side to side; giving in to the heat of the moment, I bit down a little harder, releasing a greater flow of blood. Some of it trickled past my mouth. I raised away from her, but judged that the bleeding wasn't heavy enough to be harmful. With my fingers, I smeared the blood around her throat, first staining her pale skin like paint on a canvas, then licking it clean again. She cried out and demanded more of the same.

Tumbling through my mind and but partially formed was an urge to go beyond this, to somehow carry us just a little distance farther along this path to something even better.

Now I drew my reddened fingers across my own neck and lifted her head that she might kiss it clean as well. She was so caught in the frenzy of the moment she did so without the least demur, licking and biting in imitation of my actions. She could not pierce me in the same manner, but her touch was maddening. Fingers once more at my throat, I now tore hard at my skin, trying to break it.

My nails raked in and I felt the razor-edged sting of success. My blood pattered down on her breasts. The sight and smell of it sent me hungrily back to the wounds I'd made on her. She bucked and moaned as I drank from them, sending her into another peak of pleasure. I tasted the wine she'd had earlier, felt its drowsy strength taking a firmer hold on my body.

I pushed away with an effort. The wine's effect was all the more potent since I'd not had drink in so long a time. Sleep would overcome me if I continued like this, and I wanted no sleep, not now. I wanted, needed, desired better and knew its achievement was very close. Staring at my blood bright upon her fair skin, I understood its import, understood why I'd made myself bleed. She could drink from me, allowing me to ascend to an even greater level of feeling. I wanted her to take my blood, I wanted her to take and then return it again. Nora had done as much for herself, had she not?

The slashes I'd given myself burned. But if I put Yasmin's cool mouth to them . . .

That would not be right, though.

My movements were slowing, turning sluggish. I had to hurry or the moment would pass; it would be too late for either of us. Her arms came up, trying to pull me close again, to guide my mouth back where she wanted it. She had no idea yet how much better it could be for us. I did.

But . . . it would not be *right*.

Doubt made me falter, made me think despite the wine's influence. Never before had I been taken to the physical point of wanting so badly to share my blood with another;

I'd never allowed myself to go that far because . . . because . . .

. . . *it would not be right.*

A few more fat drops struck her flesh. A thin stream of it ran from my neck, leaving a hot red trail into the hair of my chest. It would be so easy to cradle her against me, to press her lips against my throat, to let her touch be the means to sweep me out of myself for a time.

I wanted . . . and could not have. Not this way.

Eyes burning from the frustration I thrust myself fully away from her, sinking straight to the floor. She mumbled something that sounded like a protest. I ignored her. If only she'd just fainted like Samar.

The room dipped once and righted itself. *The wine*, I thought with a stab of anger, scrubbing my face roughly with the back of one hand. I was light-headed yet sleepy, and the leaden feeling yet possessed the rest of my body. Most definitely the wine.

And the bloodsmell.

It teased and tugged at me. Yasmin's hand fell upon my shoulder, fingers weakly pulling as she asked me to return to her. Sweet heavens, but I wanted to; the girl would have me drain her to death so long as the draining pleasured her. It would do that all right. Well did I remember what it was like to be kissed in that manner, and how I'd hated for Nora to stop.

Removing myself from the immediate temptation of Yasmin's blood, I literally crawled back to the pool and slipped into the water. Remarkably, it was still hot. Some way must have been found to maintain the heat other than constantly pouring in fresh steaming buckets. I wondered if Mandy would part with the name of the one who had designed this miracle so I could have such a bath for my own.

Gladly did I concentrate on such mundane distraction, forcing myself to make use of it until my body calmed, and

I could rely on my mind to start thinking again. Not that the thoughts awaiting would be especially comforting.

As my hair was already fairly soaked, I pulled off the ribbon that kept it tied back and completely immersed myself. Instinct made me take a deep breath before going under, but it was hardly necessary. Without the need to regularly breathe, I was able to stay down as long as I wished. It wasn't all that long, though, the water getting into my ears bothered me. I rose to the surface and tried shaking the stuff out again, with indifferent success.

My movements caused Samar to stir. She lay where I'd left her, half in and out of the pool. There was some blood on her throat, but the wounds had closed. Cupping water in my hands, I cleaned her off, which made her wake up a bit. I didn't want to deal with her at this time, though; in answer to a whispered entreaty from me, she swiftly fell asleep again.

I lightly touched the marks I'd left on her. They were small and would give her no trouble. She'd likely had worse from other patrons, or so I told myself. For all the delight that ever passed between myself and my mistresses, I could not help but feel a pang of remorse for having to bring this necessary injury to them. No more than a pang, though. I'd borne such marks as well during my times with Nora and knew they did not hurt; it was only shameful to have to mar such otherwise unblemished skin.

Faint as it was, I could yet smell the blood hanging in the air, but its effect on me was not as it was before. Though pleasant to the nose, the scent of food is less potent to a man once he has a full stomach—unless he's in the thrall of gluttony. My own fit seemed to have passed, thank God.

Yasmin was also starting to recover as well. She moved as though to sit up and murmured a sleepy question concerning my whereabouts. I heaved from the pool to see to her.

God, but she looked like she'd been murdered. Her throat and breasts were a horrific mess, but most of the blood was mine, so I wasn't worried. She only wanted cleaning up right away lest someone else see her or there'd be no end of trouble and alarm. Again, I whispered soothing words to make her forget and sleep, then carried her to the pool. There was water aplenty to completely wash away the evidence of my passion.

Near-madness, more like.

My head was quickly clearing, making it difficult to see how I could have forgotten myself so thoroughly. I wanted to blame the wine. That could easily excuse my actions, but my conscience wouldn't allow it. The wine had had its influence, but the fact was that I'd come too close to losing control. By God's grace or the devil's own luck, I'd found enough strength to stop things before it was too late. Who was I to impart this condition without warning, without consent, to another? I had not the right to pass it on no matter how glorious the physical fulfillment might prove.

As for Nora . . . well, Nora hadn't been as careful or considerate with me.

No, not fair, for I clearly recalled all that happened between us that night when we'd first exchanged blood. It had been a very deliberate act on her part. She'd asked if I trusted her and I had. If only she'd trusted me in return and given over the knowledge of the change that lay ahead, she'd have saved me much fear and sorrow.

Perhaps she thought her condition to be unique to herself, that it could not be passed on. But if such were so, then why not exchange blood with her other courtiers and afford herself the fullness of carnal pleasure all the time? No, there was some other reason involved. I'd been special to her, or so she said. She might not have wanted to share it with the others, only me. She might not have known I'd become like her and had thought there would be no need to explain things. Perhaps her ignorance about this unnatural state was equal to my own.

Horrible thought, that. I shook it right out of my head.

I carried first Yasmin back to the settee, then Samar, laying them close together and pulling over them some sheets I'd found to spare them from becoming chilled. They made a sweet picture, like two black-haired angels. I went to the chair where they'd put my clothes and found my money purse. They were honest girls, I noted, neither had filched so much as a penny when they'd undressed me earlier, but then Mandy had ever been very strict about that at her other place of business. I placed a guinea each in their hands as they slept. Aware of it or not, they'd performed above and beyond their usual duties for the house and deserved a special vale for their trouble.

The wound I'd made on my neck reminded me of its existence by a prickling itch. I started to scratch and halted just as my fingertips made contact with the flesh. *Close, Johnny Boy, close.* I might have opened it up again. To eliminate the problem, I vanished for a moment so it could heal. The vanishing was strangely difficult, taking much longer than usual to accomplish; I blamed it on the lingering effect of the wine.

The fire had burned low. I saw to its replenishment for the sake of my drowsing houris, then sought the solace of the bath once more. There was time enough and then some for me to loll and soak in its welcome heat and clean off the last of the blood. The water had turned a bit pink. I tried to think of some way to explain it, should anyone ask, then thought better of it. Say nothing and let them come up with their own reasons, but chances were no one would even notice.

Resting my head on the most shallow of the steps so my face was out of the water, I let my body relax and float. The pool was just large enough for it. I had nothing remotely like it at home—though that might change—and would enjoy the luxury while it was yet mine to have. Already I was forming plans to return to this earthly paradise next week. I might indulge myself with the company of but one lady, though, and see to it that she not partake of any wine or spirits until afterward. Much safer for both of us that way.

Notwithstanding the turmoil of soul my lapse of control had thrown upon me, I was well content with Oliver's munificent gift. I felt tired, refreshed, weak, and strong all at once. Not an easy combination to attain, but wonderfully satisfying. I'd have to think of a suitable thank you to give him in return.

As I mused on possibilities, my quick ears caught the distant beginnings of a commotion taking place elsewhere in the house. Raised voices, from both men and women, but nothing really alarming. One of the men was drunk and singing a bawdy song, sometimes even in key. A little row was only to be expected in a brothel, even in those as well run as this one. Mandy had vast experience in dealing with them, and like any sensible procuress, would have several bully boys in her employ to enforce the peace.

The song soon died away to drunken laughter, then loud talk that progressed up toward my end of the hall. The men had imbibed just enough to make them randy, but not so much to prevent them from doing anything about it, I judged. I hoped their ladies for tonight were as hardy as Mandy claimed, for these noise makers would likely give them a strenuous time of it.

I relaxed again, glad that they were someone else's problem and not mine.

Wrong you are entirely, Johnny Boy, I thought with disgust as the door to my chamber abruptly opened. Water sloshing about me, I sat up and turned to face the intrusion.

There were three of them, all masked, but that caused no alarm in me. Titled men often wanted anonymity while cavorting outside of their class, and I assumed this lot were no different. They were cloaked, gloved, and muffled to the ears, and their hats obscured the rest. All I could see was a bit of mouth and nose and little enough of those.

The men spilled unsteadily into the room, still laughing at whatever obscure jest had just been made. I debated whether it was worth the trouble to call for assistance or deal with them myself.

"We're in the wrong room," one of them observed, stopping to stare at me. "Not unless they've got uncommonly ugly wenches here."

"That's a man, not a wench," said another with heavy humor. "Though it might not make any difference to you."

The third member of the party whooped in appreciation. For the joke, I hoped. I tried to look past them to see any sign of help, but the view was blocked by their bodies.

"Gentlemen," I said, "as you can see, this room is already occupied—"

"Right you are—by us," declared the wit. "So you can just remove yourself."

I ignored his ridiculous command. "Perhaps your room is just next to this one. If you but look, I'm sure you'll find some very impatient ladies waiting for you there." Quite an assumption to make on my part, but I wanted to be rid of them. There was a draft coming through the open door.

"Don't I know you, sir?" he asked peevishly, stumbling forward.

"I doubt it, sir." Two more steps and he'd be in the bath with me.

"Yes, I do, you're Percy Mott, aren't you?"

"My name is Barrett, and I'd very much appreciate it if you—"

"His name's Barrett, lads."

And with those words, spoken in an unexpectedly stone cold sober voice, the comedy forthwith and bereft of no other warning changed to calamity.

Like an idiot, I still tried to finish my sentence, but the words died on my lips when from the folds of his cloak he smoothly drew forth a primed dueler and aimed the muzzle right at me. Though not faster than thought, he was certainly faster than *my* thought. I had less than an instant to react, but the pure shock was sufficient for me to waste it. Few others would have had the presence of mind to do aught else but stare as I did for that blink in time between seeing his pistol and the tardy arrival of comprehension of his purpose.

But there it was: a blink and nothing more.

Then, at the distance of two short paces, he fired right into my chest.

The roar of discharge did not impress itself upon my senses so much as the powder smoke. The acrid stuff seemed to fill the whole room more thoroughly than the deafening noise. I saw, rather than felt, the ball reaming through me, leaving behind a great blood-spurting hole. My body gave a violent jerk, then collapsed, pitching heavily forward into the water. I had no time to even bring my arms up; I could not feel, much less control them. With all my inert weight I struck the shallow step with my forehead, feeling and hearing the shattering crack of the impact with my whole being. Paralyzed, I lay as one dead for an unutterably long period during which I lived lifetimes of undiluted agony.

Voices and shouts and alarms went unheeded somewhere above him. In the confusion the pistol shooter and his companions would find easy escape.

But he didn't care about them.

It was impossible for him to care about anything.

He simply was not able.

All inner awareness had been brutally compressed down to nothing, and what had once been Jonathan Barrett was replaced by a blazing sphere of misery. He didn't exist anymore, only his pain. Perhaps in a hundred years or so when the pain went away he might think about returning, but no sooner.

His body floated facedown, bobbing and bumping against the sides of the bath, arms and legs dangling and useless in the bloodied water. People swarmed into the room, raising more noise. Somewhere a frightened woman wept, another tried to calm her. A large man seized one of Barrett's arms and turned him over, then dragged his motionless body from the pool. Others stooped to help or backed out of the way. Water streamed from Barrett's nose and open mouth. His open eyes were fixed in place like those painted on a doll.

He could not move, only lie where they left him. The humiliating helplessness should have brought him great distress, but nothing, no thought or action from within—for both were beyond him—no pleas, no prayers, no tears of anguish from without could break past the bloated wall of pain that had fixed itself between him and the rest of the world.

The large man pressed an ear to Barrett's immobile chest, then pronounced him dead. Comments were made about the blood in the pool and the singular lack of any kind of wound showing on the body. Other people joined the press to see for themselves and ask what had happened. They questioned the two girls who had been with Barrett, but could learn nothing useful since both had been fast asleep. Then all talk stopped when an unanticipated tremor ran through Barrett's body, and it gave a powerful cough, dislodging some water clogging its throat. This inspired a fresh bout of commotion as they concluded, with reasonable doubts attached, that he might be alive after all.

The wall of pain was marginally shrinking, but Mr. Barrett was too prudent a man to rush right back into things again. He waited, in no hurry to try answering the frantic questions being flung at him by these absurd strangers.

They weren't inside his body; they had no hint as to what it was going through, and until the ordeal was finished, they could damned well wait themselves.

Then his cousin Oliver was there next to him, and care and concern for this one man's fear prompted Barrett to attempt a response. The wall of pain between them was thinner, perhaps enough now to allow him to speak past it and be heard.

" 'M all ri—" he mumbled, lying.

That held things together for a little, kept them busy. Coverings were thrown upon his nakedness, a pillow was slipped under his head. The jarring involved in the latter nearly sent him farther away, but hovering just within him there existed a vague but compelling need to remain where he was. Exactly why was out of his ken for the moment.

"God, he's cold as a corpse," Oliver urgently observed to no one in particular.

"This will help," said a woman.

"No, don't do—"

But the deed was already done. Someone—probably the woman—poured what seemed like a gallon of brandy past the lips of Mr. Barrett.

"Told you," she said with more than a small degree of smugness in her tone as Mr. Barrett's otherwise numbed and lax body twitched and rolled over into a fit of forceful and messy coughing.

That burning, vile, *hideous* excuse for drink accomplished what all the coddling and sympathy could not— brought me straightway back into the thick of things, groaning and cursing and holding my exploding head. This caused some relieved murmuring among the crowd. A man who could still curse his pain had a good chance of surviving it.

Exhausted by the business, I eased onto my back again. Whatever good feeling had been mine while in the company of Yasmin and Samar had vanished completely. I was shaken to the core and trembling despite the coverings heaped over me.

Between weakening spasms as my body sought to rid itself of the poisonous brandy, I managed a feeble scowl for my benefactress, Mandy Winkle, who knelt on one side of me with a flask in her hand. She scowled right back, but with much more ferocity. Couldn't blame her for it, this sort of row could not only get her closed down, but land her in Bridewell.

Oliver regarded me with much more compassion (mixed with barely controlled terror) and strove to find out if I really was all right and if I might give an account of what happened to me. I assured him of the partial truth of the one, but had to be circumspect about the other.

"One of the bastards shot at me." My voice was so faint I hardly knew it.

"Shot *at* you?" he echoed.

"Missed. Hit my head when I ducked." Dear God, but hadn't I just? I wasn't able to decide which had suffered the worst of it, my head or my chest. They pounded and ached for all they were worth, though in different ways. One at a time I might have managed with considerably less hardship to myself and others, but both at once had been too much.

"Who was it?" demanded Mrs. Winkle, bristling with anger. Whether it was for me or for my attacker was hard to judge.

"Don't know. Masked. They were all together. You must have seen. Did you not know them?"

Some of her anger faded. "They were new ones or pretended to be so. I've an eye for faces, but that doesn't work when the face is covered. Why in God's name did they shoot you?"

I could not give a good reply, only adding again that I'd not been shot. A blatant lie, for I'd been caught square in

the chest, but it was important—I remembered why, now—
that I maintain the fiction that the shootist had missed.

"You must be wrong, sir," she said, glancing at the
pool. "There's blood aplenty in that bath or my name is
Queen Charlotte."

I followed her gaze and saw the water was not a faint
pink as before, but a decidedly nasty and unmistakable red.
The pistol ball had inflicted a substantial portion of damage
to my flesh, but that same flesh had quickly healed itself,
a miraculous but painful process made worse when my
head struck the tile steps. Either injury should have caused
me to vanish, thus sparing me from much discomfort, but
I had a lurking suspicion the wine had yet again mucked
things up.

Oliver stared at me all wide of eye and open of jaw. I'd
told him in full about my past experiences with pistols and
rifles, and he'd apparently just worked out what had really
happened. Afraid he might blurt something, I fastened him
with my gaze and shook my head once. He gulped and
cleared his throat.

"Nosebleed," he pronounced in good imitation of the
pedantic tones used by all physicians when they were absolutely certain about something, particularly about
something beneath their notice.

"Nosebleed?" asked Mandy.

He nodded emphatically and with a delicate touch pried
one of my eyelids up with his thumb as though he were
giving a normal examination to any of his other patients.
"Oh, yes. My poor cousin is frequently subject to them.
Alarming, but harmless. This one must have been brought
on by this unconscionable attack."

Mandy snorted, either in acceptance of or derision for
his diagnosis; it was hard to say. She then noticed all the
people who had crowded in and barked an order for them
to remove themselves. While she was occupied, Oliver
caught my eye and mouthed the word *Mohocks*, drawing

up his eyebrows to make it into a question. I nodded once. We frowned at each other.

"I very much would like to go home," I whispered.

"Are you able to?" he asked, astonished.

"I should be. And if not, I will be anyway."

Mandy had overheard. "Lord bless you, sir, but you can stay until you're more recovered." I could see in her face that this invitation was anything but what she really wanted to say. Hers was a reluctant hospitality, her desire for us to immediately leave coming hard against common Christian charity and the natural wish not to lose a client with such deep pockets as my cousin.

"You're very kind, but it's best that we go so you can put your house in order as soon as may be."

"Perhaps," Oliver added, "you might have one of your men hire a carriage from somewhere to take us home."

Not quite successful at hiding her relief at this proposal, Mandy promised to see what she could do and left to do it. On her way out she cleared the room of remaining stragglers.

Oliver continued to kneel by me, playing the part of attending physician, but as soon as the door closed his shoulders drooped and he released a great sigh. He favored me with a very close look.

"Are you sure you're all right?"

"Yes, though I've been better. I just need a little time."

"What *really* happened?"

"I was shot. Dueling pistol. You'll likely find the ball still in the bath."

He went back on his heels, biting his lip. "Dear God. And there's no mark on you. How can that be?"

"I'll ask Nora, should I get the chance."

"And I shall thank her, should I get one as well. If not for her you'd be—" His gaze flicked to the pool, then he suddenly rose up to pace the room. He'd passed the point of being able to hold in his emotions any longer and was in sore need of expressing them. "Of all the vicious, cowardly . . ."

I rested and let him rant against my would-be killer. I'd have indulged in some myself, but was yet feeling a bit frail. Strength would soon return to me in full measure, if only peace of mind could come as well. The horror I'd been through had made that impossible, nor would I know peace again until I'd dealt with the instigators of this outrage.

When Oliver had divested himself of the worst of his anger, I asked for his assistance to stand, which he instantly provided. The pain in my head was more of an unpleasant hindrance than the one in my chest, for it affected my ability to balance. I excused myself to him and sought relief by briefly vanishing. Again, though difficult to achieve, it worked a charm on both complaints, but upon returning, I found I'd traded two specifically located hurts for an overall weariness.

"You look perfectly awful," he said. He didn't look too well himself, but at least he was dressed or nearly so with only a partially tied neckcloth and some buttons left undone. He must have finished early with his evening's entertainment.

"Which is exactly how I feel, but I think a little refreshment from any stable in the city should fix me up again." Something unpolluted by wine, I silently added.

He looked at the pool again. "But I thought . . . that is . . . didn't you . . . with the girls?"

"As it happens I did. That's my blood, not theirs."

"Oh, that's all ri—I mean . . . but I thought when you were with them you . . ." He turned a fierce pink about the ears.

Good lord, no wonder he'd looked so odd when Mandy had pointed out the state of the water. "I'm not so wasteful as that, Oliver. Now stop being so miserable. What's in the pool happened when I was shot. I need to replace it soon, then I'll be fine. Are the girls all right?"

"I don't know. I suppose they must be."

"Look into it, will you? They were asleep, but may have seen something after the shooting."

He was reluctant to leave me, but though tired to the bone, I was able to fend for myself. I was dressed, feeling the better for it, and ready to leave at his return.

"They're right as rain, though quite frightened," he said. "They didn't have anything to tell me, sad to say. The wine they drank left 'em fairly befuddled so they're only just now understanding what's happened, and even they can hardly believe it."

"Then including you that makes four of us."

He grunted. "You must have made an impression on them, Coz, for they were most concerned about your well-being. I tried my best to assure them of it. I think they'll have a warm welcome for you the next time."

"Much good it will do either of us. Mandy Winkle won't let us within a mile of the place after this."

"Oh, she'll settle down. She's not happy over what's happened, but knows none of this is your fault. We had a short talk, and I fell in with her idea that the men were thieves after your purse."

"That's some good luck."

"Don't crow too soon about it. She understands more than she's letting on to the others. If the bastards were real thieves they'd have been busy stealing from everyone, not roaring through the place with their playacting, then blazing away once they'd identified you. Mandy knows this, knows they were trying to kill you, but she's not keen to let it get out. It's bad for business. You're not planning to report this to any magistrate, are you?"

"Much as I'd like to, it wouldn't be practical. I've nothing to tell them that wouldn't eventually do injury to our family if the whole story got out. Besides, the courts generally keep daylight hours."

"Then that's a relief for all of us, as Mandy's not keen having the law in, either. We'll also not have to worry about her carrying tales. She's as close as a clam when it suits her."

That was good to know. "What did you see of any of this?"

"Damned little. I was in one of the dry rooms toasting the health of the wench I'd been with when I first heard them." From that point his account was similar to my own experience, of hearing the progress of joking and laughter up the hall that ended with a pistol shot. "Then it was women screaming and people getting in the way of each other. I saw the last of the bastards tear past me—he was in a mask so it must have been one of 'em. Didn't think to stop him or give chase, just stood there like a sheep." He scowled, going pink again with shame.

"Thank God for that," I told him, causing him to look up for an explanation. "They might all have been armed. If they've got the kind of cowardly brass to walk in and shoot a man in his bath, then they won't think twice about cutting down another trying to stop their escape. You did well by doing nothing and I'm glad of it."

That seemed to ease any hard feelings he'd taken on himself for his lack of action. He shrugged. "It wasn't just any man in his bath, y'know. It was *you*. They made a special point of getting your name first. Why would strangers try to murder you?"

"Because they might be friends of my enemies?"

"Ridley and Tyne? I know, stupid question. Of course it has to be them."

"I can think of no others bearing me a grudge, but for my influence to have worn off so fast . . ." Granted, I hadn't all that much experience in changing the dispositions of others, but I couldn't fathom how either man could have shaken free so quickly.

"Maybe their friends had some influence of their own. Nothing like falling back in with ill company to make bad habits easier to resume."

I nodded, having no better suggestion to make.

"But how could these fellows know where you'd be? All that lot who chased us from Ridley's place were afoot. Then again, it may not have been all of them. Just one man on a horse could have followed us this far and we'd not have noticed him."

"Then it's best we get home to Elizabeth in case—"

"Good God, yes!" The mention of her name and the hint that she might be in peril got him moving almost too fast for me to keep up. I wasn't too worried for Elizabeth's safety, though; the men had been specifically after me. My present concern was the possibility of there being some immediate endangerment to Oliver since he was in my company.

But I learned Mandy had ensured the street outside her door was clear of everyone except her own lads. A fearsome-looking lot, they saw to it that we were safely loaded into a very smartly turned out carriage and sent well on our way without additional incident.

"Well-a-day, but I think this is Mandy's own conveyance," Oliver said admiringly as he took in the silk and velvet trimmings within. "Certainly gives one an idea of the sort of profit she turns. Did you see the horses? They looked like racers, we'll be home soon enough if not sooner in this wonder."

As the hour was getting late the streets were fairly clear of the worst of the crowds. I might have been able to make better time on horseback, but not by much. I could have certainly arrived faster by floating home on the wind, except for being much too tired for now to try. And cold. I made some sort of a reply of agreement and wrapped my cloak more tightly around my shivering body. It didn't seem to help.

"Uncommonly kind of her to lend it to us, don't you think?" he asked. "I'll have to find a way to thank her—aside from going back after a decent interval and dropping another purseful of guineas on her. What do you say?"

He was only trying to cheer me again. That had been the whole reason behind our going out, after all. It had succeeded very well up to a point. I shrugged, unwilling to speak through my chattering teeth.

"Here now, it's cold, but not that cold. You must have gotten too used to the heat and now this outside air is hurting twice as hard as it might. I told you that bathing was dangerous to your health—in more ways than one it seems. Your hair's still wet, too. If you'd just shave your head and get a wig like the rest of us you wouldn't have to worry about catching a chill."

An ugly gasping sound came from me, suspending his prattle. The gasp came again; I choked, trying to force it back into the icy depths of my belly. Desperate, I sucked in air and tried to hold it; it hiccuped out again.

"Here now," Oliver repeated, but in a tone very different from the mock scolding he'd just used. "There's a good chap, you'll be all right."

I felt a fool and was bitterly embarrassed, but there was no helping it.

"You've had a dreadful shock is all," he told me. "Nothing to worry about. There's a good chap."

The hiccups wrenched away from my futile effort at control and turned into true sobs. I doubled over, unable to stop, and wept into my folded arms. Oliver put a steadying hand on my shoulder and kept it there the whole time, occasionally giving me a reassuring pat and telling me in a low voice that I'd be fine, just fine. After a long, difficult bout of it, the sobs came less frequently, then not at all. Sitting up slowly with all the grace of an old man, I leaned well back into the seat, feeling absolutely wretched.

"Sorry," I mumbled. It hardly seemed, nor was it in truth, an adequate apology.

"For what? Finally having a reaction?"

"It's so bloody stupid of me to be like this." My vision was so thick with tears I couldn't see a damned thing. I fumbled out a handkerchief and roughly scoured my face as if to wipe away my mortification.

"You give me the name of any man who could do better given your circumstances and I'll adopt him for a favorite cousin. You've been through a terrible ordeal; why shouldn't you be upset?"

"It's not as though I'd never been through others."

"Those others don't matter as much as the one you've just had, and don't tell me you can get used to someone trying to murder you, because that has to be impossible."

"But I just *sat* there and let it happen. How could I allow it?"

"Allow it? Listen to yourself, you great ninny. You act as if it was your own fault the man did what he did. Do you really think that?"

After a minute I was able to answer. "No, I don't really think that, but I *feel* it. There's a difference."

"Yes, I understand the difference. None better. You recall how I was the night of Mother's funeral? I was in a pretty state then, was I not?"

He'd not said much about that night, of how he'd been in much the same condition I presently found myself, and the incident that erupted between us, but his mention brought it vividly back to mind. I'd seen him at his worst, just as he saw me now.

"You knocked some sense into me then," he went on. "Am I going to have to return the favor?" He looked as grim as a tax collector.

I felt another hiccuping gasp coming from me, but this time it was the precursor to a laugh, not a sob. As with the weeping, I could not stop it, but unlike the weeping, Oliver was able to join in. When at last it died away, I found I was no longer shivering.

Thanks be to the Almighty, all was safe and secure when we got home. Elizabeth had gone upstairs, but was not yet asleep, and the commotion of our return brought her down again. She had but to glance once at us to know something was seriously amiss. Orders were flung at servants who were still astir, and as they scurried off my good sister swept us into the parlor and saw to the building up of the fire herself. Just as one of the maids brought in a tray loaded with a hastily thrown together tea, Jericho magically appeared, stripped us of our outdoor things, and replaced them with dressing gowns and slippers. Without being asked, he unlocked the cupboard where the household spirits were kept and placed the brandy bottle on the table next to Oliver's chair. By the merest raising of one eyebrow and cant of his gaze he silently inquired if I should like a serving of my own special drink as well. I shut my eyes briefly and shook my head once. I'd see to it myself later. He nodded and stood to one side so as to listen in. Not one of us had any thought of dismissing him.

"You look worse than ghosts," said Elizabeth, rounding on us. "What on earth happened?"

Oliver made the first attempt to deliver an answer and initially tried to shield our reputations by passing Mandy Winkle's place off as being a public bath house—a fiction that lasted all of two seconds with Elizabeth.

"I understand your wish to protect my sensibilities from being shocked," she said. "But I'd appreciate it more if you just be as plain in your speech with me as you would be with Jonathan. Things will go a lot faster if I don't have to interpret what you're really talking about."

While Oliver went red and blinked a lot, I took over the task of relating the incident to her. Of course I left off a large part of it, for my business with Yasmin and Samar

had nothing to do with the actual shooting. Elizabeth went
very ghostlike herself upon hearing of the attack and my
consequent injuries and had to be well assured that though
shaken, I was mostly recovered in the physical sense. Her
own reaction matched Oliver's, being composed of equal
parts of fear, relief, and fury. Once she'd expressed a portion of each to the world at large, she then plied the same
questions already plaguing us: Who were the men, how had
they found me, and why should they want to murder me?

The who and possible why of it were fairly obvious, but
the how was more elusive. Jericho quietly excused himself
at that point. Just as we'd concluded that we must have
been followed from Ridley's flat, he returned accompanied
by our two footmen, both looking exceedingly uncomfortable and crestfallen.

"Didn't mean no 'arm, I'm sure, sir,'' blurted Jamie, the
younger of them. " 'Ow uz we t' know 'e weren't a proper
gennl'm'n?''

"If I might clarify things, sir,'' said Jericho, stepping in
before the boy could go further.

"Clarify away,'' I said, with a wave of my hand.

In a few succinct words Jericho related his formation of
the idea to check and see if the other servants had noticed
any strangers lurking about the house that evening. None
had, except for the footmen, who, in light of Elizabeth's
instructions to be watchful, had made a quick circle of the
house and grounds before turning in for the night. Coming
around to the front they met, as by chance, a very well
dressed, well-spoken gentleman who said he was in need
of a physician, and asked if Dr. Marling was at home. Having become used to such inquiries, they saw no harm in
telling the man the doctor was away that evening, adding
that he might be found at Mandy Winkle's. The gentleman
seemed to know of the place, gave them each a penny vale
for their trouble, and walked off into the darkness.

"We din' think twicet 'bout it, sir, as there's alus someun

comin' 'round to fetch the doctor at all 'ours.'' Poor Jamie
looked to be close to tears. "Then when Mr. Jericho 'ere
told us that someun 'ad tried shootin' you, sir—''

"What did he look like?'' I asked.

Jamie and his companion offered a flood of information
on the man; unfortunately none of it was very specific or
useful. He'd been muffled to the ears against the weather
like most of the upper-class male population of London. He
could have been any one of our many friends, but between
us, we decided he was most likely from Ridley's crowd.
Only a Mohock from the upper class could have combined
easy manners with such ruthless action.

Oliver sourly admonished them to be more careful and
to report any additional incidents to Jericho. "I could dismiss the both of you on the spot without a character and
no one would blame me for it, but you'd only inflict your
ignorance all over some other luckless master and then he'd
come after *me* with a pistol. Off with you, and if you've
any wits left, use them sharp the next time a stranger talks
with you or your next billet might be in the King's navy.''

They fled without another word.

My good cousin diluted his brandy with a little tea and
drained his cup away, making a fearsome face. "Damnation, but if I didn't sound exactly like Mother just then.''

"You weren't anywhere as severe with them as she
might have been, so take heart,'' I said.

"It's myself I should be severe with, standing by and
talking about taking you to Mandy Winkle's with the two
of 'em hanging about with their ears flapping. Those
damned Mohocks came straight back here when we slipped
'em and waited. Good God, we'll be murdered in our beds
next.''

"I think not,'' said Elizabeth. "At least not right away.''

"Come again?''

"They're probably off having a celebration of their own.
After all, they think they were successful. Until they learn

better, they're under the clear impression that Jonathan is dead.''

That shut us all up for a time as we thought it over. Then Oliver began to laugh.

''Well-a-day, but won't they be in for the shock of a lifetime when they find out differently?''

''Until they get over it and try again,'' I put in, sobering us all. ''And who's to say they might not try for you as well? Or Elizabeth?''

''By heavens, if they do—''

''They won't. I'll see to that before another hour's past.''

''What?''

''There's plenty of night left; I've time enough to track down Ridley and his crew and sort them out for good.'' That was putting it in the most mild of terms. When I found them I'd probably wring their necks. And enjoy it.

Elizabeth must have sensed the anger churning inside me and gently touched her hand on my arm. ''Stay home, little brother. Please. You've been through too much already for one evening.''

''Yes, and it's to prevent my going through any more of it that I must go out again as soon as possible. As you said, they'll all be congratulating themselves over my demise. What better time to deal with them?'' My every instinct was against waiting. If I left things until tomorrow evening, who knows what mischief Ridley's friends might plan and accomplish while I slept through the day? There was no reason to think they'd limit their activities only to the hours of darkness.

''He won't go alone, Elizabeth,'' Oliver said, standing up.

''Oh, yes, he will,'' I countered.

''But, Jonathan—''

''Believe me, Coz, there's no better man I'd want along to help, but I'd be distracted worrying for your safety. Mine I need not be so concerned about. Besides, you know perfectly well I can travel alone a lot faster and with much less notice."

"You'll still need help once you find them, or do you propose thrashing the whole lot all on your own?"

"I'm not thrashing anyone unless they force it on me. First I find Ridley and make sure he is indeed the one behind this attack."

"Surely there's no doubt over that."

"Not in my mind, but I also have to see why my influence didn't last on him."

"How will you find him, though? If you wait till the morrow I can—"

"Not one minute more. I'll go to his flat again. He may have returned by now, and if not then to Arthur Tyne's. I was too polite with the butler earlier, this time I'll get some names out of him." Perhaps I'd wring his neck, too.

"What will you do when you find them?" Elizabeth asked, wearing a troubled expression. "Not that I give a fig for their welfare, but I wouldn't want your conscience troubling you later with regrets."

My conscience is my own business, I thought.

"It makes you too difficult to live with," she added with a crooked smile.

I looked at her. She was trying to be light, but her eyes told me the lie of it.

"What will you do?" she asked again.

I patted her hand. "Not to worry, I'll stay within the law." *Or try to,* I added to myself, shrugging off my dressing gown. Jericho was already holding my cloak ready in the entry hall.

"That did *not* answer my question!" she bellowed after me as I hurried from the room.

CHAPTER
-8-

I'd not noticed the wind before quitting the ground. Insubstantial as I appeared to be, skimming across the sky like a wisp of cloud, there was yet enough of me left to feel its effect and have to fight it. But my strength had returned, so the struggle was more of an annoyance than a trial. A clandestine stop in a nearby stable had provided me a swift and much needed physical recuperation. Normally I'd not bother courting the risk of discovery by supping on a neighbor's stock, but our driver and lads were wide awake and like to remain so for longer than I'd wanted to wait. Rather than influencing them all to sleep I simply went elsewhere for my meal. With its red fire still fresh on my tongue and glowing hot in all my limbs, I found a recuperation had taken place in my heart as well as my body, inspiring me to an even greater determination to sort things out for good and all with Ridley and his ilk.

Rooftop and tree, park and street, all rushed beneath my shadowless form as I sped in a nearly straight line from Oliver's house toward the dingy square where Ridley lived. Even though my memory of how to get there was from a much lower perspective than the one I presently enjoyed, I had no trouble finding the way. Unwilling to give up the advantage of so fine an outlook, I solidified on the roof of his building to have a good look at things before going in.

The square below was as quiet as could be expected in London, even at this small an hour on a winter night. A few figures paced along on their own obscure errands, some wearing rags and their walk unsteady, probably from gin, others more respectably garbed, but no less tottery in their gait. I dismissed them from notice, peering closely into the darkest corners within my view. All were empty except for a narrow gap between buildings where a tart was busy earning some money. If her expression held any clue to her true thoughts, then her patron had no gift of talent for his purpose whatsoever. After ascertaining by his humble clothing that he wasn't likely to be part of Ridley's circle, I left them to it and partially vanished.

Moving down the front of the building I found what I guessed to be the window to Ridley's sitting room, it being hard to see anything through the glass while in this state. But it was the work of a moment to vanish altogether, seep through the cracks, and reform again just on the other side of the closed curtain.

I'd found the right flat. All was dark, all was silent. Apparently he was not yet home. Probably out getting drunk or plotting new crimes, the bastard. I drew breath for a soft curse to express my disgust and stopped cold.

Bloodsmell—so thick on the air I could taste it. The hair on my head quivered to attention, and my knees wanted to give out as a shudder of recognition tore through me. I knew it to be human blood.

So strong was the urge to leave, I nearly faded away and shot back through the window again. When my nerves settled to the point where I could think, I held as still as possible and listened. I sensed many other people in the building, but none in this room or the next. I was very much alone. Moving cautiously and with leaden feet toward the bedroom door, I paused at the sight of a bold red smear marking the threshold. It was like a line drawn by a bully daring me to cross.

But the bully was dead, I found, when I worked up the courage to look.

The curtain for the window in here was pulled aside, allowing me ample outside light to see every horrid detail. Ridley was sprawled on his back across the bed and very much the source of the bloodsmell. His throat was cut. The blood from that fearful wound saturated the bed linens and his clothing, for he was fully dressed, and a puddle of it stained the floor. His white face was turned to one side, toward me. His were eyes partly open, sending the hackles up along my nape, for he seemed to be aware of my presence. It was fancy only, as I discovered when I stepped farther into the room, and his gaze remained fixed in one spot. Not that that brought any comfort to me; my teeth were chattering again.

It required a great effort to master myself and closely examine the room for any sign of who might have killed him and why. Ridley must have had many enemies, considering the life he'd led; I was almost certain one of them had had his fill of the man and committed the deed. Almost, for this death coming on the heels as it were of Clarinda's failed scheme struck me as being too highly coincidental for belief.

The room was bare of anything that might be helpful. It was strewn with his clothing and other personal items in such a way as to confirm he had no servant to see to his daily upkeep. Thrown into one corner was the discarded costume he'd worn to the Bolyns' masqued ball where so much mischief had sprouted. I turned this and other things over with a gingerly hand, for I was reluctant to touch any of his property, as though what had happened to him might somehow taint me in turn.

Ridiculous thought, but there it was, joining hard and close with the leaden suspicion that I had somehow caused his death.

I searched through every cranny but found nothing that shouldn't be there. Hidden in one of his boots was a small purse with some guineas and a few smaller coins. I guessed it to have been a sort of emergency fund and put it back. Beyond that there were no papers—no letters of any sort, not even a discarded bill, which was rather odd, though I didn't exactly know what to make of it.

Going to the next room I had to find a candle. There wasn't enough light coming past its window's closed curtain to serve, and I wasn't going to change it lest the rattling of the rings on the rod be noticed and remembered later by his neighbors once word of this matter got out. Though it seemed very unlikely, someone might hear me moving around and be curious enough to investigate, and I had absolutely no desire to draw attention to myself or these rooms until I'd finished with them. With shaking fingers I coaxed a spark from my tinderbox, begrudging even that small noise.

The single small flame was all I needed to resume my search, but if anyone had asked what I might be looking for, I'd not be able to provide a good answer.

The sitting room was not the same as I'd left it, at least to the best of my recollection. If only I'd paid closer attention earlier I might have been able to notice more. Two things did leap forward: A chair was no longer pushed against its table, and an empty brandy bottle and glasses now on the table had previously occupied the mantel. Had the murderer shared a drink with his victim to work up the courage to kill? Or, the deed done, had he come out here to revive himself for an escape? There were four glasses, all the ones in his possession, all with traces of brandy at the bottom. Four murderers? Five, if yet another drank right from the bottle. Even six or more if they shared. Six Mohocks had chased me earlier, but why would Ridley's own men kill him? Or had those six been part of some rival group of troublemakers?

I could carry this no further without more information.

It would be instructive to speak with the other tenants to learn if they'd heard or seen anything, but any inquiry on my part would place me in a most serious position. I could influence people into completely forgetting my existence, but only for a time, and then might they not talk amongst themselves of the gentleman asking questions about a murder prior to the discovery of the body? Might that gentleman be the murderer himself? London was not so large a city that I could hide in it forever.

Ridley's acquaintances would afford another and probably better outlet for my questions, but with them lay the same danger—unless from them I might learn the name of the killer. Then could I influence the fellow into turning himself in and confessing, keeping my own vulnerable self safely removed from necessity of appearing before a judge.

All these thoughts rushed through my mind as I searched, each examined and put to one side like the items I sorted through, none of them being too terribly helpful to the present situation.

Except for the chair, table, and brandy being out of place from my earlier visit, and the fact there were again no papers to be found, nothing else seemed amiss in the sitting room. There was no more reason to delay a closer look at the most important source of information remaining to me.

I returned to the bedroom with the candlestick in hand, making sure to keep it well below the level of the window. There was close work ahead, this little light was wanted to scour away any and all shadows. There was a risk someone might see from the street, but I was willing to take it so long as I missed nothing of import.

Careful to step well over the smear of blood at the entry, I squatted and held the candle near and determined the stain had been caused when someone had stepped into the pool by the bed and then tracked it to this point. Easy enough to follow the trail he'd left, he must have realized it, then tried to wipe the blood from his shoe by scraping its sole across the wood planks of the floor.

I looked closely at the puddle next to the bed and could make out the scuffing indicative of someone having had at least one of his shoes in the mess. Why would he find it necessary to stand in that spot? In my mind I put myself forward to stand in the same place to try determining the answer. It came quickly. Ridley must have been sitting on the other side of the bed with his back to whoever else was in the room. That unknown man must have certainly leaned forward across the bed, perhaps with one knee on it, and one foot anchored on the floor for balance. With a knife in his hand, he could drag its sharp edge hard through Ridley's throat, then retreat, letting the body fall toward him. Thus would he be spared of the initial spray of blood; it would instead strike the wall Ridley faced. Indeed, to confirm this there was a fearful splashing all over its otherwise plain surface. Anyone who had ever seen a hog hauled up by its hind legs for butchering would understand how the blood would spurt from a man in much the same manner and take care to avoid it.

Then might the killer have stood a moment over his victim, looking down at the final struggles to hold on to life, waiting until it had all run out. Ridley's hands and arms were all covered in dark, dried gore. He'd put them to his throat in a futile effort to stay the flow. His last sight must have been of his murderer backing toward the doorway.

Going around the narrow bed, I now began a reluctant search of Ridley's pockets. It was impossible to avoid contact with his blood. Though my appetite was so completely altered that blood had become the single support of my existence, in this case I felt the same kind of pitiful repugnance any other man might feel. So distracting was it that

I could barely control the tremor in my hands; I nearly missed the thin fold of paper secreted deep in one pocket of his waistcoat. Surprised, I carefully drew it forth, turning it over once.

The outside surface was very damp, but it had been closely folded so the inside part had been fairly well protected from damage. Given the fact no other paper was in the whole of the place, I hoped that this one piece would provide some important insight to his death.

It did, but not in a form I could have ever expected.

I took it into the other room to spread it flat on the table. The staining had ruined a portion of what was evidently a letter. The upper half of the page was gone, the ink and blood blending and obscuring everything. The lower part was yet readable:

. . . an unsettling, dangerous fellow. I do not believe it will reflect badly upon my manhood to admit I harbor a certain cold fear of this Mr. Barrett and of what he might do. He is very handy with his blade, as he proved to my chagrin at the Bolyns', though I was very intoxicated at the time. Certainly upon reflection I realize now how my drunken remarks coming from so befuddled a brain insensed him to the point of giving challenge that night. But I doubt his defeating me then has ended the matter, for he and his cousin, Dr. Marling, have made it obvious they bear me much ill will.

I hope that by inviting Barrett to meet with me he will hear my sober apology and we might then calmly settle the differences between us, but if not, then I expect we shall have to have another trial of honor. As I am not yet fully recovered from the cut I got at the previous encounter, I cannot be certain the outcome will prove favorable to me, unless he relents and gives me leave to delay things until I am better able

to defend myself. If at the conclusion of my conver-
sation with him I must cross with him again, then I
should be very desirous that you act as my second as
you did before. I don't reckon him to be quite so ill-
bred as to force a conflict between us without going
through the proper forms, but in the event that I am
wrong, I hope this letter will find its way to you so
you will let others know the truth of things.

The letter had the usual closing compliments and was
signed by Ridley.

If I had been cold enough before for my teeth to chatter,
now was flesh and soul chilled so solidly that I could hardly
bring myself to move or think.

The monstrous unfairness of it was the first thought to
blossom to mind. The missive contained just the right
amount of truth mixed with lie to be perfectly plausible,
especially to anyone not in possession of all the facts.

The second bud to sprout was the absolute certitude that
anyone finding the letter on Ridley's corpse would come to
the reasonable conclusion the meeting had not gone well,
and Mr. Barrett had foully murdered his host, taking a cowardly and dishonorable revenge for past grievances.

And the last bloom to burst forth was the urgent need to
quit the premises and take myself directly home as quick
as may be. Recognizing my own panic, I forced myself to
stop and consider the even greater need for caution. Had I
left the moment upon finding the body, I'd have missed
this damning letter—what if another such item yet remained?

Pushing the cold, choking fear back down until it was
an icy knot twisting deep in my belly, I made another, much
more thorough, search of the flat and Ridley's corpse, this
time looking for *anything* that might somehow connect me
to the crime. I went so far as to turn him over and check
through the bedclothes and felt a wave of relief mixed with

revulsion when I found nothing more. Only then did I dare
put out the candle and leave, never once stopping until I
reached the sanctuary of home.

"Goodness, that didn't take long," said Elizabeth, looking up from her book with no small surprise. "We thought
you'd be away for hours yet. Did you not find him?" Then
she took a second, longer look at me and rose from her
chair by the parlor fire. "Jonathan? My God, what's happened?"

Oliver, who had been much at his ease dozing in his own
chair, also stood. I must have been in a very poor state
indeed for them to wear such expressions, and neither improved when I stumbled out with the bad news. Their initial
stunned disbelief followed by a lengthy period of shock and
horror as I told them of my discovery was in every way a
match for my own reaction. None of us wanted this burden,
but stuck with it we were, and none was more anxious than
I to be rid of it as quick as may be.

Over the course of the next hour I was questioned,
requestioned, and the letter I'd taken from Ridley's pocket
was read over and over again, inspected and discussed
down to the most minute detail. None of it changed the fact
that Ridley had been murdered, and the letter was meant to
blame me for the crime.

"It explains why there were no other papers in the flat,"
said Elizabeth. "Anyone with half a brain would notice the
lack and thus be doubly sharp to pay attention to this one.
It might be thought you'd cleaned everything out yourself
with the idea of disposing of just such a threat."

"But why should Ridley write a letter and then not send
it?" asked Oliver. "Just so it could be found on his
corpse?"

"If Ridley did write it. His killer may have penned it
instead."

"That's hardly likely. Anyone familiar with Ridley's fist

would spot it for a forgery, wouldn't they? Perhaps he was
tricked into writing it. He might have been told to do it as
a devilry against Jonathan, then once finished, his throat's
cut and . . . well, there you are.''

"Yes," I said. "There I am, dancing a jig at Tyburn or
leaving the country forever as fast as sail can take me.''

"And you think Clarinda might be connected to this?''

"Who else would have a reason? She hates me enough
for how I ruined her plans.''

"But she's locked up at Edmond's.''

"And probably has friends outside who could still help.
Ridley might not have been her only lover, y'know.''

"Oh. But if they're so cosy together, why then would
she want to kill him?''

My gaze dropped and dragged over the floor. "Perhaps
because I was trying to change him. And that could be true
whether or not Clarinda's involved. Suppose some of his
friends came by to invite him out to a night of prowling
and making trouble, and he turns them down?''

Elizabeth shook her head. "That's no reason to kill a
man. Besides, such an action would have been a sudden
and reckless thing, but the clearing out of the flat and this
letter indicates a great deal of planning. Also, if Ridley
could be induced to write such a letter in the first place to
make mischief, then it's likely he wasn't as heavily influenced into good behavior as you thought. He may have
possessed the sort of mind and will to be able to resist better
than any of the others you've dealt with before.''

Oliver cleared his throat. "You're not planning to take
any of this to the authorities, are you?''

"God's death, man, and get myself arrested on the
spot?''

"I just wanted to be sure," he said, unoffended by my
reaction. "Well, then, what are we to do?''

"Try to find out who did kill him, while avoiding all
connection to the crime.''

"That may be a bit difficult."

"I'm well aware of it."

A glum silence settled upon us until Elizabeth finally threw it off. "You're forgetting the attack made upon you at Mandy Winkle's and those men who chased you from Ridley's earlier."

"I've not forgotten; I just haven't wanted to think about it," I muttered.

"It's time you did. Certainly the two are linked together."

"Then please enlighten me," said Oliver.

"Let us suppose they saw Jonathan going in and out of Ridley's flat on that first visit this evening, and gave chase just for the sport of it. Then when they went up to see Ridley themselves, they may have had a falling out, forced him to write the letter to put the blame on Jonathan and killed—no, that doesn't work at all, or why should they try to murder Jonathan in his bath later? They need only wait for the body and the letter to be found and laugh themselves sick while the law took its course."

My gaze lifted from the floor. "You almost have it."

"What, then?"

"All right, assume they saw me go in and come out, gave chase and went back to see their friend—then discover Ridley's *already* dead."

"Oh, *hell*," Oliver whispered.

"They wouldn't need to search the body for any letter, but naturally conclude I'd just cut his throat. They have a quick talk among themselves, cleaning out Ridley's brandy, and decide to come after me in a fit of revenge. One of 'em sets himself to watch our house, finds out we're at Mandy's, and the next thing you know I'm being hauled from the bath like a dead rat. None of that could have been planned by the real killer; he couldn't have known I'd come calling that evening. He'd meant for the body to be found and me to get the blame, which is as it turned out, but not in the way he'd expected.''

"But if Ridley was already dead when you called, how could you go into the flat and not notice a dead body? You found him quick enough the second time.''

"The second time I stayed long enough to draw a single breath of air. The scent of blood is what led me to the body. I must not have breathed at all the first time. I was in there and gone in but a matter of seconds.''

He sat back to digest this.

Elizabeth, more used to the eccentricities of my condition, found it easier to take in. "Good God, if that's true . . . to think Ridley was lying there dead all that time . . . ugh. I wonder when he was killed, anyway?''

"Perhaps just before dark and a little after,'' I said.

"Why do you think that?''

"The curtain in the bedroom was open and the only candle I found was out in the sitting room. The killer would have had light enough to do his work until the sun went down. He cleans the place of other paper, shoves the letter into Ridley's pocket, and when it's dark enough to hide his face and form he goes off to wait for Ridley's friends to come over for a visit so they will find the body, not knowing how things would really turn out. They see me leaving the place and assume without reading the accusation in the letter that I'd done it.''

"But he gets what he wants; Ridley's dead and you're blamed.''

"Only by the Mohocks, and for the moment they think *I'm* dead.''

"Until they learn better and make a second try,'' said Oliver. "Thank heaven you found that letter or the magistrate's men would be hammering on our door any minute now to take us away.''

"Ridley knew his killer,'' Elizabeth said, again breaking

into the short silence that followed as we counted our blessings. "Who of his friends could do such a thing?"

"Any one of 'em, as far as I'm concerned," Oliver grumbled. "The letter was to go to that pasty-faced gull who was his second at the duel. His name's Litton, if I got it right. He's not too smart, but loyal as a lapdog to Ridley. If you want the names of any of Ridley's other friends— such as they are—you need only go to Litton to get them."

"I have to," I said. "You know where he lives?"

"No, but I can find out—unless he's been murdered in his bed as well."

"Not likely, or why write a letter to him? He's needed to raise a hue and cry against me."

"What about Arthur Tyne?" asked Elizabeth, looking at each of us and getting an answer from neither. "He was Ridley's cousin and closest friend, close enough to him to be willing to help murder Edmond and Jonathan. Where's he gotten to in all this?"

I spread my hands and shrugged. "For all I know he might have been the one who shot me."

"For all you know he may have cut Ridley's throat himself."

"I doubt that, though stranger things have happened," said Oliver, shaking his head. He turned his gaze on me. "Weren't you going to talk with him as well?"

"It will wait until tomorrow night. I'm much too shaken for further rambles."

"Then perhaps I should have a turn."

"No, you should not!"

"The very idea!" exclaimed Elizabeth.

"I just want to help. Why should Jonathan do all the work?"

"You'll have work aplenty tomorrow finding where Litton is without getting caught at it."

"Without getting caught?"

"You'll have to pretend not to know anything about Ridley's death."

"Yes, I suppose that would be rather odd if I—"

"Odd? It could be fatal, dear Cousin. Promise me you won't risk yourself in any way."

Well, Oliver was as soft as a down pillow when it came to Elizabeth, so he readily gave his word to use the utmost caution in his inquiry. "Tell you what, I can call on Brinsley Bolyn. He knows everyone and can keep his mouth shut when he has to. All I need do is get him started about that duel and let him run with it. He'll probably blurt out the address of Litton and all his relatives without my even asking."

That satisfied Elizabeth, but I saw another problem arising. "That letter was meant to bring harm to both of us, Coz. I may be out of the way of injury for now, but you could be next."

"Or any one of us, for that matter," he added with a glance to Elizabeth.

"Therefore, I propose you move your household to someplace safer until we understand exactly what—"

"*Move?* You think the danger is that great?"

"Certainly I do, and until I learn better, it's wise to expect the worst, is it not?"

"But we're in the heart of London."

"So were Ridley's lodgings."

"Well, his was hardly a decent neighborhood—"

"And you think his killer or killers incapable of traveling to this one?" I tapped the spot on my chest where the pistol ball went in. "Here was I delivered ample proof that they know exactly how to get around the city."

He sucked in his lower lip and nodded.

"We have to think in terms of safety and are in need of a fortress. I can think of none more suitable than Fonteyn House."

"Surely not!"

"It's removed from the city, has lots more servants to keep an eye on things, and a good high wall with a gate."

"May I remind you that none of those things prevented Ridley and Arthur from invading the place earlier."

"But that was during the funeral when the gate was open and no one was expecting trouble. Things will be different this time. It won't be forever, just a night or two until I can sort this business out."

"You're really serious that we should go?"

"So much so that I'll send Richard and Mrs. Howard off there alone to keep him safe."

That was enough to stir Elizabeth to a decision. "Then my mind's made up. That child will have my company, if no one else's."

Thus did she decide for Oliver, who immediately fell in with the idea. "We can start packing a few things tonight."

"Not too much," I advised. "I think we should be as deceptive as possible so this place looks like we're all still at home and nothing is amiss. Load any cases you might want to take into the coach while it's still in the coach house. When you leave, it should be separately and by different routes. Elizabeth, Richard, and Mrs. Howard can take themselves away in the coach at some time in the morning as if going on another shopping expedition. You can take your horse, pretending to go on your usual round of calls. The servants can leave by ones and twos throughout the day—"

"But what about you?" he asked. "You'll be helpless in the cellar all that time."

"I'm well hidden, and it's not likely for anyone to look there, anyway. I should be safe—the Mohocks think I'm dead, so why should they look for me? Besides, they're not likely put themselves in jeopardy by breaking into the house in broad daylight."

"How do you know?" he muttered.

"I don't, but it's an acceptable risk. More than acceptable."

"I'm not easy in my mind for you to be completely unguarded," said Elizabeth. "What if we ask Jericho to stay until you wake? That way he can answer the door and put off any callers. It will make the house appear more occupied."

I was reluctant to put Jericho in the way of any peril. "Only if he is made fully aware of the danger and has one of the larger footmen for company. Jamie will do. He's as big as a house and can redeem himself for talking to strangers. Once I'm up for the night, then off they go."

Oliver was sucking his lip again. "But could you not just leave for Fonteyn House tonight and save them the trouble?"

"I could, but I plan to be here tomorrow evening to keep watch."

"*Alone?*" Oliver looked ready to offer me some serious argument on that point.

I gently waved him down. "Yes, alone, and I've an excellent reason for it, if you but hear me out."

He worked his mouth. "If I do that, then you're sure to talk me into something I won't like."

"Only if you let me.'

"I won't, then."

But in the end, he did just that.

When I awoke the next night it was to a disturbing near-silence, the sort that would have otherwise given me alarm had I not expected it. I was aware of mice going about their business, the scratch of a tree limb brushing against the walls outside, and the tiny creak of my own bones in their sockets, but nothing else. Rising from my pallet on the bags of earth, I traveled invisibly up through the empty floors as usual to my room, reforming just in front of Jericho, who had been waiting for me. He was long used to these appearances from thin air, and without batting an eye in my direction finished shaking out the clean linen he'd picked for me to wear.

"Evening, Jericho, how went the day?"

"Tolerably well, sir," he answered. "Everyone left for Fonteyn House without incident, except for some loud objections from Master Richard when he understood where he was being taken."

"What? He didn't want to go back there?"

"He was simply reluctant to leave without the carpet."

"Carpet?"

"The one you bought for his playroom. It seems he's rather fond of playing rough and tumble over it and insisted his recreation would be seriously limited if he had to leave it behind."

"Well-a-day! Think of that!" I was absurdly pleased with myself.

"He insisted it accompany him for his stay."

"Tell me everything he said, every single word." Since I would be bereft of our regular hour of play tonight, this second-hand accounting of my son's activities would have to do for now. Jericho was well used to this, too, for I always asked him to provide me with all the details of Richard's day, at least for those times when their paths intersected. Jericho didn't mind any of it, for while he spoke at length of domestic things, I would then sit still long enough for him to give me a proper shave.

"Miss Elizabeth's new spinet finally arrived," he said. "It was just as well young Jamie and I were here to take charge of the delivery. The maker's sent along a man to see that it was in perfect tune, a rather abrupt Frenchman, but he knew his business."

"You mean it's not likely he might have been a spy for the Mohocks?"

"No, sir. All he had mind for was the spinet. He played it very well. I complimented him on it in his own language, which surprised him, and after that he was somewhat less abrupt in manner. He let it be known that he was a teacher of music for diverse instruments, as well as dance and deportment and should anyone here be desirous of lessons he was available for hire.''

''A French musician hanging about the place? That's just the sort of diversion Elizabeth needs, I'm sure. Handsome fellow, was he?''

He knew I was joking and raised both eyebrows in agreeable response. ''Passable, I'm sure, though I cannot pretend to be an accurate judge of male comeliness. However, I was thinking you would wish rather to hire him as an instructor for Master Richard.''

''I'd have to meet him first. Isn't it a bit early for that? No, I suppose not. Elizabeth's offered to teach Richard the spinet, but suppose he wants to play a fiddle instead? He could learn French at the same time. Well-a-day, but look at me, I'm talking myself into hiring the man already. I'll have to look into it all later; this other business at hand wants clearing up first. What else happened today? Any news on Ridley?''

Jericho had been apprised in full of my wretched discovery the night before, though if we three had said nothing to him, I'm sure he'd have heard about it anyway. Oliver was right about the man's uncanny ability to know all that was going on.

''There was a notice in one of the papers of the incident, sir. You may read for yourself.'' He gave me the germane sheet, and I squinted at the tiny print.

''Doesn't say much. After all the hue and cry, it only identifies him as Thomas Ridley, Esquire, and says his throat was horribly cut under mysterious circumstances. You'd think they'd have more details. There's not even a speculation on who might be responsible.''

''Upon consideration, that lack is in our favor.''

''You're right of course, but still . . .''

"I would venture to guess that the murderer may be experiencing the same sort of frustration as yourself."

"Really? How so?"

"Looking at this article, he might expect to read that you'd been taken into custody because of an implicating letter found in Mr. Ridley's clothing."

"Yes, I see it. He's probably grinding his teeth wondering what's gone wrong."

"Unless he's learned from Mr. Ridley's Mohock friends that you were killed by them. Or so they believe. The papers had no mention of your misfortune."

"I should say not. A scion of Fonteyn House shot in a brothel? Unthinkable! They'll assume the family closed ranks with Mandy Winkle to hush it up for the time being. I daresay this Mohock tribe will all be frightfully confounded when I start showing my face around."

"One might hope as much, sir, but please go carefully. Miss Elizabeth and Dr. Oliver were most concerned for your safety."

"No more concerned than I am myself. You can tell 'em I'll be extremely careful. Anything else on this?" I gestured with the paper.

"Only that his death is the talk of London society. There were several callers today. Some of Miss Elizabeth's new friends were disappointed that she was not in, and very disappointed to know you were unavailable as well."

"Marriage-minded females with their mothers?"

"Yes, sir."

"It's all from that damned duel. I should have let Ridley kill me."

"Yes, sir."

"Anyone else?"

"A few gentlemen to see Dr. Oliver came by before he left, and I had opportunity to entertain their servants and learn all the news from them."

"Which was?"

"Little more than what was in the paper. The general opinion they held, which for the most part was the same as their masters, is that Mr. Ridley, in light of the double life he led, had it coming to him. Speculation on the culprit ranged from it being one of his Mohock cronies to a jealous husband to a cheated procurer."

"Doesn't want for variety. Wonder which, if any, is the correct choice? Did Oliver offer an opinion as well?"

"The doctor thought it best to pretend total ignorance of the issue and let his visitors do the talking; thus did he learn all there was to know. He was very pleased about the ploy and asked me to mention it to you."

"Then you can pass my admiration for his wit on to him in turn."

"I will, sir."

"Did he find out where Mr. Litton keeps himself when he's not playing the second at duels?"

Jericho drew a scrap of paper from his pocket and gave it over. "Here are the directions as they were given to him by Mr. Bolyn."

"That's hardly a half-mile from here. You can tell Oliver this will be my second stop on my evening rounds, I'm calling on Arthur Tyne first—and yes, I will be careful."

"Very good, sir. Any other messages?"

"If I think of any I'll deliver 'em myself, though he and Elizabeth are not to wait up for me as I'm not likely to be by unless something extraordinary happens. Otherwise I'll just leave a note on his writing desk and you can give it to them tomorrow. Are you finished with me? I'm ready to set sail from port? Excellent. Time you got away yourself. Have you the means?"

"Jamie and I were going to walk to Fonteyn House."

"Walk? I won't hear of it. Take this and hire yourselves a cart or some sedan chairs."

"I don't think that would be very proper, sir. Jamie might think himself above his station if he—"

"Oh, hang that. These are exceptional times. If he shows any signs of snobbery you deal with it as you please, but I won't have you walking all the way out there on your own after dark. Mohocks aside, it's just too dangerous. Be sure to take one of my sticks, and see to it Jamie has his cudgel."

I saw the both of them off out the scullery door. From there they were to make their way past the stables, down a back lane, and then emerge onto a street some distance from the house. It was the same route the other servants had taken; I hoped that it was still safe. Just to be sure of things, I followed them the whole time, albeit from a height. Neither they nor—presumably—anyone else was aware of my presence, as it's most unheard of for a gentleman to take the evening air by taking *to* the air. Once they were aboard a hired cart and lurching in the right direction for Fonteyn House, I left them behind and returned, making a high circle of the neighborhood to see that all was well.

No loitering dandies, no unfamiliar carriages, chairs, or coaches lurked in the area. I wasn't sure if I should be relieved or annoyed when I slipped back inside the house.

My plan called for me to wait about the place a bit, making sure lights showed in the windows and moving them from room to room to give the impression all was normal. Then would I make another near-invisible circuit of the street, looking for spies. After a reasonable period— or until my impatience got the better of me—I would venture forth as though to take a walk and see if that drew anyone's notice. Going to see Litton might do it for me, but if need be I'd try attracting attention by walking all the way to Arthur Tyne's home, ostensibly to offer condolences, but primarily to interview him. Should he prove ignorant of all these doings, I would at the very least get from him and Litton the names of others who might be more helpful.

After a quarter hour of pacing and peeking past curtains every few minutes, I decided the house was entirely too quiet for me. Lighting more candles did not seem to help, though they gave the place a very occupied look to any watchers—much good it would do me if there was no one out there watching. Perhaps I'd counted too much on the villain's abilities. That or I was just too eager for trouble to start.

Not wise, Johnny Boy. Not wise at all.

Another few minutes crawled by while I examined the new spinet. Elizabeth had done herself proud, for it looked to be a very superior instrument. I was sorry to have to deny her the pleasure of playing it now that it was here. My own clumsy fingers picked out a simple tune remembered from long-abandoned childhood lessons. The sound coming from it was beautiful enough to my untrained ears; how might it be once she sat down and called forth its full potential?

My speculations were cut short by a fearful pounding on the front door that made me near jump from my skin. Now, that was unexpected. Were the Mohocks going to try for a bold attack after all? I peered through a window to see who it might be and rocked back on my heels in surprise. What on earth was *he* doing here?

I hurried around to the entry and opened the door to the full force of Edmond Fonteyn's baleful glare.

"Thought you had a butler," he growled, not deigning to cross the threshold. "Never mind that. Throw on something and come with me. I want to talk with you, but not here. Come along with you."

Too bewildered to question him before he turned and walked off, I had the choice of doing what he said or calling after him and insisting he return. Well, he looked to be in a pretty foul mood already, so there was little point in adding to it. If nothing else this might draw the eye of any watchers. I caught up my heavy cloak from where Jericho had laid it out, jammed on a hat, and grabbed my sword cane. Slipping into the cloak was made more difficult when I realized something heavy was in its inner pocket. The thing banged against my side and caused me some puzzlement until a quick look confirmed the weight to be my Dublin revolver. Jericho had, indeed, thought of everything.

Edmond had traveled in his coach, but he'd left it standing before the house and was stumping off down the street even as I twisted my key in the lock. I came even with him and asked him a reasonable question concerning his business with me.

"Someplace less public than this first," he said, and kept walking. We went by Mr. Dunnett's little watch house. I passed a quick greeting with him, noting with pleasure the man had treated himself not only to a new cloak, but a thick muffler and gloves. He bade me a cheerful good evening in return, but was allowed no more than that because of the quick pace Edmond had set. Apparently he was fully recovered from his misadventures at the funeral.

I thought he was heading for the Red Swan—yet another surprise—but instead he proceeded on to Hadringham's Coffee House. Happily, the smells associated with this place of refreshment were somewhat less objectionable to my sensitive nose than most, and I followed Edmond inside with hardly a qualm. Within all was warm and smoky, the very timbers permeated through with the exhalation of countless pipes of tobacco over the years. Quite a few patrons lingered at the many tables even this late, for the establishment was a favorite meeting place for the local illuminati. It provided a place to enjoy the exchange of good conversation with one's fellows, the same as a tavern, but without the resulting drunkenness and debauchery. There were other places to pursue those when the mood struck.

The gentlemen scattered about the main room looked up to see who had come in; one or two were familiar faces since I occasionally came here to pass the time when it pressed heavily upon me. I acknowledged each with a polite bow while Edmond dealt with a waiter. He ordered and got a small private room and two dishes of coffee, then told the waiter not to disturb us further. The man had barely set down his tray before money was thrown at him and he was practically booted out.

"This sounds serious," I ventured to say as Edmond closed the door rather hard.

"It damned well is serious," he snapped back. "I want to know what the devil is going on."

"Could you be more specific?"

From his coat pocket he drew out a folded newspaper and slapped it on the table before me. Though different from the one I'd seen earlier, it was open to a story about Ridley's murder.

I did my best to emulate the proper reaction of one who, though the news be bad, has already heard and discussed it at length with others. Not a difficult ruse to maintain, since it was true. "This is a terrible thing, but I know no more about it than anyone else."

"That account mentions the duel you had with him, 'Mr. Barrett of Fonteyn House.' "

I looked at the print and saw that was exactly how I'd been identified. Oh, dear. More notoriety. Father would hardly be pleased when he heard, Mother might leap into one of her fits, and Edmond was positively furious. "The duel is a matter of fact. I can't help if some fool put it in print. All I can say is that I'm as shocked as anyone about the murder."

"Are you now?" He all but loomed over me. "And who do you think is responsible?"

" 'Fore God, man, are you implying—"

"You told me this whole business with Ridley had been taken care of and a few days later he turns up with his throat cut."

"So you assumed *I* had something to do with it?" I felt
my face going all hot and red as the anger flared inside.

"I haven't assumed anything yet. That's why I'm here—
to find out what you know. I don't care if the bastard's
dead or not or even who killed him, but when the family
name is dragged about in public in connection to such a
scandal—"

"Oh, yes, certainly, the last thing this family needs is
another scandal." I couldn't keep the sarcasm from welling
up and spilling over into my voice.

Edmond pushed his face closer to mine, freezing his gaze
to mine with the same sort of intensity I'd used often
enough to force my will upon another. "Stop to think a
minute and you'll see the sense of it." His tone was low
but not at all benign. He looked as if he wanted to break
me in two. "If the law somehow connects Ridley's death
to the goings-on after the funeral, then checks into my
household and finds out about Clarinda, she'd cheerfully
talk her head off to get back at us all even if she goes to
the gallows for it."

Now did I realize why he was so angry. It was his way
of expressing a very real fear. "There's that," I said, easing
back into a calmer voice and posture. "But you know very
well Clarinda is too fond of her own skin to put it at risk."

He grumbled something that might have been an unwilling concurrence for my logic and finally backed away.
Despite my lack of need to breathe, I wanted to indulge in
a sigh of relief as he put more distance between us by
pacing the room. Resisting the impulse, I glanced at the
forgotten coffees, which were cooling. Soon they'd be too
cold to drink. Just as well, given my limits.

"Have you questioned her?" I asked.

"Of course I have. She claims to be ignorant of the incident and put on a pretty show of tears at the news."

"You think she lied, then?"

"The woman doesn't know how to do anything else,

except lift her skirts to anyone in breeches.''

I gave him a sour face, but might as well have frowned at a wall for all the effect it had on him. ''Perhaps I can talk to her and learn a bit more than you did.''

''What makes you think she'll tell you aught?''

I wasn't ready to confide to him about my talent for influence just yet, if ever, and so came up with what I thought to be a plausible excuse. ''If I let her think I'm worried, afraid of this business, she might be tempted to gloat a little.''

He snorted with scorn. ''Yes, I'm sure she'll jump at the chance to do that and thus tell all.''

''It's worth a try. Look, I've some errands to do tonight, but I could come by tomorrow evening. Perhaps the magistrates will have Ridley's killer in custody by then and all this will be unnecessary.''

He grumbled and growled, but finally gave his assent that I could see her. ''But you've still not answered me. What do you know about this?'' He tapped the paper with his fingers.

''Enough to think the law should seek out his friends for his killer, not his enemies.''

''Who? Arthur Tyne?''

''Possibly.''

''Then I hope to God you're wrong. He'd be worse than Clarinda if he ever started talking.''

''If he's guilty of this murder, he's not likely to bring it up in conversation.''

''He is if he's a fool, and he did not impress me much with his wit at the funeral. Just to be sure, I believe I should go see him.''

''*That* would be a very bad idea.'' He favored me with another scowl, but I was growing used to them. ''You want to avoid a scandal, so the best course is to stay as far away from Mr. Tyne and his ilk as you can for as long as you can. He's not in your usual circle of friends, is he?''

"Of course not."

"Nor mine. We'll just go on as though nothing's amiss and this business will simply pass us—and the family—by. But if you go barging in and stirring things up, that could change faster than the weather."

Edmond had no liking for the suggestion, if only because it came from me, but in this case he reluctantly saw the sense of it. The magical word *family* had worked well to persuade him to caution. I'd have to remember to invoke it more often.

"I shall take myself along now," I said, rising. "The evening is wearing."

"What sort of business can you have then?"

He'd probably think it anyway, no matter what I told him. "Just a bit of wenching, dear cousin, nothing more. There's a very fine lady not far from here. I'm sure she can get you an equally fine companion should you wish to come along. Or we can share, if you like."

By means of a most contemptuous and forbidding sneer he gave me a perfect understanding that going with me to such an assignation was the very last thing he desired to do.

"Another time, then," I said with a bright, guileless smile, picking up my cane. At the door, though, I felt a twinge of guilt for my impudence and turned. "Edmond, I know you're upset over all this, but there's nothing to worry about. There's even a chance the murder has nothing to do with Clarinda."

"I don't believe that," he said flatly.

"Neither do I, but there is a remote chance. Hope for it, but keep yourself prepared for the worst."

"And just how do I do that?"

I pulled out enough of the Dublin revolver for him to see what it was. "Get yourself one of these if you haven't already, and watch your back. If Clarinda's involved in some way, remember she holds no love for either of us.

Make sure your servants are trusty and fully understand the
virtue of bolting the doors and windows, and though I hope
to God it's unnecessary, give them instructions to notify
me or Oliver immediately should anything inimical happen
to you. Left without, she might persuade one of them that
she's mistress of her own house again and thus gain her
freedom.''

He pursed his lips and frowned, but he was listening.

''Otherwise, put an ordinary face to the world and carry
on as usual.''

Brave words, I thought during a quick walk back with
him to his coach. To ensure our mutual safety, we agreed
to go together. On the way I gave the street a thorough
inspection, finding nothing of note, and made a casual inquiry with Mr. Dunnett when we passed him again. He said
all was quiet, and considering the vale I'd given him, I
knew his report was to be trusted. Edmond grunted approval at this evidence of my own caution.

I saw him into his conveyance and felt significant relief
after the driver had clucked to the horses and driven them
all away out of sight. My worry had been Edmond would
find a reason to go banging on Oliver's door and discover
the house empty. Then I'd either have to explain it or influence him into not caring, and both would delay me for
longer than I'd planned.

Rushing into the house, I went from room to room, putting out the candles I'd left alight. Normally I'd not be so
foolish, but Edmond's arrival had surprised me, and I was
too used to there being servants around—neither being
much of an excuse to give to Oliver for burning down his
home. There was no harm done, thank God, and the place
had looked occupied for Edmond's benefit, but the time for
such shamming was past.

Locking the door again, I found my conscience yet
smarted over him. I should have told him at least some of

what had happened so he might be even more prepared for trouble. But before I did that, I hoped to make it altogether unnecessary. Far better it would be for all concerned if I could clear everything up tonight, and I would, God willing. If the Mohocks or the killer or both would not come to me, then I was surely going to come to them.

It was getting near to the dark of the moon, but the sky had cleared, and what few stars were visible between the city smokes served well to light my way. I felt rather exposed walking along like a normal man, and would have much preferred to rise up and take to the sky. I'd become quite spoiled. Though not so vulnerable to the world's hurts, I was yet as subject to a certain amount of anxiety as anyone. With all that had happened, my nerves were unsettled to the point that I wanted to start at every unexpected sound, and in this precarious state of mind, all sounds seemed unexpected.

I told myself not to be a blockhead and forged onward, determined to cleave to the plan I'd placed before Oliver and Elizabeth. All I had to do was follow it through. I had only to visit Arthur Tyne and hear his story, then, depending on what I heard, call on Mr. Litton or one of the Mohocks and finally sort things out.

But it had made so much *more* sense when argued before a cozy fire in a well-lighted room.

Close upon my approach to the crescent-shaped row of houses where Arthur resided, I half expected to garner some sort of notice. By this time my unease had become so much of a familiarity that it had surprisingly transformed itself to aggravation. If a round dozen Mohocks had leaped out to confront me, I'd have certainly yelled my head off, but would have also perversely welcomed the attack as a sign of progress. However, I proceeded unscathed and somewhat disappointed straight to Arthur's door.

I delivered a brisk knock and waited. Though the hour was rather late for a call, I knew the rigid rules for genteel society were likely to be very bent where someone like Arthur was concerned. I knocked again, but no butler answered.

Damnation, if I'd come all this way for nothing . . . I stepped well back from the door to see the upper windows. One of the curtains twitched. Quick as lightning, it passed through my mind that Arthur, far from being the perpetrator of Ridley's murder, might likewise be a target for harm himself. If so, then he'd have good cause to skulk in his own house, and have especially good cause to avoid me should the rumor have reached him that I had done the deed. I could knock all night and get no reply.

The lamp by the door was unlighted. A favorable thing. I glanced once up and down the street. Not completely empty, but no one seemed to be paying much mind to me, and it was very dark. To the devil with it. I vanished and ghosted through.

The entry was very dim even for my eyes. All the curtains were drawn, and very little outside light seeped inside. I sniffed the air. No bloodsmell, thank God. I listened, hearing nothing on this floor. Some stairs leading up were on my right. Rather than announce my presence by the scrape of a shoe or finding a squeaky tread, I made myself transparent and floated to the next landing, solidified, and listened again.

There it was. The intervening floor had muffled the sound of his breathing.

Beyond *that* door. Soundlessly I glided toward it, taking form only when I was on the threshold. I peered in.

It was a bedroom. A single candle burned on a table by the bed. By the window, his back to me, stood my man. He had one eye pressed close to a very slim opening in the curtain and his posture was such as to indicate his whole attention was upon the street below. Had he seen me vanish? Not that it mattered; I could make him forget, and now was a good time as any to begin.

''Hallo, Arthur.'' The devil was in me, else I'd have had mercy and given him some gentler warning of my intrusion.

He fairly screamed as he whipped around. I gave an involuntary jump at the sound and hoped it wouldn't disturb his neighbors to the point of investigating.

And then . . . I didn't give a tinker's damn for any of them. The dunce who was pressed against the far wall panting with fear was Arthur's butler.

''*Damnation!*'' I snarled. ''Where is your master?''

Under the circumstances I was much too optimistic about getting an immediate response from him, and too impatient to wait for him to calm down and collect himself. While his knees were still vigorously knocking one against the other, I stepped close and forced my influence upon him, once more demanding an answer.

''N-not home,'' he finally choked out.

''So I gathered. Where has he gone?''

The combination of his fear and my control was a bad one. His heart hammered away fit to burst. I relaxed my hold on his mind and told him to be easy. It worked, after a fashion, and I was almost able to hold an ordinary conversation with him.

''I don't know,'' he said in a faded voice after I'd repeated my last question.

''When did he leave?''

''Earlier today.''

''Did he know about his cousin's death?''

''Cousin?''

''Thomas Ridley.''

''I don't know.''

Well-a-day. And I thought it was impossible to keep anything hidden from one's butler. ''Where are the other servants?''

''Dismissed.''

''What? All of them?''

''Yes.''

"Why did he dismiss them?"

"I don't know."

"Did he dismiss you?"

"Yes."

"Why are you still here?"

The answer was not instantly forthcoming, having stopped somewhere halfway up his throat. And little wonder, I thought, once I'd looked around the room; the man had been so terrified not just from my sudden appearance in the house, but because I'd interrupted his thieving. Two bundles lay on the bed, one tied up and ready to carry, the other open to reveal a pile of clothing, some trinkets, and a couple of silver candlesticks. I also noticed why I'd mistook him for Arthur, for he'd donned some of his former master's clothing, a silk shirt and a dark green coat with gold buttons.

"You'll not get a good character doing that, my lad. A noose more like."

He didn't disagree with me.

I spent the next quarter hour in a weary bout of questioning, and though plagued with headache for my efforts, learned a few very interesting things.

Arthur had been somewhat mysterious in his behavior for the few last days, being rather quiet and subdued. Nothing odd in that, considering the injuries he'd suffered along with the effect of my influence, I thought. He'd kept to his room, resting for the most part and refusing to see a doctor for his condition, which was rapidly improving. Today he'd recovered enough to walk to his favorite coffee house to read the papers there as was his usual habit. Hours later he'd returned a changed man, being very nerved up and restless. Pale and abrupt, he ordered the packing of a traveling case, had his horse brought around, and mounted up. He then summarily discharged the entire household and rode off without another word.

This had astonished the lot of them, to say the least.

Some departed immediately after packing up their own belongings. The kitchen staff saw no reason why the food, wine, and spirits should go to waste and walked off with all they could carry in lieu of their unpaid wages. The butler, left ostensibly in charge, made no objection and let them plunder at will. Once gone, though, he had his own plan to enrich himself by lifting whatever choice objects Arthur in his haste had left behind.

The pickings were lean. No money, not even a stray silver snuffbox was to be found. If it was small and valuable, Arthur had already taken it. However, he'd left behind some very fine clothes and some other, less portable things, enough to keep the butler in comfort for the next year, longer if he decided to strip and sell the household linens, too.

And though I pressed him until the sweat ran down his face, he could not tell me or offer the least clue on where Arthur had gone.

Disgusted at this turn, I asked where Arthur kept his papers and was directed to a downstairs room that served as a sort of library. I told the man to continue his business, and pay no mind to me, and in fact he could forget he'd even seen me at all. I had no care for his thievery; he could do what he liked so long as it did not interfere with my own searching.

The library had few books, certainly not in the numbers I was used to having about. Some of them had to do with law, indicating what Arthur had read for when he'd been at university. I'd heard nothing about him to indicate he'd taken up practice, and thought it likely he was merely biding his time on a quarterly allowance until coming into his parental inheritance like so many other young men of our generation—that or hoping for a rich marriage.

The writing table he used as a desk held an untidy pile of paper, mostly old invitations, bills, and household accounting. It was very haphazard; some of the stuff was months out of date. I found a few letters from his family, who were presently enjoying the Italian climate, but no other correspondence. A note from one of his Mohock friends with a name and address would have been useful, but none were to be found. I pocketed a letter from his mother on the small chance its address might be of use later, then checked the fireplace. He'd burned paper there recently. The stuff missing from Ridley's flat, perhaps? The ash was very thoroughly stirred and broken up so there was no way to tell what it had been. I couldn't think why he'd want to kill his own cousin, though; their fellowship of murder had struck me as being thicker than cold porridge. Perhaps Clarinda could clear things up.

Or Litton.

I'd wasted too much of the night on this project. I'd best get along to see Ridley's lapdog before he got frightened and disappeared as well.

This time I took to the sky—after first ascertaining the event went unobserved. The wind was not so bad tonight. My progress was swift and exhilarating, but I had little mind for enjoyment of it as a diversion. Perhaps later, after all this business was past, I'd be free to explore and appreciate, but not now.

As Litton's place was so close to Oliver's I decided to delay going there just long enough to look in on our house and street. All was quiet and normal for the latter, not so for the former. Immediately upon my touching to earth and growing solid I saw the lights showing past the edges of the drawn curtains. Of all the infernal cheek—had the bastards invaded our home and were even now plundering it like Tyne's butler?

Of course, Edmond might have come back . . . but no, his coach wasn't waiting for him. More likely Oliver had gotten tired of waiting at Fonteyn House and returned to see how I'd progressed. Blast the man. I'd tell him a thing or two about putting himself at risk—if it was Oliver.

Just to be safe, I let myself inside without using the key and listened hard. Someone was in the sitting room. The door was open and the golden glow from many lighted candles spilled out into the hall. I heard the crackle of flames in the fireplace, and a faint step or two, then came a few experimental notes from the new spinet. Good God, Elizabeth? Fingers ran up and down the scale, faltered, missed a note, then stubbornly resumed.

I drew my pistol—in case I was wrong—and hurried forward, intending to surprise the player. But when I rounded the doorway and saw who stood within, the surprise doubled and redoubled back upon me. I stopped, turned to stone with disbelief.

The woman standing before the spinet was not my sister, but Nora Jones.

She looked up, blank-faced at first with startlement, then her features relaxed into warm recognition. That slow smile, that bewitching smile, the one she gave to me alone emerged to light her expression.

I'd forgotten, forgotten, *forgotten* how beautiful she was; my heart gave such a tremendous leap that my chest hurt. I staggered forward a step. I tried to speak, but the words wouldn't come out. Through a blur of tears I saw her coming toward me, arms outstreteched. She whispered my name. I wanted to shout hers, but it was hopeless. Giving up, I simply held her hard and close as we wept and laughed at the same time.

CHAPTER
─9─

Eventually we had to part, if only to look at each other. She touched my face with one hand, even as I touched hers, and probably for the same reason: to reassure herself of my reality.

"I got your letter," she finally said. "The one you left in my house. I didn't know you were in England or I'd have come sooner. I'm so sorry."

"It doesn't matter."

"Can you forgive me for what I did at Cambridge?"

I could forgive her anything now that she was here and told her as much, swiping at my eyes with my sleeve.

"I had to do it. You needed to go home, and I had to take care of Tony Warburton and—"

"Never mind. It's past. Other things . . . there are other things to speak of. Oh, God, there's so much to tell you!"

She smiled up to me, a little one, wavering between joy and tears. I'd missed how her lips curled in just *that* way. I kissed them, softly. The hunger for her was very much with me, but there would be time for that soon enough, I hoped. For now I was content to hold her close.

"Where have you been? I've had Oliver searching for you for more than a year. Are you all right?"

"Of course I am."

I pulled away to look at her. "But Tony Warburton said that you'd been ill. *Are* you all right?"

"I'm fine, as you see." She covered her hands tightly over one of mine. "You spoke to him, then?"

"Almost as soon as we landed in England—I thought he might tell me where you were. You've been trying to help him all this time, haven't you? Oliver said that you'd been in Italy with the Warburtons, and—"

"Then you remember *all* that happened that night?"

"Every minute of it."

Lifting my hand, she kissed it. "And I'd hoped to spare you from—"

"It's nothing, now. It doesn't matter. You're here and well, and that's all that's important to me. Why did he say you were ill? I was so worried for you. Is it to do with his madness?"

"No, no, he must have been speaking of my aunt. Mrs. Poole took sick just before we left Italy. We've been living quietly in Bath since then."

"Very quietly indeed. Why, then? No one in our circle had any word of you. I was coming to think you'd dropped off the face of the earth—or something awful had happened to you or you were purposely hiding for some reason."

"For one such as myself privacy is very necessary. I have to maintain a certain distance from people, as you well know."

"But so much distance? And for so long?"

"I'd had my fill of society. It was empty without your company."

For this I embraced her again, laughing. It promised well for us both to know she'd missed me. I was sorry about Mrs. Poole's sufferings, but within was a selfish gratitude that it had not been Nora. My arms wrapped around her, I gave heartfelt thanks to the heavens for her present and continued well-being.

"How fares your aunt?" I asked, at last recalling my manners.

"The waters there have been a help to her, thank God," she answered. "She's recovered enough that I thought of coming back to London. I sent one of my men to check on the house, and he found your note telling me to see Oliver. I came as soon as I could. No one's here, though. What's going on? Where's Oliver? Why are all the servants gone?"

Suddenly remembering the Dublin revolver I'd been holding all this time and why I was holding it, I leaned over and put it on a table. There was no chance that I would complete my dark errand tonight. Compared to Nora, the importance of finding and dealing with Ridley's murderer lost all impetus. Tomorrow would do just as well for that unpalatable task.

Her eyes went large at the sight of the weapon, bemusement drawing up the corners of her mouth. "What on earth? Jonathan?"

"This may take awhile. You've walked into the middle of a very bothersome situation. I'll explain everything, I do promise." I gently led her over to the settee. We seated ourselves, each turned slightly so as to better regard the other. I wanted to look at her all night—that, and other things. "So much has happened I hardly know where to begin. I've so many questions for you now."

"And I for you."

I gave a short laugh. "I've the feeling yours will be easier to answer. You go first."

She fell in with my humor. "Well, is your family all right? The war news—that letter you got from your father . . ."

God, that was ages ago. "They're all fine or were when I left last September. Father's decided to move the family back to England. That's why I'm here now, or part of the reason. I'd have come back to you no matter what—you have to know that, but—''

''I know.''

''—but I was afraid you didn't want to see me again. You made me forget, and I didn't know *why*. And I couldn't underst—'' I caught myself. This wasn't the best way to go about it, plunging into the middle with questions sounding too much like accusations. One thing at a time. ''My—my sister Elizabeth came over with me, I can't wait for you to meet her. She very much wants to meet you.''

She stiffened. ''You *told* her about me? About us?''

''Of course I did. I had to—in order to try to explain what had happened to me.''

''What ha—I don't understand.''

''I didn't either at first. And I was so frightened then.'' I was frightened now. The words were trying to stick in my mouth again. Rather than fight them, I took her hand and pressed its palm flat against my chest. I knew she would sense the utter silence there even as I perceived the stillness of her own heart. ''*This* is what's happened.''

She went absolutely quiet, and her color drained away. She shook her head, first in doubt, then in denial. ''No . . . it cannot be.''

''I'm like you, Nora.''

''No, you ca—no, oh, *no*.'' She pulled her hand away, stood, and backed quickly from me, shaking her head the whole time.

I reached out, but she drew farther and farther off until she bumped against one wall. She stared at me as one stricken and said nothing. ''What is it? What's the matter?''

She would only shake her head and stare.

''What is wrong? For God's sake, settle yourself and *talk* to me!'' All I wanted was to go to her, but some wise instinct told me to stay as I was and not make the slightest move. She was like a terrified bird ready to take flight. Why was she like this? Why was she afraid of me? I softened my tone. "Nora, please . . . I need you. I love you. For all that's happened I have never stopped loving you."

Trembling now, she made an effort to steady herself. At least she was listening.

"Whe-when?"

"A year ago last August," I answered, divining her meaning.

"How?"

I touched my chest. "I was shot . . . here. When I woke up, I came to realize I was like you. Those times when we exchanged blood . . . that's how it was passed on, wasn't it?"

She nodded once.

"Since then I've been living as you live—"

"Feeding as I feed?" she demanded sharply, voice rising.

"No, not exactly."

There was no breath left in her. Her next whispered question was inaudible. I only saw the words forming on her white lips.

"I'm sorry, what did you say?"

She swallowed hard and breathed in through her mouth. "Have you . . ." another swallow, another breath. "Have you killed anyone?"

I gave back a blank stare. "*Killed?*"

"You heard me."

Certainly I had killed, at Mrs. Montagu's when I had to save Father and Dr. Beldon from those damned rebels, at Elizabeth's house when I'd shot Ash and thrown Tully like a doll across—but how could any of that matter to Nora? Could she somehow know what was going on here in London? Have heard some garbled story about Ridley?

"In my own defense, in defense of others," I began, but stopped, seeing the dismay taking hold of her features. "Nora, what is it?"

She closed her eyes, refusing to meet mine.

Comprehension, ponderous, slow, and appalling, finally dawned for me. "Dear God—I obtain what I need to live from horses or cattle. You don't think I'd kill someone for their blood?"

Oh, but that's exactly what she was thinking if I read her aright. Had I not come close to it with Arthur Tyne? I'd been injured, starving, and mad for revenge of my hurts, but still . . .

"I'd not do that. I'd *never* do that! You must believe me, Nora."

"Never?" Her voice was high with doubt.

I nearly groaned, but nothing less than the truth would serve either of us well. "I almost did. Once. He'd nearly killed me, and I had to take from him to save myself . . . but I didn't kill him. I let him go."

"Who?"

"No one important, no one unimportant. Just a man."

"And what of women?" she murmured.

Here did I begin to blush. "Well, I—I've not been celibate, but no woman I've been with has ever suffered for my appetite. Do you know so little of me to think I would hurt anyone for the sake of my own pleasure?" I'd had the hard lesson of that only last night. Never again.

"That's the whole point, Jonathan. You've *changed*. The abilities you have now put you above all other men, beyond their laws, beyond their punishments—"

I responded with a snort of disbelief. "I think not, dear lady."

"Then you just haven't fully grasped it yet."

"Ah, but I have, with both hands, and just as quickly ungrasped it."

"You're still young."

"So my sister tells me, but I'm no fool. Is that what's upset you? You thought I'd turned into some sort of murdering bully?"

"It's not that simple."

"I think it is, but for pity's sake, be assured I am the man you knew before. Perhaps a little wiser, even. Believe me, I've been all over this subject of bullying with my father and sister—"

Another stricken look took her. "Your family *knows*?"

"Only Father, Elizabeth, Oliver, and, of course, my valet Jericho . . ."

She continued to stare.

Impatience got the better of me. "How could I *not* tell them?"

"And they . . . accept you?"

"Of course they did, once they got over the surprise."

"They must be marvelously understanding."

"I'm not saying it was easy for any of us, but between the choice of having me like this or buried and rotting in the churchyard, they had no trouble making their decision. In fact, they want to thank you for what you did."

"*Thank* me?"

"For all the trials we've been through, this change brought me *back* to them, and for that we are all grateful to you. My condition has given me a greater appreciation for life, theirs and mine together. I know how precious and fragile it all is, how quickly and easily it may be destroyed by a careless hand. I think the whole point now is not so much that I've become like you, but whether or not *you* can accept it yourself. I pray that you will."

"I have no choice," she said unhappily.

This low temper of hers baffled me. "Don't you?" I snapped. "Did you not make a choice that time? You took me to your bed and we made love and you gave your blood to me. Did you not choose then to make me as you are? Or was I just a convenient means to increase your own pleasure?"

"*No!*" She raised her fists, all frustration. "Oh, but you don't understand anything."

"Then *help* me to do so!"

But she said nothing. My anger had accomplished that much.

I suddenly wilted in my seat, and turned from her, overcome for the moment by the black pall of fading hope. She was afraid, and I could not fathom why. "Forgive me, Nora. It's that I've waited so long to see you. I have so many questions, and you're the only one who can possibly answer them. But if you can't or won't, I shan't press you. I'll respect whatever reason you have, even if you don't share it with me."

A long time—a long silence—later, she asked, "Do you really mean that?"

"I've made it a habit to only say what I mean. It's no guarantee against my making a fool of myself, though. Perhaps I'm being a fool now, but better that than for me to distress you in any way. Obviously this has been a shock to you, and an unpleasant one; I don't want to make it worse."

"A shock only," she said. "More than you could ever know or guess."

I hardly dared to look at her, but did. She'd relaxed her tense posture and was no longer trembling. That was some little progress. "Will you talk with me, Nora? Please?"

Another long silence as she looked hard into my face. Then she nodded.

I closed my eyes with relief. "Thank you." I remained where I was so she might make the first move. That wise instinct told me she was still quite capable of taking flight, and it was best she advance at her own pace without any push to hurry on my part.

Very guarded and pulled into herself, she perched on Oliver's chair by the fire. I would have to be careful and slow. Difficult, for the strong urge rose in me to enfold her in my arms and try to give comfort. Later, perhaps, if and when she was ready for it. Now was not the time.

"Where shall we start?" she asked, clasping her hands together. She reminded me of a schoolboy about to be tested on a disagreeable topic.

Though the question wanted to leap out as a bellowed demand, I made my voice mild. "Why did you not prepare me, tell me this would happen?"

Her gaze dropped to the floor. "Because I didn't think it ever would."

"What do you mean?"

"You're not the only man I've loved in that way, Jonathan."

"There was another?"

"Several others, long before you."

This was hardly news considering how much she enjoyed the company of her gallants. As skilled as she was in making love, she'd have had to practice with and learn from someone, or many someones. All past and done with to be sure; there was no reason for me to be jealous, but all the same I couldn't help feeling a familiar barbed thorn trying to sprout in a dark place in my mind. I firmly ignored it.

"Others with whom you exchanged blood?" I prompted.

"Yes."

"So they could be like you?"

"Yes. But when they died . . . they stayed in their graves. It *never* worked."

"One must die for the change to occur?"

She nodded. "Over the years I came to think I would ever be lonely, that I could never share this existence with anyone else. That being true, then it wouldn't matter sharing my blood with those I truly loved. It was done for my pleasure—for our pleasure—but also I always hoped that *one* of you just might cheat death as I had. Jonathan, of them all, you're the only one who's ever come back."

Silence between us. Thick, viscid, and perturbing. "Wh-why? What makes me different?"

"I don't know."

"You have to know!"

"I don't! I don't even know why *I* came back!"

My mouth was like sand. "Nora, how did you die?"

She shook her head. "I'm not ready to speak of that yet."

Her voice was so hushed and suffused with pain, I gave up for the time being any thought of pressing her on the subject. A disappointment, and now came to roost the distressing notion that she did not possess the answers to all my questions. I'd feared that possibility. Since it was apparently becoming a reality, I would have to make the best of it. I nodded acceptance and squared up my shoulders. "Well, then. You didn't think any of your lovers would return, and yet you still hoped on? That's why you'd exchange blood, in that hope. Shouldn't you have given any of us some sort of a warning, though?"

She shook her head decisively. "I did once, and when I lost him forever I could not do it again for any other. It would have been too hard to bear."

"How so?"

She grimaced, then looked at me. "Pretend it's that night again, that night I shared all with you, only instead of taking you to my bed and letting it happen as it did, I first explain what I want to do and what might happen to you after you die. Would you not have second thoughts?"

"Possibly, but I'm sure I'd have done it anyway."

"But since none of the others had ever come back, I'd only be filling you with false hopes, the kind so brittle and sharp that when broken cut you right to the bone."

"None of that would matter to me, though, since I'd be dead and uncaring of the business."

"Not so for *me*, dear Jonathan. I told all of this to the first one, the first man I truly fell in love with. I explained everything to him, the consequences, the possibilities, everything there was to know about this—this condition. He had no objections, quite the contrary, and we lived and loved until the year the plague came. Right on his deathbed he was making plans for both of us for his return—only he never returned.''

Tears. I'd seen her weep with sorrow but once before. Now did they stream down her cheeks.

''I miss and mourn him to this day. Losing him was made worse for me because of the hopes we'd had. He was so certain that he made me certain, and when I lost that . . . it was too much. Ever after I thought it best to live for the present and not the future. It made the partings when they came . . . easier.''

''For you.''

''For me. I was ever the one left behind.''

''Until now.''

She gave me a look such as would crack my heart.

''If this is what you've hoped for for so long, then why be afraid of me?''

''B-because of the one who made me like this. I was not born this way. He was my lover and shared his blood with me.''

''Who?''

''You don't know him and likely never will.'' She brushed impatiently at her wet face. ''He fed on people, on women. Said he loved them, said he loved me, but that he couldn't control his hunger. He killed to feed his hunger.''

Understanding flooded me. ''Dear God, no wonder you—oh, Nora, I'm *not* like him, and may God strike me dead before I ever become like him.''

''But he said he couldn't help himself, that he *had* to—''

''Then he was either mad or a liar.''

''Perhaps so. When I came back from death, I feared I'd soon be killing, too.''

I felt a sharp chill stab through me, but made no sign of it. ''And did you?''

''No. It wasn't in my heart to do so. I came to believe it was because I'm a woman and made of softer feelings.

I ran away before he knew of my return."

"To England?"

"France. I knew the language. There I came to see I need not live in fear of what I'd become, that this life could be very pleasant for myself and others, and there I first tried to make another like me."

"But all the while fearing he'd kill for blood like the first man?"

"I'd grown so desperate, was so wretchedly *lonely*, I was willing to sacrifice the lives of others to ease that loneliness."

I tried to imagine such solitude. My own experience with it was limited. I knew what it was to be alone, recalled certain miserable patches while passing from boyhood to manhood, but I'd never endured the kind of isolation Nora described. Even in my worst moments of missing her I knew I'd not have remotely considered taking or even risking the life of some unknown person in order to see her again.

"It must have been wretched, indeed," I whispered.

"It still is."

"Was," I hazarded, adding a note of hope to my tone.

"I don't know."

An honest response. "Then time alone will prove to you I'm no monster killing to feed an uncontrolled appetite."

A smile, so brief it hardly touched her lips. "He was mad or a liar or both. You are not like him. If you were you'd not be so kind to me."

" 'Tis love, not kindness."

"People change. We've been apart for a very long while."

"I've not changed where my feelings for you are concerned. You've been in my thoughts constantly, and not just because of the questions I want to ask you. The years we were together here—you've touched me as no other woman could, Nora. Can you tell me they meant and mean nothing? Or have you changed? Or have you . . . have you found another?''

A sharp look. ''No, I've not.''

''Well, then. Do you love me?''

Eyes shut, then open. ''Yes. Always.''

I closed my own eyes, grateful, humbly grateful for that blessing. The heaviest burden of all had just lifted from my heart. But when I looked at her again, I saw she was yet watchful. ''Then tell me what troubles you. Why are you still this way with me?''

''You'll learn of it sooner or later.''

I gestured, silently urging her to go on.

She looked at the floor. ''You know how I live. How I take a little from my cavaliers, and in return they gift me with the means to maintain my household. You know how I must keep them under the control of my will so there is no chance of rivalry amongst them, for each other or for me, else they'd be fighting or worse.''

''Such as what happened with Tony.''

''Yes. Have you done the same kind of thing yourself, bringing people around to your will?''

''Necessity forced me to learn to use that talent.''

''Talent or curse.''

''Both, then. What of it?''

''I cannot use it on you. It only works on those who are not like us.''

I shrugged. ''Again, what of it?''

''Don't you see how it is for me?''

I tried, but gave up, shaking my head.

''Because of that . . . talent, I am able to control others exactly the way I want to suit my interests, never mind their own.''

''But you've never abused it to my knowledge.''

''Have I not? With you? Jonathan, I can *control* them, and at the very last I was forced to control you so you would forget certain things, but now that you've changed—''

"You can't control me. Yes, I do see your meaning, but why would you want to?"

"It's not a question of want but of need. That's why I'm uneasy, fearful. With the others, with the way you were then, I always had that ultimate advantage. I could always be safe from any and all harm, always guide and determine things for my convenience, always avoid being hurt. Now that you've changed, I'm as vulnerable to harm from you as any normal woman is with a normal man."

"You can't think I'd ever want to hurt you," I protested.

She shifted ever so slightly in her chair, not meeting my gaze. It was answer enough.

This was a grievous blow. I bit back the pain as best I could. Nora had ever been the strongest, most confident of women. Now did I see the foundation of that strength and with that came an insight on why she was behaving this way. "You were bitterly injured in the past, were you not? By the one who changed you, perhaps? You must have, to think so badly of me."

Her expression grew dark. From what memory? "You see the face God gave me, because of it I'd ever been property in the eyes of others, a thing to be bargained and haggled over like a piece of cloth in a market and never more so than with him. In the end, when I'd changed, his control over me ceased to be. It was the one thing that saved me so I could leave him. But ever afterward there were always men wanting to possess me, tell me what to do, kill or die for me. I wanted only to be loved, not owned, and using my will on them was the one surety I had for achieving something close to that love."

"You risked this with your first love, did you not?"

"*Because* he was my first. I didn't know as much then as I did later. Things are different for me now."

"Things are different because your life is your own—"

"Then are women no longer property, bought and sold into marriage by custom or law or betrayed into the same by their own feelings? Am I not now betraying myself to you because of my feelings?''

''Or entrusting yourself, knowing that I would never willingly harm you.''

''You say that now, but later, when you become jealous . . . I can't abide it. It's ever been the cause of all my sorrows.''

''Then I shall have to give it up,'' I said lightly. ''I only want to make you happy.''

''I cannot live with you, Jonathan, if that's what you want.''

''But can you live without me? How long have you waited to share this life with someone? Will you let past fears and hurts control you now that you've a chance to give up the loneliness? Or have you grown so used to having things your own way, having things so perfectly safe and orderly that you don't dare love for real? I'm taking the *same* risk, Nora. Think of that.''

She did, and blushed.

''I'm not the man who hurt you. I am *this* man. He loves you more than life, and will do anything to preserve your happiness. You trusted me once before, did you not? And asked me if I trusted you. You once said you did not want a puppet. Well, here I am!''

Her eyes had grown wide, her mouth pursed; she was silent for so long a time I worried I'd said too much. ''You're not afraid,'' she finally murmured.

''Only of losing you. But if that is what you wish—''

''No!'' Very quick, very soft. She tucked in her lower lip and looked away. Betrayed by her feelings, no doubt, as was I.

''Nora?''

''You'll not try to keep me.'' From the hard, deliberate gaze she now fixed on me this was a statement, not a question.

''Only in my heart.''

"And not judge or be jealous of me and what I do."

"If you'll do the same for me."

"I will not marry you."

"Your love is all the marriage we need. Should you cease to love me, then we'll part if you wish . . . but I hope to heaven you won't."

"Your word on this?"

"On my honor as a gentleman. And yours?"

"If my word alone before God will serve. I lost my honor ages ago, and I'm hardly a lady."

"You are and ever will be in my eyes."

That made her smile, bringing one to my lips in turn. Tentatively I extended one hand to her, palm up. As placation, as offering, as a plea, as all or none, for her to take or refuse as she chose.

She slipped her hand into mine.

Thank God.

Now was the time. I stood and drew her up to me, holding her close as I'd wanted to for so long, able to finally give her the comfort she very much needed but had been afraid to accept. Perhaps she thought my change had altered things between us, and though I didn't see it myself, I'd respect her experience. It was that or lose her. Never again.

Unlike our first night in her bed, I was now the experienced seducer, not she. Many beginnings suggested themselves, but only one was the best of all choices for this moment. A few kisses and caresses, then I unbuttoned my waistcoat, loosened my neckcloth, opened my shirt. I waited, looking at her.

She laughed, softly. "Like old times?"

"Yes," I whispered. "If you would."

Putting forth her hand, she let her spread fingers trace slowly up my bared chest. "I should like to do more than that . . . if you would."

Nothing could have better pleased me. As for pleasing

Nora . . . well, I was determined to do my finest or die trying.

In a few short minutes we'd freed ourselves of most of our encumbering clothing. Being much taller than she, I made things more equal by stretching out on the hearth rug, dragging her down on top of me. There was more voice in her laughter now, I was very glad to hear.

The body remembers what may fade in the mind, and mine fell unresisting into the patterns of the past, recalling her likes and needs without a word being said. To be sure, our time apart did add exceedingly to our mutual desire. We kissed and touched, hands everywhere, limbs entwining as the warmth kindled and grew between us. Soon the fever of it seized me with greater heat than I'd ever known before, and Nora was tearing at me like a wild creature.

Even in the extremes of passion with other women, I had to always be mindful of my unnatural strength so as not to bring harm. Now I was suddenly aware of the hard muscles of Nora's own body and the realization I could venture more with her and do no injury . . . and she with me. I'd often suffered a bruise or two from her in an excellent cause; now were we both free to exercise ourselves fully, and did so with abandon.

I nipped at the velvet skin of her breasts and throat with my lips only, though my corner teeth were out as were hers. The sight of them in such a state had ever bought on arousal for me just as strongly as the sight of her body; I wondered if she had a similar reaction. Apparently so, I soon concluded, for her responses to my actions increased in aggressiveness and demand. We rolled and groaned and bucked against one another like animals. One second I was on her, the next she was on me. Neither of us hesitated, but hurtled forward without pause or waver.

Then was she truly on me, hips grinding away as though independent from the rest of her, pushing me up into her

body. This suited well for her initial climax, and as it overtook her she fell forward, moaning, digging her teeth hard
into my throat that she might prolong it. My blood surged
forth, engendering for me a consummation more sharp, joyful, and delirious than those times past when I'd once
merely pumped seed into her. She drew on me, her mouth
hot, demanding all and taking more. Gasping from it, I felt
my very life rushing out, but made not the least stirring to
hinder its flow, so caught was I in the ecstasy of the act.
If she wanted to drain me to a husk, then so be it; I was
hers to have.

Her frenzied movements eventually slowed, but she continued to drink, pulling strongly on the vein she'd opened.
It was wonderful; I'd never known anything to match it. It
was keen and blinding, harsh and blazing. Brain and body,
mind and spirit, all my being turned itself over to the pleasure. If it went on like this forever, then I'd have no need
of heaven.

My sight clouded over. The glow from the candles
merged with the shadows; the room seemed filled with a
golden fog. It lay warm upon my skin like sunlight.

I held still except for stroking a lazy hand up along her
bare back. As more and more of my blood went into her,
even that easy motion became too much of an effort. My
arm went lax and dropped away. I could not lift it again.

She's killing me, I thought. But that inner revelation did
not alarm me in the slightest. I'd already died, and not
nearly so marvelously as this; I had nothing to fear.

I fell into a kind of sleep close to that which came upon
me during the day when I was not on my earth. This was
without the bad dreams, though, and much more sensual. I
was soaked through, submerged in a sea of absolute bliss.
Waves of it overwhelmed me each time she swallowed. I
sank far beneath its crystal surface, not caring if I ever
come up again.

"Jonathan?"

I hated to respond, to have any interruption, but when she whispered my name a second, then a third time, I finally looked at her.

Her lips were red from my blood. Her eyes burned like living rubies. She ran one hand along my face, fingers brushing into my mouth, against my teeth. Some part of my lethargy tumbled away, and though weak as a kitten from what I'd given, with her help I slowly sat up. She yet crouched over my hips and now wrapped her legs around behind me, locking us together.

"Your turn," she murmured, letting her head fall back.

I could just see the swollen vein waiting under the pale velvet. The scent rising from it, the bloodsmell, pierced through my somnolence. My mouth sagged wide. Hunger and lust became one. Impossibly, for I'd thought myself past it, the fever rose up and seized me once more.

She made a shrill cry when, for the first time, I gouged into the virgin skin of her throat. Her whole body arced into it, pressing, holding, pulling me tighter as I swallowed a great draught of her blood, eagerly reclaiming that which she'd taken from me. My member flooded with new strength. Hips rocking back and forth, she sighed, her breath warm in my ear.

Another draught—no tiny drop carefully teased out and slowly savored, but a flaming mouthful of life's own purest nectar. I drank, deep and long as I could not do with anyone else. She clung to me, shuddering in time to it, one hand on the back of my head to push me harder, more deeply against her throat. I drank until her moans dwindled, hushed, and finally ceased, and she lay limp and unresisting against me like a sleeping child. Then did I stop, holding fast to the last quivers of pleasure as they echoed through me.

Some considerable time later we summoned sufficient will to sort ourselves a bit. Nora rested next to me on her

back, serene and smiling; I lay on my side, head propped
on one hand that I might gaze down at her. The candles
were low, the fire nearly gone. A faint glimmer from the
embers remained. Not enough to give warmth, but we had
no worry for any chill.

She'd not changed except to become more beautiful in
my eyes, and after this night she was above and beyond all
other women for me. Though she saw it differently, our
shared condition had altered nothing about my feelings toward her. If she felt the need to set limitations—such as
they were—on me, on whatever future awaited us, to feel
safe, then so be it. Ultimately, I knew only with the passage
of time could I show myself worthy of the fragile trust
she'd just placed in me. That trust would be tested sooner
or later; she'd said as much already. When the test came I
prayed I would be wise enough to recognize it and put to
rest all her fears of jealousy and betrayal.

The testing would likely have to do with her cavaliers.
She might expect me to come to resent them, for I did not
see her giving them and their gifts up. Not so much because
of the loss of money and blood they provided, but because
of their importance to her sense of freedom and confidence.
If I made offer to fully support her—as I could well afford
to do—she'd not welcome it. I could and would never ask
her to cease seeing them. That would violate our pact and
drive her from me in one witless move. I'd given my word;
I would hold myself to it no matter what.

As for the pleasure they gave her and got in return . . .
well, I'd ever had the decided advantage since my days at
Cambridge. She may have dallied with them, fed from
them, enjoyed their company, affection, attention, and
money, but she loved and went to bed with me. So things
would be now, I expected, but even better. Without her
imposed influence in my mind, I might be subject to a pang
or two of jealousy, but I'd just have to live with it or lose
her. I could no more resent her diversions with others than

she could my sporting with the ladies at Mandy Winkle's—
though that sort of pastime might be less frequent for me
now that Nora had returned. Compared to her, the other
women were little more than a charming temporary distraction.

But the future I contemplated would be with us soon
enough and take care of itself. The present had just been
and continued to be very agreeable. As to the past . . . there
was too much of it that was yet dark to me.

I wondered about this man who had rendered her change.
What sort of tyrant was he, and why had he been so cruel
to such a woman as Nora? Or to any woman for that
matter? To kill others to sustain one's own life . . . ugh.
Through no fault of my own and in the most extreme of
circumstances I'd come close to doing it myself and could
understand such hunger, but thankfully, heaven had spared
me from committing that particular sin. Apparently this
monster wantonly murdered, excusing his abominations by
claiming it was beyond his control. What rot—and Nora
and I were the solid proof of it. It sickened me that she'd
known so evil a man, had endured his touch. Certainly it
was a tribute to her inner strength that she was as recovered
as she was from what must have been a terrible ordeal.

Where was he now, and was he yet a threat to her? If
so, then he was in for a great surprise for here in me was
her own special champion. When she was ready I'd question her more closely on the fellow. I'd question her on
quite a lot of things. God knows, I'd barely started yet, but
there was time for it. Now that we were together again,
there would be plenty of time for talk.

"Shall we dress?" she asked, cracking her eyelids a fraction to see me.

"So soon? But it's been such a long time, my dearest."
I leaned over to kiss her forehead, my free hand making
very free with one of her breasts.

"That it has, but I'm ill-prepared tonight."

"Not that I could tell."

"I can. I'm so feeble I shall have to find refreshment—no, don't you dare tempt me, Jonathan."

"But it's your turn to take from me, is it not?" My hand had wandered down to an even more intimate area of her person. She writhed about, but did not retreat or make me stop. "It will refresh us both, I'm thinking."

"Perhaps so, but I couldn't—oh! Well, perhaps I could. But only to make things even between us. We can't tolerate much blood loss, you know."

I'd tolerate her draining me to the dregs as long as it was this gratifying.

This time were we slower, more gentle with one another. Nora's kiss was soft and lingered long, taking my blood away gradually, and giving back a joyful quickening to my senses so intense that I hovered perilously on the edge of a swoon from the elation.

It had not been like this for me since our time at Cambridge. I'd missed it, craved it. Small wonder I'd been so tempted to want Yasmin to do this to me; I was glad now to have pushed away from her. It had been for the girl's own good, but aside from that responsibility, I realized her efforts, enchanting and exquisite as they might have proved, would have been but a poor substitute. Only Nora could give me such perfect fulfillment.

As always, it was over too soon, alas. She could go on for the rest of the night and it would have still been over too soon, but this would have to suffice until our next meeting. She ceased taking from me, licked one last time at my wounds, and with a sigh settled into the crook of my arm. I was in no hurry to move, both for the opportunity to hold her and because I'd grown weak again; not nearly as bad as before, but it seemed best to indulge in moderation until I'd restored myself at some neighbor's stable.

"I'm glad you shaved," she said, lightly touching her

lips. They were a bit puffed and reddened, not from blood this time, but from the constant friction against my skin.

"So am I." I was also careful about touching my neck. She'd exercised great delicacy on me for the last hour or more, but for all that the area was rather tender. Nothing a quick vanishing wouldn't take care of, though. Later, perhaps, when I was more recuperated. "When next we do this, I should like to lay in a good supply of beef or horse blood. Then we won't have to stop."

"An excellent idea, my dear. I shall look forward to it."

"Then let it be soon." If I could have moved I'd have tried loving her again. Sweet heavens, but it had been so damnably long. But she was with me again, and things promised to be better than ever between us.

"Was your death painful?" Her question, breaking into my thoughts out of nowhere, startled me. "If you don't wish to speak of it—"

"No, it's all right. I've just never talked about it before. I didn't want to cause Father or Elizabeth any discomfort, and it's not one of my favorite memories. But to answer, yes, it was, but it was very quick. I've had worse since then."

"What could be worse?"

"If I told you we should be here all night."

"Have you anything else to do?"

"Yes, but I fear it would be too physically taxing for both of us."

"Rogue. You've yet to explain why you were stalking around your cousin's empty house with a pistol."

"Dear me, yes. Are you awake enough for a long listen?"

"You must know by now we don't sleep like other people."

"Indeed I do, and what a trial it was to learn that."

She put her hand on my cheek. "I *am* sorry."

I kissed her palm. "It's all right. I understand now. Past

and done. Time to move forward." I paused a moment to
think and compose ... where to begin? At the beginning?
And where and when might *that* be? I supposed on the hot
August morning when Beldon and I had our unfortunate
encounter with Lieutenant Nash and those Hessians. I'd
never asked Nash why he'd been blundering about the island with a pack of German soldiers. They should have
been with their own officers. I suppose he'd been forced to
use whoever had been at hand to hunt down the Finch
brothers. Would things have gone differently for me had
Beldon and I left a few minutes earlier or later? Or if I'd
worn another color coat?

Past and done, I thought. Thankfully, because of Nora,
I still had a future. One with Nora in it. That was all I ever
wanted or needed. Turning on my side again, I put an arm
around her and commenced telling her everything.

Interruptions upon such a lengthy recital are inevitable,
but Nora kept hers to a minimum. Still, it seemed a remarkably long while before I thought to pause, and the
fancy was becoming fact the next time I noticed the mantel
clock. The dawn was too close for me. Now that Nora was
here, the dawn would ever be too close for me.

We'd quit the hearth rug and dressed ourselves. This time
she sat next to me on the settee, as close as she could get.

"I hope you don't mind about the others," I said, after
a diplomatically brief mention of how I'd dealt with my
carnal needs with other women.

"You were careful with them?" she asked. She did not
seem in the least bothered by the subject. A relief, that.

"Always. Perhaps more so than necessary."

"I'm glad to hear it. You seem to have fared well in
your change just by following your own best judgment."

"And what I recalled of your example ... though I never
once saw you vanish."

"I don't do it often. It tires me."

"Why is it we can do it?"

She shook her head. "I don't know the why, only that we can. Perhaps it's to allow us an easy escape from our graves at night and a quick return to them in the morning."

"It was very useful to me that first time, but I've not been back to my grave since. I can't abide closed-in places even now."

"For which I cannot fault you."

"Why do we have such awful dreams without our earth to rest on?"

A shrug this time. "I could not say."

"Elizabeth thinks our return to life requires some sort of a compromise, that we must carry a bit of the grave along with us in exchange for leaving it."

"That sounds as good a reason as any I've ever considered."

"Why are we not permanently harmed by weapons?"

"I'm not sure. We heal so fast, and we vanish to heal. The two might be connected in some way."

"Why do we not reflect in mirrors?"

"I don't know. Perhaps we're invisible to them the way we're sometimes invisible to people, only it's beyond our conscious control. In some parts of the world it is thought it's because we've lost our souls, but I don't believe that."

It did sound foolish. "Why is crossing water such a hardship?"

"Because it separates us from the earth?"

"Not fair, a question for a question."

"Better than my saying 'I don't know' to you all the time."

"What *do* you know, then?"

"To always have a goodly supply of earth with me, to always and ever be prepared for calamities like fire, flood, and gossips, to make sure my servants are loyal, discreet, and well paid, to always be home an hour before dawn . . ." She had quite a list of things, most I already knew, all of them exceedingly practical. "Will that suffice for you?" she asked when finished. "There's more."

"It seems more than enough."

"Not nearly enough, I fear. I cannot reduce all my experience down to but an hour of talk."

"Nor can I give all my questions to you in one evening." Of course there would be many more evenings ahead for us, but I was of a mind to fill them with other activities than lessons. This brought an idea to mind, though. "Dearest, you asked me earlier to pretend it was our first night to exchange blood. I'll ask the same of you. If you had explained all to me at that time, what would you have said?"

She thought for a while. "Well, I would have first asked if you had ever heard of *nosferatu*." Quite the foreign word it was to judge by her intonation and accent.

Under her intent gaze I cudgeled my brain a moment. "A Baltic seaport, isn't it?"

CHAPTER
~10~

She looked at me, perplexed and gaping for an instant, then suddenly exploded with laughter, fairly rocking with it. While glad to provide her so much amusement, I was also annoyed at not understanding the reason behind it.

"Nora . . ."

With an effort she managed to restore her poise again, but each time she glanced at me, she seemed ready to burst out again. "I'm sorry. So much has happened tonight I must be giddy."

"Think nothing of it," I said dryly. "Just tell me where *Nosferatu* is and what it has to do with things."

"It is a what, not a where, and it's the name we are called in some parts of the world."

I scowled, pronouncing the unfamiliar syllables in my mind. "Can't say I like it much, then. Sounds like a badly done sneeze."

More sudden mirth. This time I was able to join in to some extent. When the latest fit passed, she said, "There are others you just might know: *upier*, *murony*, *strigon*, *vrykolakas*, *Blutsäuger*—"

"Wait—I heard that one from some Hessian soldiers . . .

don't like it much, either—especially the way they spoke it.''

"There's more. I've studied. The common name you might know in English is 'vampire.' ''

I mouthed the word experimentally. It was just as strange as the others she'd named. "Can't say that I do.''

"Oliver Goldsmith mentioned it in his *Citizen of the World.* Have you read of it?''

"I fear not.''

"Well, it was more than a decade and a half ago. I'm as eager to add to my knowledge of this condition as you are and have assembled a nice little collection of all the books I've found with allusions to and reports about vampires. I'll let you browse through it if you like.''

"Indeed I would.''

"However, what you will read and what we are have ever been two very different things. Many of the accounts of vampires are mixed in with hauntings, grave robbing, devil worship, demonic possession, and some goings-on so ghastly or nonsensical it makes you wonder if people have any wits at all. I'm sure we're linked to it because our drinking blood disgusts and frightens them so much. That's why I have to be so careful about keeping my needs a secret. In the past I'd have been burned for it or had my head cut off and my heart torn out. It could still happen in certain places.''

"That's utterly horrible. Who would do such a thing?''

"Any number of otherwise upright God-fearing people. We're different from them, we drink blood to live, therefore we must be evil. I've often thought of writing up my own account of who and what we really are, setting things down correctly for good and all, but for the deep roots of the superstitions and the fact that I've so little real information. The man who changed me was not too forthcoming with his knowledge—''

Either, I silently added.

"—and I have no wish for him to know I'd returned."

"He thinks you're dead?"

"I certainly pray so. I've not seen or heard of him for many years. It would be a good thing for the world if he were dead, but considering how the change toughens us, I would not expect it. It grieves me, for it means he's still probably killing others, but there's nothing I can do to stop him."

"Perhaps the two of us together might do something about him."

She pursed her lips and glanced away. "*That* is an undertaking I should have to think over very carefully. He's dangerous."

"So am I. So are we both."

"I wouldn't know where to start looking for him, though I suppose I could learn how. Let me think on it, Jonathan. There's so much more for you to learn first, anyway."

"Such as?"

She stood, as smooth and as supple as a cat, to stretch as much as her corseting would allow. I stayed where I was, watching appreciatively. There was a portrait of Oliver's late father over the mantel; Nora went for a closer look, then gestured at it. "Do you recall the painting of me in the antique costume?"

"The one in your bedroom? The one that makes it obvious the artist was in love with you?"

My reward was a smile. "That one, yes. What you need to know is that was not a costume, but real clothing. *My* clothing."

Now was I smiling. "What are you saying?"

"The painting was done over a hundred years ago. Just as you see me here, so was I alive a hundred years ago to pose for it."

I shook my head. Was she joking? But her manner was entirely serious.

"It's a lot to take in, I know, but I've not gone mad.

This is a very hard truth, the hardest I shall ever impart to you. Please trust that I hardly believed it for myself when I learned of it, so I'll not take it amiss if you don't believe it, either.''

''You're telling me you're over one hundred years old?''

''Yes. Our condition makes it possible. I've not aged since my death years and years ago.''

''And . . . when was that?''

She tucked in her lower lip. ''No, I'll tell you later. You're still trying to accept it. Best if you think it over first. You may take as much time as you like. In a decade or two your friends will finally convince you.''

Her plain-spoken bearing alone was starting to convince me. ''This is no jest?''

''No.''

''We do not age?''

''I think it has to do with how the vanishings heal us. It keeps us young.''

''But that's impossible.''

''Our very existence should be impossible, Jonathan, yet here we are.''

Sitting in one spot, staring at nothing, and no doubt looking like a stunned sheep occupied me for a goodly period. On top of everything else, this particular revelation was just too much to take in, but the certitude that she spoke the truth began to trickle into my overworked brain.

She went on. ''We do not age, we do not sicken—I don't know if we can even die.''

''But all things die.''

''Then perhaps we will, eventually; that knowledge is presently beyond my ken. In the meantime, please don't burden yourself thinking on it too much. I told you this because you need to know it; it's not meant to distress you.''

''How could it distress me?''

''You'll discover that soon enough.''

"Tell me now," I said, straightening myself to fix her with a direct look.

She turned away, placing her hands on the mantel. "The sad fact is we outlive our loves. That was another reason why I wanted you to forget me. Had you remained in England, we might have lived on together. The years might have passed, with me staying as I am, and you growing older and older . . . then dying. I've been through it before. At times it has almost driven me mad.

"When you got that letter from your father, I hated the thought of losing you, but it seemed better to let you go on with your life. Then would you always be alive in my memory, young and vital as I'd known you best. It was a hard parting for me, but easier than watching the years eating at you. Because of this unnatural lengthening of life and youth, I've had to learn to live one night at a time, to enjoy and cherish whatever time God grants me to be with anyone I love; otherwise I should have truly gone mad years ago from all the losses."

Simple words, simply said, and the appalling possibilities began to yawn before me. That I, too, would live on, that those I loved would age and die while I remained young and strong . . .

She looked back and saw the anguish creeping over me. Coming to sit by me again, she took my hands in her own. "This is the heartbreaking burden we carry that outweighs all the advantages we possess."

"But can—can we not exchange our blood with others? Make them like us?"

"Yes, it need not be done in a carnal manner. I've tried. But except for you and myself, it's never worked."

"Then we must discover what has made us different from them. We must."

"But—"

"Look, Oliver's taken it upon himself to study all he can of my condition. He might be able to help."

She appeared to be dubious over that idea, but made no immediate objection.

I listened to the tick of the clock as a silence settled between us. Would time have a different meaning now that I knew it had no effect on me? Yes. Decidedly yes. Knowing I had so much of it and those I loved had so little, time with them was now more precious than my soul's rest.

How old was Nora? Was she more than one hundred? Possibly. Probably. Sometimes she'd say things, odd things . . . I'd never paid them much mind before. There was a bad habit that wanted correcting. She spoke of the plague, but there hadn't been anything like that in London since the Great Fire. Her portrait, the clothes she'd worn, even the artist's manner of painting, those should have given me ample warning. Perhaps she'd worked her influence on me yet again, keeping me from becoming too curious at the time. Well, I was immune from her influencing, so that was all over and done. The temptation to press her for more information was there, but perhaps not wise to attempt just now. She was right that I was still taking it all in. When she was ready—or rather when she judged me ready—she would tell me more of herself.

"You do understand that we are not fertile?" she asked.

I stirred, dragging my thoughts over to this new subject. "I came to think as much when I failed to expel seed the first time I bedded a lady after my change."

"Does it trouble you?"

"In honesty I can't say I've really missed it—in regards to my achievement of satisfaction, that is; what I take pleasure from now is so much superior than what I experienced before my change that I might be troubled by a return to my previous state."

"A fortunate blessing, that."

"Most fortunate. Though I may no longer procreate, the desire to do so is apparently unimpaired. Quite to the contrary, since the enjoyment is so increased, the desire to have

the enjoyment is also . . . increased. Or so I have found it.''
God, but with that thought invading my mind—and particularly—my body, I abruptly wanted her all over again.
Tempting, but dangerous. She'd have to leave soon, far too
soon for what I wanted to do. Kissing each of her hands
would have to do for now, and a poor substitute it was to
be sure.

She favored me with an affectionate smile, for she could
certainly read the thoughts that had just flickered over my
face. ''Yes, I know all about the desire. We are at least
allowed fleshly pleasures, if not the usual outcome of them,
though this exchanging of blood we do is our own way—
our one way of propagating.''

''But for its success to also be such a rare occurrence
would seem to make it a pointless pursuit—except in terms
of expressing affection or giving and gaining pleasure.''

''Are you going to ask me why it is so?''

I gave her a wry glance. ''Not unless you have an answer.''

''Sadly, I do not.''

''Then I shall not bother to try.''

Soft laughter from her. She seemed very easy in her manner. Now would be the time to introduce a difficult subject
of my own.

''Nora, are you sure you don't mind the other women
I've known?''

''If I did, then I should be a great hypocrite.''

''There were other women before I left England, as
well.''

''I was ever well aware of them, my dear. Though discreet with me, you and Oliver made quite a name for yourselves around Covent Garden back then. The gossips had
a fine time discussing your adventures with the ladies
there.''

Her tone was light, so I pushed ahead. ''You need to
know about one lady in particular, though.''

"Do I?"

"It has to do with why I was carrying the pistol."

"She has a jealous husband? There are other, less forceful ways of dealing with such problems."

"It's more complicated than that. . . ."

I then told her about the family Christmas gathering.

And about Clarinda.

And Aunt Fonteyn's death.

And Ridley and Arthur's attack.

And finally, about Richard.

All in all, she took it rather well.

"Cousin Jon'th'n!"

For such a little boy, Richard had quite a bellow. My attention was immediately swept to the top of the stairs where Mrs. Howard firmly held him, else he'd have launched himself down their length to give greeting. As one footman closed the entry doors of Fonteyn House behind me, I threw my discarded cloak to another, then shot forward and up to the landing.

"Hallo, laddie! Hallo, Mrs. Howard," I said, grabbing him away from her and raising him overhead. He squealed and giggled fit to burst, kicking his legs. "I've missed you. How have you been?"

"Very well, thank you. Will we go back to Cousin Ol'ver's now?"

I glanced at Mrs. Howard, who appeared interested to know as well. "Not this evening, I fear."

"When?"

"I don't know."

Nora's arrival had seriously diverted me from necessary business, and would likely delay things again tonight when I talked to Elizabeth and Oliver. I felt badly for all the trouble I'd put them to, for they'd vacated the house and waited all this time for nothing since I'd not accomplished all my errands. But faced with a similar circumstance I doubt anyone else would have chosen differently. Nora had returned at long last; no matter that she'd come at an inconvenient time so long as she *had* come.

I'd been reluctant to part with her this morning, and very unwilling to let her go home unescorted, but she'd insisted, saying she above all people in the city was safest from its dangers. In that I knew her to be wholly correct, but it was still a wrench to say good-bye and just let her walk away. Perhaps this was a test of my promise not to infringe upon her freedom.

If so, then I failed miserably, for tired as I was, I took to the air and spied on her progress.

It was brisk, for she had ever enjoyed a good walk in the past. She was stopped not once, but several times by men. Obviously an unescorted woman was fair and easy game for such predators as roamed about during the darkest hours of the night. But each time she encountered one of these miserable brutes, she spoke fearlessly to him. He would then step out of her way, allowing her to continue on without so much as a backward glance for him. Obviously she was most adept at influencing them, else she'd have come to grief long ago.

I did nearly go solid again when three drunken villains spied her and lurched across the street to cut her off. She'd never be able to influence that many at once, or so I assumed, and prepared myself to dive to her rescue and explain things later. But by the time they got to her, she was, quite literally, no longer in sight.

From my high vantage I tried to find her again, but my vision was limited in this form. I'd only taken my eyes from her for an instant when I'd seen the trio first take notice of her. By the time I'd looked back, she was gone. This confused them as much as it did me, until I understood that she must have vanished to avoid them.

Well and good for you, Nora, I thought, headily relieved I did not have to play the hero after all, and feeling foolish that I'd dared even this much. The lady could take care of herself and had done so for better than a century without any help from me. I went home.

Just before retiring to the cellar for the day, I'd left a note in the consulting room addressed to Jericho instructing him not to come by in the evening, that I'd be over directly upon my awakening. A second note for Elizabeth and Oliver promised them I had news, but it was still not safe to return. Someone apparently found and delivered my missives, for Oliver's home was again a silent place when consciousness returned to me at sunset. I quickly dressed and had a thorough look 'round the street for unsavory loiterers. None were to be seen, but whether that was good or ill remained to be discovered. A short walk convinced me I was not being followed, and taking a quick turn in between some buildings where I would not be observed, I vanished and floated high. The wind was fresh and in the right direction; I rode it like an eagle to Fonteyn House.

"You like it there at Oliver's?" I asked my son.

"Yes, sir."

"What about this place?"

"It's all right, but you weren't here."

I hugged him tight, dangerously close to choking on a lump in my throat. "Well, thank you very much. Tell me what you did today."

"We went rabbit hunting, but didn't catch any, and then I played steeplechase."

"You want to play it again?"

"Yes, please!"

"All right, time to mount up." After a number of complicated moves, involving turning him upside down and sideways—much to his delight—I finally got him on my back. He clamped his arms hard around my neck, and I took solid hold of his legs, then we were off.

Fonteyn House, being much larger than Oliver's, afforded us a longer, more interesting course to follow. At

his whim we galloped through the lengthy halls, chased a
few of the more nimble maids and some of the younger footmen, and otherwise won our combination race and foxhunt.
We ended up in the nursery. Mrs. Howard's supervision of
that area was as competent as ever, for the room was in good
order, warm, and—remarkably for this house—cheerful.
Several candles were alight; certainly they were the most
helpful in chasing off the shadows. In the middle of the floor
lay the square of carpet Richard had insisted on bringing
along. Some toys were scattered over it; I noted with a glad
heart the painted wooden horse among them.

Richard was anxious to show me something, else we'd
have had a second circuit of the house. As soon as I'd put
him down, he pushed the toys out of the way and told me
several times to watch him. I put on an attentive face and
obeyed.

Crouching on all fours at one edge of the carpet, he
tucked his head down and rolled forward, heels over head,
making a complete turn. He looked at me expectantly. I
applauded and told him he was very clever, and if he would
be so kind as to give a second demonstration that I might
admire his performance once more. He immediately
obliged.

After many additional exhibitions of this new skill, he
started to look somewhat red in the face and dizzy, so I
asked if he would teach me how to do it as well. This struck
him most favorably, and he was soon issuing orders like an
army sergeant. I had to position myself just this way, put
my head down just that way—he was quite the expert. Finally I was allowed to roll forward. My long limbs being an
impediment to such games, I tumbled over with a less than
graceful form and crashed flat on my back with a thud. The
noise impressed Richard, so I added to it, wailing that I'd
near broken my spine, and I'd never achieve his expertise at
this game. He said I only wanted more practice, so with
many a groan I tried again, finishing with even more noise.

"Jonathan?"

Still on my back with my head toward the door, I had a topsy-turvy view of Elizabeth looking down at me. Oliver stood behind her, craning his head over her shoulder to see.

"Hallo, sweet sister and most excellent cousin! Oof!" Richard had thrown himself on my stomach.

"He's gone mad," Elizabeth pronounced in solemn tones. "Not stark staring, but God have pity on us all the same."

"Not mad, just somewhat delirious. Oh, you'll tickle me, will you?"

Richard giggled, again digging his fists into my ribs, responding with more laughter when I threatened to pinch his nose off. Fearlessly, he thrust his face forward, daring me to do my worst. I told him it was no sport that way, stood up—with him clinging to one of my legs—and stumped about the room complaining about my astonishingly bad limp. When I was on the carpet once more, he slipped free, laughing, and started to bolt off, but I caught him 'round the waist and lifted him high, which was very well received.

"You'll upset his stomach with all that larking about," Elizabeth cautioned.

"I'm fine!" Richard yelled, rather muffled as his petticoats engulfed his face. By now I held him by his heels, and his arms dangled loose toward the floor.

"Can you walk on your hands?" I asked.

In answer, he put his palms to the floor, and letting him have just enough of his weight to feel it, I paraded once around the room.

"Excellent, laddie! I've never seen better." Reaching the carpet, I eased him down until he lay flat, red-faced, and puffing. He'd catch his breath in a minute, then we'd start all over again.

"What about the Mohocks?" Oliver demanded during the respite. "What happened last night? Did you see Arthur?"

"I saw—well, this isn't the time or place to tell you what happened."

Oliver, interpreting this in the worst possible sense, went pale and grim. "Good God."

"No, I don't mean—that is—I've much to tell you but not about what you think. I just can't say anything until—"

"Quite right," agreed Elizabeth. "You'll get no sense from him until he's had his nightly dose of Richard."

"I'll come to the blue drawing room as soon as I can," I promised.

"Soonest, if you please," she told me with an arch look.

Of course they'd be eaten through with curiosity having waited all night and all day for some word from me. The note would have only stirred them up rather than satisfied. Damnation. I hated having this matter encroaching on my time with Richard.

Time . . .

No. That was yet too dark a topic to think about. Nora was right to live within the short increments of a single night. Considerations of future sorrows could wait until their arrival; best to cherish the present while it was here.

Unfortunately, the present was all too brief. Having little else to do that day, Elizabeth and Oliver had spent most of it keeping Richard fully occupied, or so he informed me when he recounted some of his adventures at rabbit hunting. He'd summoned quite a burst of dash at my coming, but was fast losing hold of it, particularly after a second bout of tumbling over the rug. As an alternative to all the exercise, I offered to read aloud from his collection of chapbooks. One of the maids turned up with a cup of ass's milk with honey for him. Mrs. Howard, who had made herself scarce so we could play unimpeded, must have ordered it. The girl stared at us closely, nearly upsetting her tray while putting it on a table.

"Have a care," I said, schooling myself to patience.

She'd likely noticed Richard's resemblance to me and my own to him and was having trouble dealing with it. Well, Edmond had warned me about this sort of thing. I wearily wondered if I'd end up influencing every servant on the estate just to spare us the complications of gossip. The maid finally scuttled out, with many a backward look. Silly creature.

"Tastes different," Richard said, looking dubiously into his cup.

"That's because it's from the country. The asses here eat better fodder than their city cousins, so their milk is bound to be different. It's not sour, is it?"

"No. Sweet."

"The cook must like you then and put in extra honey in your honor."

I found a chair, settled him on my lap, and read as he drank. Both worked a charm; by the time I was a quarter through the reading, he'd nodded off.

Though I should have rung for Mrs. Howard and popped him into bed, I lingered a bit, holding him.

He was so precious. In every sense of the word and beyond, until words failed, he was the dearest of all the treasures a generous God had ever bestowed upon me. Precious, for his own sake alone, but also for being my son, the only true legacy of my life as a normal man, if not also the most heartbreaking; for if my acquired agelessness proved true, then in all likelihood I would long outlive him. Ahead of me lay the awful prospect I would outlive everyone I loved. Nora's gift was not a mere mixed blessing, but could also rightly be called a curse.

She tried hard to make that clear to me last night.

Once Nora was over the happy surprise of the boy's existence, she went all sober again, finally divulging afresh the grim inevitablity of pending heartache.

"Why are you so anxious to sadden me?" I asked.

"I'm not, but I've lived through this without knowing

any of it and have ever regretted my ignorance. Now that I know better, I do all I can to treasure the time I have with those I love and strongly urge you to do the same. Life is so damnably *fleeting*, and not everyone is able to see how carelessly they squander their little portion of it. Empty mundanities crowd their days, their thoughts, their actions, and before they're aware of it their lives are spent and gone forever. I never waste time in futile argument over trifles, but rather cling to the joys I can share and give however great or small they may be. Never, *never* forget how long your time is compared to the brevity of others.''

So I held my son and there and then said a humble prayer of gratitude for Richard's life, a plea for his continued health and happiness, and asked to be given the wisdom to provide both to him to the best of my ability. My eyes had misted over by the time I got to the *amen*. Sniffing, I rose and gently lay him on his bed, then just watched him sleep for a while. The rise and fall of his breast, the soft patter of his heart, the pure translucence of his skin, all held me in thrall until Mrs. Howard came back from wherever she'd gotten to and asked if all was well.

''Exceedingly well,'' I answered. ''Fell right to sleep on me.''

''He had a very busy day what with the rabbit hunting with Mr. Oliver and Miss Elizabeth. They didn't find any, but I think it was more for the exercise and to pass the time than to put anything on the supper table.''

''I shall have to thank them for looking after him. I should like to hear about the rest of his day, but it will have to wait 'til later.''

''Yes, sir. Will we be returning to Mr. Oliver's house soon?''

''As soon as may be. I thought you liked it in the country, though.''

''Indeed I do, sir. If we could stay on here until your father and mother arrived from the colonies it would suit me well enough.''

But it would hardly suit the rest of us to be deprived of Richard's immediate company. On the other hand, if the Marling estate could be made livable, Mrs. Howard would have her country home within a few months. I kept this news to myself for the moment. Mentioning it would lead to more conversation, and I very much needed to be elsewhere. I wished her a good evening, pressed a light goodnight kiss on Richard's brow, and hurried downstairs.

The next hour was an interesting one for Elizabeth and Oliver as I broke the news to them of Nora's return. Elizabeth jumped up to embrace me, for she saw I was in a mood to rejoice, and Oliver grinned and pounded my back in congratulation. Then did they sit again to ply me with a thousand rapid questions, and I did my best to give good replies.

"In Bath all this time?" Oliver shook his head, bemused. "She must have been living quietly indeed. A number of our circle goes there for the waters. Strange none of 'em saw her."

"Not so strange when you consider she's only up and about at night. It was Mrs. Poole who took the waters, and she's not as noticeable as Nora."

"What was the lady suffering from?"

"Nora didn't say. There was so much else to talk about. . . ."

And I talked about it to them—leaving out, of course, the spritely dances Nora and I had enjoyed on the hearth rug. I also left out the business of not aging, thinking it better to introduce that subject at another time. Having barely taken it in myself, I was not prepared to rationally reveal the details to others. Perhaps Nora could be persuaded to tell them, since she knew more of it.

"What did Nora think about Richard?" Elizabeth asked after I got to that point in my tale.

"Oh, she's very pleased about the whole business.

Thinks it's just wonderful, seeing how things are for me now.'' Thus did I delicately allude to my infertile state.

Elizabeth understood, briefly tucking in her lower lip. ''Is—is she unable to bear children?''

''Sadly, yes.''

''*Sad* is an inadequate word for it, little brother. That poor woman.''

''Unless one considers that I'm something of an offspring of hers,'' I added.

They did, to which Oliver said: ''Very 'something of,' Coz, if the achievement of this condition is as rare as she says.''

''We're hoping your medical knowledge might be helpful in explaining why this is so.''

His eyebrows jumped. ''You do expect a lot from me . . . but I'll do all I can, of course. What did she think of Clarinda, though? I mean about the boy's conception taking place while you and Nora were still . . . well . . . *you* know.''

''She was not jealous if that's what you're worried about. At most she only questioned my taste. But I told her I was after all very young at the time.'' Unspoken was her reply that I was *still* very young.

''That's a relief. You've enough complications in your life already. Did you tell her anything about our recent troubles?''

''Seeing how closely they're connected with Richard, I had to tell her everything about them.''

''What does she think of it?''

''That it's perfectly horrible, and she's all for my clearing the mess up as quickly as possible. She's offered to help if she can, but at this moment I don't see how.''

''She knows plenty of gentlemen in the city. Some of them could secretly be Mohocks, y'know, and have useful information for us.''

''We discussed that very possibility, but she hasn't seen

any of 'em since she left for Italy all that time back. Her offer to help is more in the line of lending any and all aid from her household if we need it. Fonteyn House is ably defended, but it would harm nothing to have some extra eyes and ears about the place until this business is done.''

"Excellent idea. When shall we see 'em?"

"I hadn't really settled that with her, but I can go by and talk with her later.'' Indeed, I was most anxious to see her again. Last night had been a true wonder, but we had much lost time to make up.

"When will she be coming for a visit?'' asked Elizabeth. "Did you tell her how much I wanted to meet her?''

"Yes, I did, and she was a bit taken aback by it, too.''

"Whatever for?''

"This condition of being a 'vampire,' as she calls it, has made her very shy about revealing it to people. Times were when one could be burned at the stake for taking such peculiar nourishment, so you can understand why she's a bit wary. To hear that you not only know of it, but fully accept it is quite much more than a novelty to her. It may take her awhile to get used to the idea, but she expressed a stong interest in meeting Richard, so it shouldn't be very difficult to persuade her to a visit.''

"We'll have a late tea with her or something,'' she said, "with the two of you having your own preferred drink in a separate pot.'' Oliver made a slight choking sound, but she ignored him. "Where is she staying?''

"At her London house.''

"But I thought it was deserted.''

"Not anymore. As soon as she got my note, she came up from Bath in her coach with a few of her people. They'll have the place opened and aired out by now, perhaps not to the point of receiving guests, but they should have the worst of the cobwebs swept away.''

"Admirable, very admirable,'' said Oliver, who was starting to squirm in his chair. "But while I don't wish to belittle the importance of Miss Jones turning up, I shall burst a blood vessel if you don't give us any news about the business at hand. *Did* you talk to Arthur?''

Lest his growing agitation do him harm, I quickly imparted what I'd learned, namely about Arthur Tyne's hasty dissappearance. ''He must have got the wind up once he saw the story of Ridley's murder in the papers,'' I added. ''He's probably halfway to France by now.''

''If he has any sense,'' said Elizabeth. ''What about the Mohocks? Did you see Mr. Litton?''

''Not a sign of them, and I was interrupted by Nora before I could visit the chap. Oh, yes, Edmond came by just before I left to see Arthur.''

''Did he? You have had a busy time of it. What did he want?''

I told them of my conversation with our justifiably ill-tempered cousin at the coffee house. ''He said I could talk to Clarinda to see if she knew more than she was telling. I promised to come by tonight.''

''Will you be influencing her?''

''Only if necessary,'' I hedged.

Elizabeth did not approve of this talent, handy as it was to us all, and she knew what I was trying to avoid discussing with her. ''I rather think it will be very neccessary, so do be careful, Jonathan.''

''Do you want company?'' asked Oliver.

''Not unless you plan to keep Edmond entertained while I'm interviewing his wife.''

''Ulp. Hadn't thought of that, but I'll do it if you—''

I waved him down. ''No need to make such a noble sacrifice just yet, Coz. I'd be glad to have you along, but he was reluctant enough to let me in, and for the both of us to turn up might be more than his temper will bear. Besides, Edmond could heap you with questions neither of us is prepared to answer just yet, if ever. I should be much easier in my heart not to have that possibility as a distrac-

tion while I'm talking with Clarinda, and very much easier
knowing you were on watch here, keeping everyone safe.''

Happily, additional persuasion was not needed. He was
more than pleased to play the guardian and endure another
long wait at Fonteyn House rather than spend even a minute
with the grim Edmond. At my request, Oliver called for
someone to ready a horse for me. Though I could travel
easily enough to Edmond's by the same means I'd used to
get to Fonteyn House, it seemed wiser to use a more mundane form of conveyance. My recent travel combined with
last night's endeavors with Nora had left their physical impression, and I was yet a bit weary despite a full feeding
I'd made after coming back from following her. Later, I'd
have to make up for it. Neither of us would benefit tonight
if I appeared on her doorstep in less than perfect vigor. To
fill in the wait, I asked Elizabeth how the day had gone.

''Most agreeably,'' she said, and I was treated to an en-
gaging summation of the rabbit hunt. It cheered me mightily, until I realized it was yet another activity I could never
share with the boy. Deeply frustrating, but I swallowed it
back along with the dark feelings of regret and disappointment. At least I was here and able to share some things
with him and not long dead and moldering in the churchyard at Glenbriar.

Blessing and curse. As there was no escape from either,
I'd have to accept both.

All the horses in Oliver's stable in town had been taken
away to the safety of the one at Fonteyn House, including
my beloved Rolly. He was very full of himself tonight,
prancing about, hardly able to hold still enough for me to
mount. Once in the saddle, reins firmly in hand, I had better
control over him, but was not adverse to allowing him to
have his head for a short canter to the gates. The two footmen posted on watch there obligingly opened them, allowing us to pass through. If they had any wonder for how I'd

gotten inside in the first place, I heard nothing of it. I waved once to them, clucked at Rolly, and let him stretch his neck.

Floating high over the land is one thing, but it's no substitute for the shivering exhilaration of riding a horse at full gallop. Your life is in your hands, completely dependent on your skill, sense of balance, and sheer luck. A misplaced hoof, an unexpected concavity in your path, a startled bird flying up in your face, these and a hundred other lurking dangers can make for an easy disaster. Rolly and I ignored the lot and sped recklessly down the road, my laughter hanging in the air behind as we cut through the cold night. He was a splendid animal and not for the first time I blessed Father for putting him aboard the ship that had taken me to England.

Eventually, though, even Rolly had enough giddy exercise for the time being and slowed to a cooling walk. I felt the untroubled movement of his breathing with my legs; there was no sweat on his neck. He had miles more travel left in him yet, I judged. He'd recovered beautifully from the sea voyage. He was fit and ready for . . . well, now, there was an interesting speculation to dwell on.

My mind swiftly turned to the prospect of having my own estate courtesy of Oliver's generosity. An estate meant land enough for farming—or husbandry. Certainly the idea of breeding Rolly to some fine English fillies was far more tempting than tilling soil. Profitable, too. The gentry's fondness for horse racing was never better what with the royal enthusiasm for the sport. I had but to raise a single favorite to win one race to make a name for myself and better my fortune.

And there was Richard to consider. He was already showing an early love for horses that could be cultivated into an effortless expertise. What better gift could I bestow upon him than a stableful of assets in a business he might enjoy as a lifelong vocation?

But you're getting ahead of yourself, Johnny Boy. Let

the lad make up his own mind.

True. He was only four. Anything could seize his fancy between now and the time he reached four and twenty—if it was God's will he should live that long.

Live for the present, I firmly reminded myself, lest I grow melancholy again.

Very well. But aside from Richard's possible interest, I'd not hinder my own indulgence for such a pursuit. And if my son wanted to join in on the game, then he'd be more than welcome to do so.

Thus did I occupy myself with pleasant considerations, for their own sake and for the distraction they offered.

I needed it. Every mile closer to Edmond's home brought me back to the dreadful business of Ridley's murder and my own attempted murder. The sweet interlude Nora had given with her presence began to fade from mind and heart, to be replaced by the brutal memory of a masked coward raising a dueler on me with intent to kill.

Of course he was a coward, for only such a man would shoot another in the manner that I'd been shot. If and when I found him, I'd teach him a few hard lessons about the value of honor—if he had wit enough to learn. Doubtless he and his friends would be very much surprised to discover I was yet among the living.

Then there was Ridley's murderer to think about. It couldn't have been Arthur; his actions were those of a frightened man. The Mohocks were unlikely to be involved as well, since they'd been so bent on avenging their fallen leader's death. Someone had killed him and wanted me blamed, and as improbable as it seemed, I wondered if Clarinda had somehow arranged it. If she'd had a falling out with Ridley . . . though how any of it could have been managed with her locked up fast by Edmond I could not imagine.

Unless Edmond was behind it all. If so, then he was a finer actor than even the great Garrick; he'd not been the least startled to see me last night. Besides, what would be his purpose?

No, not Edmond. For lack of solid information I was growing too distrustful, not to mention absurd. A short talk with Clarinda would clear this part of things up, or so I fervently hoped. If nothing else I'd get the names of Ridley's companions from her; between her and Litton, whom I would call on later, I expected to obtain solid information to examine, explore, and put to good use.

I'd never been to Edmond's home, but Oliver had given me precise directions, and I found the gate without trouble just where he said it would be. I looked for and spied two small towers made of white stone with an iron arch connecting them overhead. Had I any lingering hesitancy that I'd come to the wrong place, it was abolished by the name 'Fonteyn' spelled out in the design of the arch.

The gate stood open, something I found to be rather disturbing since I'd been very clear to Edmond about the need to protect himself from attack. I thought he'd taken me seriously, but perhaps with the passage of a day with nothing happening, he'd relaxed his guard.

No. Edmond would not be so foolish. His nature wouldn't allow it. There was something wrong here.

Rolly had cooled enough from the walk so as to not take harm if I tied him up for a while. Dismounting, I led him through the gate and some yards into the property. The trees were thick here, which suited me well. I wrapped his reins around a low branch and, keeping to their cover, furtively moved parallel to the lane leading toward the house.

That structure was not far from the main road. Parts of it had been new when Queen Elizabeth's privateers plied their trade against the Spanish. One of the stories firmly discouraged by Aunt Fonteyn was that prize money from such raids had built it and founded much of the family fortune.

Changing fashion and the passage of time called for improvements to be made by each succeeding generation until one of them had given up altogether and moved elsewhere to build Fonteyn House. Edmond's branch of the family inherited what came to be called Fonteyn Old Hall, and if it lacked a certain freshness of design, it made up for it in history. There was a strong tradition one of the great Elizabeth's ministers had spent the night here, possibly with the lady of the hall while her husband was away fighting the Armada. Aunt Fonteyn had, not unexpectedly, discouraged that story as well, preferring to state it was but a rumor and far more likely Elizabeth herself had been the guest. But as the other legend was more amusing, no one really believed her.

As I came closer I picked out the different architectural styles, one atop the other, each an attempt to obliterate the one below. Sometimes such combinations work; this was not one of those times. No wonder Edmond was such a stick if he had to live in this place. One could only hope the interior was more attractive.

All seemed quiet, but then I wasn't sure what sort of trouble I expected, people running around, waving their arms and shouting perhaps? Not here that I could see. The grounds about the place were serene; lights showed through some of the lower windows as normal as can be. I found one with open curtains and peered into some sort of parlour. No occupants, just an ordinary chamber with too much old furniture. I was tempted to ghost my way inside, but did not relish the prospect of explaining my sudden presence to Edmond or, failing that, influencing him to forgetfulness. If something was seriously wrong, the best way to discover it was to ring the front bell and see what happened.

Except the house had none. Instead, I made use of a massive brass door knocker in the shape of a ship's anchor. With its obvious link to ships and ships to privateering, I'd have wagered that device had given Aunt Fonteyn much annoyance whenever she saw it. The thing clanked like the chains of hell, loud enough to be heard through the whole rambling house.

No one came forth to answer, though. I looked about for a carriage or a horse, for some reason why the gate had been left open. None was present. Perhaps they'd been taken around behind the house. The graveled drive carried the impress of wheels, of course, but I could not tell much more than that. It could have been from Edmond's own carriage for all I knew.

I knocked again, the sharp sound hurting my ears. The house was big, but surely there was some servant lurking close by to answer. I could not imagine Edmond keeping any laggards in his employ. Perhaps I should check around the back. The kitchens and stables would be . . .

The door swung open, cutting short my invasive plans.

The man who answered was not a servant, or so his garb instantly told me. He scrutinized me up and down with a bland eye and invited me in. Stepping past the threshold, I studied him just as closely. Dark clothes of good cut, a well-fitted, well-dressed wig, and a calm, commanding eye marked him as some sort of professional man. Ruddy skinned and a few years older than I, he wore enough Flanders lace to brand him for a dandy, but the frivolous effect was offset by the gravity of his demeanor. He was likely to be a lawyer, then, probably one of Edmond's cronies. He looked to be lately arrived himself, for he still wore his cloak and hat and carried his stick.

"Where is Mr. Fonteyn?" I asked guardedly.

"I was just determining that myself," he replied with an air of puzzled amusement. "We'd had plans to take supper together, but he wasn't available when I arrived. I sent the butler off to find him. My name is Summerhill, by the way," he added with a bow.

"Mr. Barrett," I said, returning the courtesy. His easy manner did much to reassure me. Edmond must have had the gate open in expectation of his visitor. Not a wise thing to do, I thought, planning to mention it to him at the first chance. I'd worked myself into a great worry over nothing.

"Barrett?" Summerhill appeared surprised. "But you're— "

"Yes, Mr. Fonteyn's cousin from America." Thus had I come to introduce myself to those people who had heard my name but were unable to place where they'd heard it. Usually, though, I connected myself with Oliver, not Edmond.

Summerhill took this in with more interest than I thought the subject warranted. I suppose I was growing tired of it. "Well, well, I've not met many Americans," he finally said.

"You're not meeting one now, sir, for I have ever been an Englishman."

"Then you are yet loyal to the King?"

"And like to remain so, sir. My family has no desire to involve themselves with a mob of radical lunatics determined to send themselves to the gallows."

He managed a small laugh. "Then you disagree with this notorious declaration that all men are created equal?"

"There are some points in that document worthy of note, but overall it doesn't even make for a good legal argument. Too many broad and impossible to prove assumptions. Besides, the conflict they started isn't about equality, but their reluctance to pay their lawful taxes. By heavens, if it hadn't been for Pitt's intervention in the war twenty years ago with the French, I might this moment be babbling to you in that language, so I for one don't mind rendering to Caesar his due."

Summerhill laughed again.

I'd given the entry hall a careful look 'round while I spoke, but nothing at all seemed amiss. Part of the original Elizabethan core of the house, its ceiling was a good two stories overhead; this and the walls were heavy with black-stained oak trim and white painted plaster work. Off to the right leading up to a gallery was a steep staircase with a thick balustrade made of the same dark wood. Ponderous furnishings and dim portraits of the long departed lent the room an air of determined respectability. Some walls had obviously been cut into to allow access for later additions, and though all very well kept and polished, it had the same unfortunate cobbled together effect as the exterior. Still, if one was of an optimistic turn of mind, one could say that, in terms of variety, it lacked for nothing.

"Wonder what's keeping that dratted butler?" asked Summerhill.

"I wonder what's keeping Edmond." He'd said nothing last night about having a supper guest, but then why should he?

"Will you be joining us?"

"I think not. I've just some brief things to sort out with him, then I must be away to another appointment."

He grunted. "A pity, I should have enjoyed hearing more of your views on the American situation. It's strange, but I've met many an English gentleman with great sympathy for their cause, yet the ones from America are entirely against it."

I detected a trace of an accent in his speech. "You speak as one who is not from England, sir."

He gave a deprecatory chuckle. "Oh, dear, but my foreign roots betray me again. I was raised by English parents in Brittany, sir, and I fear the mix of heritage and place has left an indelible imprint upon my speech."

Blood rushed to my face. "My apologies, sir. I meant no offence when I spoke to you about the French language a moment ago."

"Not at all, sir. I am not in the least offended, but found it most refreshingly honest and amusing."

That was a relief. "You are too kind, sir. May I inquire how you are acquainted with my cousin?"

"Again, you take me back to my roots. My family has

ever had a connection with shipping. Mr. Fonteyn sees to
the legal necessities of my firm.''

Shipping . . . that would explain Summerhill's ruddy
complexion. The stray idea entered my head that he was a
smuggler and seeing personally to the delivery of a cask or
two of duty-free French brandy to a valued customer.
Thousands of otherwise law-abiding English subjects readily shunned the practice of paying the King's tax on certain
goods, but though I could see Oliver doing it without a
second thought, Edmond would choke himself first. I
tucked the ridiculous notion away with a smile.

"Well, perhaps I should ring for another butler to go
find the first," said Summerhill with a rueful curl to his
mouth. "Not that you are unwelcome company, sir, but I
was looking forward to my meal.''

Reflexively I sniffed the air, but detected no sign of
cooking. Of course, the kitchens were likely to be very
much elsewhere along with their myriad smells, which
suited me well enough. The miasma of cooked food was
not one of my favorites these nights.

"And I should like to get on with my own business," I
added agreeably. "I hope my cousin is not ill." But except
for the healing wounds lingering on his hands, he'd seemed
sufficiently fit last night to take on a bear.

"As do I, but to make sure—''

"Did you hear that?''

Summerhill struck a listening pose in response to my
interruption, then shook his head. "The butler returning, I
should think, and about time.''

Whatever small noise it was that caught my attention
repeated itself. It was very distant, but clear to my acute
hearing. A woman's voice, I finally determined. I looked
expectantly at Summerhill, but he seemed not to have
heard. He shook his head again.

The sound came again and I thought it contained a note
of distress, or anger. Clarinda? God's death, but I thought

Edmond would have the sense to keep her well away from the chance of discovery. Thank goodness Summerhill did not have my sharp ears or some awkward questions might be raised.

Unfortunately, the intrusion of the faint noise left us in a temporary state in which we had nothing to say to each other. So it was that in the pause the sounds insistantly repeated, and this time Summerhill heard them, too.

"I say, that's rather odd. There's something happening up there—" He broke off, his gaze drawn to the top of the stairs.

Now did I hear my mistake, for it was not one woman's voice, but two, both raised to the point of shrillness by some desperate excitement. Though the words were muffled, they were undoubtedly calls for help. Neither voice belonged to Clarinda. I glanced once at Summerhill, then hastened up the stairs with him at my heels. On the landing I paused to listen and determined the calls came from the right-hand branching, but before I could take a step in that direction, something went *crack* and the left side of my head abruptly went numb.

As did my legs, for they ceased to hold me.

As did my arms, for they were unable to break my drop to the floor.

The fall knocked the air from my lungs. I lay still, so wretchedly disoriented I could not for the moment understand what had happened.

Much to my grief, the numbness did not last. It retreated all too quickly before the onslaught of a miserably sharp agony that swelled in my head to the bursting point. The first shock of it left me immobilized, allowing an army of drums to march in and take possession. Their deafening thunder left me on the far side of merely addled. I was helpless to do anything for myself except to sprawl on the polished wood floor and start to groan.

Wood . . . Nora had said we were strangely vulnerable to it.

Summerhill. He'd used his cane on me. Why in God's name had he struck me down?

The booming of the army began to fade, and I made out the thin sound of the women again, their cries frantic, like hungry kittens. Over them I heard a door open, followed by footsteps coming toward me. I felt the vibration of their approach through the floor: a man's heavy boots, moving slowly, and the lighter clatter of a woman's shoes. Both paused not two paces from my inert body.

"All taken care of, as I promised," said Summerhill, as calm as you please.

"Of all the damned inconvenient times for Edmond to have visitors," one of the newcomers snarled.

A singularly unpleasant thrill of alarm rushed through me as I recognized the man's voice. Arthur Tyne?

The woman uttered a soft curse in agreement. Clarinda. God Almighty. What *had* I walked into?

CHAPTER
-11-

Clarinda spoke again. "That's not any visitor—that's Jonathan Barrett!"

"Impossible," said Arthur.

"But it is. See the hair—he never wears a wig."

"It cannot be," he insisted.

"Then turn him over and prove me wrong."

Hands seized one of my shoulders and I was roughly flipped around. This mistreatment was nearly too much for me. Unpleasant as it was, I fought to stay conscious and won . . . barely. Groggily and past half-closed lids I made out their looming forms: Clarinda on the left, Arthur on the right. Arthur's expression was a study in bald-faced astonishment.

"But Litton told me he was dead! He saw Royce shoot him. Got him square in the chest."

"Then he killed another man or simply missed."

"But he was absolutely certain, boasted about there being blood everywhere."

"Perhaps you'd care to bring your friend 'round here for a nice debate," suggested Summerhill dryly, catching Arthur's reluctant attention. "I got him for you. What do you want done with him?"

This induced a lively discussion. Of all the people who might have paid a call on Edmond, I was certainly the last one they expected. Arthur continued to gnaw on about how I'd escaped getting murdered at Mandy Winkle's; Clarinda cared nothing for such details, however, being more concerned with present problems over past failures.

"What in God's name is he doing here?" she wanted to know.

"Come to visit Edmond about your brat, I expect," said Arthur, having provisionally accepted the undeniable. He continued to stare unhappily at me as though I might vanish and pop up again elsewhere to plague him. Oh, would that I could.

"Unless it's about Thomas."

"How could that be?"

"You were closest to him," she reminded. "They're neither of them fools. They'd expect you to know best who would have—"

"Never mind that," he said sharply, his face going dark as he glanced at Summerhill. "The good captain has asked what's to be done about Barrett and time is passing."

Clarinda looked me right in the eye, as appraising as a butcher considering the best way to chop up a carcass. "Can't leave him alive," she concluded. "He knows who tried to kill him now."

Arthur nodded. "Very well. I'll see to it, and this time it'll be done right. Have you found that chest yet? Then get on with it. Captain, would you be so kind as to assist her?"

This last was addressed to Summerhill. My fancy must have been right. He probably was a smuggler, but come up from his ship not with illicit cargo, but to convey two important passengers off to a safe port. He'd calmly stood to one side, listening, but not interfering with their talk. He offered no comment one way or another at Clarinda's suggestion to kill me and bowed slightly in polite acquiescence to Arthur's request.

Husbanding my strength, I continued to remain quiet until Clarinda and Summerhill were gone. They hurried off up the right-hand hall where I could yet discern faint cries for help.

"And tell those wenches to stop that row!" Arthur called after them. A moment later I heard Summerhill gruffly rumble something in a threatening tone, and the cries abruptly ceased.

"Where's Edmond?" I croaked, having summoned enough of myself together to do so.

He hadn't expected me to speak. His gaze fixed on me, half-contemptuous, half-incredulous, and wholly cold. He looked very pale yet from our previous encounter and used his walking stick as though he needed it for balance, not affectation. "He's none of your concern."

"Where is he?"

His answer was a jolting dig to my ribs with one toe. His riding boots, I discovered, were made of a very sturdy type of leather. I grunted unhappily. The sudden jar reminded me all too clearly of my bursting head. Overcome for the moment, I could do nothing for myself. I'd just have to wait until the worst of it passed away; then might I be able to settle things between us more to my satisfaction.

Arthur eased down on one knee next to me. His expression was wary, but with curiosity rapidly overwhelming his caution. "Who was it that Royce killed in the brothel?" he demanded.

"He killed no one. He missed," I said through my teeth. It would do no harm to repeat the story and might just undermine any confidence Arthur may have had for his tools.

"But Litton had been so *sure*."

How good to know for certain the names of two of my attackers. Litton and Royce. Shouldn't be hard to find the third one once I spoke to either of the others. *If* I got out of this. "Probably lied to you or was drunk. Does Clarinda know you killed Ridley?"

His face went all stony, but he might as well have grinned and nodded in affirmation.

"It was her idea."

I had wondered if she'd arranged it and should not have been surprised, but was; I should not have been sickened, but felt a twist in my vitals nonetheless. "How could you murder your own cousin?"

He snorted. "Oh, he was a useful ox, very good for some kinds of work, but in the way for others."

"But Clarinda was going to marry him."

He laughed. "He thought so, too. Had himself well convinced that a woman like her would settle for a brainless brute like himself. When pigs fly—perhaps."

"But she was locked up . . . how . . . ?"

"Edmond's servants aren't all that loyal or rich. It's amazing how much a few shillings can buy from the right person. Why did you come here?"

"Your cousin was murdered, your friends try to kill me, then you run away—or appear to—Clarinda was the handiest one to question."

"You'd have got nothing from her. How did you know I'd run away?"

"Went by your house last night. Your butler told me everything."

"Couldn't have been all that much or you wouldn't have walked in here as you did."

Indeed, I thought with vast self-disgust for having turned my back on the ingenuous-seeming Summerhill. My head fairly burned along one side where he'd struck. I wanted to vanish and heal, but knew it was too soon for that. A little more rest, or even better, some fresh blood would ease me. It wasn't as bad as the last time this had happened; I was sure the bone hadn't been cracked open again, but it was quite bad enough. I had to keep Arthur talking, postponing whatever it was he planned to do to me until I was ready to deal with him and the others. "Your own loyal retainers are all gone," I said. "They picked your place clean."

He made a throwing-away gesture. "I expected as much, but it suits me. Because of it they'll not be volunteering to talk with the magistrates for fear of hanging as thieves. I took what I needed and left them to it. Now I can quietly disappear."

"With Clarinda?"

"And Edmond's money."

"Tired of living on a quarterly allowance from your parents?" I hazarded, getting a sneer for a reply. "Or perhaps you'd hoped to take the whole Fonteyn fortune if Clarinda had gotten her way with things the first time."

"I'll settle for Edmond's money chest, if the damned vixen can find it." He peered down the hall where she'd gone with Summerhill.

"Why not ask Edmond about it? Where is he?" I demanded.

But Arthur made no answer.

What in God's name had they done with Edmond? My heart sank rapidly, weighed down by the most wretched of conclusions. "What about Ridley?" I asked, hoping a change of subject might draw him out. "There was no need to kill him."

"That depends on your need. Poor Thomas was no good to us anymore; he lost all belly for the task at hand and became completely useless as well as an inconvenient witness. He'd have raised a stink about Clarinda running off with me, too. But to have him dead and you getting the blame for it was sweet. Why should you care for him? He tried his best to kill you."

He waited in vain for a reply. If he couldn't understand my horror, then I'd never be able to explain it to him.

After a moment he shrugged slightly. "Thought you'd have been taken into custody by now, anyway. Who did you bribe?"

"No one. I found the letter about me in his pocket."

His eyes flashed wide. "Did you, now? Very mettlesome of you, I'm sure, pawing through a dead man's clothes."

"Better than cutting throats. You tricked him into writing it, didn't you?"

"It wasn't too hard. When Litton and the others found him first and bolted after you, I thought it wouldn't be necessary. Pity that you've more lives than a cat. Where is the letter?"

"Burned," I said truthfully.

"No matter. It was still a clever bit of business to put you out of the way and disgrace Edmond's precious family. Too bad for you that you did find it, else you'd be safe in a cell right now instead of here."

That sounded ominous, for I was still in a poor state for winning a physical contest.

After a moment's hard staring, he grabbed my right arm. I could offer no resistance. He pushed back my coat and shirtsleeve, exposing the skin, eyeing it closely. "I *know* I caught you there with my blade," he muttered through his teeth. "I *felt* it. You bled like a pig. Where is the wound?"

"You dreamed it," I said, hardly putting breath to the words.

"*Dreamed?* No, not that. You were half dead when . . . thought you were dead, then you came out of the mausoleum and . . . and . . ." His face crimped as he tried to remember, but he'd been safely unconscious when necessity had forced me to take his blood that night. The temptation to do it again rose in me, but I wasn't quite able act upon it.

"Dream," I murmured.

"Dream indeed, and one of your making. You tried to make it seem so in my mind, to change things." Arthur leaned close, his voice dropping to a whisper. "*What did you do to Thomas?*"

I'd have shaken my head pretending not to take his

meaning, but knew better than to try. He'd not have believed me, and it would have hurt too much to move. Instead, I stared hard at him, trying to summon enough will
to influence. Our gazes locked for a little time. I felt him
wavering as I pushed, but the struggle went awry. Even as
his eyes began to go flat and blank, an appalling pain knifed
through my head. The harder I tried to exert my will, the
more deeply it carved until I could stand it no longer. On
the edge of passing out, I broke off with a sob of frustration
and agony.

Released so abruptly, Arthur wrenched away, then clum-
sily scrambled to his feet. He was much paler than before,
sweating and panting like an animal.

"Trying to do it again? You damned bastard!" He raised
his cane and gave me a vicious stab in the stomach with
the base end. My breath hissed out, and I twisted onto my
side, curling nearly double. I waited in dreadful apprehen-
sion and hurt for another blow to fall, but he held back.
Not out of mercy, I thought when I next dared to look, but
from weariness. He'd gone gray faced and labored hard for
his breath. I likely shared his appearance, but without the
desperate need for air. Even so, I wasn't able to move
much, not yet.

"What *is* that?" he snarled. "You must have done it to
Thomas, and I know you used it on me after the funeral."

Indeed. And *why* hadn't it worked on him?

"Is that what you did to turn him on us? Is it?"

Arthur's blood loss keeping him muddled, the laudanum
they'd given him, either might account for my failure to
successfully influence him. That or he was mad. I should
have foreseen this; I should have attended to him sooner
and not let myself get distracted.

"What are you?" he demanded, voice rising.

A vampire, I thought. *And a damned tired one*. I wished
Nora here. She could take care of this lout without much
effort.

"*What are you?*"

He looked ready to kill me right there and then. The mix of terror and malevolence on his drawn face was an awful sight, the force of his emotions striking me almost as solidly as his cane. All I could hope for now was one good chance to somehow seize him and drag him down to a more primitive level of conflict. Even in this injured state, I was still stronger than most men. Out of pure desperation I might be able to manage, but he'd backed well out of my reach, cursing me.

Footsteps. Summerhill's long stride, Clarinda's quick pace. Damn, damn, *damnation* to them all.

Clarinda paused in the hall doorway. "What's the matter?" she asked of Arthur.

"Nothing," he snapped, straightening with a visible effort. "Where's the chest?"

"I found it, but it's empty. My bastard of a husband hid his money elsewhere."

"*What!*" This was a grievous blow for Arthur, worse than any I might have given him. He fairly fell against one wall, needing its support.

"It could be anywhere in this house," she went on. "We could look all night and not find it or my jewels. He might have taken it to his bankers or even hidden it at Fonteyn House or with that dunce Oliver—"

Arthur started to rant to the best of his limited ability, but Clarinda forcefully interrupted.

"Don't break a blood vessel, you fool! I've thought of a way around it!"

"Have you now? And what will you do, raise your damned husband from the dead and ask him nicely if you please?"

"That's no fault of mine. If you hadn't been so impatient to be rid of him—"

"If he hadn't tried to shoot me—"

Edmond . . . oh, God.

"A moment, if you please," said Summerhill calmly with a tilt of his head. Such was his air of command that the two of them stopped bickering long enough to glare at him. "Very good. Now, sir, Mrs. Fonteyn anticipated something like this might happen and prepared for it. I would recommend you hear her out."

"What is it, then?" Arthur barked at her.

His temper did not sit well with sweet Clarinda. She closed her mouth tight.

Summerhill intervened once more. "I believe there was a cabinet full of spirits in one of the downstairs rooms. Mr. Tyne looks in need of a restorative, and it may put him in a better mood to listen, dear lady."

The practicality of the suggestion won their grudging agreement to act upon it. Arthur, leaning heavily on the banister, began his descent. Clarinda followed a moment later, picking up her skirts as she delicately stepped around me.

"Where's Edmond?" I asked Summerhill when they'd gone. Damnation, but I sounded hatefully weak. My effort to influence Arthur had drained me to the dregs.

He glanced down. "Away behind the house. Not to worry, someone's bound to sniff him out after the spring thaw. We'd put you in the same spot, but that would look just a little too suspicious. Once just might be thought an accident, but twice . . ." He lifted a hand, palm out.

"Killing me will only put you all into more trouble," I whispered.

"Really?"

"I've no solid proof against Arthur about Ridley, so I'm no danger to any of you."

"I'm in no danger anyway, not with a dozen of my lads willing to swear themselves blue in the face on a Bible on my behalf."

His crew? I'd speculate later. "Leaving me here won't harm you. Tyne's just running off with another man's wife;

no one will pay much mind to that. But kill me and people will blame it on him or Clarinda or both with you as an accomplice. You can't afford the hue and cry of murder to be following you everywhere.''

"No one will blame any of us for your death, because it will really be just a tragic accident. Two in one night might cause some comment, but I think we can take that chance— or rather they will, since I'm not officially here.''

"Smuggler?''

"Merely a gentleman who advocates the practice of free trade between nations.''

"Especially if it profits you.''

"Particularly when it profits me.''

"I'll double whatever they're paying you.''

His eyebrows went up. "That would be a princely sum, but I'm a man of my word and I have given it to—''

"Triple.''

He blinked, then shook his head. "Tempting, Mr. Barrett, but if all goes well, even that ransom will seem but a trifle to the bounty we'll be collecting from the whole of your family.''

"What are you planning?''

"Not I, but the redoubtable Mrs. Fonteyn.''

"What is—''

"Soothe yourself, sir. It's nothing you ever need worry about. Now say a prayer for your soul like a good chap while you yet have the time.'' He quickly stooped and caught hold of my ankles, dragging me toward the edge of the stairs. "Mrs. Fonteyn thought Mr. Tyne might not be up to the labor of it yet—he's still feeling pretty thin—so she asked me to see to things. I've no personal grudge against you, this is just business, y'know.''

Realizing what he had in mind, panic took over. I started to kick and struggle, putting up enough of a fight to inconvenience him. He let go, and with a deft move, gave me another bitter tap on the side of my head with his cane.

Lights flashed between my eyes and the rest of the world. I heard myself pant out a last breath. My body went utterly limp.

He got a strong grip under my arms and with a great heave hauled me upright. I was maddeningly helpless. The room lurched. Sickness clawed at my belly, threatening to turn it inside out. I couldn't even gulp to hold back the rising vomit.

My legs were useless; my arms dangled loose. I had a hideous, dizzying view of the steep stairs and the entry hall miles below.

"There now," said Summerhill comfortingly into my ear as he swung me into place. "At least it'll be quick, and that's more than most of us get." He planted a firm hand in the small of my back and pushed for all he was worth.

I was flying in open space for an instant. Almost like those times when I floated.

The room tumbled madly. Almost like my game with Richard.

Then something struck me lethally hard all over my shoulders and back, like a hundred Summerhills attacking me not with mere canes but with clubs. I heard thuds and thumps, a pain-filled cry, cut short . . . then nothing at all.

Mr. Barrett lay still as stone at the foot of the stairs, his body as beyond movement as his mind was beyond thought.

His head was at an unnatural angle in regard to his neck; one of his arms was also bent in an abnormal manner under him. Some distant and restive portion of his brain was very aware of these and other, lesser injuries, but unable to do more than simply recognize their existence.

His enemies were gone.

The house around him was deadly quiet.

A lifetime crawled by before his eyelids briefly fluttered. He got a vague glimpse of black-stained wood steps stretching upward into cold darkness. Try as he might, he could not open his eyes again. It seemed an important thing to do, though he could not recall why.

After another lifetime the fingers of his unbroken arm shivered once. He'd not consciously initiated the faint movement, but felt its occurrence. When he attempted to repeat it, a white hot spike of lightning shot through his neck, forcing an unwelcome wakening upon his battered flesh. He tried to retreat back to the kind sanctuary of unconsciousness, but the pain followed, tenacious as a shadow, not permitting him any such mercy. He'd have whimpered a protest had there been air in his lungs. His fingers twitched again instead.

With them he felt the cold hard surface of the floor he sprawled over and slowly came to understand his circumstance.

He was in serious trouble.

And being quite alone now, he could expect no help.

That terrified him, the aloneness.

But he had family, friends, even a stranger on the road would be moved by pity to lend him aid. None of them was present, though, or likely to come.

Internal protests against this unfairness rose, fell, and died, but not the self-reproach. That whipped at him with a sting like sleet, unrelenting.

The aloneness worsened every ache and agony afflicting him. It made the prospect of escaping them doubtful. It drained away what little strength remained in him. Even silently praying for simple comfort seemed too great a labor to dare.

But not weeping. That he could not control. The hurts of his body demanded tears, and they flowed over his face, burning like acid.

Then he heard his own drawn-out moan of despair and thought what an altogether wretched fellow he'd become. He was less a mass of pain from all the injuries than a mass of self-pity from the misery of his own heart, certainly not the sort of son his father could take pride in and not the sort of father his own son could admire.

And unless he sorted himself out, he wouldn't see either of them or anyone else ever again.

I came fully and unhappily alert. The half dreams, half nightmares fled, leaving nothing of themselves behind except an earnest need to overcome the hopelessness they'd engendered. If the people I loved were not here, then by God I'd just have to go to them.

Somehow.

Any movement was a torment, especially movement associated with my head and neck. There was something appallingly wrong in that area, and I was fearful of making it worse. By comparison, my broken arm and assorted bruises were nothing. That damned Summerhill had thrown me around like a sack of grain and with about as much consideration. When I got my hands on him . . .

Anger helped. I drew it to me, held it fast, fed on the strength of it until it filled me, became *my* strength. There was an astonishing amount of it . . . for *them.*

Arthur Tyne. Ruthless cutthroat. Not for long. He'd wish himself dead before I was finished with him.

Clarinda. Unrepentant murderer. Instigator of all that had happened to me. Guilty mother of my innocent son. I'd bring her back and take poor Edmond's place as her jailer and be glad of the privilege.

The anger flared to fury, warming me, quickening bone, muscle, and nerve.

And for a very brief moment, it displaced the devastating agony.

I seized the chance while it lasted.

Inside, I felt a shuddering swoop, as though falling again. Something harsh blasted through my vitals like a frost-charged wind. It scoured me from end to end. The sharp edges of the world swiftly twisted, suddenly faded. I'd have cried out, but suddenly had no voice for my fear and pain.

Then it was over.

I was sightless, weightless, formless.

Without a solid body to cling to, to torture, the pain lifted and floated away, even as I floated above the floor.

I was free.

And tired. The effort to let go of the physical world had cost me and would surely cost more when I came back to it, but for now I reveled in the blessed liberty of this discarnate form. Whatever bones had been broken, whatever flesh had been torn, it didn't matter now. All would be whole again when it was time to return.

Sweet it was, and great was my desire to stay like this, but I had things to do or at least to attempt. Giving the alarm about Clarinda's escape was the most important— but only after I'd fed myself. Even in this state every portion of my being cried out for the nourishment of fresh blood and plenty of it. I'd have to find the stables.

Tentatively I made myself stretch forth.

Using the stairs as a landmark, I pushed away from them in the general direction of the front door. Soon I bumped against the opposite wall and felt for openings with whatever it was that now served me as hands. I could have tried materializing just enough to allow me some vision, but was uncertain of my ability to maintain the careful balance needed to hold to that partial condition. Instinct told me not to take that chance, lest I grow abruptly solid and be too feeble to vanish again. Bad luck for me if I did and found the door locked.

An opening, long and very thin, presented itself to my questing senses—the slender crack between the door and the threshold. I dived for it, pouring through like a river mist. It seemed to take forever.

Outside.

I felt the familiar gentle tug of the wind and rode it,

letting it carry me along the front of the house. Keeping the building's fixed contours on my left, I turned one corner, then another, trying to remember what I'd seen of the place when I'd initially approached it. One wing, two? The track of carriage wheels in the gravel drive had been to the left, but how far? Easy as this form of travel was, I'd have to give it up before getting lost.

I found a clear space and tried a partial reformation, but alas, my instinct had been right. Once begun, the process continued unstoppable until I was standing fully solid again.

Standing, but that changed quickly and with no warning; I dropped to my hands and knees, weak as a babe. Normally I hardly noticed the cold; now its talons gouged deep and held fast. I was hatless and with no cloak, having lost both in the house. The wind wasn't high, but more than enough to inspire me to movement again.

I'd come fully around to the back of the house and was not far from the drive. Its gravel path broadened until it covered most of the yard, but some places were thin, allowing muddy patches churned up by wheels and hooves to show through. The tracks could have come from whatever conveyance they'd used. My guess was—since the doors to an empty carriage house gaped wide—they'd taken Edmond's for their escape.

Where was he?

No one was immediately in sight; I saw only the various outbuildings and yard clutter one would expect to find for such a household. Summerhill had said the body was hidden in some way and that the death might look like an accident. Perhaps in the barn or the stables . . . but I had no time or desire to look. With the return to solidity came also the unimpaired resumption of physical need.

My corner teeth were well out and ready. I was ravenous.

Driven by the hunger, I got to my feet and reeled toward the stables. I could hear and smell the horses remaining

there, then I was at the nearest door and saw a half dozen
of them in their stalls. A few were curious, heads turned,
ears twitched; others dozed on their feet. I went to the closest, a bay gelding with a drowsy eye. He hardly reacted
when I slipped into his stall, and barely noticed when I
knelt and cut into the vein of his near leg.

The stuff fair streamed into my mouth. I gulped and guz-
zled, swilling it down like a drunkard with his day's first
bottle of gin. Its glad warmth, its taste, its strength *flooded*
through my hollow form, easing the last aches, healing the
lingering bruises. The chill air around me retreated before
this pulsing onslaught of hot, red life.

I drank deeply, vanished, and drank again until I was
quite filled to the brim.

Then I had to lean on the horse, fold my arms over his
back, and bury my head in them. The heavy beat of his
heart coming up through his solid frame was a welcome
comfort to my battered senses and soul. After all the abuse,
I needed to touch something that bore no ill will against
me, something to remind me that not all the world was evil.
The big animal snuffled once and shoved his nose into the
hay manger, supremely indifferent to my little concerns. I
liked him for that.

It could not and did not last long, but I needed only a
moment or two.

Encroaching upon my respite was the need for haste.

Even as I reluctantly straightened, I felt the fresh blood
had revived more than just my body. Plans for what to do
were popping into my head, demanding attention. I'd have
to find Rolly—heavens, I'd have to find the servants here,
if any were left. Surely not all of them had been bribed
into betrayal. . . .

Dear God, I'd have to find Edmond. What had they done
to him?

The anger for Clarinda and the others that had saved me
before flared up once again. It burned bright and hot, closer

than my own skin. In time, I'd hunt down and deal with the lot of them, this I promised myself.

I'd start with a search of the house and gather allies and information.

Those cries I'd heard must have been from two of the maids. Locked up somewhere, amd no doubt quite miserable over it by now. There had to be others as well, but before looking for them I'd have to clean myself, having not been particularly neat in my feeding this time. Appearance would have to take precedence over all else for the moment. The drying crusts of blood around my mouth might alarm the servants here far more than their imprisonment.

I quit the stables and went straight to the low rectangular structure in the yard that marked the well. The shape of the thing was disturbingly like a grave, being two yards long and over a yard wide. Its brick sides rose about a foot past the ground, the opening neatly covered by six-inch-thick oak timbers. A square cut into their middle was covered by a stout plank lid fitted with a lifting knob and simple latch lock. Fixed above was a sturdy winch and rope mechanism and the cranking handle, all polished by frequent use.

The lid was pushed up and open, with the bucket already at the bottom, which struck me as odd, not to mention dangerous, but that would save me from having to do the work. I put a hand to the crank and tried to give it a turn. It moved only a little way, then mysteriously stopped. The crank was free of obstructions; perhaps the rope or bucket had gotten entangled on something. I caught at the rope and tugged. It gave but a little. I pulled hard, and it reluctantly came up a few inches then sank again when the weight at the other end became too much. Far below I heard a soft splash . . . and a voice . . . a faint, faint voice?

Someone's bound to sniff him out after the spring thaw. We'd put you in the same spot, but that would look just a little too suspicious. Once is an accident, but twice . . .

Unbidden, Summerhill's words ripped through my brain; gooseflesh erupted over all my body. Oh, my God, *what* had those monsters done?

Bending dangerously over the edge of the opening I bawled Edmond's name into the blackness. I could see nothing inside. The natural light from the sky was blocked by my own form and hindered by the depth of the shaft. I *thought* I heard a reply to my calls, but it could have been my own echoes. Hope and horror seized me. I stood and stared wildly about the yard and toward the house. Help might be there, but I couldn't take the time to go looking for it. Could I do something myself? Possibly. But—and I shrank from the thought—could I even bring myself to *try*?

The inky square of the opening looked like a gaping mouth, seeming to eat all the ambient light. My acquired fear of little dark places came roaring up in my mind like a storm, paralyzing me with its thunderous force. Waking in a buried coffin seemed but a triviality compared to descent into this hellhole. Here was a place where darkness was conceived, born, lived, and thrived, devouring everything that came near it. Though fully aware that very little could ever really hurt me, imagination was the great enemy here, striking hard at my weakness. The reproachful awareness of my own vast abilities made the weakness even worse. I was a hopeless coward, dooming my poor cousin to a hideous death because I was too white-livered to— *Enough, Johnny Boy. Stop whining and just get on with it.*

I allowed myself one uncurbed sob of pure shuddering terror, then brutally pushed it away. It rolled up into a ball of ice somewhere between my throat and belly and held in place, trembling, but out of the way.

My mind was clear. Now, what to do?

The winch mechanism presented an obvious solution. Quickly I made some slack by letting out the rope to the end of its length, praying this would work. Making myself go nearly transparent, I floated up over the short wall, and drifted inside the black mouth.

The wind ceased after a few feet. My sight, ever limited in this form, perceived nothing but darkness unless I looked up. The square opening above grew uncomfortably small. Every foot I went down was worse than the last, but I forced myself on. If Edmond was here and alive, his need far outweighed my childish dreads.

I moved blindly now. My ghostly hands could just sense the impression of the bricks lining the walls and the rope in front of me. Then I was aware of the water immediately below. I reached down toward it, trying to find him. Heart in my mouth, I had the sudden hope that he wasn't here at all, that I'd made a hasty conclusion based on an error, that I could leave this awful place and . . .

An object. Large. Bobbing heavily in the water.

And, unmistakably now, someone's faint moan.

I caught at the rope without thinking. My hand passed through it. Damnation. There was no way around it; I'd have to go in, too, to get to him. Making myself more solid, I sank ever lower. First my feet touched the water, then did it creep up my legs and waist like grim death. Free-flowing streams were always a problem for me, but this tamer stuff was still perversely malignant. With cold. With excruciating, mind-numbing, body-killing *cold*.

Completely solid, my weight bore me right into it—and briefly under. Black on black, freezing, smothering, it closed right over me, shutting out everything. Disoriented, I lashed out wildly to find the surface, cracking a hand against a slimed wall. It hurt, but the pain jarred me out of the impending hysteria. I *forced* myself to hold still until natural buoyancy made me sure of my direction. A push, then my head broke free of the water. I spat and blew the stuff from my nose and mouth, sucking in cold, dank air I did not need, but instinct was trying to drive me here, not intellect. Indeed, I was very hard-pressed to maintain a solid form under these adverse conditions and had to fight an impulsive reaction to vanish again and escape.

Kicking to keep afloat, I cast frantically about for the rope, blessed link to the world above. My hands slapped instead against sodden material. My fingers closed on I know not what.

"Edmond?"

No reply.

If I could only *see*. I felt around, then unexpectedly touched flesh. It was his hand, and it was holding hard to the only other thing floating in this pit, the wooden bucket. There was no warmth to him, but that meant little enough in a place like this. Tracing up his arm, I found his face. It was above water, but only just. With all the splashing and distorting echoes I couldn't discern anything as subtle as his heartbeat or breathing. The moan I'd heard was proof enough of lingering life, though.

Trying not to disturb his grip on the bucket, I found its handle, then the chain on the handle, then the rope tied to the chain. The slack was all around me I was sure, but drifting and dangerous if it should twist about us in the wrong way.

I drew rope through my grasp like a fat thread through a needle until I came down to the knots that tied it to the bucket's chain. Fumbling badly from the cold and fright, I got my folding penknife from its usual pocket, clutching it hard lest I drop it. Carefully, with rapidly deadening fingers, I opened it. I made a loop in the rope and began sawing desperately away at it with the blade. The soaked fibers were thick, tough, and I was uncertain about the sharpness of my tool. But just as frustration set in and I began to think my teeth would do a better job, the thing finally parted.

Cramming the open knife back into a pocket, I crowded close to Edmond. Another loop, larger, this time threading the rope under his arms and around his back. Not easy, he kept trying to drift away from me, and all the time I was trying to keep both our heads above water. Though in no danger for lack of air, I'd be damned before I let that utter blackness close over me again.

I made several knots centered over his chest, talking to him, babbling out waterlogged assurances that everything would be all right and not to worry and God knows what other nonsense. Perhaps it was more for my benefit than his. He made no sound or response; I still couldn't see a damned thing, and was rapidly losing my sense of touch.

One last knot. Time and past time to leave. With a singular lack of control I disappeared completely and shot up from the well like a ball from a pistol barrel. The little protective roof was in my way, and though it slowed me somewhat I'd sieved right through it before regaining command of myself. In too much of a hurry to be vexed, I touched upon the earth and went solid again.

Water running from my clothes, I put both hands on the well crank and began turning. Easy at first as it took up all the slack, it halted as Edmond's weight became part of the load. I prayed the thing would support him and put my back into the work. Round and round, with the wood creaking, the rope coiling about the dowel, and my heart in my mouth, I pulled him slowly up, trying not to think of all the things that could go wrong.

Then from the square of darkness his head emerged. It lolled backward, jaw sagging; there was a nasty-looking graze seeping red along one side of his scalp. I looked away and gave another turn on the crank until his shoulders were visible. He swung to and fro ponderously, a man on a gibbet. Not trusting the ratchet pawl to hold, I reached across with one hand while bracing the crank with the other as he swung toward me again. I snaked my arm under his and around his chest, then let go of the crank. He abruptly slumped away, threatening to drop back in. I got my other arm around him just in time and *pulled*.

It was a hard hauling. He was a big bear of a man, wet

right through, and utterly motionless. His clothes snagged on the sides of the opening. I heaved him as high as I could and finally lugged him past the edge. He'd have scrapes and bruises—if he lived. I lay him flat on the cold ground and pressed an ear against his chest. For a terrible moment I heard nothing, then nearly crowed with relief when a near indistinct *thump* announced he was still on this side of the veil.

Determined to keep him here, I slapped his white face, shouting at him to wake up. He was past responding, though, and not like to do so soon unless I got him out of this winter air and inside near a fire. More lifting and dragging, this time toward what I hoped was the scullery door. Cursing like a heathen, I had to stop once to find the knife again and cut him free of the rope. It had played out like a leash and we'd reached its limit.

The door did turn out to be the scullery entry and had been left unlocked. Clarinda and the others must have come this way to get to the carriage house. That simplified things. I pulled Edmond up the step and inside, bulling through to the kitchen. My hope was that like other kitchens this would be the warmest room in the house owing to the need for a constant fire. Hope was fulfilled, I saw, when I blundered inside with my burden. For once I was glad to have the stink of cooked food assaulting my senses.

The fire here was little more than a mass of glowing coals, but easily remedied. I lay Edmond on the still warm stones of the hearth and threw on fresh dry kindling, knocking over the fire tongs and other things in my shivering haste.

The noise attracted notice. I heard a sudden loud banging and a chorus of calls for help coming from behind a solid-looking bolted door.

Edmond's missing servants.

It's amazing how much calamity can be turned about in a quarter hour's time. And what a wonderful, luxuriously

wonderful relief it is to turn one's cares over to others and
let them deal with the work.

Most of Edmond's people had been closed up in one of
the pantries, except for two women who were soon found
shut away in an upstairs cupboard. Fortunately, the pantry
door had been bolted, not locked with a key, so I soon had
everyone else out, blinking in the growing firelight after
being in the dark and asking a hundred questions at once.
All were agitated in one form or another from red-faced
anger to teary-eyed fear, but were otherwise no worse for
wear. I determined a middle-aged woman named Kellway
was in charge of them, told her who I was, and after one
glimpse at her master's desperate condition she forgot all
about her own difficulties. She instantly set things in motion, shouting out orders for brandy, bandaging, blankets,
and hot water, sending people scurrying off in every direction.

Evicting all female members of her staff but herself from
the kitchen, she commanded two of the footmen to strip off
Edmond's wet clothes. By the time things reached the point
where she would be forced to leave as well the blankets
arrived, preserving decorum. She made me strip down, also,
which I did not mind, and questioned me closely over what
had happened, which I did mind. It worried me at how
easily I was given to lying and improvisation when forced
to by the demands of an uncomfortable situation. Hardly
honorable, but certainly necessary.

Wrapped in dry blankets and with a perfectly smooth
face I told of my appointment with Edmond and of being
surprised by Summerhill and knocked unconscious.

"I woke up lying on the ground next to the well. In want
of water to ease my injury, I tried to draw some, then discovered Mr. Fonteyn was inside."

A general murmur of dismay went around.

"He'd tied the rope about himself to stay afloat, so I
managed to haul him up. The poor man collapsed just as I
got him out."

This inspired a general murmur of approval. Considering my cowardly delay in getting started, I did not allow myself to bask in their admiration.

"But how did you get so wet, sir?" one of them asked, having observed my own drenched and half frozen condition. I'd been far too thoroughly saturated for them to think I'd gotten in such a state merely from dragging Edmond around. At least the immersion had cleaned all the blood from my face.

"The bucket came up with him and was full of water. When I cut him free of the rope the damned thing tipped and slopped it all over me, then fell back into the well." I left it to their imaginations to work out just how that kind of clumsiness could have possibly happened. "You'll want a replacement."

"God bless you, sir, as if we cared about an old bucket," said Mrs. Kellway, wiping tears from her eyes before bellowing at a distracted scullery boy to keep heaping wood on the fire.

Indeed, but I wanted to account for everything. They might well have suspected me of being in on the foul deed, after all.

While Mrs. Kellway gently dabbed salve on Edmond's head wound and bandaged it, I learned from them that Summerhill, Tyne, and two men dressed like sailors had suddenly appeared in the house, brandishing pistols, then smartly locked everyone up. Not long afterward the coachman and a groom were also forced into the pantry, bearing the news their master had arrived home, but not knowing what had happened to him after their own capture. All waited in vain for him to either rescue them or join them, taking turns to listen, but hearing nothing until my noisy entrance.

No one knew how the men had gotten in, but after a quick head count by the butler, a missing footman was promptly declared to be the traitor who had likely given entry to the intruders. An enthusiastic round of invective aimed at the fellow started up, with each declaring him to have ever been an untrustworthy rogue and listing all his bad points, slights they'd suffered from him, and various other character flaws. So many piled up in such a short time I wryly wondered how the man had ever been employed here in the first place.

Under Kellway's ministrations, Edmond looked a bit less blue than before, but still unconscious. Having myself been through a similar experience of nearly freezing, I told them to start massaging his limbs and cover him with hot wet linens, replacing them as they cooled. People were sent off to fetch more water for heating and to find the household's bathtub. I meant to have him fully immersed in steaming hot water, but that good intention was dashed when a boy hefted the unwieldy thing in. It was not much more than a wildly overgrown tin punch bowl a half-foot deep. The bather was to sit or stand in the thing and have water poured over him, I supposed. Oh, for the soothing delights of Mandy Winkle's house.

"But hasn't he had enough water already, sir?" asked a dubious Mrs. Kellway, when I explained my disappointment over the limits of their "tub."

"As long as the stuff was good and hot this time. It would have warmed him all over." Then I recalled what Oliver said of people believing anything about my birthplace. "It's something I learned in America. We know all there is to know on this sort of thing there."

It worked a charm on her, and thus enlightened, she gave a sage nod of agreement.

Oliver. I'd have to go back to Fonteyn house and tell him and Elizabeth about this latest disaster. Clarinda's mischief was not over yet, I judged. From what I'd heard, she had something else planned, and we'd have to be doubly on our guard now. Edmond needed a doctor anyway, and Oliver was nearest.

I raked my bedraggled hair back with my fingers, untidily retying it with a damp ribbon. Now that work had calmed them, some of Edmond's people found time to stare at my revealed features. My sharp ears plucked Richard's name out of a medley of whispered comments. So, Edmond had not seen fit to confide family secrets to them. I didn't think that was even possible, but he'd apparently managed. Would this weaken my position of assumed authority with them? Might they not think I was somehow allied with Clarinda since I'd so obviously once been her lover? Better to leave quickly before I found out.

Then Edmond stirred and gave a thick, water-choked cough, distracting us all. I pushed in close just in time to see his eyes open.

"Thank God!" cried Mrs. Kellway, saying it for everyone.

He had a stark staring cast to his expression. Understandable, then I had a swift flash of perception and told them to gather as many candles as they could find.

"Sir?" questioned a hesitating butler.

"He's been in the very heart of hell, man, give him some light for pity's sake."

My urgency and insight got through, and soon the kitchen was brighter than a ballroom. Whether it was a help to Edmond or not was hard to tell, but certainly it could do him no harm. When his eyes looked a bit less feral, I pressed a cup of brandy to his lips. He took that down easily enough, which was most encouraging.

"Do you remember what happened to you?" I asked him. "Just nod, there's no need to speak yet."

He did nod, but ignored the rest. "That bastard Tyne. Where?"

"He got away—for now."

"Clarinda?"

"She went with him. I think they're going to try getting

away by ship.'' And would do so unless I got moving myself and arranged to cut them and Summerhill off.

"Riddance,'' he sighed out. "Good . . . riddance.''

By that I could assume Edmond wanted no more to do with her, but it was out of his hands. I had my own special plans for his wife and her charming friends. Half-formed, to be sure, but doubtless when I caught up with them the other half would be fully matured.

"Tyne shot at me,'' Edmond said, responding to Kellway's question of how he got in the well. "Dismissed the coach. Alone at the front. He and some others came up. Tried to shoot him. Saw his pistol go off. Couldn't hear either of 'em. Strange. Thought someone hit me from the side.'' He gingerly touched his head and encountered the bandages.

"Just a graze by God's good will,'' I said, pulling his hand away. "Leave it for now until a doctor can see it. Do you recall anything else?''

His eyes shut a moment, then snapped open, focusing on the nearest of the candles. "Blackness. Cold. So cold. Water. Thought I'd been killed. Tried hard to breathe. Woke me a bit. Heard you next to me, jabbering on. Wanted to box you sharp and shut you up, but I couldn't move.''

"That was after you were out of the well,'' I said carefully, hoping he'd accept it. "You got things jumbled.''

"The *well*?'' He tried to sit up, but for once the feeble state of his body won out over his disposition. "I was in the well?''

"It's a miracle, sir,'' pronounced Mrs. Kellway. "The good God and all his angels took your part tonight and saved you, and that's a fact. If Mr. Barrett hadn't been there to pull you out we'd be praying for your soul's rest now instead of for your recovery.''

He fastened his dark eyes on me, still trying to take it all in, I suppose. "How?'' he demanded.

I shrugged. "You did the real work tying the rope around yourself.''

"But I didn't—*you* were there . . . I know you—"

"And you damned near broke the winch with your weight," I pressed on, not giving him a chance to continue. "I'd have had an easier task of it if you were built less like Hercules and more like Mercury. Next time you fall in a well I'll leave you there and spare myself a strained back."

I'd hoped a brusque manner would put him off and counted upon raising a snarl from him at least. Instead, he gave me a long hard look. I'd have been worried, but his eyes were going cloudy. He put a hand on my arm and squeezed once with a bare ghost of his usual strength.

"Thank you," he whispered, then fell back into a doze.

I expected to be hanged there and then by the staff, but Mrs. Kellway only dabbed at her face again and gazed at me with the sort of unaccountable fondness usually reserved for favorite children and small dogs. "Bless you, sir, for saying *just* the right thing to him."

"But I—oh, never mind." I stood up, nearly tripping on my blanket. "Blast it. I need to borrow some proper clothes. I'm sure my cousin won't mind if I raided his cupboard."

"But, sir, you're in no fit state to be—"

"I'm quite recuperated, thank you, and someone has to go for a doctor. My horse is out front and all saddled, so if you please . . ." I'd put on a firm unarguable manner, asserting my place again after the previous near-familiarity, and it worked, at least in this household. Jericho would have offered considerably more resistance—and would have probably won.

Dry garments from Edmond's wardrobe were found, all rather large, of course, and I had to wear my own damp riding boots, but none of it was of any real concern for me. My cousin still needed help, and Oliver was but a few miles down the road.

I sent one of the stablemen to find Rolly, absentmindedly omitting to explain why I'd left my horse that far from the house. Donning my reclaimed cloak and hat (both found on the stair landing) I was ready to rush outside before anyone else decided to ply me with questions best left unanswered, when a commotion at the front door halted my progress. To my surprise, Oliver strode forcefully in past a protesting maid, looked quickly around, and spied me. Had Elizabeth gotten impatient for news and sent him along? No, that couldn't have been it.

"What in heaven's name are you doing here?" I asked, not bothering to check my utter bewilderment. But even as the words came out I knew something was dreadfully wrong. My otherwise cheerful cousin wore an awful expression and visibly trembled from head to toe. "What is it? Is Elizabeth—?"

Oliver bit his lip and gave a violent shake of his head. His hands were clenched into quivering fists, and he looked ready to burst from the extreme inner agitation he was trying hard to keep under control. "Th-they got into the house," he finally said in a voice, a terrible broken voice I'd never heard him use before.

My belly turned to water. I did not have to ask who "they" were.

"Held pistols on us all. Took him away. You must come."

"T-took who?" But in my heart of hearts I already *knew*.

"Oh, Jonathan." Tears started from his eyes. "They've kidnapped Richard."

CHAPTER

-12-

"They *won't* hurt him," Elizabeth told me. "They wouldn't dare."

"That bitch would dare anything," I whispered, staring past her at nothing but my own rage blasting against the confining walls of the room. I couldn't risk looking at her in this state. Too dangerous.

"But she won't hurt him. She'd never endanger her chance of collecting the money for him. You have to believe that of her if nothing else."

Yes, it was one thing we could trust about Clarinda, her avarice. But if she was capable of holding her own son for ransom, might she also get rid of him the moment he became useless to her? Or if once she had her money would she even give him up? Not because she held any maternal affection for him, but to make him a continual source of spoils from the family coffers. How would she treat him? How was he being treated? Like my anger, my anguished uncertainty was bottomless.

Oliver came into the blue parlour from his latest trip down to the front gates. I didn't quite look at him either as he paused just inside the door, only swung my head part way in his direction, keeping my gaze from touching his. "No news yet," he said in a subdued voice.

"We should have heard something by now," I rumbled, glaring at the mantel clock. Useless thing. Last night Clarinda had promised to communicate with us, but she'd not said *when*. Forced into hateful rest by the rising sun, I'd lain oblivious in the cellar through the whole helpless day and upon awakening was incensed near to madness to learn no word from her had come to us.

"It's only to make us more anxious," Oliver added.

And it was working all too well on me. I paced to the fireplace and back, too restless to sit. That wasn't enough, though. Hardly aware of the act, I curled my hand into a fist and smashed it into the wall above the wainscoting. I pounded right through the paper and plaster and whatever lay beyond. Something wood, no doubt, to tell from the pain shooting up from my knuckles. I pulled free, spreading plaster dust all over, mixed with the smell of my own blood. A quick vanishing and I was whole again, ready to do more damage.

"I say," said Oliver, sounding shaken. "I say—for God's sake, Jonathan . . ."

I understood now why Clarinda hadn't been overly distressed at not finding Edmond's money. With or without it, she'd planned all along to take Richard away; he was her surety of a clean and profitable escape. She'd made careful arrangements, indeed, and had smoothly carried them out with Summerhill's help. Last night Clarinda and her friends had forced themselves into Fonteyn House in much the same way Edmond's home had been invaded, with help from a turncoat inside.

In our case it had been one of the maids. The same one who had brought Richard's milk. He'd fallen asleep so quickly because of the laudanum she'd put in it. A half full phial of the stuff was later discovered hidden away in her bed. Thank God she'd not given him the lot, though what she'd done was harsh enough. I'd been right there *holding* him while it had done its work. I should have sensed something was wrong. I should have *known*.

At about seven of the clock, apparently in accordance with instructions from Clarinda, the traitorous maid then snuck out to the front gate to distract the guards there from their duties. So successful was she in her mock flirtations that Summerhill and two of his sailors had the easy advantage of them, knocking them senseless, then the whole party came rolling onto the grounds in Edmond's carriage. They halted far enough from the house so its noise would not be marked, and went in through a door the maid had left unlocked for them.

Summerhill and his men kept everyone in place at pistol point while Clarinda rushed upstairs to fetch the sleeping Richard out of his nursery bed. Mrs. Howard had pleaded and finally screamed at her to desist. Clarinda knocked the tiny woman to the floor with one swipe of her hand. With Richard's unconscious form wrapped in a blanket, she carried him down to face Elizabeth and Oliver.

"We're going on a little trip," she told them with a smile. "Not a long one, for children can be so tiresome when traveling. You may have him back again if you like."

"What do you want?" Elizabeth asked, her voice thin with fury. Oliver, though infuriated himself, had the presence of mind to hold tight to one of her arms to prevent her from charging into their midst and possibly getting shot for her trouble.

Clarinda continued to smile unnervingly. "I judge this little man to be worth much more than ten thousand guineas to you, but that's all I want for him. You have all tomorrow to collect it together. When you've got it, tie a white rag to the front gate. Don't do anything foolish like trying to follow us or calling in the magistrates or I promise you'll not see your dear nephew again. This is a family matter. Just keep it quiet and within these walls and all will be well for him."

When asked if she understood, Elizabeth nodded, giving Clarinda a look that should have burned a hole right through the woman's skull. A pity for us all that it had not.

The invaders, along with the maid, then backed their way from the house. Arthur Tyne had driven the coach right up to the entry doors by then, and from his high perch covered the watching household with a pistol until Clarinda and the others were aboard. Summerhill climbed up with him to take the reins, and off they cantered.

Jericho, driven by his own anger and outrage into taking a chance, broke away from the house to follow the coach, avoiding the curving drive and making a straight line short-cut through the grounds to reach the gates. Alas, he did not get there in time to close them and delay the party, but was at least able to report they'd turned south. Since Edmond's house lay to the north and east, a rider could go there and fetch me back without putting Richard into additional danger. Oliver was mad to do it anyway, to find out how she'd escaped and if anyone had been hurt in the process. Thus when he arrived, he had his traveling medicine box with him, which was fortunate for poor Edmond.

Since then, Oliver had been kept busy running back and forth between Fonteyn Old Hall, Fonteyn House, and his bankers in London. The latter had been understandably curious about why he had need for such a tremendous amount of money, but had turned it over to him all the same. Clarinda had calculated well; it was more than enough to set her up in royal style wherever she wanted, but not so much that it could not be readily collected together. As soon as he had it, Oliver sped home, pausing at the gates to rip away his own neckcloth and tie it to the bars for the signal. Since then, Jericho and others of the household—including the now recovered and quite angry Mrs. Howard—had spent the time in futile watch for any sign from Clarinda.

"I . . . I brought along some help," said Oliver, dragging me from the wretched past to the wretched present.

"Who? Edmond? I thought he was still confined to bed."

"And so he is." Oliver now came in the room and stood aside. "This way, dear lady," he said.

Nora swept in, arms stretching out to me, and my whole world turned right over.

We clung to each other without speaking, she giving comfort, me shamelessly taking it, and for a few moments all was well. I choked on some long held back tears, but she said everything would be all right, and that gentle re-assurance was sufficient to keep me from completely break-ing down. When I next looked up, I discovered Oliver and Elizabeth had tactfully departed, allowing us some privacy.

"Oliver told me all that's happened," she said. "I'll do anything I can to help."

"It's a godsend just to have you here."

"He's worried about you. Said you were in quite a bad state last night." She glanced at the hand I'd put through the wall. "It seems you still are."

"The day's rest took care of my body, but not the tor-ments in my mind."

"That's how it's ever been for me. I've seen wickedness, Jonathan, but nothing to measure to this. All that I have is at your service."

"Bless you for it. Just looking at you gives me new hope. Between the two of us we have an army." But an army held in abeyance, forced to near-unbearable waiting until word came from Clarinda. Damn the woman.

Seeming to sense my thoughts, Nora embraced me again, then asked if I was up to introducing her to Elizabeth.

"What?"

"Oliver just rushed me right in. I don't want to be rude."

There was more here than simple etiquette, I knew. She wanted to help and would begin by trying to distract me out of myself. A change of subject, a resumption of innocuous social obligations, perhaps then I wouldn't feel the brutal, raging emptiness of guilt tearing my heart to bits.

I glanced at my knuckles with their smears of drying blood and dusting of plaster. *It's better than beating at the walls, Johnny Boy.*

Swallowing back the cloying self-pity, I said, "God bless you, Nora," then went to fetch my sister and cousin.

We all assumed a kind of defiant desperation, resolutely carrying on in a nearly normal manner against the strain of the situation. I say nearly, for we were drawn tighter than a fiddle string and like to snap at the least noise, real or imagined.

Because of this shared adversity, Nora forgot about any trepidations she'd confided to me earlier over meeting Elizabeth. Both ladies took to each other, but I'd expected as much, knowing them so well; still, it was heartening to see them getting on together.

Of all things, Oliver was the one who proved to be the most shy around Nora.

"Because of what she did, don't you know," he said, when I went aside to ask why he was holding his distance from the group. He touched his throat with nervous fingers. "I mean, *you* know. All this while a chap's not even aware of it. Doesn't seem quite right."

"That's why she stopped with you. Stopped a long time ago."

"And made me forget it. Couldn't have me carrying that sort of stuff around in my head and not expect me to mention it to someone sooner or later. She didn't have much choice, did she, though? Notwithstanding, I feel rather peculiar about it."

"You should talk to her, then."

"Well—ah—well, I'm not so sure about trying *that*. Besides, she already apologized to me about it, y'see, when I went to fetch her over here. Bringing it up again might seem ill-mannered."

"True. Then perhaps what you need is some ordinary converse with her to help you see there's more to her than what you've experienced in the past. I will tell you it means a great deal to Nora that, knowing what you know, you've still extended a welcoming friendship to her."

"Does it?"

"This condition isolates her dreadfully. I've been given to understand that she's only ever rarely found people who freely accept it. She was quite thunderstruck when I told her how many knew about my change. For her to be drawn into a circle of friends where she is free to be herself and not have to lie or influence to avoid a fear-filled reaction is a great comfort to her soul."

"Is it, by God?" He looked at her with new eyes. "But she seems so confident with herself."

"That's from years of practice." I dared not guess how many years, nor did I share this thought with him. "Just be easy with her, Oliver, as you are with me, and be her friend. She'll ask nothing more of you, I promise." My gaze darted significantly to his neck and he went beet red.

"Uh—ah—well, of course. Be glad to do it, Coz. If you're sure."

"My word on it."

Then I jerked my head around, as did Nora, being the first to hear. Elizabeth and Oliver froze to listen and perceived it for themselves: the sound of quick footsteps in the hall without.

Jericho had stationed himself by the front gate for much of the day, keeping watch with others for Clarinda's promised message. Sweating and breathless from his run, he burst in holding a thin oilcloth packet in one hand. No need for him to say what it was; tied to it was a scrap of white cloth. We rushed him like thieves falling upon a treasure. This time I recognized Clarinda's bold handwriting; it was addressed to Elizabeth, which seemed odd until I remembered that they thought me to be dead. With a great effort of will I gave it to her to open. I couldn't have done it anyway, my hands shook too much.

She tore at it and unfolded the oilcloth. Inside was a single sheet of paper bearing but a few lines, which she read aloud:

> *"Come to the town of Brighthelmstone by this time tomorrow night. You'll find* The Bell *to be a most agreeable place to lodge. Don't forget to bring along your special gift for R."*

"No signature," said Elizabeth. "And it's vague enough to be no more than an innocent invitation. She's not risking herself here."

"That's fine for her," grumbled Oliver. "Where the devil is Brighthelmstone?"

"A little seaside town about fifty miles south of London," Nora told us. "I stopped there once years ago after a storm on a channel crossing drove our ship off course. Afraid I don't remember much about it, though."

"I'll wager *they* know all about it, especially that Summerhill rogue. Our going there will make it very easy for them to make their own crossing once they get the money, unless they have us running off to some other place. Clarinda will lead us a merry dance before this is done."

"Not to worry, she doesn't yet know the tune is about to change."

"Jericho," said Elizabeth, "did you see who left this?"

He'd recovered somewhat from his run. "Only a glimpse of him, Miss. We heard a horse galloping up from the southern branch of the road and presently saw it. His rider was all cloaked and muffled. As he came even with our gate, he threw down the packet, turned the horse, and went back south again. He'll be halfway to the Thames by now."

"Damn," I said. "I should have been there. I could have followed him, caught and questioned him."

"And have possibly put Richard in more danger," said my sister. "You'll have your chance at them, little brother, when they turn up to collect their ransom. Until then we'll do what we're told and give them no suspicion or excuse to hurt Richard."

I nodded, seeing the sense of it, but wanting to pound more holes in the wall. Then my heart sank as another difficulty raised itself to mind. Though I could gallop all the way to this seaside town in one night given the proper changes of horses, no delays, and a guide who knew the road, I'd still have to find some kind of safe shelter before the next sunrise. The limits of my condition chafed at me as they never had before. I imparted these thoughts to the others.

"Now that *is* dangerous," Oliver said. "You talk like you're going to run off on your own. I won't hear of it. We've more than time enough to get there by coach if we leave right away. Elizabeth and I can look out for you during the day, and by the time you wake tomorrow night we'll be there."

"Besides," Elizabeth added, "they might have people watching the roads and inn, and if you arrived so openly that would put the wind up them."

My impatience to go forth and do something was such that I was ready to offer argument against all this sense. But even as I drew breath to do it, Nora touched her hand to mine.

"My coach," she said in a gentle tone, "is completely enclosed."

We all stared at her.

"Quite sheltered from the light, very comfortable to sleep in for the day, and all ready to go," she continued. "Will it do?"

Oliver's face lighted up with unchecked admiration. "Well-a-day, I should say it's just the thing. Miss Jones, you are truly a wonder."

"Thank you, Dr. Marling," she said with a gracious smile.

The five of us—for Jericho insisted on coming as well—were ready to leave within half an hour. Along with Nora's coach and driver, we saddled four extra riding horses, provisions for the road, and, of course, the ransom money. Mrs. Howard wanted to come, too, being quite tearful about it, but after a short discussion, I convinced her she would be the best help to us by staying behind. I would not have objected to her presence, but for the fact of Nora's and my condition. All the rest of the party were in on the secret, so there was no need to guard our speech or actions with them, but with Mrs. Howard in tow, the poor woman would certainly hear or see something she shouldn't. I had no wish to further influence her into forgetting things.

Nor was it necessary to influence her to stay, for she accepted the inevitable with snuffling grace, and pressed into my hands a little bundle of Richard's things: extra clothing, some chocolates wrapped in twists of paper, and his toy horse. The sight of the last item near brought me to tears, too.

As for Cousin Edmond, we'd not yet said anything to him about the dark business, and didn't plan to until it was done. He was still weak from his awful experience, and Oliver thought it better for him to learn about it after the fact, lest he lurch from his sickbed and try to interfere. He'd probably burst a blood vessel when he did find out, but we'd deal with it then, having enough problems to occupy us for the present.

We gathered together a goodly number of firearms and a store of powder and lead for the journey. England was as civilized as any country in the world, meaning we had plenty of justification to defend ourselves against the many thieves prowling outside the family circle. Oliver packed his duelers and small sword; Elizabeth and Nora each carried their muff pistols; I had my Dublin revolver and sword

stick, and lent my own duelers and small sword to Jericho.
Nora's driver had his own weaponry ready to hand. Any
highwayman foolish enough to stop us would be in for a
very disagreeable surprise.

It occurred to us that Clarinda might have arranged to
waylay our party at some point along the road and simply
take the money. Against such a chance, I would ride up
with the driver to play the lookout, and Jericho planned to
take my place come morning.

The journey was not an easy one for any of us, but I
found it particularly difficult to endure. Once the whirl of
preparation was done and we'd set out, I had nothing to
occupy my mind except the constant worry for Richard. I
was not disposed to pass the time with Nora's driver. That
dour-faced individual sat silent the whole while I was with
him, speaking only to the horses. He seemed to know his
business, though, never once stopping or slowing to ask
direction and never expressing even a hint of an opinion
about our irregular expedition. An excellent man, I thought.

He took the southern road, for all we know following
the exact route of the messenger who'd brought the packet
to our gates. Even at this time of night London's streets
were something of a snarl. He kept to the westernmost
roads to avoid the bulk of the city and skirted 'round the
west and south sides of St. James's Park. He then made his
way through a number of turns before finally coming onto
Bridge Street and thus Westminster Bridge. The water
crossing was hard, as usual; I found myself pressed back
into the solid barrier of the coach as it took us forward over
the Thames. With a tight grip on the bench, I shut my eyes
and concentrated on not vanishing and not being sick as
we passed over the wide, stinking swirl of gray water.

Then we were free of it and on Bridge Street again, but
only briefly, for it soon became the New Road, and we now
rumbled through empty farm land. An astonishing change,
that, being in a crowded noisy city one minute and in silent

countryside the next. The very air was different, no smokes or night soil fumes to assault the senses, but clean and cold and heavy with moisture. It did not feel like rain, though, and so it proved as the hours passed and the heavens spared us further problems. Not that it was an easy road, being as rutted and muddy as any I'd known on Long Island. It took some practice to balance against the irregular swaying as the coach rolled over the ruts, but I soon got used to it and was better able to keep my attention on the way ahead rather than on my seating.

The miles crawled ever so slowly under us. My impatience was such that more than once I had to fight down the near irresistible urge to float up and soar ahead. Not that it would have done any of us much good. Clarinda's note had been clear enough on the time. Even if I got to the town before dawn, nothing would be like to happen until tomorrow evening. So I ground my teeth until my jaw ached, and kept my eyes open for highwaymen. None showed themselves; perhaps it was too cold for them.

I think the others managed to sleep a little, for after a few hours the sound of voices within the coach finally ceased. It must have been lonely for Nora, being unable to escape into slumber for herself, but she made no complaint or comment on it when we stopped to make our first change of horses at a large inn. Elizabeth, Oliver, and Jericho all climbed out to stretch themselves and take refreshment while Nora made special arrangements with the chief hostler for the care of her four matched bays.

"We should be back in a day or two," she said, pressing enough money on him for a week's worth of stabling. "See well to their care and you'll have this much again on our return." Her promise, reinforced by a piercing look that I recognized, left me in no doubt her animals would be the pets of the stable.

"How are things with you and the others?" I asked her.

"Most agreeable. Oliver's been even more thorough in

his questions about me than you were that night. Quite the inquisitor, your cousin.''

''He's not annoyed you, I hope?''

''Not at all. I forgot how amusing he can be. There are some questions I'm sure he wants to ask, but his sense of delicacy in Elizabeth's presence is holding him back from too much frankness. He hardly need trouble himself, though, Elizabeth's well on to him.''

''Then you're still getting on easily with her?''

''Very easily. We won't be exchanging recipes or lace patterns or that sort of rot, but I think it likely we'll be friends long after this crisis is past, however its outcome. She's a very dear, sweet girl, brave and smart. I don't wonder that you love her so much.''

''Yes, after Father, she's quite the best, most sensible one in the family.''

''You do yourself a disservice, dear Jonathan.''

''I think not,'' I said, holding up my hand. There was still some dried blood and plaster dust clinging to my skin, evidence of my loss of restraint.

She had only a wry smile for it. ''That's only natural frustration. I don't know how you've held yourself together even this long, but hold on just a little longer. We *will* get your boy back.''

Such was her conviction and so strongly did she pass it to me that I almost thought myself under the spell of her influence again. It was enough to bolster me for miles on end, until the dawn came creeping over the vast stretch of sky on our left, and we had to stop the coach so I could take shelter within.

Nora had spared herself no available convenience in its special construction. Each bench opened up like a kind of long chest and might otherwise have been employed for the storage of travel cases. Nora had one of them lightly padded for her use, the pads containing quantities of her earth. Thus might she comfortably rest during the day. The other bench, though not so softly appointed, was cleared of the few stores we'd thrown in that I might also have room to recline. It was a bit of a press because I could not really stretch out, but no more so than in my own traveling box. It was of no matter to me; with my head pillowed on a sack full of my own earth, I passed quickly into uncaring insensibility the moment the sun was up.

The coach was quite still when I woke, though I was sharply aware of sundry noises about me: the voices of men and women, the clop of hooves, the honking of disturbed geese, and dogs barking. I cautiously raised the bench seat and peered out, giving a jump when I realized with horror someone was inside the coach. One glimpse of a dark figure crouching between the seats and I ducked, the lid slamming down with a thump, giving away my own presence.

"We're in Brighthelmstone, Mr. Jonathan," Jericho informed me in a calm, patient tone.

My hair eased back into place on my scalp. I belatedly grasped the notion that he and the menacing figure were one and the same, and the man had only been waiting for me to waken as usual. " 'Fore God, what a start you gave me."

"Sorry, sir."

Lifting the lid again, I staggered to my feet, stepped out, and let it drop back into place.

"What a row you make," said Nora, sounding rather muffled from her own hiding place.

To give her room, Jericho backed out of the coach. She emerged from her haven, looking less crushed than might be expected, though she fussed a bit about her skirts. "Much more of this and I'll take to wearing breeches," she said, swatting at some wrinkles. She gave up trying to flatten them and bade us a good evening. Jericho replied in kind; all I wanted to do was kiss her, which I did when the first chance presented itself. That pleasantry accomplished,

I had a look through the open door, but could see little enough past Jericho. Part of a muddy yard and what looked to be the windowless side of a large brick building made up the totality of our view. The coach's closed and latched windows hid the rest. Nora sat on her bench and signed for me to take the other. Until we knew better, we dared not show ourselves yet.

"What's the news?" I asked Jericho. "Are we at the Bell?"

He'd brought a lantern with him and set it on the floor between us. "We are, sir, and have been for quite some time. We found a sitting room had been reserved for Dr. Marling or Miss Barrett and party by a well-dressed gentleman calling himself Mr. Richard."

I stiffened at the name. Was Clarinda indulging in some tangled attempt at humor or simply tormenting us? Probably both.

"We've been resting there, waiting to hear something from Mrs. Fonteyn. Dr. Marling thinks the man might have been Captain Summerhill from your description of him."

"Perhaps Arthur Tyne is still too feeble yet for such errands, that or they prefer having Summerhill taking the risks."

Jericho lifted one hand to indicate his lack of knowledge on that point. "What matters most is for you and Miss Jones to remain unseen here in the coach for the moment; the whole of this inn must certainly be under watch."

"We have a way of leaving without anyone knowing about it," I reminded him.

He nodded. "True, sir, but it will not be necessary, we'll be departing shortly. This was left with the innkeeper not a quarter hour ago." He presented me with a sheet of paper. I held it so Nora could read as well.

At your earliest convenience, do come and take the view at the Seven Sisters. The way is sure to be dark,

*so bring lots of lanterns and keep them lighted. Don't
go too near the edge between the fifth and sixth Sister,
for the chalk crumbles easily. Be sure to bring R's gift.*

On the reverse side of the paper was a map and directions
with a small circle to indicate our destination.

"The Seven Sisters?" I asked after a moment's study.
"What's that, another inn?" The markings and place names
meant nothing to me.

"They're a series of chalk cliffs on this side of East-
bourne," said Nora. "A long way for us, I fear."

"At least a dozen miles, according to the landlord, sir,"
added Jericho.

"Then what?" I said with no small amount of bitterness.
"A note telling us to turn around and go to Land's End?"

"Dr. Marling expressed a similar sentiment; however,
Miss Elizabeth thinks their purpose in bringing us here may
be to see how obedient we are to their orders. So far we've
done nothing to merit reproach."

"Let us hope they think so, too," I grumbled.

Another cold night, another cold, jolting ride. Despite my
complaining, I also thought—fervently hoped—this would
be the end of it at last. Surely Clarinda would be as anxious
to collect the money as I was to rescue Richard. Besides,
she might not want to press us too far lest we finally rebel
and seek outside help.

After we quit the Bell and finally Brighthelmstone altogether, we paused long enough for me to climb up to sit
with the driver again. He had to go north a few miles to
find and follow a thready east-west road through the downs.
The softly rolling countryside held no beauty for me, but
rather I imagined spies lurking in every fold of the land or
modest clumping of hedges. They could well be there, too,
either Summerhill or some of his men, watching from a
distance. The night was moonless and overcast, but by observing the driver I determined there was just enough light

for ordinary men to see by. The noise and movement of
our coach and all the horses were visible against the pale
chalky soil and dead grass; the lanterns were but an extra
insurance for them. I kept my face well covered against any
chance of recognition.

"Almost there, sir," the driver announced, and I asked
him to slow and stop the horses.

The land ahead rose on either side into two great rounded
hills with a well-defined valley between. In the near distance I spied more such formations, a large one to my right
and several more of varying sizes undulating away to the
left.

"The Seven Sisters," I said, making it half question, half
statement.

"If the map is right, sir. Can't really count 'em from
here."

The wind was high, carried a strong sea smell, and was,
as ever, cold. It pounded at my ears and would have torn
my hat away if I hadn't already tied it fast with my woolen
scarf.

Not a place I care to linger, I thought as I clambered
down from my perch. The others came one by one out from
the coach and stood with me.

"Do you see anything?" Elizabeth asked, directing her
query equally between Nora and myself.

We stepped away from the lanterns on the coach and
carefully looked all about us.

"Nothing and no one," Nora answered after a moment.

I pointed at the lowest part of the little valley ahead.
"There's something white."

"White?" asked Oliver, stepping forward. "Like a
rag?"

"I can't quite make it out. Who's for having a better
look?"

They all were, it seemed. Oliver and Jericho carried lanterns while Nora and I led the way, with the coach slowly following our little party. We trudged as best we could over the uneven ground, until the white object became more clear to us. Someone had gone to considerable trouble building up a substantial cairn using chalk shards gleaned from the immediate area. Just over a foot high at its peak and several feet across, a length of white cloth had been placed in its midst, well anchored so as not to blow away.

The sea sound came to me now, strong and unexpectedly loud. The land, even in this depressed point, slanted up and away from us, cutting off the view beyond. I walked past the cairn and abruptly halted, realizing I was getting close to the brink of a fearful drop. Far past the ragged edge of eroded chalk was the vast restless shadow of the sea, dark gray under a gray sky.

"I'd say this was the place," said Oliver, catching up with me.

"Have a care," I told him, stepping back several yards and holding out one hand as a warning. "The earth is badly crumbled here. Clarinda mentioned it in the note."

"So she did," he said, frowning. "And very decent of her, I'm sure. Now what?"

I looked left and right up at the crests of the hills, half expecting armed men to appear and come bearing down on us like a barbarian hoard.

"Jonathan, we've found something," Nora called, drawing us back.

Oliver's circle of light joined theirs where Elizabeth and Jericho stared at the cairn. I followed the line of their gaze to the white rag, which was not held in place by the weight of the chalk, but from having one end tied to a partly buried leather pouch.

"It must be theirs," said Nora. "That hasn't been left in the weather."

Jericho started to drag it out, grunting when it caught on something. He freshened his grip and pulled hard. It came free, at the same time revealing the impediment. The pouch had a long carrying strap, and the strap was wrapped around a man's arm.

Thus did we discover Arthur Tyne's body.

The grim disinterment did not take long; we all worked at it. Shaken as we were after the first terrible shock, the activity was necessary to keep from thinking too much, or so it was for me. My worry of the moment was mostly for Elizabeth and Nora, on how this might affect them—until I came to understand they were far more concerned over my well-being than their own.

"Shot," said Oliver after a brief examination. "Clean through the heart."

"Why would they kill him?" asked Jericho, brushing dust from his hands.

They looked to me. As if I had any answers. "Perhaps he slowed them down."

"Or Clarinda didn't need him anymore," said Elizabeth. "Or this Captain Summerhill was more to her liking."

"Whatever the reason, they wanted us to find him, to know how easily . . . how easily and how willing they are to kill."

Oliver stood. "Clarinda's *not* going to let them touch Richard." He said it firmly, as though he believed it.

Any reply from me would have either been a lie of agreement or throwing the hope he meant to impart back in his face. Instead, I gestured at the leather pouch. "Anything in it?" I asked.

Jericho plucked it up and pushed back the thing's flap. "Yes! Some paper . . . here!" He hurriedly unfolded it, holding it flat against the wind so we could read.

Put the gift in the bag, then throw it over the cliff. R will be waiting below if you want him. There's a village about a mile east of this point with a path down to the beach. Go there, then come west again. Use great care and caution lest harm befall you.

I left my lantern and tore back to the cliff. The closer I got to the edge, the more perilous the footing. I didn't care. Oliver called out to me, but I chose not to listen. The last few feet I fell to my hands and knees and crept up to the fragile brink.

Oh, but it was a well-considered spot for them. From this more immediate vantage I saw how the Sisters, a series of hills overlooking the sea, seemed to have been sliced down the middle by a giant's knife to reveal their chalky vitals. The knife had been a jagged thing, for the cliff sides rose high in long irregular vertical slashes, marred with many cracks and few if any ledges, impossible to climb up or down. At their base far below ran a wide strip of beach, covered with fallen debris from the cliffs, broken stones, seaweed, and other tidal flotsam.

On that beach I now spied several figures, a boat, and waiting out in deeper water, a small ship.

"What is it?" Oliver demanded. He also dropped to his hands and knees, crawling the remaining distance to join me. "What do you see?"

"They're down there," I said. "The lot of 'em, I think. There's their ship. Do you see it?" I pointed.

He squinted. "I think so. Where are they?" A pause as I pointed again. "No, sorry, can't make out a thing in this murk. Damn good luck for us that you can. Is Richard—?"

"I'm looking."

The figures huddled near the boat, which had been dragged up onto the beach. I saw several men, then a woman sitting on one of the larger rocks—Clarinda. My heart jumped right into my throat, for close against her breast she held a child-sized bundle.

"God, he's down there! She has him!"

His hand fell hard on my shoulder, keeping me from going right over. "Steady on, Coz. Look at this carefully first before you go charging in."

"Your light—hold it up so they know you've come."

"All right, but I'll remind you they might want to blow my head off."

"I don't think so . . . yes, that's it! That's stirred them, they're moving about, pointing up at us."

"They'll recognize you."

"Hardly—all they can really see is your light and perhaps some silhouettes, y'know. That's why she wanted us to carry lanterns. Hah! One of 'em has a dark lantern, he's opening it—"

"Yes, I see it swinging, a signal for me I suppose. Hope to God it *is* them and not a pack of smugglers going at cross purposes with us."

The others came up with Elizabeth in the lead. "Is it Richard? Is it?"

Oliver looked over his shoulder to her. "I can't see him, but Jonathan can. Stay back now."

"Is he all right?"

"He's too far away to tell," I answered. "It's all very clever. You throw them the money, then by the time you find a way down the cliff to get to Richard they're on their ship and heading for France."

"If they even leave him behind," she said, putting into words one of my countless fears.

"They will, whether they've planned it or not."

"What are you thinking?"

"That they'll be feeling very safe from attack thinking none of us can get down this cliff. The very last thing they'll expect is for someone to turn up in their midst and take him away. I'll be on them and out before they know what's happened."

"You'll be . . . but it's too danger—oh! Never mind. None safer here than you and Nora."

"True, but I will be careful, dear sister, if you'll do the same for me."

"Gladly, but for God's sake tell us what you're planning."

My brain fairly hummed with ideas now that I had a definite and visible goal to go after. "Oliver, I'll want you to shout at them and get them to come closer to the foot of the cliff. Say that you've got the money and for them to be ready when you throw it down, but instead of the money, I want you to fill the pouch with the rocks from the cairn."

He grinned. "They won't like that."

"Indeed. I want all their attention on you. Distract them as much as you can, get their hopes up—it will be that much more of a frustration to them when they find their treasure is a false one."

"But won't it further endanger Richard?"

"No, because by then I'll have him. You have to keep them busy for as long as you can and give me the time to slip in close and get to him."

"But Clarinda will have them on you first thing."

"No doubt, but after ten paces they won't know me from the rest of the shadows. This darkness will be in my favor, I'll be able to run where they can only stumble. The lot of you need to have your pistols ready, too. A few shots and—"

Oliver shook his head, outraged. "And chance shooting you or the boy? I think not! We can't see a bloody thing from up here and could hit one of you by accident."

"I can help on that," said Nora. "I'll be able to direct your fire." She looked at me. "I assume you just want them busy ducking while you get away, because it's not likely we'll any of us be able to hit someone on purpose under these circumstances."

"Exactly, a few shots straight down the cliff should be enough to send them scurrying for their boat, though I'd be well pleased if you should happen to drop one or two of 'em by accident. Once you see me get Richard you open up and distract them from pursuing us. If they were fools enough to give us the high ground, then we'd be fools not to use it. If they do shoot back, with the distance and the dark you should all be fairly safe, but keep your heads low, and be sure to put out the lanterns. Right, then.''

My sudden energy to do something was contagious. Jericho and Oliver hurried to the coach to get the pistols and powder. Elizabeth began putting rocks into the pouch.

With a hand on my arm, Nora stayed me from helping. ''Remember he won't vanish with you. You won't be able to bring him up the cliff in the same manner of travel you'll use to descend.''

Damnation, but I wouldn't. ''Then I'll make for that village in the note. Leave the riding horses here and send your driver ahead with the coach. You can catch up with us later.''

''Very well—but Jonathan, the shooting. If one of the pistol balls should hit you while you're holding the boy . . . it will go right though you to him. You're taking an appalling risk with his life.''

And did I not clearly know it? ''F-for all I know he might already be dead.'' I pointed to Tyne's partially uncovered corpse. ''But if alive I'm ready to do anything to get him away from those monsters. I'll take that chance rather than leave him with them.''

Her hand tightened, then fell away, and she said nothing more.

When all was made ready, I gave my sword stick and Dublin revolver into Elizabeth's keeping, knowing they would only be a hindrance.

''You should at least have the pistol,'' she protested.

''It takes two hands to bring a new chamber to bear on the thing, and I'll need both to carry Richard.''

''Then God go with you, little brother.''

I saw her prayer echoed in the faces of the others and suddenly felt a wash of fear. Not for myself but for my helpless son. What if my actions brought him harm instead of deliverance? What if, God forbid, I got him killed? If I truly wished for his safety would it not be better to let him go? My brave words to Nora seemed but a hollow pretension. Clarinda could not possibly be so heartless as to hurt her own child. Surely some of the worry for him she'd expressed to me had had some tiny seed of sincerity within. The sensible thing would be to give her the money and hope for the best. It was entirely reasonable, much more preferable than the wild, perilous, half-thought-through plan I'd just improvised.

Much more preferable, but for the voice within telling me—all but screaming at me—to ignore sense and let my heart lead in this matter. Against all reason it cried alone. Undeniable, my instinct told me this was the right thing to do, the one thing I *had* to do.

But that did not make me any less afraid.

Confidence is an intensely ephemeral quality, flooding you fit to burst one instant and miles away the next leaving you dry and gasping in the emptiness. I was wretchedly parched by the time I'd eased my way down the cliff face to crouch immobile in a jumble of water-smoothed rock.

Oliver was already calling down from his now distant perch. He couldn't keep them occupied forever while I wavered between sense and folly. Perhaps in some distant corner of my mind I'd anticipated this hesitation, and that's why the pouch was filled with rock, not money. For then against its discovery would I be forced to take swift action.

But no matter the reasons—the time had finally come. Working or not, my heart had taken up lodging high in my throat, and I wasted several precious moments trying to swallow it back into place.

I'd drifted down and lighted just to the east of the men

on the beach. The whole area seemed horribly bright, and I quailed each time a head swung in my direction. None of them saw me, though. None. What was like day to me was pitchy midnight to them.

"I don't think the pouch is big enough," Oliver bawled from on high. "It's sure to be too heavy to throw very far."

"Do the best you can, Dr. Marling," Summerhill bawled back, sounding unflappable and thoroughly in control. He was turned away from me, but I recognized his voice and bearing. He stood a prudent distance from the base of the cliff, cane in one hand and dark lantern in the other. He'd covered its light over; Oliver wouldn't be able to see him at all.

"Silly ass," grumbled one of two men hovering close by.

"Long as 'e's a rich ass," put in the other, identifying the object of comment as my cousin and not their captain.

I slipped off my cloak, hat, and scarf, forsaking their protection for ease of movement. Then did I also forsake solidity and float low over the ground, skirting Summerhill and his men, as substantial as a ghost and just as silent. My vision limited, but still better than theirs, I made a straight line toward the boat and Clarinda.

Changes had taken place. She was no longer seated on a pile of rock, easy to get to, but was in the boat itself, with six more men standing around it. Richard was in her arms. My instinct had been true. She'd had no intention of leaving him after getting the money. No surprise was left in me concerning this woman, only fury, which carried me forward—just in time, it seemed.

No sooner was I started than Summerhill shouted something to the men, and they turned upon the boat and began shoving it into the water. I heard curses for its coldness and rebukes to hurry as "the Captain 'uz comin'." I hurtled toward them.

And was stopped.

It wasn't quite as severe as falling off a horse at full gallop, since my body was not solid enough for bruising, but the shock was just as brutal.

The sea. The damned sea.

I was hard pressed to cross free-flowing water normally; in this near-nebulous state I'd *never* do it. The limits of my condition utterly prevented me from pushing so much as an inch farther.

No time for thought about the consequences—I reformed and plunged up to my waist into the surf. By comparison, the freezing immersion in Edmond's well had been a summer lark. This winter sea was so icy that the cold burned my skin, seeming to eat right through to the bone like acid. I must have cried out from it, for two of the sailors so diligently pushing the boat turned to look.

In no frame of mind to be polite or careful, I was on them like a storm, knocking them out of the way and devil take the hindmost. My hands found the gunwale, grasped hard, and I heaved up and into the boat, sprawling over the ribbed bottom, water streaming from my clothes.

Clarinda half stood, but the craft bobbed crazily, forcing her to sit again. She gave out with an abortive screech, whether from the sight of me or from the danger of falling in, I could not tell. I had a single image of her staring at me, wide of eye and with a sagging mouth, of her trying to back away while holding tight to her precious bundle, of Richard's dark head poking out from the illusory protection of the blanket she'd wrapped around him. His eyes were shut fast. Asleep or made insensible by more laudanum?

And then the narrow boat was full of men, cursing, shouting, all their anger and fight centered upon me, the unexpected intruder. I had no thought for anything but to get to Richard, though. They were merely obstacles in the way, inconvenient, but surmountable. Even as a man raised

a pistol level with my face I kicked out with one leg and
knocked him right over into the water. Two more had slid
aboard, one of them falling upon me more by accident than
design because of the boat's now very erratic rocking. They
got in one another's way in the confining space, and I took
advantage of it by striking the nearest senseless, then pushing him back against his friend.

The way clear for a moment, I found my feet and surged
forward again. Now Clarinda let go with a fully realized
shriek. I heard Summerhill distantly barking commands,
trying to instill order upon the chaos, and succeeding. There
was one man left with the wit and speed to act; he bent
and picked up one of the oars, bringing it hard around with
intent to clout me flat with the thing. Fast as he was, the
movement seemed slow to my perception. I caught the
stave of wood before it could do me harm and wrenched it
from him with a strong sideways twist that sent him over-
board.

The last man had recovered somewhat from being
pushed, tried to drag me down, and promptly discovered
himself to be on the wrong end of the oar for his trouble.

The boat had drifted far enough from shore that Summerhill and his ruffians were no immediate threat. The rest
of the men were unconscious or floundering. None stood
between me and Clarinda now. Unsteady from the boat's
motion I moved closer to her.

"Give him to me," I said, reaching out with one hand.

She half rose, but could not back any farther away.
Thrice now I'd returned from the dead, from the fight in
the mausoleum, from the attempt in the bath, from the push
down the stairs in her own home, the last being the most
impossible to deny. What thoughts were in her mind I could
not guess, but the emotions were obvious, being equal parts
of rage and terror. Her white face contorting into something
inhuman, she lifted Richard's limp form high, and hurled
him into the sea.

Of all the horrors that had run through my mind since she'd taken him, this had never once shown itself. It was too abominable. My reaction was without thought, instantaneous. I swung the end of the oar wide and hard toward her. I had an impression of it striking her head, the impact traveling up the wood to bruise my hand, of her swift and abrupt drop; impression only, for by then I was diving into the corrosive water after my child.

No time to register the pain, all my effort was concentrated on maintaining a solid form against the overwhelming urge to vanish. He was not far, little more than five yards, but they might well have been miles for my slow progress. I lived lifetimes until my hand thrashed against the edge of his blanket, eternities until I found his small body in the mass of soaked fabric. I got his head clear of the smothering water. After all this his eyes were yet shut. Dear God, no . . .

The shore. Where? That way. Close and too far. Hurry.

More eternities until my toes brushed and caught on the rocky bottom. Staggering, holding him tight, I lurched from the sea's caustic grasp, then fell to my knees. Sobbing with dread, I tore away his wet clothes, searching his pinched blue face for sign of life. Pressing my ear to his chest I forced myself to silence, listening with all my soul.

There, I thought I heard it . . . a faint flutter like a bird's wing. His heart. His *living* heart . . .

"You murdering bastard," said Summerhill, almost conversationally.

I looked up at him, up into the barrel of his pistol.

"You—" he broke off, recognizing me. His aim wavered as amazement finally penetrated his imperturbable armor. I'd seen such uncertainty before, such hesitation; it would not last long. With Richard close in my arms, I rose and bolted like a deer.

Ten paces, I'd said. Ten paces and they'd lose me in the dark. I'd been wildly, fatally optimistic, and Richard would be the one to suffer for my misjudgment.

Shots. A veritable hail of fire.

I ran faster.

A second volley.

I flinched and sought shelter behind the low mass of stones where I'd left my cloak.

"Run!" someone called in a thin, faraway voice.

Nora.

I glanced up the cliff. Yes. They were firing down at Summerhill and his men, scattering them, giving me the chance to get clear.

"*Run!*" Elizabeth now, strident with urgency.

I swept up the dry cloak for Richard and fled east, threading madly between the stones, skidding, nearly tripping, but always rushing forward, and never more looking back.

EPILOGUE

It was a fine, clear Christmas Eve, not too cold, not too windy. Tomorrow promised a continuation of the good weather, though I'd be sleeping right through it, as always. No church for me, alas, but we'd made a merry party of it tonight having trooped out for evening services. I had innumerable blessings to be grateful for—though some weren't fit for the peace of the sanctuary, like my grim thankfulness for Clarinda's death.

But others, like Richard's recovery, brought me to kneel before God with sincere and humble gratitude.

Thus far the boy had shown no ill reaction from his kidnapping. Clarinda had apparently kept him drugged for nearly the whole time, as he had nothing to tell us of the experience, not even a stray nightmare. I know, for since then I'd lately taken to watching him in his sleep when the mood struck, sitting close by with a book and alert to any change in him that might indicate distress. Mrs. Howard complimented my zealous concern and at the same time reproved me for being overly protective. I smiled and told her she was right, but begged her to indulge me until I felt more secure about his safety.

Richard continued healthy despite his plunge in the freezing sea water. I'd run nearly the whole way along the beach to the tiny village mentioned in Clarinda's note and had all but broken into its one tavern seeking help. One look at us and our bedraggled condition and the owner's anger changed to instant compassion as he took us for shipwreck survivors and roused the rest of his house to beneficent action.

As fires were built up, broth was heated, and our clothes were set out to dry, I improvised a poor tale of an overturned boat for their many questions. This inspired even more queries as they wanted to know where the boat was like to be found, why I'd been out at sea at night, how I'd upset the boat, and other annoying details. I was spared from additional bad lying by the timely arrival of Nora's coach driver, soon followed by Nora herself and the others. Oliver, taking charge as the one doctor on the premises, pronounced that I was too addled for talk and told me to rest while he tended Richard, something I was more than glad to carry out. What with the number of our party and all obviously being well to-do, the interrogators retired to watch and draw their own conclusions about the strangeness of the situation.

We stopped long enough on the return trip for Oliver and Jericho to re-bury Arthur Tyne. His improvised grave went undiscovered for more than a week and was quite a mystery to the Brighthelmstone magistrates as was stated in the one paper we found that reported the incident. The man's murder was popularly blamed on smugglers or pirates, and in a way the conclusion was perfectly right. Certainly no one of us ever stepped forward with further information for the inquiry.

Oliver stayed on in Brighthelmstone and kept an ear open to all the news. When talk came of a woman's body found on the beach near the Seven Sisters, he went along with the rest of the curious for a look and, putting on a convincing show of surprised sorrow, proclaimed her to be his long missing cousin, feared lost at sea. Thus was he able to bring Clarinda back for internment in the family mausoleum. Her terrible head wound was dismissed as having been caused by a rough encounter with the rocks when she'd washed ashore. So far no one had connected her in any way to Arthur Tyne.

I was thankful also for Edmond's full recovery from his own dance with the Reaper.

He eventually got the full story of all that had happened from me—or most of it. There were certain aspects I chose not to include, like my extra-natural abilities and the exact manner of Clarinda's demise. I baldly perjured myself, saying she'd fallen and hit her head in the boat during the fight. He grunted, and asked no other questions. The official story given to the rest of the family was that Clarinda had run away from him and drowned at sea by misadventure—something just scandalous enough to put off deeper inquiry. Edmond, already in mourning for Aunt Fonteyn, didn't have to change much of his outward show of grief, only to extend its duration. I think he did grieve in his heart for his wayward wife. Apparently he had been happy with her, once.

I was also thankful for the end of all persecution from Ridley's Mohocks.

It was but small work to find Royce and Litton, his would-be avengers, as well as a few others who had been connected to him. Though the task of reforming the lot of them into good citizens seemed rather too overwhelming, I was willing to take it on, but upon discussing the prospect with Nora, I gladly adopted her suggestion. Rather than trying to convert them, I simply instilled in each an irresistible desire to take a grand tour of the Continent. Some were bound for France, others for Italy, and none was like to return anytime soon. They could have Europe and all the rest of the world if they'd but leave me and mine in the peace of England.

The only dark spot was Summerhill's escape.

Oliver was yet busy making diligent inquiries about him. It seemed the captain was from Brittany as he'd said, and had in the past engaged Edmond's services for certain legal matters, none of it connected with smuggling, though. Edmond had little to add about the man, except to say that Clarinda had taken to him. As Clarinda had taken to quite a number of men, Edmond had paid no more attention to this particular indiscretion than the others. Since she had been adept at using, then discarding a man when another more useful one appeared, I wondered whom she might have had waiting when she'd finished with Summerhill or if he had indeed been her final aspiration.

It mattered not now, but I would keep my eyes open for the captain. He'd bear watching against future mischief, I thought.

But for now, all was peace. We'd moved back into Oliver's home in town, once more leaving Fonteyn House to the care of some trusted servants. The parlour fire roared with warm comfort for the body, while the excellent sermon we'd recently heard did the same for our souls.

Nora and Oliver were seated near the fire showing Richard how best to toast bread. Elizabeth was at her spinet, engaged in learning a new piece of music, an occupation that held her attention only until Jericho came in with a tray laden for tea. According to the others, supper was too long a wait for refreshment. Elizabeth played the hostess and served all but Nora and me. We thought it best not to indulge our own specific appetite in front of an actively curious four-year-old.

"I hear Jericho gives a good report of a certain French dancing master," Oliver said. "What do you say to sending for the fellow after the New Year, see if he suits?"

"Indeed?" I arched an eyebrow at Elizabeth, the obvious source of my cousin's information, since I'd imparted it to her only last night as but a distant possibility.

She shrugged prettily. "One can't start too soon in teaching a boy the finer points of gentlemanly behavior."

"He's very much the little gentleman now," I said in mild protest. "Though I might consider employing someone. In the not so near future, mind you."

"Brother, you just don't want to share him with anyone else."

"A palpable hit," said Nora, correctly reading my expression. "Keep pressing, Elizabeth, he'll call for quarter in another minute."

"Let's play fox hunt," said Richard, his bright face covered with toast crumbs and butter.

"There's a perfect example of the need for someone to teach him proper manners." Elizabeth wiped at the boy's face with her handkerchief.

"Example? He just wants a game." I winked at him, a silent promise to steal him away at the first opportunity.

"Yes, but he must learn to say 'excuse me,' and 'may I please' when breaking into a conversation."

"Excuse-me-may-I-please play fox hunt," said her resolute nephew, his voice somewhat muffled by her efforts at cleaning.

"A quick learner, is he not?" I asked, and no one offered to disagree. "Come here, Richard, time to ride to the hounds."

He broke away from Elizabeth, leaping onto me like a monkey.

"Gently, Jonathan, not so much bouncing, he's just eaten."

I promised to be sedate, keeping my word for almost one whole circuit of the house. Richard's enthusiasm carried over to me, and I forgot about caution in the face of fun. We galloped as madly, as noisily, as joyfully as ever before, so much so that I paid scant mind to the outcry that followed when Jericho answered a knock at the front door.

Just as I cantered into the parlor by way of the servant's entrance, I saw Elizabeth and the others suddenly rushing out the main door into the entry hall. I stopped, hearing more exclamations and outcry, the happy kind. I felt myself kindling to a unique, near forgotten warmth at the sound of a voice, low and clear and very much loved.

Father. Father has come at last.

"Left your Mother at Fonteyn House with all the mourning," he was saying. "It's true then? She still wasn't believing it when I had the head groom take me here. This will be hard. At least Beldon's there to help. Yes, Beldon and his sister came along, quite the mixed blessing on the crossing. . . ."

"What's wrong, Cousin Jon'th'n?" Richard tugged at one of my ears.

"Nothing, laddie. You're about to meet someone very special."

"Who?"

I swung him around so as to seat him on one arm, and with a flock of birds flapping around in my belly, walked toward the entry hall.

They were all gathered about Father, Elizabeth still holding tight to him as he shook hands for the first time with Oliver. Nora stood close by awaiting introduction; Jericho also hovered near, his face alight with genuine pleasure. The lot of them looked up and fell silent as Richard and I came in.

Father broke into a great smile at the sight of me and stepped forward, arms open to embrace . . . then he faltered. A most amazing expression possessed his face as he stared first at me, then at Richard, and perceived the *exact* resemblance between us. His mouth dropped open.

"Welcome back to England, Father." I lifted Richard up to get a better hold on him. "I—ah—I have a bit of news for you. . . ."

P. N. ELROD

"Offers deft touches of wit, beauty, and suspense.
Entertaining."   —*Publishers Weekly*

__**DANCE OF DEATH**   0-441-00309-5/$5.99
In P. N. Elrod's latest novel, the vampire Jonathan
Barrett meets the mortal son he never knew he had.
__**DEATH MASQUE**   0-441-00143-2/$4.99
__**DEATH AND THE MAIDEN**
                                    0-441-00071-1/$4.99
__**RED DEATH**   0-441-71094-8/$4.99

THE VAMPIRE FILES

"An entertaining blend of detective story and the
supernatural from a promising new writer."
                              —*Science Fiction Chronicle*

__**LIFE BLOOD**   0-441-84776-5/$4.99
__**BLOODCIRCLE**   0-441-06717-4/$4.99
__**ART IN THE BLOOD**   0-441-85945-3/$4.50
__**FIRE IN THE BLOOD**   0-441-85946-1/$4.50
__**BLOOD ON THE WATER**   0-441-85947-X/$4.99

Payable in U.S. funds. No cash orders accepted. Postage & handling: $1.75 for one book, 75¢
for each additional. Maximum postage $5.50. Prices, postage and handling charges may
change without notice. Visa, Amex, MasterCard call 1-800-788-6262, ext. 1, refer to ad # 535a

Or, check above books	Bill my:	☐ Visa ☐ MasterCard ☐ Amex	
and send this order form to:			(expires)
The Berkley Publishing Group	Card#		
390 Murray Hill Pkwy., Dept. B			($15 minimum)
East Rutherford, NJ 07073	Signature		
Please allow 6 weeks for delivery.	Or enclosed is my:	☐ check ☐ money order	
Name		Book Total	$
Address		Postage & Handling	$
City		Applicable Sales Tax	$
		(NY, NJ, PA, CA, GST Can.)	
State/ZIP		Total Amount Due	$

𝕾urrender to the 𝖁ampire's 𝕶iss
SPELLBINDING NOVELS OF THE NIGHT

ELAINE BERGSTROM

"Bergstrom's vampire is of the breed Anne Rice fans will love."—Milwaukee Journal

__*DAUGHTER OF THE NIGHT* 0-441-00110-6/$4.99

Elizabeth Bathori casts a shadow of terror across Europe, bathing in the blood of the innocent in search of immortality. Thousands fear her, but few know the source of her inspiration— the kiss of the vampire Catherine Austra.

__*BLOOD RITES* 0-441-00074-6/$4.99

__*SHATTERED GLASS* 0-441-00067-3/$4.99

LAURELL K. HAMILTON

__*THE LUNATIC CAFE* 0-441-00293-5/$5.99

Preternatural expert Anita Blake mixes business with pleasure when she investigates the mysterious disappearances of a number of werewolves...and falls in love with the leader of the pack.

__*CIRCUS OF THE DAMNED* 0-441-00197-1/$5.99

__*THE LAUGHING CORPSE* 0-441-00091-6/$5.99

__*GUILTY PLEASURES* 0-441-30483-4/$5.99

"You'll want to read it in one sitting–I did."—P. N. Elrod

Payable in U.S. funds. No cash orders accepted. Postage & handling: $1.75 for one book, 75¢ for each additional. Maximum postage $5.50. Prices, postage and handling charges may change without notice. Visa, Amex, MasterCard call 1-800-788-6262, ext. 1, refer to ad # 486c

Or, check above books   Bill my: ☐ Visa ☐ MasterCard ☐ Amex _____
and send this order form to: (expires)
The Berkley Publishing Group   Card#_____
390 Murray Hill Pkwy., Dept. B   ($15 minimum)
East Rutherford, NJ 07073   Signature_____

Please allow 6 weeks for delivery.   Or enclosed is my: ☐ check   ☐ money order

Name_____   Book Total $_____

Address_____   Postage & Handling $_____

City_____   Applicable Sales Tax $_____
                                        (NY, NJ, PA, CA, GST Can.)
State/ZIP_____   Total Amount Due $_____

ACE
New Releases

__*BRANCH POINT* by Mona Clee 0-441-00291-9/$5.50
"A time-travel adventure in the tradition of H. G. Wells."—Julia
Ecklar, author of *Regenesis*
In time travel, there is a starting point, an end point, and a point of no return.

__*DAGGER MAGIC—A NOVEL OF THE ADEPT*
by Katherine Kurtz and Deborah Turner Harris 0-441-00304-4/$5.99
"Kurtz and Harris have created a charming and unusual detective!"—*Locus*
The enigmatic Adept, Sir Adam Sinclair, and his fellow enforcers of Light
must thwart the rebirth of the Third Reich.

__*ORCA* by Steven Brust 0-441-00196-3/$5.99
"Entertaining!"—*Locus*
New in the bestselling series featuring Vlad Taltos, assassin-for-hire! Vlad
uncovers a financial scandal big enough to bring down the House of Orca—
and shatter the entire Empire.

__*HAPPY POLICEMAN* by Patricia Anthony 0-441-00321-4/$5.99
"Thoughtful, strange, witty...a pleasure!"—*Analog*
Six years ago, the world ended. But in Coomey, Texas, the alien Torku
keeps things going with VCRs, Twinkies, and cryptic advice. But after six
years of living within the paisley barrier erected by the Torku, even a small
town can go stir-crazy. Crazy enough to covet...and to kill. *(April)*

__*THROUGH THE BREACH* by David Drake 0-441-00326-5/$5.99
"Classic."—*Orlando Sentinel*
Beyond an impenetrable membrane lies another universe with all of the
riches of the Federation. The only point of entry is Landolph's Breach,
where most men have never returned. *(May)*

Payable in U.S. funds. No cash orders accepted. Postage & handling: $1.75 for one book, 75¢
for each additional. Maximum postage $5.50. Prices, postage and handling charges may
change without notice. Visa, Amex, MasterCard call 1-800-788-6262, ext. 1, refer to ad # 578

Or, check above books   Bill my: ☐ Visa   ☐ MasterCard ☐ Amex
and send this order form to: (expires)
The Berkley Publishing Group   Card#_____
390 Murray Hill Pkwy., Dept. B   ($15 minimum)
East Rutherford, NJ 07073   Signature_____
Please allow 6 weeks for delivery.   Or enclosed is my: ☐ check   ☐ money order
Name_____   Book Total $_____
Address_____   Postage & Handling $_____
City_____   Applicable Sales Tax $_____
                                            (NY, NJ, PA, CA, GST Can.)
State/ZIP_____   Total Amount Due $_____

Join the

P. N. ELROD
FAN CLUB!

(A.K.A. The Teeth in the Neck Gang!)

The only club officially sanctioned by
P. N. "Pat" Elrod, find out the latest
news on her signings, personal
appearances, and more. Get the
nitty-gritty details on all her books
and future works. Got questions?
Elrod has a Q & A column just for you!
You get: a personally autographed
membership button, I.D. badge, and
a multi-page quarterly newsletter—
all for just $10.00/year or $12.00
overseas! Send your check or money
order (U.S. funds) to:

The P. N. Elrod Fan Club
P.O. Box 100362
Fort Worth, TX 76185

Name:_____

Address:_____

City:_____ ST:_____ Zip:_____

(Please print to ensure proper delivery)